Double-wide

Other books by Michael Martone

Michael Martone

Double-wide

Collected Fiction of *Michael Martone*

QUARRY BOOKS

AN IMPRINT OF
INDIANA UNIVERSITY PRESS
BLOOMINGTON & INDIANAPOLIS

Publication of this book is made possible in part with the
assistance of Robert Olin, Dean, College of Arts and
Sciences, University of Alabama

This book is a publication of
Quarry Books
an imprint of Indiana University Press
601 North Morton Street
Bloomington, IN 47404-3797 USA

http://iupress.indiana.edu

Telephone orders	800-842-6796
Fax orders	812-855-7931
Orders by e-mail	iuporder@indiana.edu

© 2007 by Michael Martone

The paper used in this publication meets the mini-
mum requirements of American National Standard for
Information Sciences—Permanence of Paper for Printed
Library Materials, ANSI Z39.48-1984.

Manufactured in the United States of America

Library of Congress Cataloging-in-Publication Data
Martone, Michael.
Double-wide: collected fiction of Michael Martone /
Michael Martone.
p. cm.
ISBN-13: 978-0-253-34828-9 (alk. paper)
ISBN-10: 0-253-34828-5 (alk. paper)
1. Indiana—Fiction. I. Title.
PS3563.A7414D68 2007
813'.54—dc22
2006024237

1 2 3 4 5   12 11 10 09 08 07

For Theresa
Η ζωή

We were United World Federalists back then.
I don't know what we are now. Telephoners, I guess.
We telephone a lot—or *I* do, anyway, late at night.

Kurt Vonnegut, Jr., *Slaughterhouse-Five*

Contents

Acknowledgments

The author thanks the editors of these magazines for originally publishing the fiction reprinted here:

Colorado Review, Exquisite Corpse, Harper's, Iowa Review, The Florida Review, Epoch, Sycamore Review, High Plains Literary Review, Story, Arts Indiana Literary Supplement, North American Review, Yellow Silk: Journal of Erotic Arts, The Crescent Review, The Laurel Review, Indiana Review, Denver Quarterly, Sun Dog, Madison Review, Northwest Review, Telescope, Luna Tack, Shenandoah, Seems, Antaeus, The Antioch Review, Pig Iron, Ascent, Minnesota Review, Benzene, Mississippi Valley Review, Indiana Writes, Black Ice, and *Aura.*

Alfred A. Knopf published *Alive and Dead in Indiana.*

The Johns Hopkins University Press published *Safety Patrol.*

Indiana University Press published *Fort Wayne Is Seventh on Hitler's List.*

Broad Ripple Press published *Pensées: The Thoughts of Dan Quayle.*

Zoland Books published *Seeing Eye.*

The author thanks his assistant, Erin McMillin, and Lee Ann Sandweiss and the folks at Indiana University Press for finding *Double-wide* a home back home in Indiana. And credit, credit, credit to Marian Young who makes the deals.

Double-wide

Tool Box | An Introduction

Monkey Wrench

I blame it all on the Thor Power Tool Case, the reason this book exists. In the matter of *Thor Power Tool Company v. Commissioner of Internal Revenue* that came before the Supreme Court in 1979 (the year I graduated from the Writing Seminars of Johns Hopkins University and started publishing stories) one may find what is the matter with the present-day book publishing business. *Thor Power Tool* has had a profound effect. The short answer: the case eliminated a long-standing tax dodge. After 1979, it became much more expensive for publishers to carry inventory from year to year. As a result, publishers began to cut print runs in order to minimize inventory and began to dispose of that inventory more quickly. Books went out of print soon after they were printed. And if a book did not generate a high enough profit to offset this new tax burden, it was pulped before the end of the fiscal year. Where once a publisher's backlist—the inventories of small but steadily selling titles—was the company's main asset, it now became a liability. And the frontlist of blockbuster books that could justify in revenue their sustainability received the commercial publisher's complete attention. The result? Books that once used to be in print for years were now out of print in a matter of months. So, my own first book of stories, *Alive and Dead in Indiana*, which was published by Alfred A. Knopf in the spring of 1984, was, by that Christmas, turned into cellulose house insulation.

The book you have in your hands is a reconstitution of sorts of the many past shreddings and mulchings my several books of fiction have endured. This is not the first time these stories have found their way back into print once they were out. In the table of contents of *Double-wide*, one may read a kind of fossil record. *Fort Wayne Is Seventh on Hitler's List*, in its two editions, was a paperback version of *Alive and Dead in Indiana*, cleverly avoiding the severe consequences of *Thor* by lodging with a generous Indiana University Press, a nonprofit press not so pressed by the tax code. Or so I thought. But even not-for-profit presses have felt the need to account their accounting as their university and foundation patrons have insisted these concerns pay more and more of their own way. So here is to you, IU, for the resuscitation yet again of these constantly dying stories. In *Double-wide* we are now into double overtime.

Snap Line

In Russia, there are writers fond of saying that they all come from beneath The Overcoat. It is Gogol's story, "The Overcoat," they are talking about as the primal influencing fiction informing all that follows. The issue of influence for me is not so sartorially clear. I have worked in Alabama for ten years and have watched my local students struggle anxiously with the influences of the writers of the region, struggling to absorb, abandon, build upon the likes of Faulkner, O'Connor, Welty. In the South there is never any question that one writes about the South. The South is seen as a subject. Not so much Indiana. Why would one write about Indiana? I often answer that, well, someone has to, and leave it at that. But it is more complicated, of course. If there is a coat I have been trying on all these years, it's Billy Pilgrim's Dresden jacket. Mr. Kurt Vonnegut, Jr.'s unstuck character of *Slaughterhouse-Five* leads the parade. Mr. Vonnegut seems to have worked out the particular problem of being a regionalist from a region-less region. The adhesion of the unstuck.

I like to think there are two basic strategies for the out-flowing migratory Hoosier, two stories in answer to that nagging question, where you from? The first is Bill Blass's disguise that takes on the big city, takes it and the bigger world by storm. The fashion guru from the south side of Fort Wayne out-New Yorks New Yorkers. David Letterman, on the other hand, wears his trumped up bumpkin nature on his sleeve. Stories of sacking at the Atlas, his mom's pies, the abiding love for the Jim Nabor's version of "Back Home Again."

It's tough, is all I'm saying about what to do with this particular material. Are these "Indiana" stories? I don't know. Am I an Indiana writer? Maybe. Kind of. I now have lived more years outside the state than I lived in it. But I keep coming back. Pilgrim indeed. You remember the scene in *God Bless You, Mr. Rosewater* don't you? That chance meeting of wandering Hoosiers far from home? "I'm from Indiana too." All the vectors that have taken me away seem to lead me back again, a strange string theory unraveling. Warped space, time unstuck.

Grappling Hook

My father worked all his life for the phone company, in the switch rooms where when you dialed the number you wanted you were connected to it. As I reread these stories I noticed a lot of telephony. I suppose you could read that as a desire to be connected, the phone lines themselves an elaborate analog stitching together of a people constantly on the move. But there is that other "telephone." I am thinking of the game of whispered messages, ear to ear, passing from person to person that transforms the original message into a shadow of itself. The message tweaked, bent, made new.

Those actual wires, cables, are disappearing now, replaced by digital cells. More and more, we all bear witness to that the telling contemporary juxtaposition: a group of people together all animatedly speaking on their cell phones to someone else someplace else.

The most frequently uttered first sentence of cell phone usage is:

Where are you?

Wireless has left our actual addresses unmoored, so we drift and seek a homing beacon. We still seem to need a fix on location. Pin it down. A context to gab.

Stories are short performances of connection, composed and consumed in private. One never knows if they will "take." One hopes so. But so much is left out by design, left out in the hope that so much is already there, understood. One of the stories reprinted here is narrated by Harlan Sanders who at the time of its first publication was alive and selling fried chicken. He is now dead. So it goes. And more and more people believe that the Colonel was always a mere cartoon creation on the side of the bucket. Information degrades, gets lost in the transmission's static, its fuzz. So it goes.

I said (didn't I?) that this was a fossil record of some real and imagined past. But maybe it's more like a 13-year hatch of cicada who emerge from their shells grappled to tree trunks, clapboards, and masonry—papery remnants of their sawing songs coming at you invisibly from the leafy canopy.

Box Cutter

FEMA trailers still race through Tuscaloosa in convoys of three or four on their way to the Gulf Coast and New Orleans a year after Katrina. Most of the ones I see are coming from Indiana straight down I-65.

This introduction is all about metaphor, about the slant way art approaches life and the way the fiction here is skewed. Why *Double-wide*?

I come from Indiana which is, among other things, the double-wide, RV, fifth-wheel, van conversion, mobile home capital of the world. Everywhere there are those stubby little trucks hauling halves of houses, the open side wrapped in plastic. Wide load. Flashing lights. Fields of mutating vans. Fiberglass and Plexiglas. I grew up on a vast flat plain where houses and parts of houses shuttled back and forth between factories made of prefabricated parts. Where cars transformed into houses. Where houses found wheels.

In this landscape of impermanence, who carpenters together the mobile homes and vans? The Amish. They come from their farms, 80 acre oases in the shifting sands of mobility. They bring their skills, their craft, honed for a life of subsistence and sustainability, to an enterprise that is cheap, quick, temporary. I like to think of this uneasy marriage, the symbiosis of care and expedience, craft and crate, greed and gift. I like to think of my stories as these hobbled habitats, finished by hand, cruising the interstates, oversized loads, still settling.

A trailer is not just a trailer. A house is not just a house. Indiana is not just Indiana. And I'm not just me. Robert Frost wrote that a poem should mean at least one thing and, at least, one thing more. Exactly. Kind of.

And things should be used over and over. Let's all go quarry a few new bricks for our outhouse from that coliseum in downtown Rome. I myself cut and pasted in, moments ago, several paragraphs here from something I wrote years before. But then, this book is all about cut and paste, held together by that very American anxiety, that tension of moving on or staying put. These fictions are about many things, but one thing they are about is that: the moving on and the staying put.

From Alive and Dead in Indiana

Highlights

This is my office. The clock on the wall is mine. It is in the shape of a black cat. Its tail hangs down. When the tail moves one way with each tick, the cat's eyes move the other way. Usually, I am home by now. This is my salt tank and those are my fish. Those are my couches. Those are my chairs. This table is for the kids and their little chairs. This cigar box full of broken and dull crayons is mine. I am waiting for Mrs. Gustafson to bring Bobby in after football practice so I can fit him with a plastic mouth guard. The Formica table top and the waxy scribbles are mine. The stack of magazines is mine. This *Highlights* is mine, and no one has circled the hidden pictures in the Hidden Pictures. I have already found the comb in her bonnet and the bird in the elbow wrinkles of the man. I have yet to find the spoon, the light bulb, the banana, the pencil, the loaf of bread, the carrot, the ball, the vase, the mitten, the umbrella, the ladder, the iron, and the flashlight. It is a picture of the gingerbread man running away. They hide everyday things in a picture of a fairy tale.

I treat kids, mostly, and the roller skaters who wander in from the boardwalk with a chipped tooth from a fall. A bloody incisor in the palm of my hand. I wear a smock with bunnies sometimes or bees. Bright colors, never white. I keep rubber spiders in the light wells to cast shadows overhead. Mobiles twist in the salt breeze. I warm the explorer in my hand. Have three flavors of fluoride from which to choose. I let the children use the hand mirror and look at my teeth. I keep a treasure chest behind the desk filled with plastic dinosaurs, airplanes, and toy soldiers. They bring me their baby teeth. They think I am the tooth fairy. I give them quarters and take the teeth home to Suzy, who says one day she will think of something to do with them. But I find the teeth everywhere, little bits of bone. They will last longer than anything else in the world. The smiles I see here in the chair are all spotty, only temporary. What future do I see in it but braces, orthodontia? All my work gone when the kid's eleven. The baby teeth just hold open a space in the head. Washing out a mouth I tell its owner to rinse and say my name into the funny sink next to the chair.

I have very large hands. My paddles. A hand going through the water has the same amount of surface area whether the fingers are open or closed. They proved that in wind-tunnel tests. They were always proving things about the water in the air.

It's all the same. Thicker and thinner.

I could feel the water. Get its feel. I could feel the water splashing into the gutter on the other side of the pool. I could touch the wall before I touched it. I could feel feeling going out of my fingers and spreading through the pool like dye. I could feel the molecules slamming into each other.

But my hands are too big for a dentist. My hands make my patients gag. My fingers can't tell between a premolar and a molar. When I wash my hands with the green soap before I touch a patient, for a second I feel the old feeling. I leave my hands wet. "Open up," I say. Underwater, my hands are two fishes. I watch them through the milky light.

I think Suzy was happiest when she was being saved. The books I did on swimming always had a section on lifesaving. She was always the victim. She has the pictures Leifer did. The close-up of the carry where I have pinned her arm behind her. Her other arm is thrown up over my shoulder. Floating dead, her eyes are closed. It is quite tender, actually, the way I am looking down at her, my head cocked to the side, my other arm riding above her breasts. Her makeup perfect, even wet. The longer shot as I drag her along. Our bodies all broken into lines by the water I am sculling. My head and her face above the water. Her hair is trailing into the ripples of water. In one, I am carrying her by the chin as I would someone unconscious, but her eyes are open, her eyelashes wet. What was I saying to her? My double-jointed thumb was pulling her mouth down and tight. Then there is the series where I am lifting her out of the pool. Holding her hands on the edge with my own as I climb out. Then bending down to pull her up and over. Pictures are what marriage is all about.

On the boardwalk, the men and women grind by on roller skates. In dry swimsuits, they swim along, arms paddling backward. They float down sidewalks. It is another liquid, a thinner medium. There was a dance once called the swim. They dance it with their eyes closed as they slide past. Antennas grow from their ears, little backpack radios, earplugs, headphones.

"All I want to know is can you do it?" he said from the chair. I'd told him what I was going to do.

"Do what?" I asked.

"You know, man, with the filling. You hear about it."

"Those are accidents," I said, mixing the cement.

"Well, make one happen. I want my molar to pick up KABC. But it doesn't have to be that station. I just thought it would be the easiest. All those watts."

When I was swimming, I couldn't hear a thing. But maybe the ocean. Like the one in the seashell. A sound like metal. You can hear the tide sizzle on the beach. The skaters hiss along. Their eyes closed, their mouths working.

Swimming laps, I would imagine a woman walking on the water a few steps beyond the reach of my stroke. Sometimes, she would trip on a wave and, if she stumbled completely, look at her elbow as if she had scraped it. Sometimes, she would drop pieces of her clothes as she walked. Around her feet would be circles that would expand and disappear when she walked. As I was about to touch the wall, she would step out of the pool as if she were stepping ashore from some boat.

She was not the most interesting thing to think about. So I would begin thinking about the woman the others were thinking about.

I am worried about tooth dust. I can see it floating in the air, in the rays of sunlight coming through the window. It is fine and fluid. What will happen after years of breathing it? The mouth is a filthy place. But the dust. I can see it as I walk through it. Feel it eddying around me, closing in behind me. You can write your name on it on the tray; the instruments are grainy with it. It is getting thicker. When I use the high-speed drill, the patient gripping the arm rests from the pitch, I can see little puffs of dust from the tooth.

It smells awful.

Worse than burning hair.

No one thought I would make it when I went back to school. I had done nothing for four years between the Olympics. I went up to Canada, but it was the last time I wanted to talk about swimming. The records wouldn't hold. And they kept asking me, "Do you think your records will hold?" I went back home and flew my radio-controlled glider up and down the coast. I would spiral it up and stall it out, tip the nose over and bring it to me like a hunting hawk.

I watched video tapes with Suzy of all the races in Munich, and finally ran out of things to notice. My right elbow bent when it should be extended on the recovery stroke of the two-hundred fly. Suzy would watch Carson, and I would look past the TV at my poster on the wall.

Before a meet you shave down. Some guys do it quietly, others loudly in the shower. The chest, the tops of the feet, the insides of the thighs, the small of the back, even the crotch. Everything is shaved. Doc had boxes of blades and razors. There was a wall of mirrors, and the guys leaned over the sinks toward them, plucking eyebrows, earlobes, and nostrils, then giving in and shaving the eyebrows.

Some would use Neet. Some would use only a razor. It was like peeling off skin when you did it right. You felt faster, seamless, streamlined. The team from Tennessee shaved their heads and held up their feet to show us the soles with the nicks from where they'd shaved. Well, well. They dared us to touch their scalps. I walked over and poked a finger at someone's bald temple.

"It's in your head," I said.

That is when I started my mustache.

I had a little comb I would use before taking my mark. But I still shaved everything else. I got used to my body that way. When I stopped racing, it was like becoming a man all over again. I grew old in a couple of weeks.

I have dark hair. Sometimes, still, I am surprised by the hand I see working in a mouth. This is my hand. I'll watch Suzy bathing and shaving her legs, raising one out above the soap bubbles like a commercial. She lets me shave the other, knowing how good I am with a razor. Her skin is very soft. When we shower together, I make her lift both arms at the same time, and I shave both her underarms at once.

I cannot remember learning to swim. I like to think that my father threw me in someplace and, as he waited for me to come to the surface, turned to my mother and said, "We have a fish on our hands." If I were a fish I would want to be the kind that has a migrating eye. The eye itself turns the body flat as it comes loose and wanders over the head to the other side of the face. I would think about that while swimming laps. Growing gills, webs, flukes. Evolving backwards. Or maybe the mouth would migrate to the side of the head so I wouldn't have to turn to breathe. Better yet, a hole in the middle of the shoulder blades. No teeth at all.

While I swam, parts came loose and floated free. My nipples slid down my chest. My chin sheered away. My toenails shed like scales. There were fingers in my wake.

I was always thinking of something else. Of one more thing. When I talk to a patient in the chair, before an answer, the mouth is going open, and I can see the tongue still working back in the mouth. The patient makes funny sounds. The teeth, never quite right, float in the gums, washed forward like plastic bottles in the surf.

Suzy got the idea from a television commercial.

It was a floor wax commercial, but in it they machine-gun the glass cockpit of a jet. You can see the white bullets bouncing off. The ingredient that protects the cockpit is in the floor wax. Suzy thought we could make a clear plastic wall out of the same stuff and embed the medals in it. That way you could be sitting in the breakfast area and look out to the living room out to watch the television through the clear plastic wall. The medals, she said, would seem to float in the air. I looked into it since I couldn't think of any other way to display them. All the time I was thinking about burglars machine-gunning the wall, the gold suspended in front of them. You could knock on the air in front of you. But they told me the plastic would turn green with age. And what would I do when I moved?

I started swimming every morning when I was five. I turned from the window and picked up my rolled towel to go with my father to the pool before dinner too. Outside my friends were walking away. My mother had turned them away at the door. He is going to the pool. He is going to the pool. Our parents would be on the decks sunning or in the empty stands reading summer books in the middle of winter. It was always summer. And the light was always reflected from below, aqua and turquoise. It was always summer. My hair was always wet or had those furrows the comb left after I combed it wet. And I thought I was lucky I wasn't blond, I mean, so the chlorine wouldn't tint and shine my hair. At college, there were no children. So I would walk off the campus into the neighborhoods or go to the playground and watch the children. There were lots of children in Bloomington. A teacher shooed me away once.

These were the children who had been the test groups for toothpastes. Crest was invented in Bloomington. The unmarked tubes, the new brush, the special tablets that stained the teeth where you missed. All of them brushing together in the school cafeteria after lunch. Those children had been the ones to rush in and say, "Mother, mother, only one cavity!"

We carved teeth in dent school from blocks of clay the size of sugar cubes. When I dream, I dream of two things—teeth that are as large as my head and drowning.

When Suzy yawns, I can see the fillings in her back teeth. I'll tell her to hold it and take a look in the light the lamp on the end table puts out. She will go right on watching television. I can see it reflected in her glasses.

"When are you going to file my teeth again?" she asks.

She asks me about striped toothpaste and how they get the stripes in it to come out right.

I do recommend sugarless gum.

If you watch television in the right light you can see yourself watching in the glass. I think television is not so much like an eye as a mouth. I look and look at it, and I don't know why others see it looking back at them. It's a mouth, all right. When we go out Suzy turns off the television and brushes her hair while looking at the green glass. Her long straight hair begins to float away from her, drawn by the static of the screen. I like to watch her.

Under the water, as I would go into my turn, I would see Doc's face, green, in the window. There was a window in the pool wall so he could watch us underwater. Pushing off, you planted your feet on the glass. He watched us and took our picture. Around the pool, on the walls, are still pictures of me swimming different strokes—the same strokes stopped at the same point or a series of one stroke instances apart, from all angles. My head coming out of the water as my arms pull on the fly, head on. What am I looking at? Doc's book was called the *Science of Swimming.* He developed interval training and hypoxic training. He defined the two-beat crawl stroke and the principles of fluid mechanics. He saw the Bernoulli principle in my stroke. I developed my stroke on my own by trial and error. When I came to Indiana as a freshman, Doc asked me how I pulled my hands through a crawl. I told him: a straight arm pull down the middle line of my body. When I saw the first movies, I saw myself using a zigzag pull with my elbows at ninety degrees. How did I develop such good mechanics when I didn't even know how I swam? Doc said I was a motor genius, and he strapped lights on my fingers and toes that flashed as I swam and made light-tracings of my stroke on film.

What I did all at once, swimmers now watch in pieces.

Doc could never get the pieces fine enough. Two pictures that looked identical to me looked years apart to him. They were a slice of a second apart. Like that puzzle in children's magazines where the quintuplets are really twins and three are impostors.

He no longer recognizes me now that I am not in college.

They say one day Doc was surprised by his own picture in a recent team portrait.

I remember the lights on my fingers and toes. I remember the batteries on my back.

There is this bar in Bloomington, Nick's, we would go to after practice in the morning. After telling Doc that we had a class to go to. We'd make our way down Kirkwood against the flow of students heading toward the old campus and their first class of the day. As they would close in behind us we would hear them say, "Swimmers."

Swimmers.

Nobody ever said, "Mark!"

Sitting at the bar, we could look out to the street and the students heading east. Across the street they were building a little mall on the corner of Dunn. Bloomington looked like Indiana then. It probably looks like California now. The stone replaced by redwood, outdoor cafés where the bars with neon signs had been. And roller skaters gliding to school instead of townies leaning into the wind.

The windows at Nick's were painted over with diagonal panes to make it look English. So we saw all this through diamonds.

You drank your beer from old jars.

They sold beer by the pound at Nick's.

She misses the interviews.

Plimpton was the last, four years after all the wins.

We showed him around, ran the tapes and films.

He was interested in what I was going to do now. I told him I was going to be a dentist, and he didn't believe me. I could live on the razor money, he said, sell goggles.

"You could pretend to be a dentist, George," she said, "and come to Mark's office." On the televised interviews she sees now, she watches the wives and girlfriends, how they kiss and hold on to the men who are talking. She likes the ones who never look at the camera but stare up at the men.

I ask my patients questions while we wait for the blocks to take. If their mouths aren't full of cotton, they try to answer. It is hard to talk when half of your face is numb. Lips and tongue and jaw are disappearing. I answer the questions for them as they nod their heads.

I keep them in a lock box at the bank. What can you do with them? I read somewhere in my textbooks about the place in the body that stores gold salts. Like the thyroid and iodine. If you suspect a lesion, you administer some radioactive salts and watch the iodine coat the throat. You need just a little bit of iodine. The same with gold. There is always a little bit in the brain. That is where it concentrates, in the thalamus, the seat of emotion. I think about this when I am flushing out a filling, filing it down. There are little shavings on the back of the tongue. In the brain, too, a little cavity, a missing piece. If the iodine is not there, you go all puffy. I don't remember what happens if you are deficient of gold. Sad, I guess.

I think of the medals on my chest, pure and heavy. You could bend them and rub off a mark like the crayon color of gold. Not like the metals I mix now—the silver amalgam. Silver expanding, the tin contracting, the copper's strength, and the zinc for flow. All mixed with mercury. Not like gold. Gold is perfect. Gold does not discolor if kept clean. It resists crushing stress. It keeps an edge. It will not fracture.

I think about my medals in the bank vault. Perhaps, if times get tough, I will have them flattened into foil and rolled for the pellets I need.

Could I ever drown? Could I ever forget that much? Is it really like breathing? I am like the cartoon character who has walked over a cliff and hasn't looked down yet.

I watch all the cartoons on Saturday so I can discuss them with my patients. To drown would be the only death that would make sense. The thing that makes you, kills you. The thing that serves you right. The hunting accident for the hunter. But I wonder if I could let myself or if the water wouldn't toss me back. No, it won't be the water that I'll drown in, it will be the swimming.

Someone has colored in Goofus and Gallant. Blue and red faces. *You should hold the gate open for your little brother. You should help him find his shoe.*

I have found all the hidden pictures in the Hidden Pictures and have circled them all with purple Crayola.

Bobby has yet to show up.

This is a nice life—being here, the crayons, the teeth in my pocket, Suzy home.

Everybody Watching and the Time Passing Like That

Where was I when I heard about it? Let's see. He died on the Friday, but I didn't hear until Saturday at a speech meet in Lafayette. I was in the cafetorium, drinking coffee and going over the notes I had made on a humorous interp I'd just finish judging. The results were due in a few minutes, and the cafetorium was filling up with students between rounds. I had drama to judge next and was wondering how my own kids had done in their first rounds. So, I was sitting there, flipping back at forth through the papers on my clipboard, drinking coffee, when Kevin Wilkerson came through the swinging doors. I saw him first through the windows in the doors, the windows that have the crisscrossing chicken wire sandwiched between the panes. He had this look on his face. I thought, "Oh my, I bet something happened in his round." He looked like he'd done awful. He'd probably flubbed a few words or dropped a line or two, or so I thought. I once judged a boy making his first speech who went up, forgot everything, and just stood there. Pretty soon there was a puddle on the floor and all of this in silence. The timekeeper sat there flipping over the cards. So I spoke up and repeated the last thing I could remember from his speech. Something about harvesting the sea. And he picked up right there and finished every word, wet pants and all.

They were corduroy pants, I remember. He finished last in his round, but you've got to hand it to the boy. I'd like to say the same kid went on to do great things. But I can't because I never heard. So I tell this story to my own kids when they think they have done poorly, and I was getting ready to tell Kevin something like it as he came up to the table. Kevin was very good at extemp. He's a lawyer now, a good one, in Indianapolis. He said to me then, "Mrs. Nall, I'm afraid I've got some real bad news." And I must have said something like nothing could be as had as the look on your face. Then he told me. "Jimmy Dean is dead. He died in a wreck."

They'd been listening to the car radio out in the parking lot between rounds. That's how they heard. "Are you all right, Mrs. Nall?" Kevin was saying. Now, I'm a drama teacher. I was Jimmy's first drama coach, as you know. I like to think I have a bit of poise, that I have things under control. I don't let myself in for surprises, you know. But when Kevin said that to me, I about lost it, my stage presence if you will, right there in the cafetorium. Then everyone seemed to know about it all at once, and all my students began showing up. They stood around watching to see what I'd do. Most of them had met Jimmy the spring before, you know, when he came home with the *Life* photographer. They just stood watching me there with the other students from the other schools kind of making room for us. Well, if I didn't feel just like that boy who'd wet his pants. Everybody watching and the time passing like that.

But you were wondering where I was, not how I felt.

I suppose, too, you'd like to know how I met James Dean, the plays we did in high school, the kids he hung around with and such. What magazine did you say you're from? I can tell you these things, though I don't quite understand why people like yourself come looking for me. I'm flattered, because I really didn't teach Jimmy to act. I have always said he was a natural that way. I think I see that something happened when he died. But something happens, I suppose, when anybody dies. Or is born for that matter.

I guess something is also gone when the last person actually knew him dies. It's as if people come here to remember things that never happened to them. There are the movies, the movies are good. It's just sometimes the people of Fairmount wonder what all the fuss is about. It isn't so much that the grave gets visited. You'd expect that. Why, every time you head up pike to Marion, there is a strange car with out-of-state plates bumping through the cemetery. It's just that then the visitors tend to spread out through town, knocking on doors.

Marcus and Ortense, his folks (well, not his parents, you know), say people still show up on the porch. They're there the glider, sun up, when Ortense goes for the Star. Or someone will be taking pictures of the feedlot and ask to see Jimmy's bedroom. Why come to the home town? It's as if they were the students in tile cafetorium just watching and waiting for this to happen after the news has been brought.

People are always going through Indiana. Maybe this is the place to stop. Maybe people miss the small town they never had. I'm the school-teacher, all right. I remember everyone. I have to stop myself from saying, "Are you Patty's little brother?" "The Wilton boy?"

That's small town.

The first I remember him, he was in junior high. I was judging a speech contest for the WCTU, and Jimmy was in it, a seventh grader. He recited a poem called "Bars." You see the double meaning there?

He started it up kneeling behind a chair, talking through the slats of the back, you know. Props. It wasn't allowed. No props. I stopped him and told him he would have to do it without the chair. But he said he couldn't do it that way. I asked him why not. He said he didn't know. He stood there on the stage. Didn't say one word. Well, just another boy gone deaf and dumb in front of me. One who knew the words.

I prompted him. He looked at the chair off to the side of stage.

Couldn't speak without his little prison. So he walked off.

"Bars" was a monologue, you see. In high school, Jimmy did a mono-logue for me, for competition. "The Madman." We cut it from Dickens.

We took it to the Nationals in Colorado that year. Rode the train out there together for the National Forensic League tournament. As I said, it was a monologue. But it called for as many emotions as a regular interp which might have three or four characters. You never get more than five or six characters in a regular reading. But Jimmy had that many voices and moods in this single character. Could keep them straight. Could go back and forth with them. He was a natural actor. I didn't teach him that. Couldn't.

I know what you're thinking. You think that if you slice through a life anywhere you'll find the marbling that veins the whole cake. Not true. He was an actor. He was other people. Just because he could be mad doesn't mean he was.

You know the scene in the beanfield. Come to the window. There, you see that field? Beans.

They used mustard plants in the movie.

And here, we know that Jimmy knew that too. Beans are bushier. Leave it to Hollywood to get it all wrong.

In the summer, kids here walk through the beans and hoe out the weeds. They wear white T-shirts and blue jeans in all that green. Jimmy walked too when he was here.

That's the town's favorite scene. Crops. Seeing that—those boys in the bushes, white shirts, blue pants. How could he have known how to be insane? Makes me want to seal off those fields forever. Keep out everything. You can understand that, can't you?

It was quiet then. Now the Air Guard jets fly over from Peru. I notice most people get used to it. At night, you can hear the trucks on I-69 right through your bed. I lost boys on that highway before it was even built. They'd go down to the Muncie exit and nudge around the barricades in their jalopies. Why, the road was still being built, you know. Machinery everywhere. Imagine that. How white that new cement must have been in the moonlight. Not a car on the road. This was before those yard lights the rural electric cooperative gives the farmers. Those boys would point their cars south to Indianapolis and turn out the lights, knowing it was supposed to be straight until Anderson. No signs. No stripes on the road. New road through the beanfields, through the cornfields. Every once in a while a smudge pot, a road lantern. That stretch of road was one of the first parts finished, and it sat there, closed for years it seemed, as the rest of the highway was built up to it along with the weight stations and the rest stops.

I think of those boys as lost on that road. In Indiana then, if you got killed on a marked road, the highway patrol put up a cross as a reminder to other drivers.

Some places looked just like a graveyard. But out on the unfinished highway, when those boys plowed into a big yellow grader or a bulldozer blade or just kept going though the road stopped at a bridge that had yet to be built, it could be days before they were even found.

The last time I saw Jimmy alive, we were both driving cars. We did a little dance on Main Street. I was backing out of a parking slot in my Buick Special when Jimmy flashed by in the Winslows' car. I saw him in the rearview mirror and craned my neck around. At the same time, I laid on the horn.

One long blast.

Riding with Jimmy was that *Life* photographer who was taking pictures of everything.

Jimmy had on his glasses, and his cap was back on his head. He slammed on the brakes and threw his car in reverse, backing up the street, back past me. He must have recognized my car. So out I backed, cut across the front of his car, broadsiding his grille, then to the far outside lane where I lined up parallel with him.

He was a handsome boy. He already had his window rolled down, saying something, and I was stretching across the front seat, trying to reach the crank to roll down mine on the passenger side. Flustered, I hadn't thought to put the car in park. So I had to keep my foot on the brake. My skirt rode up my leg, and I kept reaching and then backing off to get up on one elbow to take a look out the window to see if Jimmy was saying something.

The engine was running fast, and the photographer was taking pictures.

I kept reaching for the handle and feeling foolish that I couldn't reach it. I was embarrassed. I couldn't think of any way to do it. You know how it is—you're so busy doing two things foolishly, you can't see through to doing one thing at a time. There were other cars getting lined up behind us, and they were blowing their horns. Once in history, Fairmount had a traffic jam.

The fools. They couldn't see what was going on.

Jimmy started pointing up ahead and nodding, and he rolled up his window and took off. I scrunched back over to the driver's side as Jimmy roared by. He honked his horn, you know. *A shave and a haircut.* The cars that had been stacked up behind us began to pass me on the right, I answered back. *Two bits.*

I could see that photographer leaning back over the bench seat, taking my picture. I flooded the engine. I could smell the gasoline. I sat there on Main Street getting smaller.

When the magazine with the pictures of Jimmy and Fairmount came out, we all knew it would be worth saving, that sometime in the future it would be a thing to have. Some folks went all the way up to Fort Wayne for copies. But Jimmy was dead, so it was sold out up there too.

I wasn't in the magazine. No picture of me in my car on Main Street. But there was Jimmy walking on Washington with the Citizens Bank onion dome over his shoulder. Jimmy playing a bongo to the livestock. Jimmy reading James Whitcomb Riley. Jimmy posing with his cap held on his curled arm. He wears those rubber boots with the claw buckles. His hand rests on the boar's back.

Do you remember that one beautiful picture of Jimmy and the farm? He's in front of the farm, the white barn and the stone fences in the background. The trees are just beginning to bud. Tuck, Jimmy's dog, is looking one way and Jimmy the other. There is the picture, too, of Jimmy sitting upright in the coffin.

Mr. Hunt of Hunt's Store down on Main Street kept a few coffins around.

That is where that picture was taken.

In Indianapolis, they make more coffins than anywhere else in the world. The trucks, loaded up, go through town every day. They've got CASKETS painted in red on the sides of the trailers. You wait long enough downtown, one'll go through.

See what you have made me do? I keep remembering the wrong things. I swear, you must think that's all I think about.

What magazine did you say you were from?

Jim's death is no mystery to me. It was an accident. An accident. There is no way you can make me believe he wanted to die. I'm a judge. I judge interpretations. There was no reason. Look around you, look around. Those fields. Who could want to die? Sure, students in those days read EC comics. I had a whole drawer full of them. I would take them away for the term. Heads axed open. Limbs severed. Skin being stripped off. But I was convinced it was theater. Look, they were saying, we can make you sick.

It worked. They were right.

I'd look at those comic books after school. I'd sit at my desk and look at them. Outside the window, the hall monitors would be cleaning out the board erasers by banging them against the wall of the school. The air out there was full of chalk. I flipped through those magazines, nodding my head, knowing what it was all about. I am not a speech teacher for nothing. I taught acting. I know when someone wants attention. The thing is to make them feel things before anything else.

I taught Jimmy to kiss.

I taught Jimmy to die.

We were doing scenes from *Of Mice and Men*. I told him the dying part is pretty easy. The gun George uses is three inches from the back of Lenny's head. When it goes off, your body will go like this—the shoulders up around the ears, the eyes pressed closed. He was on his knees saying something like "I can see it, George." Then *bang*. Don't turn when you fall. After your body flinches, relax. Relax every muscle. Your body will fall forward all by itself.

Well, it didn't, not with Jimmy. He wanted to grab his chest like some kid playing war. Or throw up his hands. Or be blown forward from the force of the shot.

"Haven't you ever seen anything die?" I asked him.

"No," he said.

"It's like this," I said, and I got up there on the stage and fell over again and again. I had George shoot me until we ran out of blanks. It was October, I remember, and outside the hunters were walking the fields flushing pheasants. After we were done with the practice, we could hear the popping of shotguns—one two, one two. We hadn't noticed that with our own gun fire.

Hunting goes so fast and that's what irritates me.

Jimmy was so excited, you know, doing things you couldn't do in high school. Dying, kissing. That's how young they were. Kids just don't know that acting is doing things that go on every day.

"Just kiss," I told Jimmy after he'd almost bent a girl's neck off. "Look," I said, taking one of his hands and putting it on my hip, "close your eyes." I slid my hands up under his arms so that my hands pressed his shoulder blades. His other hand came around. He stood there, you know. I tucked my head to the side and kissed him.

"Like that," I said.

I quieted the giggles with a look. And then I kissed him again.

"Do it like that," I said.

Even pretending, Jimmy liked things real. No stories, action. He was doing a scene once, I forget just what. The set for the scene called for a wall with a bullet hole. Jimmy worked on the sets too. I was going to paint the hole on the wall, and Jimmy said no. We waited as he rushed home. He came back with a .22, and before I could stop him, he shot a hole in the plywood wall.

I tell you, the hole was more real than that wall. I remember he went up to the wall and felt it, felt the hole.

"Through and through," he said. "Clean through and through."

The bullet had gone through two curtains and lodged in the rear wall of the stage. I can show you that hole. If you want to look, I can show you.

Right before he died, Jimmy made a commercial for the Highway Safety Council. They show it here twice a year in the driver's education class. The day they show it, I sit in. The students in the class each have a simulator. You know, a steering wheel, a mirror, a windshield with wipers that work, dials luminous in the dark.

Jimmy did the commercial while he was doing his last picture. He is dressed up as a cowboy, twirling a lariat. Gig Young interviews him. They talk about racing and going fast. Then Gig Young asks Jimmy, the cowboy, for advice. Advice for all the young drivers who might be watching. And I look around the class, and they are watching.

It is the way he begins each sentence with "Oh."

Or it's the lariat, the knot he fiddles with.

That new way of acting.

What is he thinking about? Jimmy was supposed to say the campaign slogan—*The life you save may be your own.* But he doesn't. He looks toward the camera. He couldn't see the camera because he wouldn't wear his glasses. I can see what is happening. He is forgetting. He says. "The life you save may be—a pause—"mine." Mine.

I guess that I have seen that little bit of film more times than anyone else in the world. I watch the film, and he talks to me, talks to me directly. I have it all up here.

He kissed me.

He died.

Leave his life alone.

I know motivation. I *teach* motivation. I teach *acting*.

Pieces

I parked that night in a lot across the street from a restaurant I wanted to call on the next day early. I had gotten into Fort Wayne late, having driven all day from my home in Corbin, Kentucky. I had made a side trip crossing the Ohio at Brandenberg to Maukport, then on to Henryville, Indiana, where I was born and grew up. It was for old times' sake. No one knows me there now. I talked with no one. Climbing north, I had this sense of things starting up again. It was already hot. They were running, and I took my place in the stream of white-haired travelers hauling those silver trailers, driving those new finned cars, passed only by Negro children being driven south out of the cities to Grandma's place on the land in Mississippi or Alabama. These are the times of real migrations. With the warm weather and those new highways, people had started to move. I was on the road all the time and hadn't seen anything like it. Not since the thirties.

The traffic put me late in the city. I got my bearings from the bank building downtown. I'd been here before a few years earlier in 1950. I found Anthony Street, and followed the overhead trolleybus lines, a main street, and must have even followed a trolleybus because I remember thinking they still have these, the smell and the sparks and the sound of sliding metal. Fake lightning. And there might have been real heat lightning that night and lightning bugs.

The elms looked real sick in the streetlights. I didn't have time to find a place, or money if I had found one, having not much more than enough for gas and a bit extra, just in case. Nor am I so inclined. I like sleeping in a car, especially my car. I have my spices. And there was a change in the weather that night. So when I spotted the Hobby House Restaurant— and I had some trouble since it was locked and dark—I pulled into the lot across the street which had a huge sign still on that late. It was a painter's palette with three brushes poking through tile thumb hole. Each dab of paint was lit up by a different color of neon.

It wasn't a paint store but an ice-cream parlor. Each color a flavor of ice cream, I guess. The sign burned and buzzed to high heaven, but I was able to settle down in the backseat with beaten biscuits and my scales.

I weighed my spices and herbs in the pools of colored light for the next day's meeting.

The palette was on some type of timer.

At midnight, it went out and silent just like that, even though no one was around to switch it off. And there was lightning that night but no thunder. It flashed as I put my things away in the dark.

Am I telling you too much? These things might not be to the point of the matter. But give me a little room to build up speed.

I'm sixty-six years old, which should give me a pretty good enough excuse for acting this way.

I can remember fifty years ago as if it were yesterday. I can't remember yesterday.

The maps in my time you had to read. *Three miles from the county line, turn left on the macadamized road, an old Indian trail, and at four and a half miles, with redbarn on the right, take another left. This is county road 16. Oil mat.* Roads weren't lines then. Give me time and I'll make the turn.

I sell a recipe for fried chicken. That's what brought me to Fort Wayne that night. I used to have my own place in Corbin, and I couldn't complain. Business was good because my cooking was good. Country ham, black-eyed peas, red-eye gravy, okra and string beans, watermelon pickle, hoe cake, baked apples. Duncan Hines wrote me up in his *Adventures in Good Eating* before the war. Gave directions. The shed on your left, the fence on your right. That kind of thing. He got you right to my door. No Worcester Diner, tablecloths, and gravy boats. And the thing was in place. I even had a root cellar with roots.

Eisenhower's defense highways put me out of business. I sold it all for a big loss. My wife said that it was about time we went south anyway, and she wanted to head down that new 75, a clear shot to Florida. SEE ROCK CITY on every Barn and birdhouse. But I wasn't going to manage on my Social Security wearing Bermuda shorts, thinking twice about buying this pack of Beechnut gum. A few years ago, I taught a good friend of mine, Pete Harman of Salt Lake City, how to fry chicken with this recipe and every indication was that the chicken did a job for his business.

There are some other places too. Other men who have heard about it. They would send me four cents, a nickel a bird. But it was nothing I worked at or thought about. And now these cars were passing my place. Though I couldn't see the traffic, I could feel its steady rumble through my feet. Those roads are so big you can hear things like you can over open water.

My last good days were feeding the crews who drove the graders and dozers. Their hard hats were lined up on the rack by the door like skulls. I'd rather wear out than rust through. So I got on that road, joined the rumble with the Pete Harman deal in mind. I put a pressure cooker, the spices and scales, my apron and knives in the backseat of my '53 Pontiac. It had an amber Indian head on tile hood, and it handled like a boat I shipped out over that sound.

It was no great adventure. I'm an old man, after all.

I started by cooking for my family. Time to get out of the kitchen and take it on the road since the road had up and gone.

It's not so strange. You fellows are fretting right now about what to do with your folks, I bet. I had to make up my own mind, had to make a little money.

So I hadn't met her yet. Instead, I am in a parking lot in Fort Wayne, waiting for this restaurant to open up for breakfast. A crew of high school kids is tarring and repainting the lot. They are making noise as they close off a section with rope laced through the handles of gray sealer cans. I'm the only car in the lot. It's a big lot. They lay down the parking stripes that look like fish bones on the tar. I can see the painter's palette sign is turquoise. Down the way is the baseball stadium where the Pistons play. There are big silver pistons on the press box. I know beyond the stadium is a road being built.

The elms look even sicker in the daylight. More like willows than elms. The restaurant has the look of being open now, though I haven't seen anyone unlock the doors, and, sure enough, cars start turning in. I start mine and drive across the street carefully as the traffic is picking up. I park and go in. I like the place. The walls have stained, knotty pine paneling. The tables have red checkered tablecloths and each, no matter how large, is set for two. There are wagon wheels on the walls; half-wheels are buried in the backs of booths; the chimney lamps on the tables rest on little wagon wheels. The coffee is streaming into pots.

In the restroom, I wash my face and shave quickly. I have very little beard. The room is well lit and clean. Before going back to my booth, I knock on the women's restroom door. When there is no answer, I peek in. It's the same story, clean and bright, a couch for nursing.

It is a breakfast menu. Combinations of eggs, ham, potatoes. They have steak, hash, all the juices, and a specialty—a doughnut with its hole teed up in the center, glaze dripping from one to the other. But I order lunch—a hamburger, fries, and a Coke.

"No problem, hon, but the deep fryer's not on till eleven. Hash browns okay?"

Everything is fine.

There's a regular clientele. Coffee is poured before anyone asks. Conversations are picked up where they left off the day before, morning papers left behind to be picked up. So are large tips. There are men in uniforms. They use their fingers and dip their toast. They stack their own dishes. This feels like home.

"Here, let me heat that up for you," the waitress says, pouring coffee with a smile.

Even though it is crowded, it is comfortable. There are dining rooms closed off. I can just sit, drink the coffee, and read your local news.

After the morning rush has left for work, what remains are the old men talking about the weather, a feeble-minded boy sweeping up, and my waitress with the bright glass coffeepot still steaming in her hand. I ask to see the owner. I know his name. At first she looks at me as if I've betrayed her hospitality. Then she reads me as a salesman, smiling as she says, "All right, I'll get him, wait right here."

The owner comes through the swinging doors, out from his office. He is followed by my waitress, who brings him coffee as he sits. I get right to the people we know, talk about the National Restaurant Association, mention the new highways. He's at a disadvantage when I make my pitch. I could be his father. I ask him to let me make some chicken for him. What's he out but some shortening and flour? That's right. I stayed on to cook for him and then for his customers. Then we shook on it, and I taught his people in the kitchen how to do it. Next thing was to make arrangements for getting the ingredients mailed and him sending all the money back home.

It wasn't until I was back on the road again that I saw her hitchhiking. At first, I thought she might be a boy. She wore pants and had her hair up short. She had a small roll at her feet, a silver frying pan tied up on it. She stood, thumb out, too far from the road. But I saw her. She grabbed her things and ran to the car and opened the door without looking in first.

"Where you going?" I asked her.

"Wherever you are."

Fair enough. I put it in gear and got back on the highway. It didn't take her long to notice.

She said, "Jesus, what's that smell?"

I told her what the smell was and what I was doing on the road. I didn't ask anything because I felt she didn't want me to, nor could I tell from her looks whether she had been on the road for a while or if I was her first ride. She didn't say a word when I pointed the car toward Michigan. Maybe she didn't know. Maybe she didn't care.

It seems to me there aren't any real crossroads anymore for most people. Most of us are going against the grain. She had nothing to decide, only tendencies. I had taken her up. Your part of the country is a funnel of flat land with a bias. I worked as a ferryboat captain on the Ohio. A small boat. Ferried autos and walkers from Jeffersonville to Louisville. I made the trip once an hour, seven hours a day. I heard about Mark Twain and read some of his books. I wanted to be a river pilot like him. I took to wearing white suits like his. Piloting that boat, you could feel what I mean. The Ohio wants to sweep you west.

She said, "You're from the South, aren't you?"

I said that all depends on what you mean. Some people will say the South starts at 38th Street in Indianapolis.

The accent, the funny suit. I knew she was thinking of it all. The greasy diet, the in-breeding. I don't mind. On these trips, I let people think what they think. It's good for business. My age helps too. But I try not to go on about what I've done or seen. Let them imagine what they want.

I'd say she was a city girl. Movie stars on her mind. She probably thought the road led somewhere, that it was not just for the nation's business, the national defense. The "big road," you call it in Kentucky. The road to town. The road that leads to something different. As I think of it now, I didn't understand her half the time. She was restless on the seat, read the road signs to me, wanted to play games with license plates. I said she should follow along on the maps I keep in the glove box. She didn't want to.

There were things I didn't want to be with her but couldn't help being because they are what I am. An old man, a salesman, a gentleman, her father. But she needed to be talked to. The country whizzing past needed to be filled up with fun. I have advice, though I try to hide what I mean. I've done my share on posses walking through field stubble and dragging rivers while dogs bawled. Maybe I wanted to scare her, but I say I didn't.

She put on her sunglasses so I couldn't see her eyes and slouched in the seat against the door. It wasn't locked, but I held off from doing anything about it. We went on miles that way, me lecturing. She leaning into the unsafe door. Finally, I reached across the seat behind her. Pushed the button down. She didn't say a word except "Thank you."

We were traveling through the lake country near the Michigan line. The trees along the road would open up to water. I talked about me then.

I couldn't help myself. I had made a sale. Like that waitress, I just wanted everybody served. I left home when I was twelve. I told her that I had worked on farms, been a streetcar conductor, was in the Army in Cuba, worked jobs that disappear. I studied law by mail waiting on the ready track of freight yards. Boiler was my light. I was a justice of the peace in Little Rock. Sold insurance and tires. Headed the Chamber in Columbus, Indiana. You can check that out if you want. I'm not really from the South, you see. Not from anywhere.

"Yes," I said. I pulled it all together, a piece here, a piece there. Yes, I have seen things. I rode the reefers and the blinds, saw a man frozen to the metal of the baggage car when the tender threw water picking it up on the fly. I was on a train with ballast in my pockets. Then I said something I thought she could use. *Never get off where there is no shade.*

I meant that.

She asked me when I left school, and I told her when they started in with algebra. If X was what you didn't know, then I didn't want it.

She lost interest after that. She turned to look out the window at the orchards being sprayed.

We were heading, though she didn't know it, to Mackinac Island in the straits. It's at the top of Michigan. The road is like a lifeline through the state's palm. It was there we got mixed up in a troop convoy. On maneuvers, I guess. Reserve Guard. I had seen convoys in the south-bound lane with their lights on, antennas bowed over on the jeeps. The trucks have a round-shouldered look, like they're hunching down the hot highway. We came up on their replacements heading north. The last vehicle was a jeep with MPs in white helmets in it. I scooted around, and then around the next deuce and a half. I blew my horn. I could see the cops shaking their heads, yelling and pointing. They weren't happy to have their string broken up. I tucked the Pontiac in between two trucks, waited for the lane to clear, then leapfrogged another truck.

I could see, when I swerved out there to pass, that the line went on for what looked like miles ahead. She perked up when we started passing. Rolled down her window. Took off her sunglasses.

As we got along deeper into the convoy, she waved to the boys. I could tell they knew right away she was a girl. Some drivers sped up to get a good look, pacing us and not letting me jog around. I could see the jeep of MPs in the rearview. It was working its way up the line behind us. They passed when we passed, eyes on us.

She yelled out to each truck. How far you going? Where you going? And then she would listen for a boy to shout how good-looking she was. I kept my eyes on the road. Listen to them, will you?

Laughing.

I felt sad seeing her reach out so far and trying to hold hands with some boy while the wind blew.

But I got to the head of the line, and that was that.

It was dark in Mackinaw City. A storm was on the lake. We could see the white in the water. Here was the end of the world as far as I was concerned. Even the roads ran out.

Across the water there was an island with no cars, restaurants that might sell my chicken. We'd take the ferry in the morning. I arranged for a cabin. It had a small stove and a sink. I grabbed some food from a grocery just as it closed. Then I cooked dinner, using her skillet. I took my knives and started cleaning chicken, telling her I'd been cooking it since I was six. I told her about Momma peeling tomatoes all day for Stokely-Van Camp in Henryville. I told her about May apples, greens, sassafras buds. I let her help, showing her how to peel a potato, snap the skin off the garlic with the flat of the knife. She was helpless, and I asked her why she brought the pan along anyway. She had seen pictures of Johnny Appleseed when she was a kid. She was serious, she said, about leaving home. I was cutting an onion. I can cut an onion, if it is a good onion, in such a way that it stays whole for a few seconds after I am done slicing. One instant it is whole, the next a pile of a hundred pieces. She had me do this several times. You have to know what to do with it once you have it, I said, thinking of her frying pan, of the onions, well, of everything. We were both crying tears we didn't mean. We ate in silence. She said she loved the food. Everybody does.

The storm boomed on outside. I don't think she knew where she was. Not just that moment—an old log cabin with an old man—but where in the world. Maybe if she knew, she would have considered turning back. The highway was pretty slow after all. Camping with her family all over again. I looked at her as she looked at the fire and wondered if she would be telling stories about this ancient man crossing roads with chickens. She asked me what held the onion together in the first place and if I ever tried to put it all back together like a puzzle.

I slept outside in the back seat of the car. She hadn't said one thing, not one way or the other. There are certain lines I don't cross. I hadn't offered her candy, only stone soup. To me it is all the same. When my belly's full, so is the rest of me. Maybe she just didn't have the words.

Outside the Pontiac, it was bad. The chief's head flashed. I went to sleep in the smell of sage and fresh ground pepper.

In the morning, it was all there. My spices, the storm, the girl in the cabin.

We drove to the ferry. But we could see from the water that no one was going anywhere. We got out and stood around. Some places you never reach.

I asked her what she wanted.

She said, "Let's just go. Just keep moving."

We headed south down 131. Nothing to talk about. No sun to give her a clue to the direction. The tin of the pressure cooker whistled as we drove.

It is the pressure cooker that is the secret. No waiting. Eight minutes to cook your goose. Didn't she know how much danger she would have been in if she hadn't been with me?

We crossed back into Indiana. Sleeping, she didn't wake up til I slowed for an Amish buggy around Nappanee. Horses and wagons were everywhere on the roads and in the fields. I got the car wheels to straddle the manure. That part of the country is the way Henryville was when I was growing up. Broad-brim straw hats and beards, suspenders and serge. Lordy, what I've seen. Now she wasn't half an hour away from where I picked her up in Fort Wayne, but she was way back in time. She was losing ground. She made me pass a wagon real slow as she stared, from behind her sunglasses, deep into the bonnet of the lady driver. She wanted to know what they were doing in the fields. Why they looked the way they looked. It was all so far away to her.

Not much farther up U.S. 6, she said here was where she would get out. All she had to do was say the word. She thanked me. I pulled over and stopped, got out and fetched her roll from the trunk. We'd parked next to a muckfield planted in peppermint. It had already been cut and raked into rows. The air reeked of it and onions in a field nearby. No shade in sight. She hadn't gotten a thing from me but a ride down the road. I told her to be careful.

I was able to look back at her a long time since the peat fields are so flat. I wondered if she realized what a difference a few feet make, that just this side of Fort Wayne is that continental divide turning the river back on its tributaries and dividing up the country as sure as the mountains out west. She probably didn't know how it all fit together. A small rise on the plain could cut her off forever. I turned a corner and never saw her again. I drove the rest of the day and night only stopping for gas.

Now it's your turn to tell me what this is all about. Who was she? Has something happened? Have I broken some law?

All the time I was with her I could see she didn't know word one about drummers or bums or bindlestiffs. But who was I to tell her? The roads are different now. But what's it to do with me? I'm glad that part of my life is behind me.

Alfred Kinsey, Alone after an Interview, Dreams of Indiana

I could never tell a dirty story. There is the one about the new convict and the numbered jokes, but that is not the type of thing I am thinking about. Well, anyway, the new convict calls out a number, and no one laughs because some people can't tell a joke. Pomeroy used to laugh at that one, probably more out of respect than anything else. I was, by that time, a kind of authority.

In the fall, Clara and I would borrow a car and head out of town on a Sunday. The leaves would be turning. I like the way fall works. The leaves not turning really, only the green going, and the carotene showing through for once.

We always saw it on our way to Brown County, saw a car pulled off onto the shoulder, occupants out there picnicking or napping near an overlook. And with the leaves forgetting themselves all around us, so would we. We'd try to get a look at the parkers. All this nature, but what we wanted was a look at each other. I always used this anecdote to teach my beginning classes the concept of species recognition. Interbreeding population is the last distinction before variety, I am convinced. It is the only instinct. Our heads are literally turned.

Martin kept expecting the women to lift their blouses. He was always saddened by the disparity between the public and the private history. He never doubted which was true. I remember him going over the histories of his classmates at Indiana. With the files open before him, he just sat there shaking his head. He had believed everything his friends had told him.

The first warm day and the whole department would head out to the quarries around Bloomington. Imagine in the first days of spring, their spouses within reach again, everyone is on the lookout for the return to life of some specific fauna. All these men, knowing the oestrus of their special species, have these females next to them on crazy quilts. Our peculiar nature. Look at them. Their heads bent to the obscene buzz of zoölogy. The University spelled zoölogy with that pesky umlaut overhead. The mark the Prussians left behind after drawing out the blood. There was a white dust on all the leaves from the gypsum factories. Spring in Indiana. The cut and tumbled blocks of the abandoned quarry must have looked like ruins to a German scholar. This was a new world for me. Let them find a story here. Clara was next to me, white from the winter but already tanning. The rocks were warming up. I had just turned associate, and felt secure. So I stopped them before they could get their killing jars from the car. Yes, I stopped them by taking off my clothes and diving headlong into the pool of someone else's reflection.

We could talk shop in the most public of places because of the code. I would say, "My last history liked Y better than CM although Go in Cx made him very ez." That type of rendering made everyone more comfortable. That was during McCarthy and the Customs Case. Our books could not be sent through the mail. The Institute and the University were very sensitive. We had recently lost the Rockefeller money. No one was laughing at anything.

Clara and I, during the first hot summers in Bloomington, would walk its streets and alleys, mildly interested in the bees collecting around the backdoor rubbish bins of restaurants. Pleased when we distinguished characteristics readily. Family, order, class. The tiny mass of Latin, yellow and brown, lighted on the red bricks. Their abdomens pulsed and touched. The wasps scribbled on the surface of a pool of water. Genus, species, variety. We went to Dunn Meadow and turned the oak leaves over in our hands, recognizing the wasp by the disruption of the cells, the black gall on the dull side of the leaf. Rummaging through campus to where the Jordan River disappeared underground, we read the leaves until it was too dark to see the beauty marks, left, and grabbed a bench on Kirkwood. From there we watched the couples collect under the yellow lights of the Von Lee as they waited to buy their tickets. We saw them touch each other. We did not care who was watching us watching. Paying no attention to the miller in the light or the cricket in the dark, we rounded the corner to the Book Nook, empty and quiet between terms. The soda jerk behind the counter told us again where the speaks were this summer as he screwed his towel into the glasses while I sat down at the piano where Hoagy Carmichael had composed "Stardust" and played Chopin and Beethoven, without distinction. We closed the place, circled back to ours, and, without turning on the lights, stumbled by the sheets of insects under glass, the cotton and the chlorides, the spreading boards and pins, and, with nothing left to identify, fell in bed with the house as hot as it had been all day.

My secret was never to show surprise. I told my interviewers to assume that everyone had done everything. Anything that could be imagined is humanly possible. We had only to ascertain when and how many times.

Clara would sometimes bring my lunch down to Jordan Hall when the Institute was just setting up house. "Honey," I said to her, "this building will some day house more pornography than the Vatican." We laughed. She always understood when I was joshing. We sat on the steps where Dellenbeck liked to take our picture and watched the young men across the way strip down to the waist and knock off for lunch. The WPA was building Sycamore and the Auditorium, and the CCC was adding a wall around the campus. Everything was done in the local limestone, which would turn from pink to gray in winter. That summer those boys with their farmer's tans molted into men. Thomas Hart Benton used some of them in the murals he did for the Auditorium. I took his history when he was on the campus. That afternoon we shared a lunch Clara brought, back in the woods where the river traced through the exposed bedrock. He wore overalls and talked about Missouri. Clara sat with her legs curled under her skirt. He stretched out his hand and touched her cheek saying, simply, "Bounty."

Pomeroy thought I derived some pleasure from keeping secrets. That was the psychologist in him talking. I never would reveal anything, of course, nor hold anything over anyone's head. It wasn't power that interested me.

I remember when Pomeroy broke my code, found and read my history, and Clara's and the children's. Of course, I was upset. But it pleased me even more that he was so willing to learn.

Her waist was gone. She was white in the moonlight. I remember, because the curtains were gone. Laundry. The baby was showing and had already moved. It was past the time we had agreed upon to do anything more. Her waist was gone, and she was a different creature. But it was summer, I remember, because I would stay up after she went to sleep and listen for insects. She had longings for cream puffs. I could keep nothing from spoiling. She could no longer move. There was no surprise. The introduction of love is its own undoing.

I told my researchers that there were only three ways a subject could not be reporting accurately. He could exaggerate, conceal, or remember imprecisely. Our methods took care of all three. The number and speed at which we ask our questions took care of most problems. No one could prepare a life, especially a sexual one, on the spur of the moment. The rest was in the follow-up, to see if the same story could be told twice.

I no longer ask myself certain questions. Donald died the year of my first Biology. It was Mill, I believe, who began his autobiography with a reference to his father's book on India. Author and Father. At the Institute, we interviewed each other every year or so. I have gone through my sexual history over twenty times. I've never found the slightest inconsistency; my stories match from year to year. The repetition makes everything clearer in my mind. In others, this justifies our methodology. The story is to remain the same. I am not so sure in my own case. I have been over everything again and again, but no single night presents itself to me as the one during which Donald was conceived. *Sexual Behavior in the Human Male* took ten years to write, and I can still recite the seed of that story. I even remember what the woman wore, the pearl at her throat. Perfection out of irritation. She was one of the students in the marriage course. In conference, she asked me how much passion she should expect from her fiancé. And I didn't know. Not then. Donald was three when he died. My first son. Some passion spent long ago.

I told my interviewers that some subjects would make advances. I prepared them for this as best I could. I knew it would happen. I had instructed them to remain impassive, always impassive. Nothing cools ardor more than impassivity. We did not want to lose the oral history, though. We did not want to lose anything.

There were about fifty different measurements taken on each specimen of gall wasp. And this was only morphology, not phylogeny, host relationships, geographic distribution, life cycles and history, or gall polymorphism. I no longer had the time for the rest of it, and couldn't find a graduate student so inclined. I was caught up in the other work. By this time I had finished two books on the Cynips. That was enough of a contribution.

I remember watching Clara once as she measured the third segment of antennas. She would still work on the plates with water colors and go over the Leach drawings after the children were in bed. She would use the colored pencils to write me notes. I told her the new study interested me more. No more pictures to draw. "Imagine," she said, "the illuminated manuscript of this. A different box of colors." I gave the rest of the specimens to Harvard and went to the field again, collecting.

That man in the West Side bar in New York, I remember every word. "I am Dr. Kinsey, from Indiana University, and I am making a study of sexual behavior. Can I buy you a drink?" What could he say? I took his history. He was a homosexual prostitute and was so pleased that I had been telling the truth that for years after that he encouraged his friends to be interviewed. I took his history. I got it. But what impressed him more, my innocence or my knowledge?

I always hired interviewers with stable marriages. It was the nature of the work. My experience of Americans led me to believe that they were skeptical of those who cannot keep house and home together. Of course, we had to travel a great deal, we really did, and then be alone with those consenting adults in any little bit of privacy we could find. Very little was lost on us.

Clara stayed behind with the children. I left with the men, and Clara finished the pictures she had started years before of the gold hands on the abdomen of Sphecids.

So many people wanted to tell me things. I let them. I simply let them talk. That was what was important. Let them hear themselves. I just listened. They wanted to tell me secrets so that someone knew they kept them, that they had secrets to keep. When the study started, I, of course, interviewed myself, following my life until its history ran out. Clara's history, the one Pomeroy came across, was contrived from the things I knew. She could never tell me things. I made it all up.

There are many ways of saying yes. I have trained myself to hear them all. When I interviewed, the code we used could represent every subtlety by making each different affirmation a different word. There is even a yes that means no, of course, and the many ways of saying no. This is all I have needed to understand the lovers of the world.

Winter in Indiana. The brown oak leaves stay on the tree through the winter. The dry leaves say yes. The stones turn from pink to gray. I will die of this enlarged heart, my doctor says, because there is no time to take the rest I need.

Whistler's Father

To get to the fort, you have to cross the St. Mary's River on an arched footbridge made of concrete and steel. The bridge is steep enough to make you lean forward. There is nothing moving on the river that needs this kind of clearance.

The St. Mary's runs down under the Spy Run Bridge, and then it meets the St. Joe River, to form the Maumee, which flows on to Toledo and Lake Erie.

The fort is built on the tongue of land between the two rivers. So it floods a lot. But this summer they've lifted the rollers down on the Anthony Street Dam, and the rivers are almost dry.

I can see the Three Rivers Apartments down by the confluence from here, the elevated tracks built over the old canal, and the whole sweep of Fort Wayne's skyline-bank towers, the golden dome of the courthouse. It is the kind of picture they like to show before the local news. Along the river, I can still see some piles of sandbags from the spring's flood and the lines each crest left through the summer. The riverbed is beginning to dry and crack below the levee. I like to stand here each morning on my way to the fort and watch all the flags go up on the buildings downtown.

I work at the fort. The bridge is supposed to make it easier for the visitors to imagine they're walking into the past. You have to leave your car on the lot next to the ticket booth and cross the bridge to the fort. Spy Run, after it crosses the river, goes right by the fort, but they do it this way instead. The ticket booth is also a gift shop with little brass cannons, postcards, pens, and pencils. There are racks with all the literature. At night the bridge is closed off. There is a gate made out of cyclone fencing that hangs way out over each side of the walkway so nobody can climb around it. I think it's funny, a little screen fence protecting a fort.

The oak logs of the fort are white and unweathered. They would have been unweathered then. It is always the summer of 1816.

We do all the regular things other places do—like dip candles, card wool, spin, and weave. The soldiers make shot and clean their weapons. Someone plays the fife. The children hold their ears when we shoot off the six-pounder. But we're not saying all the time, "This is how they make stew on an open fire" or "This is where the men sat and read their Bibles."

Everybody plays a person, somebody who was really here in 1816, and we make up stories to get the facts across. Otherwise, we just go about our business, answer questions when we can.

"Do you think Polk will be President?" We just look at each other and scratch our heads. "Who's he, mister?"

There are fifteen stars on the flag and fifteen stripes. Running out of room. The Congress is trying to figure out what to do next.

When I head in the gate, Jim is working out the flogging with Marshall. There was a flogging on this day in 1816.

I am George Washington Whistler. I'll die during an epidemic in St. Petersburg, Russia, in 1849.

I was in Russia as an engineer, building the railroad between St. Petersburg and Moscow for the Czar, making harbor improvements, looking over the dockyards. One of my sons will be the painter James Abbot McNeill Whistler, who was in London when I died. He was only sixteen. That's why you never see a portrait of his father.

In the summer of 1816, I am sixteen too.

My father designed and built this fort, the third and last American fort on the site, as well as the one that was standing here in 1800. That's the fort I was born in.

Most of what I know about George is all going to happen to him after he leaves here—his marriage, his work on the border between the U.S. and Canada. That doesn't help me much now. So I just do what I think a sixteen-year-old would have done back then. I fetch things. I haul water. I whittle. I run across the compound while the soldiers drill. I tag behind Jim, who is Major John Whistler, my father, until he pretends to send me on errands. I sulk in the corner of his office while he lectures on strategy and boasts of the fort's design to a group of visitors. I gripe about school to the other kids. We've got some books from the time—primers and things. Or I tell them about how it was when we walked here from

Detroit. Most of all, I talk about leaving and heading off to the military academy at West Point.

That's what's going to happen to my person pretty soon, and that's most of what I know, things that will happen soon.

Late in the day, with my chores all done, I'll go down to the river and skip a few stones. The people crossing back over the bridge will be able to see me there on the bank.

Most of the other people who work here—the soldiers and their wives, the settlers, the traders—are history majors out at Indiana-Purdue University on the bypass. They are always telling me a new fact they've come up with in the library—like a diary that mentions something a person did, or what was in a letter found folded in an old book. They're always building things up from just a few clues. My sister, Harriet, for instance, is supposed to have been a real gossip and mean. That's what they decided from some letters they found along with a recipe for cornbread. She fretted greatly over Major Whistler, our father, who seems to have not gotten along at all with B. F. Stickney, the Indian agent, or with his son-in-law, Lieutenant Curtis. I've seen Jim—who is really a professor out at the campus—have yelling matches with the man who plays Mr. Stickney. Visitors will come through the gate, and the two of them will be shouting. Major Whistler is out on the balcony of his quarters. Mr. Stickney is over by the hospital. It's something about the payments and the sale of alcohol.

Nobody tells the visitors what they're getting into. They just have to catch on. It must seem like these are real fights at first. The visitors move around, trying to get out of the way, and I ignore the whole thing. So we're pretending all the time, and as the summer's gone on, the little things we've started with have been added to.

It takes all day to do everything we've invented to do.

One soldier shoves me up against the flagpole every morning to show how nasty he was supposed to have been. Someone else does nothing but stay in bed in the hospital. He dies all summer. But he's been gaining weight.

We are always saying how we could really use people who can speak French the way they did back then.

This is educational for everybody. The fathers are always quieting their sons saying, "Listen to this," as the Sergeant Major pats the barrel of the howitzer and tells his little story about Fallen Timbers. The women and the girls hang around the kitchens and out near the bower down by the river, where the ladies from the fort do the laundry. Sometimes people will help weed the plots of vegetables or churn butter. They'll add a few stitches to the quilt.

The college kids who work here get credit, I think. Or write papers. Something.

Everybody who visits is interested in sanitation.

I take people around to the privies, point out the chamber pots, tell them how it was a real problem in the previous fort during the war and the siege.

"Here is the gutter that Major Whistler, my father, had dug around the parade ground for the water to run off."

I've learned a lot too about history and speaking in front of people. I like talking about these things and having people listening. I like it when they nod and whisper to each other. The little boys look at what I'm wearing.

Kids my age will try to trip me up, asking about hamburgers or the Civil War. But I haven't made a mistake once. Well, once I did, but the guy who asked didn't know I did, so it was all right.

I'll be a senior next year at North Side High School, which is up on the banks of the St. Joe near the site of a French fort. Fifty years ago, when they dug the foundation, they found an Indian burial site. That's why we're called the Redskins. My teachers think this will be good experience. They wrote good recommendations for me. My own father isn't so sure, but he is happy I have a job and that I work outside.

To him, it's a summer job, that's all.

Lieutenant Curtis, who is my brother-in-law by marriage to my sister Eliza, has mustered the garrison together for the morning assembly and flag raising. The orders and officers of the day are posted, regulations concerning fraternization and venereal disease are read. He goes on a bit about B. F. Stickney, thinking aloud about the man's character. The men are at parade rest. They're dressed in the hot wool uniforms or the white fatigues.

The flag is popping.

There is already a large crowd watching.

Behind the crowd is a file of late arrivals going in and out of the buildings.

Before we opened, we talked about fudging a bit, holding up the flogging until we had enough people to make it worthwhile. That won't be a problem now. It's something we always have to work out since the visitors aren't around for the whole day usually. We don't want anyone to go away without seeing a special event, a rifle firing or the band playing at least. But we can't be flogging every hour on the hour.

"Next flogging in twenty minutes."

We try to be true to the facts we have. The trouble is that the visitors see a few hours of what took years to come about. So it's kind of hard to explain why they're whipping this man today. It's funny that more people don't ask.

It is all done by the book—down to the knots and the tattoo the drummer's doing. I am sitting on the roof of the magazine. The magazine is the shed where they kept the powder and munitions. It was supposed to be brick, so it wouldn't burn or blow up. But there were just too many trees around. Major Whistler sodded the roof instead, and the grass is long and green.

The magazine is near the east wall. Between the *thwap, thwap* of the whip and Marshall's screaming, I can hear the traffic going by on Spy Run.

The street is on the other side of the wall. Cars honk at the sentry in the blockhouse from time to time as they go by. The real fort was on the other side of the river, near where the apartments are now, up on the high ground. That's how they got the land to build this fort. It's on the flood plain along with all the parks.

There is a lot of flood plain when you have three rivers running through a town.

One of the first jobs I did in the spring was sandbag the fort during the flood. We pumped the water out into Spy Run and back into the river. But the water really didn't go anywhere. I was happy to work three days and nights without pay. It was a good way to get to know the people I was going to work with. And it was a big flood, a hundred-year flood, and I was in it with historians.

That night the President's helicopter was beating around overhead. Its spotlight was dancing all around and lighting up this little clearing. There we were, passing heavy wet bags. The water was rippling into waves from the rotors. Looking up I could see the rain pouring through the beam of light. Jim still worries about rot damage to the wood, termites and such, but everything is green and cool this summer, and it will probably stay this way until fall.

The roof is nice with clover blooming.

Most of the people in the crowd wear dark glasses. We can't, of course. My face is tired at night from squinting. I have just started wearing contacts, so I can go without my glasses. Jim's face is lined from the weather and from worry. We're always trying to get the visitors to see how much quicker people aged then.

This will be my only summer here, you know. George Washington Whistler has to be sixteen.

Marshall's been carried off to the hospital. Lieutenant Curtis has dismissed the men, and they are dispersing. My sisters have been dabbing the corners of their eyes with handkerchiefs. Their bonnets hide a part of their faces. My father is talking to a group of visitors, slapping his gloves, in his hand, on his flexed knee talking about discipline and justice and a peacetime army, I imagine.

"Who are you?" says a little boy, calling up to me on the magazine roof.

He is wearing sunglasses with six-shooters in the upper corners of the lenses.

I tell him who I am, and he asks if I know the soldier who was beaten.

I tell him that I do know him and why he was punished.

"Can I come up there?" the boy asks.

"Nope," I say.

This isn't the only thing I've been doing this summer. I still go out. I ride around town with some of the guys from school. We make the loop from the one Azar's Big Boy out on the bypass to the other one by South Side High School. Everybody's got their first jobs, running registers or dropping fries. They cut grass on Forest Park. It gives them money for the cars and enough left over to order food and hold down a booth without getting kicked out.

Some of my friends are going to summer school, and that's what my job seems like to the others, like summer school.

We go by the Calvary Temple sign that flashes *Calvary, Temple, Calvary, Temple.*

Clinton splits off into a one-way street. We go past the old power plant and the fenced substation with wires going out everywhere. On the ribs of the big transformers are these fans pointed at the fins on the side. They are on sometimes to cool down the transformers. But at night the blades are feathering, turning slowly in the breeze.

Les always says how funny it is that they use some electricity to run the fans to cool the transformers to make the electricity. Over the St. Mary's, by the armory, under the overpass, through downtown, under the overpass, and into the near south side of the city. Coming back, we go up Lafayette, which turns into Spy Run by the bridge. We go by the fort, all dark of course, except for the lights of the cars playing along the walls, and the guys all kid me. One night, they'll break in, and it will be trouble for me. Maybe T. P. the whole place. They'll leave my name in red paint on the walls.

We head north by Penguin Point, with the trash cans shaped like penguins, and then run along the bike path on the bank of the St. Joe. We cross State and off to the right is North Side across the river. The ventilating scoops all swiveling like weather vanes left and right. That's another thing we can never figure out, how those scoops are all pointed in different directions in the same breeze. Spy Run bears down on the Old Crown Brewery, dead ahead, but turns sharp left to meet up again with Clinton. Mr. Centlivre is all lit up on the building's roof. His foot is planted on a keg like a big game hunter. We start talking about going to Ohio. But we never do.

On weeknights I keep score for my dad's softball team. I fill up the frames with little red diamonds. They're winners. It's fast pitch. They have uniforms and everything. When the ball gets by the catcher and no one's on base, he throws it to the third baseman, who always plays in. The third baseman relays it back to the pitcher, a windmiller, his ball jumping over the plate. They're sharp. I call out the lineups. On deck, in the hole.

They all ask about the fort and tell me how they mean to come by.

They work during the day, and on vacation they usually go away. I tell them there is plenty to see right here in town. But they know I am kidding.

I like the plinking sound of the aluminum hats. I like to see the white ball go bouncing beyond the lights out into the high grass of Hamilton Park, a grown man chasing after it like a kid.

I warm Dad up before the game, taking one step back after two throws. He's always very deliberate, pretending to throw after he throws. He tells himself what he's doing wrong. I can hear snatches of it. I'm all encouragements. When he's not in the field but swinging the lead bat, I hold his glove to keep it off the ground, make sure there's a ball inside to keep the pocket.

Dad takes some of us from the fort to the various parades and festivals where we've been appearing. We go all over this part of Indiana. Mom comes along to help with the maps and to look over the handicrafts. They won't accept mileage. We're all in the backseats of the station wagon in full-dress uniforms. Shakos, crossing white belts, bayonets in the scabbards. The muskets are up on the luggage rack. Mom always says, "I bet the wool is itchy."

We don't look very smart since our clothes are authentic and hand-made. You'd expect more. But we do all right in the parades, staying in step and following orders. We fire off a salute at least once.

Dad works for Rea Magnet Wire and worries about the way the car smells. As long as I can remember, his cars have smelled of copper and the enamels. He even smells that way when I get close enough to him. It's like something you were trying to melt in a pan, chocolate or butter, was just starting to burn instead.

He hangs little green paper Christmas trees from the rearview mirror, but they don't do any good. Mom asks why draw attention to it by trying to cover it up. I don't think the people from the fort notice—or if they do, they get used to it like we all do. They're nervous about the parade and how they look.

All summer I have been thinking about my chemistry problem. I'll be taking third-year chem in the fall. I've liked chem since the first class. It's the teacher, I think, and because I have a knack for it. My senior year will be organic and a special project. I've known what I wanted to do for a long time, ever since Mr. Dvorak showed us the clock reaction in an early lecture.

A clock reaction is close to magic.

The stuff in the beaker changes colors all by itself.

It didn't seem like science at all. That's why it was great for beginning classes. He poured these three clear liquids into a beaker. The liquid turned a bright orange and seemed to thicken. He kept on stirring slowly with a glass rod, clinking it against the glass beaker. All of a sudden, the orange turned black. It was just like someone had flicked a switch. He told us that a professor at Princeton had designed the reaction, and that orange and black are the Princeton colors.

Since then, I've been thinking about my own clock reaction in white and red, North Side High colors. It has to be in that order since the white couldn't cover the red.

I need to find three compounds, ABC. A and B can't react. B and C can't react. But A and C do react, and their product is a white solid. In that product somewhere there has to be something that will then combine with B, but not all at once.

I can't have pink.

For two years I've been mixing precipitates—blue-green coppers, orange potassiums, cobalt blues, the yellows. The test tubes go from clear to color, and the solid settles instantly or suspends, milky and in motion.

Iron gives red, and there are many white metals.

Dvorak says there are tables and books that just list the colors. That would save me time, but I like to see them for myself—the colors and the grades of solids, sand or silt or crystal. There's one, just a drop, that turns as it falls through the acid, a little gray worm by the time it hits the bottom. Don't worry—one day I'll say, "See?"

White, red.

My mother thinks I think too much. She's caught me staring into the sink, watching the Ajax oxidate and turn blue. She thinks I should go out more. My dad doesn't say anything but worries out of habit. We'll sit together out on the porch swing. I'll be reading, and he'll be smoking a cigar. "Boats this year," he'll say after a while. "Sailboats."

He's thinking about the Junior Achievement projects for next fall.

Rea gives copper wire to a J. A. company.

The kids make pictures of things by stringing the wire between carefully arranged pegs. Cars, trains, airplanes—all made out of thread-gauge copper wire, gold-headed tacks, black cloth for the background.

I am waving to the Kiwanis pontoon going by on the river. I can hear pieces of the talk about the beautification project, the downtown, the fort, the portage that made this spot worth fighting for in the first place. My two sisters are washing nearby, letting the crowd of visitors overhear them talk about the Major, our father, and finding him a wife, how that would make him more tolerable to live with. I go on back to the clearing in front of the gate where the rifle squad is drilling and the cannon is being readied for firing. The visitors shade their eyes, take pictures.

They've been blowing up buildings across the river downtown. It's the easiest way to demolish the vacant old hotels. From here, we can see some of it. A building turns to dust and disappears from between the other buildings. If the wind is right, there is hardly any sound, just the cloud of dust rolling away. The Keenan Hotel. The Van Ormen. Once the gun crew tried to time a firing with one of the explosions. They aimed the cannon in the general direction so it would look like we were shelling the downtown, the building collapsing before our guns. Jim said it was a stupid idea. The visitors were more interested in the drill, swabbing out the barrel, ramming, loading, the slow-burning fuse. The visitors were from out of town anyway and probably didn't know what was going on. The local people would be downtown to watch the building go.

The problem is that it is so hard to imagine this place without buildings even though so much of the old city is leveled now into fields of rubble. The view is broken only by the steeples of the old German churches.

It's easy for me to pretend I've never tasted white sugar. Basketball hasn't been invented. But I think I stick too close to the facts. Maybe I can't see much beyond the things I can see.

My friend Les isn't like that at all. He told me once of the project he'd like to do. Since energy is just matter traveling at the speed of light, he told me, what he'd like to come up with would be some kind of filter that would slow things down. Hold it up to the light and solid blocks of stuff would fall out of the air.

"That would be better than your clock reaction," he says. "You might have to pick stuff up, but you wouldn't have the mess afterwards."

And Jim has no trouble at all being someone else. It is 1816 to him. "Listen," he says, "what bird did that? One of the swallows from the blockhouse?"

He's proud of the fort's innovations—the cupola for putting out fires, the overhanging ports to shoot down on intruders crouching by the walls. He's proud that he's convinced the banks to see it all like he saw it and that he convinced the city fathers to go along. There are signs all over town pointing in this direction. See Old Fort Wayne. For the longest time, all there was of the fort was one replica cannon in the lobby of the library, flanked by a glass case with a model made out of toothpicks and paper.

It had been there as long as I could remember.

It is late in the day. The pies that Harriet and Eliza made are in the windows. I'm supposed to swipe one and take it off to the soldier's mess. The sisters search each building, rolling pin at the ready. But the men hide me from my sisters. The visitors scream with laughter as I race from one building to another a step ahead of my pursuers. The visitors are on all the porches, resting on the hand-hewn chairs and benches. The sun is hot. The sky is blue. I make it to the hospital and disappear inside just as the sisters emerge from the southeast blockhouse.

Major Whistler steps out on the porch of his quarters and shouts with command, "What in God's name is going on here!" The sisters confide to those nearby that the boy needs a mother, that he's getting too big to chase after.

Harriet is portrayed as a flirt, though distracted with the care of her father. Her motivation for wishing to see our father married again comes from her own desire to be free to find a husband. She will later marry a Captain Phelan who will be killed in Detroit. She'll live to 1872. Harriet.

Major Whistler will become the military storekeeper at Bellefontaine, Missouri. He will move with the troops to the new Jefferson Barracks in 1826, and die there in September.

Eliza will go with her husband, Lieutenant Curtis, from here to Detroit to Green Bay. She will have a child in the cradle and one in school when, one day, while washing clothes in a river near Fort Howard, she will be killed by a bolt of lightning. That's it for Eliza.

Daniel Curtis and I are eating pieces of pie in the hospital. He is there caring for Marshall. The record shows that Curtis served as the fort doctor that summer when there was no one else to do it. Had some training, had some schooling. He was liked by the Indians, having witnessed the speeches at Brownstown in 1810. He was a schoolteacher from New Hampshire.

"Stickney," he said, "is an opportunist. He is receiving money from the whiskey-traders."

The pie is very good. Made with berries from our own canes.

It is hard for me to keep from thinking about the futures of these people. I feel sorry for Curtis, though it is years before his wife's death and his bungling at Fort Howard. He will be court-martialed and discharged.

We sit and eat the warm pie in pieces he's cut with his knife. We've hidden what's left of it beneath a bunk. The man who plays Curtis winks at me a lot.

The visitors stick their heads in the door. They see us eating the pie in what seems a normal fashion. They see another log building, bare and chinked. The planking has been ripped out by a two-man saw. The only color is the leather fire bucket in the corner. It's painted blue.

Les says that it would drive him crazy.

"It's enough for me just to not think about school this fall."

We are sitting on the riverbank by North Side, down below the concrete levee. The brewery makes the air smell rotten. Cottonwood seeds are floating in the green water. I tell him it's kind of like living with premonitions all the time or ESP.

"It's neat knowing everything," I say.

The clock on the brewery has read twenty after ten since it was sold to a national brewer.

"See," I say, "they're going to let that place go right down the drain. Let it all just fall apart."

Les just grunts and heaves a rock to make the pigeons fly. Cadmium is light blue, I think, and rhodium is red but expensive. Iodine is not really black but violet. A dark violet.

We have been spying on the cheerleaders who are practicing in the parking lot by the school. We watch them from behind the levee as they work on their movements. The way they clap their hands and bounce on their toes. They climb on each other's knees and backs. They do the type of cheers you like to watch even though you can't cheer along with them. Splits and flips. They wear red sweatshirts, white skirts.

"Try and explain that to future generations," Les says. We keep watching through the afternoon, ducking down to the river when we think they've seen us. The littlest one is on the top of the pyramid. We see her skirt fly up. She lands on her feet and bounces. Falling with her from all over the formation are the other girls, landing and clapping. They bounce, no longer in unison. Applaud what they've done. Then they do the pyramid cheer again.

I like to think the painter Whistler didn't paint a picture of his father because he was like me. He didn't trust his memory, was only comfortable with a model sitting in front of him. He was my age when his father died, and he'd just started drawing.

I have a collection of postcards with reproductions of his paintings and his etchings. Les says if I have etchings, I should tell the cheerleaders to come around and take a look.

They are pictures of docks and streets in France and England—highly detailed—panes in the windows and reflections in the glass. The portraits are all very sad, though I can see that they are beautiful. They are titled after their colors and compared to music.

Arrangement in Black and White.

Blue Nocturnes.

Things like that.

The picture of his mother has a picture hanging on the wall that I can barely make out. I think it is another one of his pictures. I can't imagine what he looked like. George, I mean. Sideburns, I guess. A high collar? The Czar took a ruler and drew a straight line from St. Petersburg to Moscow.

"Do this," he said.

And Whistler did.

His father, Major Whistler, and B. F. Stickney are having it out near the gate. Everyone draws in, the garrison as well as the remaining visitors, who feel better about what is happening around them now. This is all made up, they are thinking.

"How dare you, sir! How dare you!" Stickney is saying.

The Major produces maps and indicates lands deeded by the treaty of Greenville to the Richardville clan of the Miami in perpetuity.

"There are white settlers on the land, Mr. Stickney. Here and here."

I see my father in the crowd, listening to what's going on.

I guess it looks like a dispute at home plate, both benches emptied.

Soldiers are moving in with muskets. They begin breaking through the crowd. Lieutenant Curtis holds the two men apart. His hat is knocked off his head. "Gentlemen! Gentlemen!"

I edge over to my father, who asks me what's going on. I tell him about what Stickney's been up to, selling land to families up from Kentucky, paying off the tribes, and getting the money back by tripling the whiskey prices on payment day.

I can smell the copper.

He has just come from the plant, so it's strong and mixed in with my own smell and the smell of the wool uniforms that only get washed once a week since that was regulation. My dad begins to ask me another question, but then I can see he starts to understand the way things work. So he waits for me to speak first.

He probably stopped by to give me a ride home, probably got across the bridge without paying since it's close to closing.

My eyes are very tired and I can't wait to take them out. I mean the contacts. I don't think I'll ever be able to wear them as long as they say you're supposed to.

The soldiers are pushing us all back with their muskets now. The braid on their shakos is loose. There is an eagle and a white cockade. The hats make the soldiers look taller.

My father takes a few steps back. His tie is loose but still knotted.

This is the first time he has seen the fort. I point out the gardens and the pickets and the Pennsylvania key, notched in the corners of the buildings. Cars are going by on Spy Run. Flashes of color. Engines are revved high. People are on their way home from work. We stand there on the edge of the crowd, my dad and I, listening to an argument that was settled a long time ago.

Dear John,

I am living in Indianapolis now. Like me, it has no reason for being here. The people of the state simply wanted their capital in the middle of Indiana, paced off the distance, and brought an apprentice of L'Enfant out from Washington, D.C., to make all the same mistakes in this city's plans. Streets, named after states, radiate from circles where monumental statuary bases are waiting for statues, waiting for someone to become famous enough to become a statue. Everywhere you look in this city you see these flat-topped pyramids, empty niches in building facades, friezes without faces, metopes without bas-relief. The circles here, too, were planned for defense purposes as if someone would wish to take a thing that was never meant to be. The theory was that batteries positioned in the circles could command three hundred and sixty degrees of the neighborhood. The airplane makes this all silly, of course. But, on the other hand, it is only from the air that you can see the plan, gain any perspective on the order here. Instead, the circles cause traffic jams, rotaries coursing with cars at all hours (late-model plum colored Chevrolets, it seems, are everywhere), all looking for numbered streets. There are quadrant designations too—NW, SE. It is very much like an army camp, except there are no white rocks. There are boulders on people's lawns. Blank bronze plaques are bolted on the sides of the boulders. In the summer, you can watch the husbands trim the grass by crawling on all fours around the boulders using those hand clippers. The boulders came all the way from Canada, their sides worn smooth for the plaques by the glaciers that carried them down here.

I came here looking for you. You're not dead yet, officially. Still listed as missing in action on the Lunghai Railroad en route to Hsuchow, China, 25 August 1945. I can't go back there now and look for you myself.

What were you doing in Anhwei Province? Another airfield in the middle of nowhere? I thought when you left Changsha for the last time you were on your way to Shantung Province to organize the North. I can't remember what you said to me.

The woman at the American Legion headquarters here is very kind and helpful. She tells me that I mustn't worry, that GIs are marching home all the time. Some have knocks on the head and have lost their memories. Pockets of Japanese resistance are still being turned up on nameless atolls a dozen years after the surrender. There are prisoner exchanges all the time. Priests stumbling out of the jungle. I have pretty much given up hope, though. I go on out of habit. I think you can keep someone alive. I keep. I still write often to your sister Betty on the farm in Macon. I tell her about her brother in China. She tells me about growing up with you in Georgia. The farm, she writes, has now been all planted with trees, just as you wanted it to be. Elm (though there is a new disease here in the States that is killing them), tulip, white pine, and, of course, birches that do not grow well since they are not native to the South. Your father still preaches. Your mother still plays the organ for him. Things would not be that different if you came back now.

I sit in the study room at the American Legion with the other women—widows mostly, though some are old girlfriends like me. We all have our files, the accordion type, filled with letters from comrades, maps, commendations, canceled orders. We wait for records to become declassified, for belongings or effects or last remains to appear from the warehouse searches in Kansas City. The older women wear hats with veils. The cross-hatch of the netting makes their faces look made up out of dots like newspaper photos. They remove just the one white glove, the one from their writing hand. The other glove is specked with the crumbs from their erasures. When a regular gives up her place by the window, someone new comes to take it and stays until, a few weeks or years later, her work too is done.

In front of the American Legion Headquarters building, a mall begins, and from there it stretches four blocks along Meridian and Pennsylvania to the Post Office. There are plazas and parks. There is a hundred-foot obelisk of black Berwick granite. Around the base is a varicolored electric-lighted water fountain. There is a cenotaph, gold Roman eagles and all. Halfway down the mall is the War Memorial, a replica one-third the size of the mausoleum erected by Artemisia. There is even a light on the plateau of the stepped roof that represents the eternal flame. Scaffolds, like the ones window-washers use, hang high up along the west wall of the building. Workmen are still carving the names of the Korean dead. Watching them, I hear the sound of hammer and chisel long after I see the blow. All of the buildings around the mall are made from limestone in that New Deal style. The U's are carved as V's. There is, on the part of the mall that begins in front of the Legion building, a vast vehicle park and ordnance dump the Legion supervises and maintains. Rows of 37mm antitank guns, howitzers (all spiked, the breechblocks gone), files of quad .50 mounts and Bofors guns. There are a few old Shermans and Grants, even a Stuart, destined for a park somewhere or maybe to be cemented in a town square. The Legion distributes the surplus to the local posts, to be set up on stoops and front lawns next to lighted flagpoles. The guns will be trained on the part of Main Street that is most menacing. Every city will have one. They can't all be hammered into plowshares. I can imagine a crew of drunken legionnaires scrambling from a stag, manning this fieldpiece, pretending they are walking shells toward the grain elevators. In purple fatigue caps sagging with medals, these men will crank the elevation wheel because that is the only thing that is left working, and then they'll lob a few shells toward home, the wife, the kids.

After a day of looking for you, I walk along the rows of weapons, and if the wind is right, I hear the whistle coming from the vents of the air-cooled barrels. I smoke a cigarette, watch them carve the names. It is all drab and battleship gray. Everything that is loose has been stolen. There are chalk marks on the shields and fenders. Stars glow on the armor.

I live in Chinatown here. It is on the near south side in the shadow of the Lilly pill plants. To get there, I walk around the monument circle at Market Street and cross the Crossroads of America at Washington and Meridian. Under the railroad overpass. By John's Hot Stew. I don't know why I am writing this as if you will come looking for me.

Chinatown here is the type of thing you would expect. Chop suey joints above laundries or laundries above chop suey joints. Banners hang above the street. The smells of soy and dry-roasted peanuts. Taiwanese mainly. Many from the fall of the Tachen Islands. Quemoy is being shelled again. There are animated arguments at the walls where the language dailies are posted. Children dribble basketballs along the sidewalk. Wearing scarlet, they weave around their fathers. The public phones are in pagodas. The shelter signs are in Chinese.

It is not really like Changsha, though there is a jinriksha. Most people here wear black sneakers. They miss China. I can pretend I am still there—bow to the men in sleeveless shirts and gray pants in my building, share silk thread with their wives, who sew all day. I can imagine when I leave in the morning I am on my way to the Yale-in-China Hospital again. Taste tea in a coffee cup. And I wait for you. At night in bed, I hear a train slam into the station. It is the Japanese shelling.

There is a man here who says he remembers you when you preached in Chekiang Province. He is still a Christian and insists I go to church with him, an A.M.E. in the next ward. He says he was told you joined the AVG, that all China has heard of you. He tells me your Chinese is perfect. He would not be surprised if you were still alive and preaching to many converts. Mao himself would not be able to tell you were American. I think the man says what he thinks I want to hear; he brings me fried bananas and takes me uptown on the bus to the cathedral to play Bingo.

There is one bathroom on my floor in my building. I like to sit there, steaming in the tub. I can smell the starch from the street. Do you remember the P-40 shot down over Lingchuan when we lived there? It crashed, pilotless, down the road. I remember when the Chinese peasants, hundreds of them it seemed to me, carried the cracked-up plane up the road to our house. The smaller parts, they held them above their heads. It looked as if it was coming apart as it moved. It was like the dragons at New Year's. "Here is your plane," they shouted, dropping it near the porch. We were the only Americans they knew of. You thanked them in your perfect Chinese. Sly General Wang took the aluminum from the fuselage and had his smith make the bathtub. Remember the bathtub? All we had before was the Yangtze Kiang. The way I washed your back like an Asian wife. Why did you leave with Drummond without saying anything? You wrote to Betty trying to explain. She has shown me the letters. And you wrote to your parents. In Lingchuan, in Changsha, when we made love, you whispered to me in Chinese. In Chinese. I didn't know Chinese. I don't know it. The geese flying backwards. The Eastern menagerie. And I would have gone with you to the West, to Turkestan if you had wanted. Converted the Jews. It is a place for a woman. "Look, I have a mission." Now, I have a mission, John. I had one then and they are the same. You, John. Did you, in doing your duty (and was it duty to God or to country that allowed you to leave me?), confuse your two missions? A missionary is always the best warrior. I remember the Jesuits saying mass along the road in camouflage, the host made of spinach flour. I remember the almond eyes of that Flying Tiger. I kept them above our bed after you left. I would stare back at them as they bore down on me and try to imagine its smile.

I asked for you at HQ. I waited for your letters every day at the Yale Hospital. I rode my bike back home past the quilted soldiers who eyed me along the road as they unwrapped their puttees at night, just as they had wrapped them as I went to work in the morning. Your letters never came. I always left forwarding addresses. Mailed a packet of letters to your family. I tried to write the letter that would free me. I could live with the secrets of the war you shared with me. I could have lived with you and your God and your other women. I watched you for hours as you studied the code books. A mission makes us the thing we pursue. We are what we study. I am becoming you, John. Losing me. Losing us. Losing the very reason I went looking in the first place. The way you lost yourself in a China you believed could be converted into Georgia. Why did you leave me? Was it that you could no longer understand English? Had you only the taste for the cheapest red rice?

You don't know about television. Imagine one of your radios but this one sends pictures along with the words. After my bath, if the night is warm, I go down to the appliance store and watch the televisions in the window. No one in Chinatown can afford one yet. So, people come out and they watch with me. The men wear straw hats and bob up and down to see over shoulders. The women sit on the curb or lean against the few cars and listen to the man who translates the words which come from the small speaker tucked up under the awning with the sparrows' nests. There are twenty sets on tiers all tuned to the same picture. You can watch people making sure that all the pictures are doing the same thing at the same time. You can see their heads jerk from screen to screen. I go there to watch them watch. During the day, the screens are turned off, and no one stops on the sidewalk. The televisions are watching us. "Take one home," the appliance man tells me as I pass his door. "It will keep you company." He says I will never be lonely. "Come back tonight. They will all be turned on tonight."

Then I go back to the American Legion and search for you. In my file is a new commendation from Chennault. I answer mail. Write letters. Make notes in the margins of radio traffic logs.

I do not know how many letters this makes to you. For a while after the Arbor Day I spent in Georgia, I would send them to your sister there. She would write back as you. She had practiced your hand from the letters she had from you during the war, tracing them as she grew up the way other children trace animals or flowers out of encyclopedias. We both went a long way toward believing. She cut short her hair and nails, carved our initials, yours and mine, into one of the trees. She had her picture taken by the tree while she wore your old work clothes. But the closer she got to you, the more I missed the things that she was not. Maybe I am cursed with too much memory. Maybe I write these letters as a way of forgetting. I watch the nicotine stains on my fingernails grow out as the nail grows out, and I think to myself that by the time the yellow splotches reach the tip, I will be over this. They do and I am not and I smoke more and my nails are stained. Perhaps I will clip them and send them off with this letter.

Of course, there are other men. Mr. Lee, who brings me the fried bananas and the fortune cookies without fortunes he buys half-priced at the bakery thrift shop. There's him. He clips articles for me from the National Geographic. He takes me to movies at the Circle Theatre. There is the floorwalker at L. S. Ayres, who began by suspecting me as I wandered around the mezzanine near the stamp corner. But I was innocent, and he led me to the perfume counter where he spotted my arms with samples. What could they say to me? "He is dead and gone." They are too polite for that. To them, I am a story they could tell their grandchildren. "I knew a woman once."

Recently, I met another man.

At my table at the Legion, I found a box of chocolate-covered cherries. I thought someone had forgotten them from the day before, and I tried to turn them in to the woman at the desk. She said no, they were for me. "A Mr. Welch left them for you himself." Welch's was the brand name on the box.

That night as I watched television, he appeared in the jinriksha, bedecked with flowers. "Audrey, my dear, come for a ride with me."

The men watching television looked to see him too, a tall man in a linen suit and Panama. "I am Robert Welch," he said. "It was I who left the bonbons for you." The women in the gutter clucked. "Come here," he said, "I have things to tell you about your Captain Birch." Such a nice smile. He held out a candied egg. "For you."

The men had turned back to the television in the window. The women leaned together. "I have irrefutable proof that John Birch was killed by Communists in nineteen forty-five."

Mr. Lee said, "What gives, Pops? Can't the lady watch TV in peace?"

The man said, "The meter's running, Audrey. Please, come with me. We can talk. I have been looking for you these last five years. I have good news of John Birch."

"You told me he was dead," I said.

Mr. Lee said, "Scram. Beat it, Pops." Now everyone was watching the scene in the street. The men who had been nearest the store were now in back, looking for an opening to see. Mr. Lee; sensing he was now the center of attention, continued to yell. I thanked Mr. Lee, apologized to the television audience, and got into the seat next to Mr. Welch. As we left Chinatown, the children in pajamas ran after us collecting the stray blossoms that fell from the jinriksha.

What else could I do? Another lead to track down. Such a gentle man who had given me candy, your name. I suppose that Mr. Welch, Robert, had thought I would be grateful for the truth. The truth was that the truth didn't interest me as much as a convincing lie. Later, I found out that that was his mission, truth telling. Another truth not yours, John. He believed all he had to do was tell people the truth and they would act accordingly. Not that easy.

As we clopped around and around the monument circle he told me some more truth.

This is what the man said. He said he had made his fortune in candy and then sold the business to Nabisco. He said he spent his time and money studying the spread of Communism, that he kept a little score-card in his wallet. He knew the political positions of Ghana and Kwame Nkrumah. He said he came across your name when you helped Doolittle, and that, as he pieced together your life in China, he turned up my name. My first name. Our affair. Our engagement. The mystery of your leaving. Now, as he looked for Communists, he also looked for me. He said he'd found, in your life and death, the ordeal of an age.

"What was he like, really?" This is what he asked.

I was eating the candied egg. I told him what he wanted to hear. A truth teller always has such simple notions of truth. I said, "A pious man. Deeply religious. His soldier's shell temporarily assumed. A gentleman. A happy warrior. Cheerful. A tinkerer. A lover of children. All the things you would expect from a man descended from a Mayflower Pilgrim and related, through blood, to four U.S. presidents."

I did not tell him about the rice paper, your calligraphy. The way you squatted against the wall of the hut. The bathtub.

He gave me his handkerchief to wipe the caramel from my hands. When I offered to give it back, he told me to keep it. We returned to my building and he walked me to the door.

He said, "Audrey, I must continue to see you. It is important to the Free World. You, who knew and loved John Birch, can understand what he and we should stand for."

"Yes, of course," I said.

Robert took me to the 500 after we had spent the weekends in May at the time trials. We sat in the infield while the cars shot around the track.

Before the race, he led a prayer for the war dead, cried when they played "On the Banks of the Wabash." He took me to restaurants. He praised you over John's Hot Stew. We went to Indians baseball games, to the state fair. The judge slapped the rump of a steer. He said, "A farmer, that's all John ever wanted to be."

Always at my desk, I would find some type of kiss. I could not concentrate on your file. All the women seemed to be weeping more than usual.

I smoked more cigarettes and bought Hershey bars from the stand in the lobby of the building. In all the public buildings, the Marion County Association for the Blind runs the concession. They say they know by touch the denomination of the bill. They make change easily. They sit, their creamy eyes floating in their heads, surrounded by candy. No matter how quiet I am. "Yes, may I help you?"

I buy some gum and return to my place. I write letters to the floorwalker. I tell him I did steal some stamps. "I'll never be able to see you again." Also a letter to Mr. Lee, breaking it to him gently.

One night Robert took me to his room at the Fox Hotel. French windows led out to the balcony where he had set up a white telescope. Ten stories up you could see down to the spokes of the lighted streets as they radiated from their circles. The circles were phosphorescent craters. All along the mall, the government buildings were flooded with lights. Car lots on the south side were having sales. Surplus spotlight beams waved back and forth. I looked at the city and saw if for the first time. Robert, through his telescope, searched for Sputnik.

"There, there! That's it!" He was so happy. "Look at it as it goes by."

The stars are different in Indianapolis. I can see no dragons, no bears, no crabs. My eyes came back down to the red neon of the insurance companies on Meridian.

I am sitting here now in my usual place writing you another letter. I can't say things right. I cannot wait any longer. And, now, I am here at the signature, the farewell. Who is the John of this Dear John letter? I imagine you somewhere at mail call. The names of the dead shouted out, packages passed along on fingertips. Envelopes thrown, arms reaching out. "Yo! Here! That's me!"

What should I do? Robert will soon ask me to marry him. We will honeymoon in England, the better to study the evils of Socialism. He will read to me from newspapers over breakfast. We will talk about you as would a father and a sister. He will ask me to marry him as I walk out of this building for the last time having left a box of chocolates for the kind woman at the desk. I will wear white gloves and inspect the equipment on the lawn in front of the building. The gun barrels crisscross above our heads. The grass has grown up around the tires of the caissons and the tracks of the tanks.

Robert has shown me a picture of your funeral in Hsuchow. I have it here. I will send it to you. The Japanese probably wonder how they got into this. They want to go home now that the war is over. They look over Drummond's shoulder at the casket. The Chinese, in their German-looking helmets, are drawn up in a row, bayonets fixed but sheathed. They go out of focus as they approach the camera. There are too many stripes on the flag. Is this hope? Is it just me? The one flaw that gives the deception away. The foliage looks flat, a painted flat. The whole thing staged, a postcard from a wax museum. Why was the picture taken? Can no one believe you are dead?

Why did you leave me, John? That is the heart of the matter. Robert showed me how to read the cowlick on the chocolate shells. All the assorted pieces before him, semisweet and milk, in the pleated paper cups. Each had its own dripping crest that told its center. A crown of thorns for coconut, a halo for cherries. That is what we all need. Our own Braille, like phrenology, to tell us the difference between cordials and hard centers.

I am in Indianapolis. Robert is inviting some friends to come and talk about the world, about its future, about you. I will meet them. I will be as close as they come to you.

I am going through my file of letters to a dead man. One of the first things I learned was your last words, reported by Lt. Tung:

我不能走了

Wo pu neng tsou le. I cannot go on. I cannot go on. Yet I fear we cannot live without you.

The Greek Letter in the Bed

The skull over the door is stolen from the biology lab. There are red Christmas tree lights in the eye sockets. The triangle has something to do with champagne. They don't tell me what. The TKE sign stays on all night. Sometimes, the boys from the other houses steal our light, and, sometimes, my boys steal theirs. They hide them in my suite. My suite fills up with Greek letters. I stack them against the wall with the light bulbs still warm. "You boys," I say. In their plywood frames the bulbs are the size of grapefruit and look like a package that Harry and David, the fruit people, would send. My furniture is alphabetized. When a boy comes in to talk with me about how he misses home, he parks himself on the Tau by my dresser.

These chaise lounges must be replaced next spring. The weather wrecks them here on the porch. An alumnus lends us furniture his motel can't use. We have the finest furniture on campus, and that helps at rush. But the alumnus causes problems now and then, appearing unexpectedly at house parties and telling anyone who will listen about the parties they had when he was a pledge. The boys say you are a Teke for life, but I know his only reason for being there is to watch out for his couches. He doesn't want anyone to be sick on them.

Of course, I have my own key and even my own entrance around back over the kitchen, but on nights like this one, I like to use the front door to see who is sleeping in the public rooms and the TV lounge. Make sure they're warm enough. Or I stay up with one and talk about the party. I let him make promises to me that he will never drink again. I pick my way through the bodies. Snores and sour smells. These are the unlucky ones. No one to sleep with so they sleep with each other.

The boys at Wabash call themselves gentlemen. If one of them entertains a lady for the evening, he hangs a knotted tie on the knob of his closed door. There are no locks. Late some nights, when I can't sleep, I walk through the house with my Boston. We troop down a whole corridor of doors sporting ties. Ties I've tied for them. It is the only time they are used. The boys come to my suite with the tie in their hands. I make them stand in the mirror, and I reach over their shoulders, putting together a bold Windsor as a man would do it. I never learned the motherly way of facing them. They slide their ties off, knotted, over their heads. Thanks.

I know why they send me away when they have house parties and mixers with sororities from Hanover or DePauw. One night I found my boys and their dates spread out around the house, peering in the basement windows. They ruined my borders, moss roses and impatiens. Inside, a pledge was earning all of his points by making love to a woman on the billiard table. He was being supervised by his big brother—that's part of the rules. Usually, you earn your points by vacuuming the hallways or cleaning the head. Outside, everybody hedged in between me and the windows. All I could see were two bare feet sunk in the corner pockets. The next night, I asked that pledge to sit next to me at my table during dinner. He gave the prayer and nothing else was ever said about it.

They send me away on Thursday nights so they can tell their dirty jokes and have food fights or drop eggs from the third floor landing, trying to hit the heads of pledges in the basement well below. Or the girls arrive for a football weekend. Most of the boys will be lawyers or doctors, and most of the girls want to be those kinds of wives. Meanwhile, I am with the other housemothers in a cottage off campus, playing bridge very fast, eating desserts our cooks make, and boasting about our boys. I wish sometimes we would play euchre instead. Loll says it is not seemly for housemothers to play it. She is from Sig Ep and yaks on about her dead husband. "A man," she says, "like no other man." As if she knew. "Loll," she says he said, "you are like no other woman." And he would know because he knew a couple of the other housemothers back when we were all younger. He was the football coach and most of the housemothers are local girls. I don't think Loll knows. That's when Dorcas will say, "Mighty fine Texas cake, Marcella." And Marcella will answer, "Well, thank you, hon. More nuts this time." They are partners and Loll snips at some code. It's code, all right. All of us have lived too long. Too long with boys. Too long without anything else. Room and board are free, remember. And the boys are always the same age. It keeps me young. The campus never changes. Most of the time we are the only women around. And the boys pretend to be gentlemen. I feel as I have always felt.

Here is a story I always want to tell at those card parties. When I went to Washington, I visited the Capitol. In a room that has all these statues, there is a certain spot you can stand on and hear what's being whispered on the other side of the room. Hear every word. My room is like that hall. That is how it is in my room in the house. The heating ducts and tunnels, the thin paneling and the laundry chutes must all crisscross above my bed. Nights, I hear the sounds the couples make in the rooms, and I know they are listening, too, to one another through the walls. This is what I want to tell the other housemothers. Listening as if I were on the bottom of some sea with all those noises swimming around my bed, I breathe out a kind of moan and listen to the middle of it being picked up and passed from one mouth to another, sinking back into the new wing where there are bunk beds, a couple above and a couple below, and back again. Each room adds its own layer and then it comes to me, a round dollop of sound, suspended above me. And me, the mother of pearl. No, I never interfere. That is not what a housemother is.

Thursday nights in the cottage are for buttermints and the little stadium pillows Blanche brings for the folding chairs embroidered with "Sit on DePauw." Autumn nights, we can hear the boys singing. One house might come by to serenade us, singing "Greensleeves" and "Back Home Again in Indiana." Or a wife of some faculty member will bring a covered dish and her Avon samples. But we don't have much truck with the wives. We aren't wives now, after all. Not mothers either, except to places, to houses. And because we keep houses, we are thought to be deaf and dumb. I probably am. We are for appearances only and our appearance—the same Butterick pattern in sixteen fabrics. "I thought that man would be the death of me," Loll says. "Always after me." Some nights we play hearts instead.

Nor will I tell them about that fellow, Pound, the crazy poet, and how I was the one who made him leave this place. When it is my turn to deal, I deal. But it is true. I was the woman in his room that night. Because of me he went to Europe, and that's where he got famous.

I was with a circus that fall, and Crawfordsville was the last show before we wintered at Peru. I took tickets mostly, guessed weights and ages on the little midway we had. I read minds. I stayed in Crawfordsville after being paid off, hoping to go south. I spent the first night in the open with some flyers who next day left for parts unknown. That's how I met Mr. Pound, near a mailbox on Grand Avenue. He was mailing a stack of letters; there must have been twenty. He was mailing them one at a time, reading each address before pushing each envelope in the slot. He wore a big white Panama, and he had a malacca cane. Not to mention a red beard.

"You look cold," he said. "

"I am cold," I said.

I was cold. Crawfordsville has never been friendly to a single woman. The college is all men. The town is used to men. At the circus, most of the crowd was made up of boys from the college in collarless shirts and crew-neck sweaters, hanging around an older man, a professor. What girls there were always carried an armful of dolls and teddy bears, those were just becoming popular, escorted by the boys who kept winning the prizes. I was waiting for a Monon passenger going south.

"You must stay with me," he said. "I need someone to talk to, and you'll do very nicely." He rapped his cane against the mailbox. "Besides, it will be fun getting by the housekeeper."

The day had been bright but never warm with those flat-bottomed, fast-moving clouds that seem to make the land flatter and the wind colder. Now that it was night, it had a head start to the first frost. Besides, it was nothing new. I had been in a circus.

"You must tell me my fortune," he said. I went to his rooming house. The stair was opposite the front door. His room was at the top and to the right. He went first and made the housekeeper make some tea, following her to the kitchen. I snuck in and up the stairs. The room was small—a bed, some chairs. Doilies and fringe. There was a big square pillow with a needle-worked "P" that I thought stood for his name but he said later it was for Pennsylvania, where he had gone to school. "Your girl makes you a pillow there. It's all the rage."

"You have a girl?"

"No," he answered.

The tea tasted good. It was English tea. He had some cold cornbread in his pockets. He gave me the bed and put the chairs face-to-face for himself and lit a cigarette without asking me.

"There is much literary tradition in Crawfordsville, you know. Lew Wallace, the author of *Ben Hur,* died here." He said he visited Indianapolis just to see James Whitcomb Riley, that he'd found him entertaining schoolchildren on his porch, a little girl on his lap. Mr. Riley had suggested they get drunk. And, later, they did.

"Won't she hear us?" I said.

"She thinks I talk to myself."

He must not have been a poet then. He talked about the provinces in France because he had been there the summer before. "Hills and peaks and castles," he said. "Not this flat Athens of the Midwest." He was lonely and young. You could tell that. The boys in the Teke house today would have thought him strange, a sissy. The way he dressed. He never did anything but talk to me. He told me about his friends in Pennsylvania and how he loved to take baths. There was something in his voice. The way he talked was like writing a letter. He stretched out in the chairs, throwing his head back and closing his eyes. He fretted about not being happy here or not wanting to stay in Indiana. "I shouldn't feel that way," he said. "I'm a nomad, you see. You are too, aren't you? Don't you want to stop wandering? Don't you want to stay someplace?"

I didn't. I suppose if I could have known about it then, I would have headed out to Hollywood. Instead, I went to sleep, listening to his voice, wondering why there are so few people with red hair. I never told his fortune. Were there leaves I could read? I was his fortune. Behind the red hair was a blue wall, and the ashtray and the tea tray were filled with cigarette butts.

I woke up the next morning and the first thing I saw was Miss Grundy, her arms full of sheets, looking as if she was disappointed I wasn't dead. "That man," she said. "You poor girl." He was fired that morning by President Mackintosh. I was told Ezra begged to stay. It was understood nothing happened between us and that I was not the reason he was dismissed. The trustees thought it a charitable action, suggested Wabash was not suitable for Mr. Pound. I gave Ezra my ticket, and that night he was on his way south to Indianapolis, pillow under his arm. Miss Grundy suggested the college find me a position. Next thing you know, I was centering a canned cherry in the middle of each chocolate pudding in the TKE house.

I got a letter from him, care of Miss Grundy, a few months later. "Venice, a lovely place to come to from Crawfordsville, Ind."

The other mothers wouldn't care, anyway. We swap recipes, sour cream cookies, and butter brickle bars. We plan menus and really worry about color on the plate. The price of tea in China. And the boys don't dream. The ones who know who he was and that he was here, never ask me. I hear his name sometimes after English 3. Another gentleman with a girl in his room. He forgot his tie. Maybe if I was a poet, I could tell them how it was. Instead, I am quiet at my table. The only thing I'm asked about, besides the salt, is when the letters were stolen and when they were returned. And if it's true that the skull is all that's left of the one pledge that told the house's secrets.

Walking through the halls at night with my Boston, I look at the annual pictures. Mine is the only face that never changes. My vanity. It is the same picture every year since the first year. That peek-a-boo look. I had skull-tight hair, veiled eyes, dark, bow lips. What a funny way to grow older and stay younger. The matting is the same every year—a circle for me, their sweetheart and their favorite. The boxes are filled with boys aging over four years like presidents in office. When I meet the real mothers during parents' weekends, I look for the faces in those faces. The way I stare must make them uncomfortable. "Boys," I say, "will be boys."

I saw that Pound again in 1958 when he was in the hospital. I took my vacation that year in Washington so I could try to see him. Ever since the war, *The Star* had run these articles about him because he had been here once. I didn't think I would be able to see him. I was too early at the hospital, so I waited. At two, another woman arrived. She had the profile of a face on a coin. I found out later it was his wife. She never said a thing to me but hello. She had an accent. I followed her and a man in a white coat up a metal spiral staircase. We went down a hallway. In an alcove by a window, I was introduced. He couldn't remember me, of course. But that's because he was sick.

"Indiana," he said. "Elephants walking in the corn."

He made tea. He talked about Italy. There was a chance then that they would let him go in the care of his wife. She sat with her back to the window. Other patients came up to the screen that divided us from the ward. He gave them pennies and sent them away. He wore a green visor cap like a card player or a banker. I thought of crumbs in my lap, and I brushed my skirt with the side of my hand. He talked about Idaho and maybe going there. The potato.

Other people visited. They called him E. P. He talked about poetry to them. I thought then: Had I been a poem? Maybe I was a poem. The only other visitor I recall was another woman because she was from Fort Wayne. She could remember walking the tow path on the canal. She talked to him in Greek. She told me that later. Then, I was watching two of the other patients dancing. Two men, dancing.

I gave him a pound cake meaning a little joke by it, or a token of who he was.

"It's got a pound of butter, a pound of flour, and a pound of sugar," I told him.

He smiled at that. I knew he didn't remember me.

I followed his wife and the other woman out of the hospital. The woman took me back downtown in her limousine.

"He's an old fart," she said, "but important." She said that Wabash was a good school. "I taught in an all-girls' school in Baltimore for years. I have never been back to Indiana. I must go back sometime before I die." I thought that was a strange thing to say.

I went back to Indiana on a night train. The cars were powder blue, and the trip through Ohio seemed to take forever. Have you been through Ohio? I would like to say that the boys missed me, but my vacation is during initiation in the house. That is in early January. They are too busy to miss me. I would like to say too that I was important to someone, to E. P. maybe, but that would not be true. I'm simply one of the somethings that happened to him. I didn't change myself. Or I'm left over, an extra part. The clock still runs. What happens to yeast in bread? There's no story here. He took the stories with him. I think people think sometimes that they make up their own world. There always has to be people like me in those made-up worlds. Nothing would happen if there weren't.

Did I tell you what I do when the nights are cold like this one? I put a big Greek letter in my bed and plug it in. The lights are so bright, they bleach the blankets. It looks like a person curled up in bed. When I get home, it is nice and toasty. I pull back the covers like I was opening a living thing. I look at the huge Θ or Π lighting up my bed. And my room's all upside-down because the light's coming from below. What does it look like? It looks like nothing else at all. It looks like a letter in a bed.

You must see it sometime. That skull, it never sleeps. Do you need a place to stay?

Schliemann in Indianapolis

1 April 1869

There are twelve great railroads that cross this city now, and the number will be fifteen, I am told, by the end of the year. Three lines pass behind the house I've taken on Noble Street for the sake of my case. My days and nights are filled with the ringing of bells, the huffing of the engines. I sit at this desk thinking about Catherine and my divorce from her, of Serge, Nadja, and Natasha in St. Petersburg where they will live and die on account of their mother's foolishness while all the time I hear the constant slipping of steel wheels on steel rails. There is no greater testimony for the future of this country than this ceaseless traffic. My small backyard is filled with white sand that spills from the tracks as the engineers maneuver their machines up the grade. The neighbors' laundry is always sooty, but the stones of our building are still too new to have turned color.

I have engaged the lawyers, five in all, of two firms: Hendricks, Hord and Hendricks as well as Seidensticker and A. Naltner. I believe Senator Hendricks suggested the other firm as they too are German. We filed suit just in time as the court has since adjourned and will not sit again until 1 June. The principal tenor of my complaint is being, by law, published once a week in a weekly paper of general circulation. The advertisement will run for the next six weeks. So I will sit and wait for the court to sit again, pretend I am a resident of this city, and read my challenge to Catherine in the Indiana State Journal. These are the best circumstances I have found for initiating such a complaint. If I fail here I am prepared to try Wisconsin but that will mean fall in Asia Minor and little time to begin digging before the wind turns around or the Turkish government again changes its mind.

My desire to prove my claims on the Troad had brought me to North America for the fourth time. I believe my American citizenship, recently obtained in the city of New York, will aid in my negotiations for a new firman with the Turkish government, for they will have little to do with a German and even less with a Russian. To present myself as a Greek would be unthinkable, though I believe more and more that Hellas is my homeland. I am fortunate to be able to choose my citizenship. My fortune is not bounded nor am I restricted by languages. The divorce is an afterthought, an anecdote, and this formality, this waiting, an inconvenience to be sure but an easy one to suffer to be rid of Catherine with her orthodoxies and her precious St. Petersburg. I have come to America for papers only, and I will have them. Indiana is my die, then, for my future direction is clear to me. I need only strip the mistakes of my past from me so that I am left with the golden thread.

I left New York on Wednesday last by the Jersey Central Railroad, then by the Pennsylvanian. I paid $20.00 to Indianapolis and $3.00 for baggage. For $2.50 more I had use of a splendid sleeping car called the Silver Palace. In this car were eleven silver columns; splendid silver lamps, in fact, everywhere silver-plated ornaments in great profusion; immense numbers of mirrors in silver-plated frames, excellent toilettes, magnificent carpets, silken curtains, good waterclosets and stoves, excellent sleeping apparatus. I had good company and among the rest a lady of French descent, even born in France, who had married a man of whom she severely complained saying that he is a drunkard, constantly beats and otherwise ill-treats her. She fled from him on Good Friday when she had been attacked again by this man for not having prepared for him some meat which he did not think sinful since he is from England. I lamented her sad fate but that is all I could do for her. Being without means, she is returning to her husband.

Stories such as this agitate me for I believe in marriage. That I dwell on their telling and on my own state follows from my condition here.

Indianapolis lies at latitude 39.55° and longitude 86.5°. I am 527 feet above the sea, 827 miles from New York. Though it is much colder than New York, I must find a place to bathe.

6 April 1869

I am bathing in the White River beneath a railroad bridge where the pilings have created a small beach of sand. As the trains pass overhead, wreaths of the engine's smoke descend in one piece through the laced iron struts and wooden ties. It is quite cold in the water but I believe it is doing me good. It is not the sea, as salt water is indeed healthful. It is not even a river, actually, but a shallow stream where even in its middle I can stand and wave at the passing passenger cars. And this is the principal source of water, along with a few deep wells, for the city. I asked Naltner about this. I see now, that an adequate water supply was not even a consideration for the men who founded Indianapolis. The city was built overnight. It is the newest of cities in the state, evolved from nothing save a swamp. There was not even an Indian village on the site. No one had lived here before. It is an example of parthenogenesis and pride. I am taken by this. Here are a people who build cities for no other reason than that the locations are geographical centers of arbitrarily decided governmental regions. Reason enough. There is no water here, and the past is no deeper than the White River lapping at my waist. No, no deeper than this coat of dust on my new desk.

Naltner has shown me the ruins of the dry canals, finished, after years of labor and extravagant expense, only a few weeks before the first railroad entered town. Horses were to tow barges from New York and the Great Lakes to the Wabash and the great rivers beyond. Now they are grassy ditches that fill sometime with rain. All sorts of rubble, building blocks and timber, everywhere. We rode our horses along the bottom of the perfectly straight canal, seeing nothing on either side but the abandoned banks here and there sprouting spring flowers. The lock doors, sprung open, hung on great useless hinges, and the channels stretched out of sight broken only by mounds of discarded property—furniture and stoves, bed ticking and clothing. The system was never used. The company that built it, bankrupt. There was a man who was bathing in the waterfall created by the broken trough of a feeder aqueduct overhead. He told us only to go away and leave him alone. We did and continued to follow the great cuts. Here: pickaxes, shovels, bars, wedges, and other tools. There was equipment for a drag line. We emerged finally, far beyond the limits of the city; the trench had prevented us from seeing the mean shacks at the city's edge. We came in to a field of timothy and clover, a farmer's pasture. We turned our mounts back toward Indianapolis, now only dark smudges of smoke in the distance. There was a street sign in the middle of the field, 125th Street, and stakes in the ground. We followed these signs in descending order, through the fields to town, to the streets that have been constructed.

My lawyers suggested I purchase a partnership in a local starch factory as evidence of permanent residence in this place. The house, I understand, is not enough so I have arranged to buy a fourth of a share of the

Union Starch Company on New York Street for $12,000 with $350 of it in cash. The terms are put in such a way that I will forfeit my share if the balance is not forthcoming by 25 July. By that time, if all goes well, I will be in Europe. The sum is not too great to lose.

I am reading the books Doctor Drisler suggested on the Indian languages. They are Gallatin, Buchanan, Catlin, and W. W. Turner. Perhaps, as I wait here, I can learn a few of these tongues. But my method depends upon simultaneous reading of a book printed in the new language as well as one printed in one of the languages I know. I have found no book in the languages I know translated into the Indian and no book at all of the original Indian dialect. Is there writing? I am still working on Swedish and Polish, and Naltner reminded me that I can find speakers of all my languages within my neighborhood. Yes, but what would I say to these fellows? No one must know the real purpose for my presence here. I am alone in this small house. I have outfitted it with simple furnishings. I read all day. I write letters and receive answers.

17 April 1869

Last night a hurricane blew up with such sudden force and power I was afraid this house would be knocked down. Accompanying the storm were rain, hail and lightning. I stood by my window and waited for the next illumination of a grotesque frieze: the saplings bowed, stripped of their young leaves; crazed horses with men at their harness; children reaching to grasp their mothers' skirts. Scarcely had the storm begun and the sound of its machinations drowned the puny chuffings of my backyard rail line, when a larger explosion sounded, the shock quaking the ground and seeming to take even the tempest by surprise. Soon thereafter the fire alarm rang out, and I went at once from window to window. I saw no fire from any vantage, but stood transfixed by the lightning and the unnatural tolling of the alarm. I saw again that night in San Francisco, my first trip to America. Having come to join my brother and his mining concern, I found instead I would bury him, dead from typhus, in the hillside he had sought to excavate. I am a broker. I saw an opportunity in trading with the miners while I settled my brother's affairs. I assayed ore, advanced credit, took risk. I awoke that dreadful night to a similar alarm; the windows were filled with flame. I escaped to the bay with one pud of dust on which I sat and watched the hills that city was built on blaze golden against the black sky. My brother's body lay somewhere beneath that storm of fire.

The day after the storm in Indianapolis I learned that the hurricane had collapsed the Central Railroad Freight Depot and buried nine people. Seven escaped, slightly injured, but two, one being the Reverend Daniel Ballou, a Universalist Minister of Utica who had preached at the Masonic Hall, died today. Already the citizens of the city begin to rebuild with workers making hardly an attempt to salvage brick from the previous walls.

Today the weather is again much cooler.

26 April 1869

Today was the anniversary of the foundation of the Odd Fellows society in consequence of which a great festival was held with great processions of the Odd Fellows in their uniforms or grades of distinction in the streets with many banners and much music.

I read again today my notice of divorce from Catherine. I also read her letters, the ones placed in evidence, with their botched translations which make her sound the schoolgirl. Her Russian is far more eloquent, her pleas better constructed, and I hear somewhere within her phrasing the old music. Or is it my recollection of the language itself and the time when I was new to it. I have made love to that woman in my fifth language. My vocabulary is exhausted. "My husband," she calls in her letters, "I will always be here," she says. Sometimes it is a curse to know all the different names for a thing. Husband. Wife. One longs for the dead tongues and a world that does not change. I am through trading indigo and olive oil, tea and cotton. I am finished with those winters and working through the mounds of chits and bills wearing gloves without fingers. She wants the clean touch of gold, the white hands of the banker. In Ithaca, I held the sacrificial knives. I let the ashes of Odysseus run through my fingers. I buried my hands into the very dunghill where Argus waited for his master.

2 May 1869

Sunday is a very dull day here as all of the groceries, barbers, and even the bakers, along with other shops are closed. All, that is, except the cigar depot. My cook leaves me in the early morning on the Sabbath to go to church and returns around 5 o'clock to leave for me a cold supper. She leaves again for evening services and once did not return until early Monday morning.

The shop windows are shuttered from the inside, an admirable invention of this country. I will be alone on the street, mark my reflection in an empty window. Walking, I wonder if they will ever finish with this city, this country. Everywhere are heaps of brick, tubs for mortar, scaffolding taller than buildings. Names are only half-painted on windows: bold letters, outlines, ghosts implied by the spaces. I imagine the plans and designs for these structures in the workmen's heads, a picture of what they want, their own way of joining and plumbing smuggled within their memory from the old countries. The deserted Sunday streets seem like a memory, vague but bold, not detailed enough and without people. Flower boxes have no flowers. And the citizens have disappeared from what is usually a very busy boulevard as if I'd wished them away, as if they were my creation in the first place. I have stopped thinking of them, and they are gone.

At the cigar store. His door is guarded by a wooden carved statue of an Indian. Human scale. I lean against the other post, conscious of the mimicry. I think of the porch maidens. We are the only ones on the street. The awnings are rolled. The street itself is only half paved with cobble stones. We say nothing to each other.

6 May 1869

Suddenly my plans for an easy and early divorce have been disrupted by an act of a scoundrel in one of this state's northern counties. A report of a divorce abomination has been circulated through the capital by all the newspapers. Here is the story. Some years ago a man married a lovely rich girl whose tireless efforts substantially enlarged her husband's estate. She nursed him through a recent illness. The couple had seven children. After twenty years, he fell in love with another young woman. Through false witness and perjured proof he has won a divorce in another county. There is a brief waiting period after which a divorce is granted. This allows an opportunity for the divorced party to present evidence and contest the decree. The wife had not the slightest knowledge of the affair. The time for such opposition expired. In spite of the shoddy evidence of the case and as the deadline has been reached, the court has granted the divorce, and the wife has been forced to leave her husband's house abandoning all her property. The children belong to the husband as well. News of this has spread throughout the state. The scandal has aroused cries from the pulpit and press for this woman was highly respected. There are demands the law be changed. It is on everyone's lips. My lawyers remind me that only the legislature can change the law, and it is in recess now from its regular session. Only the governor can call a special session and only then in extraordinary times. This incident, emotional as it may be, is not, they assure me, reason enough to call the bodies together. It will be the business of next year's regular session. I remain only partially convinced as all of this is new to me.

The recent events force me to read as many papers as possible in an attempt to construct the workings of this country. I read the papers printed in languages other than English as well. There is even a paper in Hebrew that is delivered. My cook—herself an avid reader of the press, as Americans believe the press to be the fount of knowledge, the means of advancement while the papers do not attempt to show that it is otherwise—now is convinced I am a Russian Jew. She speaks slowly to me in English when she brings my tea, as if I were a child.

Here, more notices of storms. We have had tremendous rains and in consequence heavy inundations which have nearly destroyed the bath at the bridge. The storms are accompanied by thunder, and the paper is filled with the sad news of persons struck dead or maimed by the flashes of lightning.

The temperature changes all of a sudden.

10 May 1869

No one believes the city exists. Learned men tell me it is all metaphor, a creation of Homer, nothing more. "You are a grocer," they say, "a dealer of dry goods." They are inaccurate when they attempt even to describe the thing before them. They see only what they have been told to see and are polite since they wish to continue their sterile diggings and the search for antiques. They believe in my wealth that it might give them aid as they scratch in a place not one meter deep. They speak of imagination. Surely they can see that the world is very old, that even the fanciest poetry contains a buried truth. The swamp on Mr. Calvert's land in Hassilk can be read. Odysseus tells Eumaeus that hard by the walls of Troy was such a swamp. And beyond the hill the continuous range of more hills.

As a general rule, classic literature is despised here owing to the universal enthusiasms for acquiring material wealth; thus classical education is at low ebb. Knowledge cannot hold out against the same desire. The colleges answer perfectly to the German gymnasiums.

Thus at every turn I am not understood. To some I am nothing but a common man. Here, a savant entombed in books and papers who is not of this world nor takes part in the life of Indianapolis. I dream of Troy. The towers and gates. Of pulling it to the surface whole, brushing it off, and placing it before them. But the Turks will have left buried only the reliefs and statues of gods and beasts as they quarried the stone. The Koran forbids the representation of living things. Let me raise these beings then and the dumb stones will fall in place.

13 May 1869

I am taken by the enormous amount of children who seem healthy and very pretty for the most part. The immigrants—German and Irish—seem to produce more than the Americans who are far less blessed with offspring. Many of these scions, I have found, are already engaged in making their own way, earning their bread while boot-blacking, running errands, selling the continuing stream of the newspapers' updated editions. I recall one lad who placed a booklet on the laps of each patron of a horse-drawn omnibus I was riding. The booklet depicted various views of the city, mostly of the capitol. He told us all that they were 3 cents apiece, 2 for 5 cents. I gave him a dollar, and he carefully counted out the exact number, calling me "Sir" and telling me that he wasn't a beggar. He exited as the car stopped and disappeared into a street crowded with children and crisscrossed over head with numberless telegraphic wires. The vegetation has rapidly advanced.

14 May 1869

My worst fears have been realized as the governor has called the legislature into extraordinary session having to do with appropriations and the passage of the 15th Constitutional Amendment that concerns voting rights. Introduced this session as well was a bill amending the existing divorce law. Its drafting was motivated by the recent sensational divorce scandal, and its passage pricked on by aroused public sentiment. The bill, if passed, would allow a divorce only after a summons had been presented and sworn to the defendant. The plaintiff must be a longstanding resident of the county, attested to. There is also a most urgent clause attached that would affect my case, since, as law, it would become immediately enforceable. A summons would be dispatched to Russia and my wife, causing an intolerable delay.

Since the inauguration of the special session, I have visited the capitol daily. I have been endeavoring to prevent this bill's passage in its present form.

The capitol itself is an amalgamation of classic columns and domes, the central one of hammered gold. The stone is the state limestone. Upon close examination there appears in the grain a solid sea of frozen invertebrates, shells and such, worms and snails, all petrified. Creatures turned to stone. I thought of the marbles on the exploded Parthenon and of finding the toe beneath my feet. I thought of the smoothness of those stones and how they would fit back together. I pointed out the teeming life to Naltner, who was there to introduce me to various legislators. He said he hadn't noticed that before. All stone was field stone to him, and he then showed me the overlarge statuary of Washington, Jefferson, and other founders draped in competently rendered togas, the periwigs chiseled to their heads. "Italians," he said.

I sat in the public gallery of the Senate along with the ladies who vigorously fanned themselves and watched the passage of the divorce bill. I had been too late to prevent it. The ladies were satisfied, applauding politely all around me. In the house the bill was referred to a committee, which would allow time to plead my case before what Naltner assured me was to be a key collection of representatives. The meeting is being arranged for a few days hence. I watched the house in session, standing by the door and its man. I am not hopeful of the outcome. The representatives behave much like schoolboys, all chewing and continually spitting. Many hold their legs up on their desks before them, and all put the laws in the most summary and reckless way.

I left Naltner there departing from him in the darkened rotunda. Again, there were more assurances. Emerging from the shadows of the capitol out into the now darkening streets of Indianapolis, I saw the veterans making their ways back to the grounds. This is where they sleep. One meets them here at every step. Men with only one arm or one leg and sometimes even worse. Both legs amputated. I saw even one whose both legs were amputated close to the abdomen. They come here for the pension accounts and do not return home. Along the streets are men in the dusty dark blue tunics. Yellow piping for the cavalry, red for the artillery. The braid and decorations are peeling from the sleeves. The hats have been stripped of their badges. They talk in groups. They light torches. They pose in the circle at the city's center, prefiguring the statutes the legislature promises to erect at public expense. Everywhere there is this blue and suddenly I realize it is my blue. I was the merchant of this color. It was my indigo warehoused from the Crimea. It was my dye in their coats. The color has bled as well. It is the exact shade of the sky at that time of the evening. The color the sky absorbs when the sun sets over a prairie, over something as broad as the sea. It is no longer Prussian blue or Russian or Austrian. It is an American blue. There are Zouaves too in faded short jackets. The fez crushed. The loose, striped pantaloons flap as the man swings by on a crutch. I am reminded of the Turks, my own adversaries, standing on the hillside overlooking the digging. The rifles cross the knees. I look out of the pit as out of my own grave, up at the guards who are smoking and talking. Nightly, I pass these crippled men wearing the memories of what has happened to them. I am aware of the elaborate procedure of my own walking. The soldiers make their way by me like shadows, but they are not shadows.

At home again, I am too despondent to open my letters. I ignore the package from Archbishop Vimbos though I know it contains the portraits I have requested.

16 May 1869

I met the legislators in the adjourned and abandoned Supreme Court room of the capitol. The room is a perfect cube. These dimensions symbolize something I am sure. The walls contain portraits of retired justices. The more recent are daguerreotypes or other photographs. Naltner explained the circumstances of my case. He explained who I am, my books, my ideas about Troy. The legislators on their part look unimpressed, their gazes as glassy as those emanating from the rows of pictures. I assured them of the seriousness of my suit. I spoke of my starch factory in the city, my recent purchase of shares in the Chicago, Burlington, and Quincy and other roads, my desire to stay in the state. Arrangements were made. They were amenable to a deletion of the urgent clause, saying they saw no difference a month or two delay in implementation would make in the spirit of the law. We agreed, as we descended the broad stairs to the floor of their chamber, that the current law was an abomination, that its abuses should be curtailed. And I did agree with them as I shook their hands in an ante-chamber, a room full of men shaking hands. I tire, though, of the pretense. I have created this elaborate life of lies. I do this in order to one day scratch in the dirt. My languages have only helped me lie in every tongue. I lie even to myself. This too is necessary. This is another thing that must be done. I am so positive I am correct. I can see so clearly. The picture of the place, that city, aches in my brain, and all these words in all the languages ever spoken cannot place stone back on stone.

I sat the rest of the day in the gallery as the debate continued below. I listened to speeches made on a variety of subjects—commodity prices, allocations, penal code, the amendment to the Constitution— while everywhere on the floor knots of men stood in the chamber's corners, at their desks and in the doorways and whispered without gesturing nor listening to what was being said.

17 May 1869

The temperature changes here are very sudden. Some days ago it was cold, and it was necessary to light heaters and put on heavy clothes. In a few days a heat wave caused the temperature to rise to 39° in the shade. On account of the humidity, the heat is unbearable and oppressive. Since the city is surrounded by swamps, the heat causes pestilential infections —ague, Isthmus fever, erysipelas. At least one-third of the population is afflicted with fevers. As a prophylactic measure, every morning I take a little quinine which I trust grants me immunity.

I will leave my daughter, Nadja, this house. It amuses me to think of her here in some far future time, perhaps reading this entry while she sits at this desk. How many railroads will there be then? Will she attempt to piece together the mystery of why her father left her so young and then disappeared into America. I had hoped to teach each of my children a special language, one only each would know. Serge, Italian. Nadja, Finnish, and Arabic for Natasha. Instead I will leave them houses all over the world. They will learn their own languages. I see her on the way across the sea, holding her hat as she stands near the railing. I see her reading this page, looking for a mention of her mother's name, her own name. Until then this house will bring an income of $144.00 minus commission to Naltner which is altogether satisfactory.

I have been at the capitol daily. Soon the bill will be read for its third and last time. Pierce's amendment which I supported was tabled due to its length. Another died for a want of a second.

21 May 1869

I am already in love with the photograph. My friend and teacher the Archbishop Vimbos, at my urgings, has sent these portraits. I had written to him in February explaining my future plans and my desire to have a Greek wife once I was free of my Russian one. I told him that I sought a wife of the same angelic character as his married sister. She should be poor but well educated. She must be enthusiastic about Homer and about the rebirth of my beloved Greece. The languages, I told him, do not matter, but she was to be of the Greek type with black hair and if possible beautiful. My main requirement was a good and loving heart.

Her image is here before me, immediately recognizable as the loveliest among tin plates of the others. She is young. Not twenty, I would guess. I fancy myself as living now only in a metaphysical world. I desire a wife who is inclined toward learning, one who would simply love and honor me and travel. I was once sensual and sentimental, but I have changed through those long winters. Perhaps a widow, I suggested. A girl, after all, finds paradise in the fulfillment of her physical desires. But the baths, the baths have invigorated me, and I have refrained from daily horseback riding while in my bachelor's state. The light on the plate turns her face silver, an icon, surrounded by ebony enamel. Her black hair. I am an old traveler and a good reader of faces. The others ring of tin, smell of mercury. In their visages is always something blurred: the eyes both closed and opened; the mouth, a smile and frown; a hand sweeping to brush back the vanishing hair. Not Sophia's face. Her eyes are clear. Her skin is bright. How like noble Paris I feel, choosing among the goddesses. But beyond the myth, the bride is no mere mortal woman. How this little piece of foil draws all the light in this dark room, the yellowing newspapers and heavy curtains. It is the only light in this dark summer. The question is still undecided which will free me to go to her. I cannot read what is before me. I find it impossible to read what I am writing. My eyes, old and weak, are drawn to her face. I wonder, does she play the piano?

24 May 1869

I have been bathing here in the river for more than a month, but it appears that there is no other amateur but me for early bathing.

There are no coffee houses here.

The weather has become very hot and the thermometer ranges between 22° and 25° Reaumur in the shade. The air is damp as it rains every day. One feels the heat double.

I visited the Union Starch Manufactory. I am part owner of the company. It is altogether a fine building being three stories made of red brick with large windows. A stream runs hard by. Everywhere, there is white steam escaping and the smell of the matter. It is a new building, completed after a previous factory was totally destroyed by fire a year ago. We have a capacity of 40,000–50,000 pounds of starch per week. But I was feigning interest. I was far more taken with the girls working, their open faces appearing in the partings of the steam. There was a lightness in my step even though the heat was unbearable and several of us were down to our shirt sleeves.

It occurs to me now how inaccurate these journals will be, not a record of each day at all but whole clumps of time. Some passages were written in passion, others on sleepless nights. How much do I carry with me? And these few facts, will they be important when I leave this place?

If all fails there is Wisconsin which has written its desire for citizens into its divorce laws. It is a part of the country that I have yet to see.

29 May 1869

To my greatest joy, 41 of the democratic members presented their resignations to the governor in order to avoid voting on the 15th amendment to the United States Constitution which gives to the former slaves the right of voting. By their resignation the House had no quorum and thus no more business could be transacted. The remaining republicans with but three democrats who remained voted then on the 15th Amendment, with but three nays, the democrats. It is doubtful it will be sanctioned by the Congress. At all events no other business could be done by the House. No further action will be taken on the divorce bill. My joy is immense. After all, I am very glad to have got an insight into the doings of these people's legislative assemblies, which presents Democracy in all its roughness and nudity with all its party spirit and facility to yield to lateral influences, with all its licentiousness. I often saw them throwing paper balls at each other and even the speaker.

1 June 1869

There are now but a few weeks before the court considers my case again and I have every confidence that the adjudication will be in my favor. I am tempted to travel once again, to see the surrounding countryside or the other principal cities of the state. Naltner warns me that the fruition of these plans might suggest my unwillingness to stay permanently here. I am a resident, a citizen. "Go," he says, "go to the local gatherings. The lectures, clubs, performances." I find the theatres dark and undecorated and do not understand the native love of humbug. Barnum, say, and minstrelsy. I brood in this room. I try not to think of Sophia and my case, but I find I wish for the remaining weeks to be over all at once. I compose list after list of questions which I post to Archbishop Vimbos: *What does her father do? Is she a good housekeeper? Can you send me a lock of her hair? In care of my address in New York. In care of my home in London. Paris.* I wait for the mails and the sound of my housekeeper's knock. "Mail," she says. "Letters." All one word sentences for my benefit. These are the longest days of the year. The sun remains at the zenith constantly. The nights are long also. They only seem to be, of course. Time.

4 June 1869

I see here in the evening at every step bright sparks in the air which are produced by the lightning bug. It is said to remain here only one month. The light is produced by the phosphoric matter which the insect carries at its back part.

I believe in progress. I witness its manifestation daily in this country and on each of my various visits. The draining of the land. The speed at which San Francisco was rebuilt after the conflagration I saw. On my last visit I traveled the south of the country, the battlefields and sacked cities. All gone now, I understand. The land planted to the future, new road right-of-ways surveyed next to the twisted rails. I visited the patent office in Washington and toyed with the models one must submit. The pavement here is, itself, new and much improved being broad, well drained with wide *trottoirs* for those on foot.

Yesterday I witnessed a demonstration of a recent invention, an engine of war. A Dr. Gatling, an inventor of farm implements, operated his gun for the citizens of Indianapolis and for the officers of the ordnance section of the United States Army. He assembled the weapon he calls a labor-saving device for siege on the broad field known as the mall. The gun was smaller than a standard field piece. It had a limber and caisson. The barrel consisted of many barrels which rotated by means of a crank similar to those found on a mill. The whole operation resembled grinding coffee. The gallery of spectators was swelled by the number of veterans of the Grand Army in the remnants of their uniforms. The local Horse, in smart tunics and busby, drilled before us as the gun was readied. The green field was turned to black earth beneath their parade. And then Dr. Gatling made a brief speech, mentioning his use of the latest ball and cap and powder. At the conclusion of the speech, those closest to him drew back, and he was left alone on the field where he proceeded to crank the machine, bending slightly at the waist, sending forth shot after shot in less than a second each, and each barrel reloading itself. This he sustained for several minutes while the ladies held their hands on their ears. At last with the ammunition exhausted and the gun silent, the onlookers broke out in cheers. Dr. Gatling, on his part, took a slight bow and swiveled his gun on its axis through 360°. It was a spectacular exhibition, and its sight has stayed with me. The use of such a weapon can be easily imagined.

Tonight the atmospheric conditions must be favorable for I can hear the sounds of animals, their bells and bleats, carried to me from the bordering fields. As I walked in the city before retiring, I turned the corner into an empty street and heard the clear bawling of a calf that must have been miles away.

7 June 1869

In this room I am surrounded by paper. There is my letter to Dr. Drisler and the Convention of American Philologists. If all goes as expected now I will miss this meeting in Poughkeepsie. Here my treatise on *The Thousand and One Nights*, seeking to disprove the claim of its Chinese origins. Around me, my fortress of newspapers and journals from which I have quarried this pile of articles, cut from the various columns. The epidemy of train accidents, a dreadful one recently on the Erie. Cures. Divorce laws. Tales of reconstruction in the South. Notices of meetings. The slow, ancient news of Europe.

I find I lose myself in reveries of Sophia, of visiting her classroom and perhaps hearing her recite the scene in the Odyssey where the girls come to the river to wash and to play. I must stop myself before I fall to the old sin of pride. Are all these things I contrived and planned ordained to come true? It is an old story. I will them into being.

12 June 1869

I have made one final trip with Naltner north from here to a site outside of a small town where a circle of mounds are located. On our way, we passed through field after field ripening into the raw commodities on which my fortune is based. We saw acreage of wheat, maize, oats, barley, and rye in the varied greens and browns. We saw fine teams of horses and mules and the various new equipment for reaping and threshing, all brightly painted. Hay was being raked and drying. Everywhere we turned there was good husbandry and honest toil. At the mounds, we discovered that all but the steepest part of the hill was in cultivation. We stood on the crown of one of the largest, looking out at the squares of fields and townships. We shared the summit with a herd of cattle which find it pleasurable thereabouts. Here the beasts escape the flies and feel the slight breeze that stirs. They are patient and, as I regarded them, I understood Hera's epithet, the cow-eyed one. They watched us while we spoke. Naltner told me of the boys of the country following behind the plows, collecting barrels of arrowheads and tools, parts of pots and bones. Most is dirt though. But everywhere I looked I saw that intelligence shaped the land. The mounds are the only rise on a broad, flat plain and so arrayed as to leave no doubt of their unnatural composition, perfect in their geometry and symmetry. "Who was here?" I asked Naltner. "No one knows," he said. There has been nothing written about them. It seems even the modern Indians, the ones who had had intercourse with white men, were at a loss to explain such things. Probably no precious metal or quarried stone. A burial tumulus, perhaps a site of an ancient battle.

17 June 1869

The Americans are wonderful wood cutters. They cut three times more than anybody else. For one laborer cuts daily two fathoms at 128 cubic feet each. They also excel in bricklaying and it is wonderful to see how a brick mason lays, in one day, 200 bricks into the walls of a building.

23 June 1869

To my greatest joy my divorce has been decreed today by the judge, Solomon Blair. His only objection was that the children were unprovided for, but as I consented to take them at my charge, it was all right. I will obtain copies of the papers, the whole proceedings, and the decree. It is to their credit that the lawmakers view marriage as a business transaction, a contract that can be dissolved. I will hasten to New York and then to Europe, to Greece. Perhaps there is still time for a walk in Asia. Perhaps Sophia will need more weaning from her parents' home, a journey to the islands, the birth places of the gods. And winging before me, a letter to Catherine who today in our house in St. Petersburg knows nothing of how her life has changed. I can see her in the front room, sifting through the letters and calling cards, sighing in her way, reaching out to pull the cord, and then thinking better of it. Her attention is arrested by a bird's song or the sounds the children are making, French with Nurse. I already know her future, have already scratched out the note that will transform her world.

Here is something marvelous. There are innumerable suicides daily committed all over the country, and they are reported in detail by the papers. Truly a mystery for everything I have seen is an argument against that course of action.

And here a notice of a meeting of the railroads to standardize time. As it stands now each small town and city sets its clock at noon when the sun is overhead so that the traveler, dizzy at each disembarkation, sets his watch anew. There are a thousand different times. The line's schedules are useless since it is a different time everywhere on earth. An observatory in Pittsburgh is to send a telegraphic signal sometime soon.

Biograph

Iced air. How do they do it? We could've gone to the Marbro, but they don't have it there. I like the sign outside here, snow on top of all the letters. Everybody sitting outside on the street, looking over at the glowing white in the light. Light bouncing off the awnings. People dying in the heat. But you got a little money, and you are in where it's cool. They must take the heat right out of the air. But how do they know which is the hot part? In the loft, one time, placing bets, I saw the guy who runs the machine out in the middle of the street looking at something he held in his hand. The drays and the trucks working their way around him. Only the trolleys creeping up to him, the motorman yanking on the bell. I couldn't hear it because the windows were closed. The iced air. Everybody squinting at the man in the street holding his hand up staring at it, at something in it. Things moving slow in the heat. Boy, it's swell. I want to stay for the whole show. Let my shirt dry out, roll my socks back up.

Everybody's sitting in the dark. Up there in the ceiling they got the little lights that are supposed to be stars. Palm trees in pots up there on the sides of the stage. Ushers in monkey suits by the fire doors. It's like in Mooresville at the Friends with everybody sitting and waiting for somebody to get up and talk. I could stand up here and tell them a story. Mrs. Mint is the only one who knows, and she's worried about getting back to Romania, thanks to the house she ran in Gary.

She treats me square. No trouble when I stay with Patty. And Patty, still married to the cop, doesn't have a clue.

Thanks me every time she smiles because I'm the one who got her teeth fixed for her.

Smiling at me in the dark.

Jimmie, she says, when you going to take off those sunglasses. You can't see the movie. She likes a man who carries a gun, but she can't say why.

The girls down where Patty works all tell her I look like him. I just laugh, buy her a diamond, tell her I work for the Board of Trade.

There's a guy named Ralph Alsman's arrested all the time because he looks like him. The story's in the papers. How he keeps robbing banks.

There's nothing better to do. Rob a bank, go to a movie, buy a paper. It's all the same.

I read the paper all the time, and I start out thinking I don't know the man. Then I think that could be me.

You have to keep your mind busy or you go nuts. Think of Homer beating it by tying string to flies he caught while he stood time on the mats in Pendleton. You go nuts without something to do. You buy a little time out of the heat.

I bet the girls wouldn't know what to do if I was him. Wouldn't want me to really be him. It only gives them something to talk about without no customers while Patty's putting on her hat and I'm leaning in the doorway waiting for her to blow.

I like Patty good enough, with her smile and all. She is nice and heavy leaning on my arm when we walk on the street. My hand will be in my pocket on the gun, and I'll tap her leg with it through the clothes. She'll smile. Our secret. *My husband, she says, only has the revolver they gave him.*

I like Patty. She'll do for now. But she's not Terry.

Sometimes, I think I see Terry in the Loop when I'm down there with a bag of corn feeding pigeons. Out of the house pretending I'm working. I'll be looking at the birds and her legs will walk by and I'll follow them up and something will go wrong.

I want to ask the doll where she got those legs from, but they just clip along through the crowd of strutting pigeons.

It's like that with a day to kill downtown. Her hand waving for a cab. And in the store windows, I see all the things I could buy that she would like. And all the other women, their hair thrown off their forehead just like hers, tilting their heads and thinking that the stuff they see will make them look like Terry. I can't go and get her. South Bend wasn't enough, and they've hidden her in some county jail. For harboring.

There has been a fire on a boat that had a party going on it. A little boy in a sailor hat is crying behind a glass window. It's beginning to fill with smoke in there, and you can't hear him cry. People are jumping off the ship. The railings are giving out, and people are falling into the water. There is a priest swimming with the boys. And then it is night, and the moon is shining, and the burning ship is shining on the water. Along the shore bodies are washing up, and people and police are looking through them.

So, you're out, Pete is saying as we drive south out of Lima. *They'll go up to the farm while we'll go down to Cincinnati.*

You're out, I say. I hadn't seen them since I got parole. I was in Lima by the time they broke Michigan City. Dumb. *I see you got my message,* I say.

We're laughing. There he was standing at the dayroom door. Too many pistols. Too many shots had been fired. Terry would be at the house. *Thanks.*

Mac is reading off directions. Left here, right, right here. Something they learned from Baron Lamm's gang. In the dark. Clark is sucking on his fingers. He shot himself. *Kind of rusty,* he is saying, his finger in his mouth. The sheriff didn't look too good.

We told him, Pete said, *that we were Indiana state parole officers.* Mac laughs. *He didn't believe us.* They laugh. Nervous. *You're out. You're out,* I say.

You should've not locked up the sheriff's wife, Mac says. *Right here.*

I tell you he'll be all right, Pete says.

It's going to be tough watching him die from across the room and behind bars, Mac says.

It's not that bad. He'll be okay.

He'd been square with me. The food is good.

There's just no going back, somebody says in the dark.

The sun is just getting into people's eyes. The light going all one color on the store windows. Mothers yanking the kids on trolleys to get them home in time to make supper. It takes longer for the men to get off and on the Toledo scales by the door. Harder to think. Almost time to go home. Not enough time to start something new. The tellers begin stacking the coins, and the hack's in the basement looking for work.

When we were together around a kitchen table planning a job, drinking beers but no hard stuff, and it would come that time of day, why, we'd all know it. And someone goes to the window and looks out, another stretches out on the davenport, reads the morning papers again. Not working.

After getting out of the pen we'd show up at the bank, 2:45 on the dot.

The bank was closed. Closed from Roosevelt's holiday and never opened. We'd stand there. Heavy in the vests and the guns. Looking through the bars and then looking real quick to see if anyone has seen us. Time thrown all off by something that happened years ago when we weren't in the world.

I hear in Mexico they go to sleep all the afternoon.

It's too hot for anything, even robbing the banks.

Then there are just two pair of hands. Blackie's throwing dice, shuffling cards, and counting poker chips. Jim's writing, turning pages in a book, and accepting a law degree. Then just Blackie's hands, his fingers tapping on a felt-covered table, waiting for the cards to be dealt. Then Blackie spreading the cards in his hand, looking them over and getting ready to bet.

Somewhere in the Wisconsin countryside and Pete saying, *That's it.* I'm feeling pretty good. We could be anywhere now. The fields all gleaned. Some shocks still standing. It's a big Buick, and the cold wind is blowing through it since we've taken out the windows.

We're going to take them to the hideout, says Mac, kidding. Meaning the two citizens we have.

Can you cook? I am asking the lady without smiling.

She's wearing Pete's coat. The fellow's got on Pete's hat.

Pete's not even cold.

After a fashion, says the lady.

So we go along watching the phone wires. Down to two and then one. Birds all puffed up on them. Then no wires at all, just the fields and the white sky.

Pete runs them out into a turned field. Mac changes the plates. Pete turns them away, back to the wind. The three of them out in the big field. Pete ties their hands and then he comes back half the way, stops and goes back to get his hat and coat.

After Greencastle, we could kick back. It had been Homecoming weekend at the college, and the stores were making big deposits. Pete feeling grand. I say to him, *Why don't we move in with you two and share a place?* He says, *Sure,* without asking the girls. At the Clarendon, we carried the bags with the guns while the boy took the rest. Margaret set out right away to bake the new money. Crumbling the bills as we made fists, then smoothing them out. All the time we talked about what to do next. Not thinking about it at all. It takes time for new money to get old. But it all fell apart when Terry didn't do her bit. She sat and made up for hours though we weren't going anywhere. One day there was no breakfast on the table. What gives?

There's your girlfriend, says Margaret.

Terry starts right up. *I can't cook.*

Well, you better start learning, I say.

Pete making a fist all the time and the green squeezing out through the fingers.

If they don't know me, they don't know how to say my name. The *g* is like in girl or gun. When they showed up from the *Star* and *News* at the farm and asked Dad what he thought about me and said the name, Dad just said, *I don't know him,* never heard of me. *But he's a junior,* they said.

That's not my name, Dad said. And he pronounced it for them.

That's all changed now, they said to him.

The old man just sat there right in front of them.

That's okay. Left all that behind. Even left that *g* behind.

Who told me that? Toms of the *Star* in Tucson while we waited for Indiana, Ohio, and Wisconsin to double-cross us. He came up to the bars during the sideshow, all those locals going by to look at us for a quarter. Pete steaming at Leach. Mac saying how great the weather was down there. Toms called me by my real name and told me the story. He asks me if that's how I wanted to be known, by the other name and all. Hell, it wouldn't do any good. It's out of our hands, just like everything else.

The police are leaving after doing nothing. They open the door, and there is a woman standing on the other side just about to knock. Shows she's surprised to see them, but she knows them all by name. She asks them if it is that time of month again. They nod and file out, the plainclothes first and then the uniforms. She stops one who is eating a sandwich as he goes by, takes out a hanky, and polishes his badge. All I had was a big bolt wrapped up in a neckerchief. I kept hitting him but only knocking off his straw hat. He'd pick it up and put it on again, and I'd knock it off. He was making that god-awful sound, and I could hear the Masons come running. He didn't have no money. I didn't know a thing then. Just a kid. Same grocer gave me a talking to when I'd swiped some jawbreakers. He knew my dad. I ran, and someone chucked a bottle after me. They found me in the barn.

It was to have been all set. But the judge didn't care. I heard he died falling asleep across some railroad tracks, a knife in his pocket because I was coming to get him.

Since the operation, it's been like I had on thimbles. Patty wonders what's happened to my fingers. She's got them spread out in front of her eyes, tired of my fortune. She says, *Well, hell. How do you pick up something like a dime?*

I start thinking about all the things I've touched. Chairs and guns and the counter I hopped over in Daleville. The glasses. The sinks. The steering wheels. The money. It's like those things remember how I felt. But me, I forgot it as soon as I let go.

Touched Terry all over. Must have left a print on her everywhere. Some cop dusting her rear, blowing it off, saying, *We got the son of a bitch.* And they're all looking at her, looking for me. All the other women too. Shaking hands with men and having them look into their palms.

You think twice about punching a light switch.

Red rushing in saying that he killed a cop at the garage. Lost the Auburn, and they got his girl. He quieted down, started in telling us all over again what had happened and that the girl could be trusted. We looked at each other's faces, knowing that we didn't look like anybody else no more. Mac looked like a banker. Pete like some college kid, he's going without a hat and wearing that floppy collar. He walked into Racine and put a big Red Cross poster on the window without anybody taking a second look. And I'm looking like a sissy bookkeeper. Putting on weight.

We got the girls to dye our hair. Thought it was funny, us sitting with sheets around our necks. I said red and let my mustache grow. Terry sitting on my lap, drawing the eyebrows in. *Didn't like your face to begin with,* she's saying. Pete telling me later about the two toes he's got grown together. And Red holding up his hand, saying, *What am I going to do with these.* I never thought about them before, the fingers he left on the railroad track in the Soo.

They're going to fry you, boy.

I could hear Pete calling from the next cell. Leach was taking me back to Indiana. I fought them off awhile and they put cuffs on too hard for it. Some vacation. There was the cop from East Chicago who ran away. *He tried to stop me,* I tell them. Where is Wisconsin's Lightning justice now? I could hear Pete screaming from his cell about going to Wisconsin and staying together and Mac calling from someplace else, *See you, John!*

I'll never see them again. I can't remember their faces. They went from Tucson to Ohio when Indiana waived the bust-out from Michigan City. They'll get it for getting me out of Lima. The last thing is voices.

So long, John. Sioux Falls, Mason City. South Bend wasn't enough. I met their Mouth on the fair grounds to pass them the money. The parachutes dropping from the tower. *Tell them I'll get more.*

Indiana flew me to Crown Point. The pilot said that over there is Mexico.

Blackie has won the boat on a bet. They sit together on the deck with the lights of the city behind them. He asks her what she wants to name the boat. She talks about having a house and family. It's old-fashioned, *she says but that is what she wants. Then Blackie kisses her, and she stops talking about leaving the city, sailing away.*

We called her Mack Truck. She made breakfast Christmas morning. The fight I had with Terry was all left over from that race driver. I told her to go back to the reservation. *Take my car.* She's packing and crying.

Pete's girl said, *A girl's got a right to choose who she wants to be with.*

But it was like I didn't know Terry no more, and she stopped being pretty.

Christmas in Florida. Even the joint had snow.

I told her to go where it was snowing, with the race driver. And she left after Red told her how to work the spark on the Ford. *I can buy another car,* I shouted at her.

It was so hot. I sat around in pieces of suits, and the girls giggled about thinking the tide was a flood. They had never seen an ocean in Indiana.

It got hotter the week after Christmas. The papers said we were still raising hell in Chicago. They blame everything on us. On New Year's Eve, people were shooting off firecrackers to see the light on the water. Pete's girl got out a tommy gun, and it rode right up when she shot it. I took it from her and fired it out over the waves, a long rip. But it wasn't any good firing at nothing. The tracers just looked so pitiful. Everybody else had girls and was heading for Tucson. I said I was going north and look for Terry. Red said he'd come along. We'd fence some bonds in Chicago.

If I make it to Mexico, I'll never see any of them again. Terry lost in the jails, Pete and Mac in Ohio. We can't pull off the magic trick again. We broke out of too many places. Even if I could walk in with this new face, there'd be no way to walk them out. The farmers they got to sit with them are taking shots at airplanes flying by. South Bend wasn't enough.

I'll never see Sally Rand at the Fair again. Have the woman I'm with tugging at my sleeve to get the hell out of there. But only half pulling, looking up at the stage too, at the feathers and the shiny pieces of paper. A thing like that. You can't stop watching the fans and balloons-because they are moving and changing and her face is floating, floating above whatever it is she's using to cover herself where she has to. The cops making such a big deal of it, standing off to the side, looking just like the rest of us looking up at the parts of her. Hiding like that. She didn't have to hide!

The alarm is ringing on the building. Red is jumpy, getting the money when a cop walks in. He thinks it's some kind of mistake. His blue overcoat is buttoned over his gun. *Just what I was looking for,* but it's trouble. There are more outside. They're lining up behind cars. *Grab somebody and go!* I yell to Red.

Someone says, *Can I get my coat?*

Out the door with the cop ahead of me and someone is calling the cop's name and the cop is running off down the street. I feel the bullet hit the vest. It knocks me back. I shoot at where the smoke is, and get hit twice more. I hear glass crashing and the alarm. I shoot some more at the smoke, see Red go down to the right, grab him, grab the money. My back is to the guns.

We get away in the car.

East Chicago still has Christmas stuff up.

Red took the bullet under his arm. My chest hurts. Red says from the back seat that being shot ain't nothing like being shot.

The ramps are crowded with people. He runs into Jim, and they shake hands, leaning forward and grabbing each other's arms with their other hands. Jim tells Blackie that he is running for DA and that Blackie's crowd better watch out. Blackie tells Jim that he's all for him and that Blackie's going straight. There is a roar from the crowd and Blackie says, Dempsey. *They talk about the fight and say that they will have to get together. There is another roar, and Blackie says,* Firpo.

Patty wants to hold hands in the dark. Puts my hand on her knee. She's got no stockings on. It's warm between her legs. We're both looking straight ahead. Watching the movie. I'm slumped down and my hat's on my lap. I'd say the man next to me is crowding me. His arm takes up the arm rest.

Her dress is nice. I think about what it's made of, stitch by stitch. What if the parts fell apart? In the shop I made double task, triple sometimes— yoking sleeves, setting collars with a Tomcat. The white thread in the blue work shirts. Thinking of pulling one thread and having the whole thing fall apart. It just feels good now, the cloth and what's underneath. She is moving.

The new DA is tired. Election night and all that. A woman breaks through the crowd and hops into the limousine after him. She says that Blackie sent her. They settle back in the seat and pull a blanket over their legs.

In Tucson, they took us one at a time, and me and Terry just getting back from looking for Indians. She stood there with her fingers crossed and her hands on top of her head. They cuffed me.

I do some shouting. *Hey, I tell you, I'm Sullivan! You got the wrong man! Some vacation,* says Terry.

They had the prints on Pete and Mac by the time I made it to the station.

I don't know them. That's what I say. The place is lousy with reporters.

The cops take me into a room where they start going through papers. They snatch my hand, turn over my wrist.

Well, what do we have here?

One bent down and undid a shoe.

The other foot, Charlie, says a guy.

They look at my heel a long time. I remember Pendleton and the foundry and pouring metal on it to get out of the heat. And then Charlie, he takes my face in his hands, and I say, *Hey.* He holds my head still while his thumbs feel through my mustache, pressing my lip on my teeth, my head down. This is *the guy,* he says.

They open the door and the reporters come in.

Guess who we got, they say.

Where's Indiana? I ask a farmer who's standing in his field. He points to the road crossing just ahead. Terry says, *You can't tell them apart. Illinois looks just the same. It'd be something if they were the colors on the map.*

I stop to change the plates and put the chains on. The roads are thawing and it'll just get worse as it gets warm. My dad won't know me now with these new clothes and hat. I want him to see Terry and the car. Hubert'll be there and the sisters. We'll hide in the barn if anybody comes. The hay will all be gone, and we can shoot baskets in the loft.

It wasn't warm enough for a picnic. But they filled the house with everyone bringing a covered dish and their own service.

I told them all about Crown Point. Once in the front room. Once in the kitchen. The kids on the porch. The men around back. Hubert took my picture with Terry. Then with me alone with the gun. Says he'll not have it developed til they catch me.

The people on the floor kicked the gas candle back and forth. Homer went in to get Red out of the vault. I'd been shot already. Green bent over where the gas shell hit him. We're all crying. I'm holding a girl when we go through the revolving door. It's my right shoulder so it's her I push against the glass.

She gives a little grunt.

Homer's behind me.

We've got people lined up all over. It's like a picket fence. Red comes out and gets hit. It's coming from up above us and behind. We all get our guns going. The people got their hands up. Lester sets them out on the Buick. Two on the fenders like deer. They're on the back bumper, the running board, between us in the car. There must be twenty.

Slow! I yell.

Homer's reading off the directions when someone on the running board says, *Here, right here is where I live.* We stop and she gets off. Cars go by honking, thinking it's a shivaree. My arm hurts, all crowded in like that. Lester's leaning out the back with a rifle. We stop to let some more off, and he gets out to spread some tacks. I'm thinking that he's getting them under our car.

Some law you got! he's yelling at the locals.

The new DA and Blackie's girl are sitting at a table in a nightclub. A woman is on the stage, singing. After the song, everyone pounds on the tables with little wooden hammers. Then we see Blackie asleep in a room. He wakes up, and magazines fall to the floor. The phone rings, and he answers it. A woman, in bed, is on the other end of the line. She asks him to guess who she saw that night at the nightclub. Blackie hangs up and looks at the magazines.

Tellers always telling you to use the next window. Not believing you unless you have a mask. Walking in the door and wasting a whole clip above their heads. Less chance of shooting maybe, but you never know when somebody will get a wise idea, think they're in a movie.

That boy in South Bend, looking at his hand where the bullet went through.

The sheriff in Lima saying, *I'm going to have to leave you, Mother.*

The bullet that killed him on the floor next to him.

Margaret so surprised when the gun went off on the beach in Florida.

All the things we didn't do too. And did.

They'd draw my face all wrong. I don't smoke. Finding out later, after Pete and Mac got shipped to Ohio, that Leach told the papers to give me all the play.

Didn't matter to Pete.

Blackie closes the door, leaving the body inside. He catches up with his bodyguard, who is waiting by the elevator. It is New Year's Eve. The bodyguard is wearing a derby.

Cops are at the door, Terry says. And I'm a Lawrence something, something Lawrence. *Get dressed,* I tell her, fitting in a drum.

I am always waking up to these things. I can't remember my name. I'd been leaving every morning, heading downtown to make it look like I had a job.

Terry's put her blouse on backwards. She's remembering what happened at Dr. Eye's.

Shots from the hall.

That'll be Homer coming over for breakfast.

Hurry up, I tell her, and spray the door.

Think about the cake the neighbor lady from across the hall brought over the first day, her husband with the pipe, saying he has a crystal set.

Down the back stairs, back out the back door.

Terry dents a fender backing out the car. I'm waiting, watching the door. The birds are noisy in the vines on the side of the building.

The DA is in his office trying on an overcoat. He tugs on the lapels. He bends forward, clutching the coat together to see where it falls on his legs. He checks to see if there is a label. He turns around in it and asks his assistant, for his comments. He looks over his shoulder and down the back of a sleeve. It could be yours, says the assistant. Yes, says the DA, standing there, thinking. He's in the middle of the room, bundled up. They bring him another coat, and the DA tries it on. The DA reaches into the pocket and finds a small wooden hammer.

I heard they let her finish her drink. Then they took her out of the bar.

She'll be out before you know it, Homer was saying.

We were on the Lincoln Highway, heading to his folks. All the little towns had banks to rob. *They're taking away parts of me,* I'm saying to Homer, who's humming. We'd been stumbling through jobs. Losing guns and money. Not even planning anything anymore. Just going in shooting. Trusting the vests.

I'm lost, I say.

Men are pushing carts of big steamer trunks through the crowd. A band is playing somewhere. There's a ship whistle blowing. The DA looks at his watch and out over the people. Everyone is waving and shouting. There is a siren and the crowd gives way. An ambulance pulls up to the dock. Blackie gets out.

The shooting started when three guys left the bar to head home. The cops must have thought they were us. Lester opened up right away.

He sleeps with that gun.

I took off up the stairs with Homer and Red. We fired some out the windows, then covered each other to get out the back, down the bank to the lake. Walking on the far side, we could hear the shots over the water. Flashes every now and then.

They kept shooting at the house.

We tied up Red's head and caught our breath. Nobody even knew we were gone. They'd upped the reward that week.

The lake was very smooth, and we could see because of the moon and stars. They had all different sizes of guns shooting at the lodge.

The DA is running for governor. Blackie is at the racetrack. He looks through binoculars. He sees her in another part of the grandstand. He goes over and sits down. She says she's worried about Jim's chances to become governor. Someone is trying to ruin him, and he won't do anything about it. Blackie tells her not to worry, that he'll take care of it. He looks at her, tilts his head, says she mustn't tell Jim they talked.

Crossing the Mississippi on the spiral bridge below St. Paul. Pretty tricky since we're coming from the north. We pick up a tail. They start shooting. I knock out some glass and shoot back. Homer guns it. Red gets it. Never lucky, Red. His head already tied up from the night before at the lodge.

We shake them on a farm road and leave the car. I hold on to Red in the ditch while Homer goes to flag down a Ford. A family out for a drive, it looks like. Homer goes in the back with them. Red says he needs something to drink. The car could use gas. I stop at a place. The bottles are cold. My hands leave marks on the glass.

A lady opens the bottles for me. I go back to the car and give one to Red and try to give one to the kid in the back.

He's had his lunch already. I don't want him to have it, says the mother.

Down on one lip of the gravel pit, a locomotive is pushing some empty cars around. Piles of snow left over from the winter. It's been easy to dig in the loose gravel and sand. They're pumping water down below. Homer slides the body down through the bushes, and we put him in the hole. We're taking off all the clothes.

You weren't there, I say to Homer, pointing out the scar under Red's arm.

It's how he missed Tucson.

I tie up his clothes. Homer has the lye, but I want to do it. Feel kind of bad pouring it on his face. Turn his hands over and pour it on his fingers.

It smells real bad.

A hockey game is going on. Lots of people hollering. But there's a man in a men's room, two men. You can see them both in the mirrors. One of them says, You wanted to see me? *The other man pulls some paper towels from the rack. He turns to answer the question. It's Blackie. He has a gun wrapped up in the paper towels. When he shoots, you see live flashes coming from the towels.*

They told me later I swallowed my tongue. Last thing I can remember is the towel on my face. *Hotel Drake* in gold. And the smell of the ether.

I should've had a local. But I couldn't stand the thought of that, of looking at them when they did it. I wanted to wake up different.

I was always waking up the same.

The dimple was gone. But I could see where it had been. And the mole left a mark.

I was puffy and sore.

I saw a picture in a newspaper of a boy that turned out to be a picture of all the boys in a high-school class, one face on top of another. It didn't look like anything, and it had all the parts. I remembered that picture, looking at my face. Rob another bank and I'd have to get rid of this one too.

I wonder what I looked like with my face all blue. No way to forget it. That's me, all right.

Homer was thinking twice, cursing the tattoo. Finally went ahead and called it a goddamn mess. Lester sitting around drinking from a bottle of beer changes his mind a couple of times. Keeps what he has. Damn doctor was probably glad to let him.

Blackie sits and sketches all through his trial. The DA is examining a witness. Blackie's lawyer starts to get up to make an objection. Blackie stops him, says, Relax, you've been beaten by the best, *smiles at the DA, who is telling the jury that people like Blackie must be stopped.*

The cops are happy to show us the guns and vests. We act dumb. *What do you call this?* we are saying.

Oh, that. That's your submachine gun. They have some .45s too.

We tell them we're from the East, doing a story on the crime wave. *Sports is my regular beat,* says Homer.

Yeah, well I've never been east, says one cop.

You should see the Fair in Chicago while you're in this neck of the woods, says the other one.

They talk it up. We listen.

I like hearing about myself. It's like being at your own funeral.

Being tourists got us in trouble in Tucson. Pete telling a cop he thought he was being followed, and the cop saying no. Tourists from the North. And I take pictures of cops directing traffic. *You look good in a uniform,* I tell them. The Sam Browne belts. The buttons picking up the light, turning white in the picture.

Pete used to say, *I wish you'd stop that. It's not smart.*

I'd say, *It's my hobby.*

We tell the cops in Warsaw we'll send them the story when we get done writing it.

The governor is in his car, racing to Sing Sing so he can see Blackie before he goes to the chair at midnight. Sirens getting closer, governor's car, motorcycles, everything speeding.

Guess who, I say to Margaret through her door. When she opens it, she knows me right away.

What happened to your face? You in an accident? I try to laugh. It's not her fault. I go on in. She's tough, but she misses Pete. I give her some money from Mason City and tell her about the tear gas and the bag of pennies. She says she doesn't think it would do any good. *You never know,* I say.

I've been down seeing my folks on the farm, I say.

She says that she reads about me all the time in the papers.

You know half of it ain't true.

It wasn't no good with nothing to plan.

She says she was at a dance when I broke out of Crown Point. She says she made sure a cop saw her that night. Says she makes sure a cop sees her every night. She tells me she's thinking about going into vaudeville. People had been around to ask.

I could hear her sister in the next room taking a bath.

It didn't matter now that we had shields. They kept shooting, and the people with their hands up got hit first. The bags were too light. I was working the inside with two guys I didn't know. They were the only ones who would work with us now. Homer was outside with a rifle and Lester by the Hudson.

We walked out and everyone started to get hit. Homer in the head from a shotgun that took the pants leg off a local. I pulled him into the car.

He said we should wear something different when we did South Bend. *New. faces. Sure.*

So we had on overalls over the vests. Always a clown. We wore straws too. Changed his luck. Pieces of straw mixed in with his hair in the hole in his head. Lester wanted to count the money again.

Blackie walks with the priest. The warden is there, the governor, two guards. Blackie says so long. Someone is playing a harmonica.

Mrs. Mint saying again over ice cream that Romania isn't a country, just what was left of a place after the war. Patty holds the cherry up for me.

I don't know anything about the world.

I'm seen everywhere.

Cops in England are searching the boats going to France. Every body that turns up is what's left of me.

I could call the Leach home, hear him stutter while he tries to keep me on the line. But it could be anybody with a gun. I'm worth too much now that the governors got together.

I'll check in with Henry Ford. Send a messenger to Detroit with a note. All the models I left on the edge of Chicago. Good little cars.

Mrs. Mint told me she's already turned the bed down back at Patty's place. But I want to stay and watch the cartoons.

The lights are going up and everybody's squinting coming out of the dark. I can see who's been next to me. And Patty crying. Mrs. Mint looking through her purse for a hanky for her. I can't keep my eyes open. Pete, Mac. I'll see their Mouth at Wrigley tomorrow, give him what I can spare from the trip.

Patty touching my hand. Then both of the women are squeezing by, heading for the aisle. The crowd is buzzing and I can smell the smoke from the lobby. It's cold in here. Just this once I'd like to open my eyes and have it be all different.

2

From Safety Patrol

King of Safety

I don't know technically what it took, but my father was the one who found the woman. The woman had been telling the children stories.

She had a telephone number a digit off one that gave a recorded story. Kids would dial, listen, wait through the commercial message. The stories were fables and fairy tales which changed daily, delivered by that voice—I always believed it was a woman from somewhere else trying hard to sound as if she grew up in the Midwest—which spoke all the messages for the phone company. It is the voice that says: We can not complete your call. It is necessary to dial a one. Please try again.

In any case, the real woman gave up trying to explain to her callers that they had reached the wrong number. At first she had thought these were crank calls when all she heard was panting. She called the telephone company. The company gave her the usual song and dance.

She had to be old and alone, a widow, a grandmother with her family out in California.

The kids would call and listen. After dialing the number, they'd exhaust their knowledge of telephone etiquette. They'd tell her to start. They began to cry hanging on to the phone, startled by this other voice, a voice that sounded frightened and confused, too.

The woman gave up trying to explain, began telling her own stories. She used the library. She bought the big books from remainder tables. She told the callers about her own grandchildren and her children. Family stories. Finally striking up conversations with the callers, she got to know individual children well enough to select something special, perhaps the same special story or a whole series. She started leaving tales unfinished so that the children would call the next day for the conclusion. She's let the children finish the story themselves. "Call back tomorrow."

This went on without parents catching on. They thought it was in-nocent, darling, their children pressing the oversized receiver to their heads, talking seriously to a recording.

Soon the calls to the real story fell off to nothing. Everyone was calling the woman. Her number became *the* number. My father, who was a switchman at the South Office then, found the woman telling the stories, found her tiny voice.

I was one of those children.

My parents have a picture of me from around that time. I am on the telephone. It is a black-and-white snapshot, but I know the wall on the phone behind me is yellow. I am in a highchair wearing only a diaper and rubber pants. My skin has that grainy finish. The cord from the phone drops behind me and looks like it runs out of my bare chest up to my arms and fists covering the receiver, my head. I am looking away, my eyes are deep in the cave of my arms. I must have been crying because my eyes are teary. There are flecks the color of the glossy coated stock of the paper in the black irises. They used to print a month and year on the white borders of the square pictures. But that was when the pictures were developed, not when they were taken. A roll of film might stay in a camera for a year. So it is impossible to say when exactly this picture was taken or why or if I was listening to anyone or if I was even talking then. It is one of only a few pictures that is not of a vacation or special event. It's the only record of that wallpaper, cornflowers in baskets, now three or four layers beneath the paint and paneling that's been applied since then. It wasn't that long ago but the telephone, the highchair, the rubber pants, the big safety pins in the diaper look rare, museum-quality, so old.

It is funny to watch people talk on the phone because only a few parts of them are involved. It's like they are off dreaming. They are somewhere else. Their eyes stare into the distance. Their bodies limply dangle from what kind of look like nooses around their necks.

I can hardly recall that woman's voice, but I know the story I liked to hear. It was the one about the man and the steam shovel who must dig a hole before the sun sets or they won't get paid. They dig so fast they forget to leave a way out of the pit. But the building is built right on top of them, trapped in the basement. The happy ending is the steam shovel becomes a furnace and the man the custodian. I asked the woman to read this story. I believe she did, and I followed along at home with my own copy of the book. I could hear through the phone when to turn the pages.

My father came home one day—this was much later—and said the company would be closing up all the windows in the switch rooms. You used to be able to see into the buildings, into the frames and switches, from the street. Now the windows are bricked over or there are steel curtains behind the windows which make them look like the buildings still have windows, like the building was like any other building. A switch room looked like a library. There were even those tall oak ladders on wheels that slid in tracks. The ladders had signs hanging from the step at eye level. They read, Look up before Moving. In the *o*'s of Look there were black dots, pupils peeled to the top of the bigger circles, eyes looking up. The switches had battleship-gray covers to keep the dust out. The covers looked like bindings, uniformed, shelved like encyclopedias. The shelves went to the ceiling. The frames to the far end of the room.

But there was always the click of the switches as the electricity looked for a way from the caller to the one called. My father could follow a call through the building. He bent his head to listen, distinguishing the sounds. The thump when someone somewhere picked up the phone, the brushes sweeping the switches as they counted the number dialed, the kiss at the end when they swung over to connect. All seven connections snapped free when the call ended and someone hung up. He always knew when something important was happening outside the building. The clicks and stutters grew, boiled, ricocheted all around the big room. Finally he would take the headphone and plug into a call using the two alligator clips. He'd listen hard to the voices and decipher the message. There was a steady rain of calls, the word of mouth. Who had been killed? What war? How many dead?

My father probably broke all kinds of rules by bringing me to the switch room in the first place. But sometimes after hours he'd get called in to troubleshoot, and my mother and I would go along. She would sit at the workbench reading *Playboy* magazines taken from someone's locker. A switch would be dissected on the table before her. Its guts spread out over the newspaper covering the spilled coffee. I collected scraps of wire from the floor. Behind the switches the wires were braided into ropes, the ropes to cables. The bright colors of each wire surfaced and sank like fish in a rolling sea.

My father always found the trouble.

Often there were voices talking over the clicks of the switches. A line had been tapped because there was something wrong. The conversations would be piped through speakers. That's what my father listened to while he worked. He listened to these conversations. No real emergencies. The ordinary traffic of chat. People checking in on each other.

When I call long-distance, when I call home now, sometimes, I'll hear one of those conversations again in the shadow of my own mundane call. I'll be talking about the weather and my father will ask if I want to speak to my mother. But I can hear another conversation in the wires, or in the air now, traveling along with mine. Someone will laugh somewhere, describe a day all differently from the one I will be talking about. It becomes too difficult to go on, I get distracted, pulled into the other conversation. "I'll call back," I say, "and get a better connection."

"Do you hear that?" I say. I listen to the whispering. I think it is the very same conversation I heard those nights long ago when my father walked up and down the aisles of switches, plucking out single wires from the mess of wires and attaching meters that measured the current's flow, the resistance.

The boxes that contained the recordings had windows, so I could see the tapes wind and unwind. Time and temperature, weather, the very things the people were talking about on speakers. I saw the storytelling cartridge, as well, spinning, spinning.

For awhile my mother liked to plant things with philodendrons. We had a potbellied stove with the heart-shaped leaves roiling from the vents and hatches and ports. Chests and dry sinks, wash basins and pitchers. She hollowed out an old wood wall phone, and the leaves coiled with the crank, the mouthpiece hung from the tilted shelf where the phone book would have been perched. She even planted the shotgun my father had gotten for her during the time he worked at night.

The gun probably never would have fired. But the idea was for her to frighten the intruders in the home, to look like she knew what she was doing. There had been a prowler in the neighborhood for a long time. My father had listened helplessly to the conversations at night, people staying up late thinking they had heard something. Sitting at the workbench in the office, a ruined switch before him, there were whispers around him, rumors, gossip. The clicks knitted up the city. Everyone talked about it and the talk came through the switches late at night, ran on the speakers, echoed in the big room.

But my mother hung the gun on the wall, somehow coaxed the vines down the barrel, and the leaves sprouted at the breech. With the room in half-light the gun looked wrapped in barbed wire.

You couldn't kill the stuff. That's why she grew it. Cuttings were always soaking in jam glasses on the window sill above the sink.

My father's phone calls would wake us all through those nights he worked. There was a princess phone in my parent's bedroom. The dial glowed with a kind of blue light the color of the taxi lights at airports. I woke up to hear my mother groping in the dark, talking to herself or my father. Sometimes, she would stay up all night instead, watching old movies. Those nights my father brought her a Buddy Boy sandwich from Azar's. I found the sacks in the morning when I got up, even found a few sesame seeds from the bun sown in the carpet around their chairs.

I like to call them when I travel. I call from the observation decks of tall buildings. There are always phones there, usually around the corners from the gift shops, away from the elevators. I like to look out and tell them what I am seeing.

When the company sealed up the switch rooms my father took me up to the roofs of the buildings after he troubleshot. At the Main Office we'd even go further up to the top of the microwave tower. The pigeons purred in a frequency lower than the transmitters nested around us. On a clear day we could see the next tower on the horizon in each direction looking back at us.

I call from revolving restaurants. Sometimes, I stay on long enough to go all the way around. Sometimes I don't remember, as the view comes around, that I'd already seen it.

Before I was going to school, the company was sending my father to schools. He called from all of the cities I visit now. This was before all the tall buildings, even before direct dial. That is one thing he went away to learn about, direct dial. He was gone weeks at a time. He brought me Tonka trucks of all sorts—fire trucks, delivery trucks, postal vans. They were all metal. The tires were rubber like tires. It made sense. That story I wanted the woman to read all the time had pictures of just such vehicles done up in a metallic crayon wash. I like construction, building. Even now next to the tall buildings are the deep holes and the bright yellow caterpillars crawling around at the bottom of them. I am one of those men you see looking through the plywood. I excuse their dust. I've rushed through a lonely lunch. I don't know anyone in this town. It is what my father must have done when he went away to school. He killed time until the class started or after it was over for the day, watching cranes being built by other smaller cranes, then the cranes building the building.

Maybe he thought about it on the long train rides back home from one of those schools and cities. Maybe it was clear from what was happening once he returned to work in the offices. He began changing things. He would be transferred from one switch room to another. Main. North. South. Times Corners. Poe-Hogland. He went to each with all that he had learned. Somewhere along the line it must have come to him. What he knew now really meant that very soon his job would not exist anymore. In a way he was wiring what he knew and what he had learned and what he was into those buildings so that the buildings would pretty much run themselves. And these things would come to pass, would happen long before he was even old enough to retire.

Somewhere about this time I became the King of Safety. I rode a float in two parades. One was on Memorial Day and one was on Armistice Day. It wasn't a float but a trailer pulled by a car. The wheels were hidden beneath skirts of corrugated cardboard painted with black and gray tempera. It was supposed to look like a brick foundation. My father rode in the back seat of the company car. He looked back up at me on the trailer. I was sitting on a porch glider. There was a Queen of Safety, too. She was bigger and older, in the other corner of the glider. A sign swayed above us, suspended from a garden trellis stuffed with red and green crepe paper that looked from a great distance like vines and flowers. Along the route of the parade on Memorial Day everyone listened to transistor radios and to the race. I could hear the tinny engines. Except for that the parade was pretty quiet. The nearest band was up ahead marching toward the Memorial Coliseum. I waved and waved. Everyone pressed their heads against the little boxes at their ears. Parnell, the street where they have the parades, still to this day has elm trees. I saw the reflection of the arching branches sweep down the rear window of the car over my father's face. The whole summer was ahead, filled with watching the city cut down trees. But all the trees survived here, came together above like a cathedral. This is what it must have been like when my parents had been children, when the city, it seemed, was entirely shaded.

My parents had sent in that baby picture, the one of me on the telephone, to a contest the company ran. I imagine the company chose the King and Queen at random out of a whole pile of snapshots, the sons and daughters of employees. The company promoted safety. I understand now that safety was something they could promote. They didn't have to sell the phone service. I think safety had to do with calling a Zenith number before you dug near an underground cable. Safety was like the flags all the soldiers ahead and behind us were carrying. There was nothing wrong with safety.

I had the crown for a long time afterward. I kept it on the globe. It fit, and I just now realize that if I had that globe I would actually know how big my head was then, hold it in my hands. A wife had sewn some sequins onto cut and sculptured carpet backing. It was elaborate and pretty, the crown. I lost it and the globe in a move.

In the summers I caught lightning bugs by slipping an empty peanut butter jar around them as they furiously beat the air. They moved so slowly. The ash at the tail end seemed to heat up like a coal in the breeze.

I had punched holes in the lid of the jar through Peter's eyes. I put grass and clover inside. In the morning the insects would always be gone. And my father said that they must have gotten out through the holes. I made the holes smaller and smaller. But still in the morning they were gone. They disappeared.

It was much later, I was gone from home then, when it struck me that my father had lied, that all the time he had been releasing the bugs and resealing the jar. It wasn't long ago that I understood that and called him up and ask him about it. He only said, "I thought you knew."

And it was the same thing with my being King of Safety. It was years after the parades. I understood my father wanted to transfer out of the dying switch rooms, find a job that would not become obsolete. He thought safety was safe. There would always be accidents. There would always be death. His child would be his introduction.

I have never been anything else but the King of Safety. I've never won another raffle or bet or game or contest. I've never been chosen or singled out. It is my one moment in life.

I have the photographs from that day. My feet did not touch the floor of the float but slid back and forth above it as the lawn glider glided. There was a little fountain, too, that had water. The company symbol on the side of the car looks kind of like a cap with ears. My father's face is in the shadow of the roof of the car, but he is looking this way. Did he get the idea about safety during the parade? Or was this just the first step as he untangled himself from the switch rooms? What had he learned by the time we pulled into the lot at the Memorial Coliseum, filled with all the old soldiers in their tight uniforms?

While he worked for Safety I tied his ties. My father sent me five or six at a time. I tied them all at one time, one after another, leaving the skinny end as long as I could so he would be able to slide the tie knotted over his head. The ties are ruined this way. He never learned how to make the Windsor knot or the half-Windsor or even the four-in-hand though I offered to teach him.

In the mirror I kind of looked like him. But I never would have bought those ties. And sometimes my mother would call, frantic because a knot had come undone. I would have to talk her through on the phone. I would look in the mirror going with the mirror's left and right, under and over. I listened to my mother struggle with the tie and the cord of the phone. She'd choke and gasp. She'd sob. I'd hear the gentle slap of the fabric on the mouthpiece. Her hiss, the hiss of the polyester.

I used to call myself person-to-person when I traveled. Really I was calling my parents to let them know I had arrived safely. The operator would say my name, and my father would say "he's not here." I could still do that, call and ask for myself, but I am older and have a credit card. I punch the numbers in after I hear the tone. That voice comes on when I finish, the one the phone company has had for years, and says "thank you."

Besides, I am up in the air when I call, on the observation decks of tall buildings.

Now I want to take three minutes and tell my parents that I can see three states and an ocean from where I am standing. The time on the phone is like the time I get on the binocular machines they have on these observation decks. One second you're looking out into the night trying to make out something. Then that black curtain they have inside snaps down. It's discipline, I say to myself. "I've got to go," I tell my parents after the first three minutes.

Once in Chicago in the black Sears Tower, I watched a formation of helicopters emerge from a park by the lake, rise and orbit the building below where I was standing looking down. "I bet that's the president," my father said. "He's supposed to be in Chicago today. I bet that's him."

I couldn't tell, but one of the helicopters drifted up until it hovered level with my floor. The men in the doorway of the helicopter looked my way steadily. "What's happening?" my mother said. She was on the extension.

By the time the woman died, the phone company had all her stories on tape. The tapes are still used. My father told me that when she was first confronted with evidence of what she had been doing, she lied. She was afraid, my father said.

When I was older and after my father was working in Safety, I asked him about the switches I had seen in the old offices, the switches marked with a twist of scrap red wire. He told me those had been hot numbers the other switchmen had listened in on. They were people in love with each other and apart. You found them easily because they were connected all night, the magnetism of the current holding the circuit fast. The lovers always thought they were being listened to, my father said, when they were.

"Do you hear something?" one would say every time there was a pause in the conversation. "It's nothing," the other would say. "It's in the phone." My father told me all this though he said he never listened like the other men.

My father was born the day before Christmas, and we always felt bad because he never seemed to get as much as the rest of us. His gifts all came at once. Christmas Eve is the one day he goes out alone. He goes to the 412 Club and Casa D'Angelo and the Hoosier Tap, where friends from work buy him drinks. One of our Christmas traditions is to worry about my father. He makes his way from one bar to the other. He never calls. It is hard to know now if it is real worry or mock worry. He always comes in around the time he was supposed to. The rest of us can eat and open presents. Every year he comes home with a new idea for a drink constructed from different food colorings and fruits. He stands over the blender, crushing ice while we tell him that this is the last year for his running around.

I have a picture of him taken on one of those nights. He is sitting slouched in a kitchen chair, under the yellow wall telephone. There is a different wallpaper on the wall. His eyes are half-closed. His hair is cut strangely. It was the only time he went to that barber. He is holding a bundle of long, thin sticks. My mother gave him switches because he had been bad that year. He looks very pleased and wise. He was feeling no pain, basking in the pop of the flash bulb. He was soaking up the abuse we were giving him, which he has always accepted as our love.

Years later my father will lose his job in the Safety Department during a reorganization. He will spend his last years with the company supervising the cutovers in the offices so that they will all have electronic switches, components, solid-state parts. "It is no big deal," he will tell me when I call.

The second parade I was in when I was King of Safety wound through downtown in early November. No one came. It was cold early that fall, and a few years afterward they stopped having that parade. I didn't wave. I huddled beneath an army blanket with the Queen. The little fountain was bone-dry. The metal glider burned in the cold. The parade moved as slowly as it had in the spring. And it was silent. The bands weren't playing because of the chill. Their lips would stick to the brass mouthpieces. The sidewalks were empty. The stores closed. The streetlights came on automatically. Everyone said that it smelled like snow.

I think now I should have been miserable. But for a long time afterward, these were the best moments of my life. My father was in the white car. I saw him watching me as I was being pulled along. The parade shuttled back and forth. It was as if we were looking for a crowd of jubilant cheering people. But, at the same time, we were restrained enough not to break this stately cadence. I felt as if something grand had been visited upon me and everything—the buildings and streets of the city—was in order and everything would be preserved and maintained by this cold. We were barely moving, and, though I do not have a picture of this parade, it felt as if we were a picture and capable of telling volumes to the people who would come upon us in the future.

The voice of the woman who tells stories is not the way I remember it. I can hear something disquieting in the voice. I believe it has to do with talking to no one but a machine.

The windows of the telephone building were bricked-in out of fear of terrorist attacks.

The prowler was arrested only two doors from my parents' house while in the act of raping a woman who lived alone.

On the Empire State Building I can go outside, stand on the platform and pretend to see my parents' house, miles away. I like the elaborate precautions, fences and pikes that curl in with sharpened points. I have been to the pit back in Indiana where the stone for the building was cut. All the way down the building would be the limestone fossils arranged in the strata of prehistoric life.

They say that time slows down during accidents, that everything becomes very clear. I have never experienced the sensation, having never been that close to death. I look west to Indiana. The wind blows my tie into my face. I try to arrange my hair. The quarry is as deep as the building is tall. I imagine reading the facade while plummeting along the side of the building. I try to imagine my brain working that fast, attempting to arrange the clams and worms into some story.

I've called home. I talked to my father. In the silences between descriptions he pushed buttons on his phone. The tones came together into simple little songs, nursery rhymes, lullabies. It wasn't much and he told me it wasn't hard to do. And time was passing.

I love this, the Empire State Building and its blown crowd of people, observing. We hold back, holding back, each toying with the idea, each of us finding inside some argument against that jump.

Nein

My grandfather writes to me about what might be the last gasoline price war ever. The price of regular is already 29.9 cents a gallon. At the Lassus Brothers station up Main Street from the Standard where my grandfather works, regular is two cents lower and another penny will come off by the end of the week. He writes about the lines of cars that inch into the station, how happy the drivers are when he leans down to the opening window. The drivers chatter on after asking for the fill-up. They recall the summer of their first car when, even then, gas was more expensive. They hitch their thumbs over their shoulders indicating five or six red tins, the size of dictionaries, in the back seat. "Those too." Some of them ask again if the numbers can possibly be right, and Grandfather bends over and explains the war to the customer. The pump dings in the background, and the bell in the garage dings as other cars pull up. The Lassus Brothers and the Gladieaux Company, the small local concerns, are gambling this last time, this winter. Since the major companies were buying out the owner-operated dealerships, the owners also went along and cut prices. Their days seem numbered anyway. Gulf and Conoco have already pulled out of the city, and Shell is wavering and has begun to offer cutlery again. With the prices this low, no one is using the self-service pumps to save the penny. So Grandfather has a chance to talk to people in the cars. The heat escaping through the windows is the only warmth he can get. The cars keep coming, one after the other. No one bothers to use their credit cards. There is no need to go back inside and run them off. There are many out-of-state plates, Michigan and Ohio. People driving up from Indianapolis are the only ones who seem to be interested in having their oil checked. In Henry's parking lot across the street and the lot by the newspaper building and along the curbs of Main and Broadway, cars idle in harmony. The running lights from other cars as they troll past the double-parked cars define the identical clouds of rising exhaust. The prices will go lower.

Grandfather has worked for Ed Harz's Standard for the last thirty years, part-time after his other job. Although he has retired from City Light, he continues to work for Ed on weekends and nights. When my mother was away at school, he would write to her from the station, sitting on the high metal stool next to the candy machine, using its top for a desk. He would send her money, telling her to use it to buy stamps and write or to have her laundry done there instead of mailing it home. He wrote these messages on the backs of pink customer receipts he found on Ed's desk, or on the reverse of flyers from the Amoco Torch Club. He writes on the other side of the big single-numbered sheet that stands for the day he worked. He has pulled it down from the three-colored Atlas Tire calendar right before he closed up. A quickly scratched note with no subject in the sentences. Some money. An order. A direction. The rest was left to the imagination. Before the price war started, I would get the same type of notes. Now, because he is so busy at the station, he writes them when he gets home or waits until after closing, sending all of his paper tip money or money he has changed into paper. The silver is usually kept for the younger grandchildren. He sends a note about the price of gasoline in Fort Wayne, Indiana. He writes that he is very tired. There is no end in sight.

I think of him at the station. It is one of those old blue and white ceramic tile boxes with glass wrapped around one corner of the front. The oil company wants to change it to the colonial brick façade, cupola and weather vane. Grandfather, on the islands, slides sideways between the pumps and oil cabinets from car to car. "What ja have? What ja have?" Or I can see him angling across the driveway, leaning into the wind. He steps over the driveway hoses that would set off the bells and works his way over to two metal display signs in the one corner of the property. One on springs rocks down and back against the wind. The other, when the wind blows, separates into three sections that swing back and forth, coming together to read in big red numbers "29.9." Grandfather wears a pin-stripe coverall. Over that is a quilted vest, not a new bulky down vest but an actual lining from a coat. On his head is a helmet liner from the Second World War he got surplus. Green wool. On its brim is his union button, a hand squeezing the light out of bundle of lightning. He is carrying a stack of plastic numbers for the sign. It is difficult in this weather to climb the little ladder to reach the sandwich sign on the pylon. It is beneath the twirling orb emblem and the slogan that reads, You Expect More from Standard, and You Get It. As he begins to change the prices, a sudden gust of wind strips the numbers from his arms and carries them down the street. The *ones* vectoring, the *twos* somersaulting to *fives*, the *eights* halving to *threes*, the *zeros* dribbling along the sidewalk. The *nines* of the state sales tax enclose everything my grandfather shouts in quotations of cardinal numbers. He chases them down the street between the celebrating automobiles. The cost is the same. The price is lower still. He writes that no one gets out to help. Everybody honks their horns at once, thinking things have never been so good.

"Think of me," my grandfather writes. "Think of me." The letters come to me in bank envelopes, business-size with the plastic window and a silver lining scrolled with insignia so that nothing can be distinguished when they are held up to the light. He is sending money. The letter is folded around the bill and then stapled so, when the letter is unfolded, I must snap the top fold up and the lower flap away from the middle section of the page and the bill extends out from the bottom of the sheet, a tongue. It is always real money, never a check or postal order.

Growing up, the grandchildren are taught never to move anything in Grandfather's house for fear of uncovering another hiding place for his money. He will not use banks except for the envelopes and free desk calendars. Even before the Depression, he refused to invest and still believes a man can weather anything by keeping his money at home. I have found folded bills under lamps and ashtrays, in the phone book. I can make out shadows of coins in the globes of ceiling fixtures, and bills silhouetted in the shades of lamps. I would have to sit in the dark living room, waiting for Grandfather to turn on the one light that would, this week, reveal nothing. All hiding places are that simple. Between the cardboard cover of an album and its plastic wrapping or inside the inner sleeve, a "crispy" would be secreted, forgotten because the record was never played but purchased only for its cover's contribution to some lost filing system. Grandfather has forgotten how much money he made, losing money on purpose in the house, buying only records for himself, and giving the rest away in allowances to his daughter and son and to their children. To me. This is the way around taxes, which he associates with death. He writes that in this way an inheritance will not be taxed but given outright. After he dies, he wants us to sell everything in the house, even the light fixtures. What we find, we can keep as if the money had slipped out of a pocket long ago and lodged between the cushions of the sofa.

My mother writes that when she went away to school her father would write, "Think of me." Now, when she closes her short notes, crowded with weather and unspoken superstitions, Mother writes, "Think of your grandfather," as unthinking, as conventional as "yours truly."

I think of my grandfather at the filling station. He is writing a short note with a black crayon on the back of a calendar leaf. He writes, "Happy Birthday to me." It is his birthday, and the only money I have has come with the announcement. He stands at the high table inside the station, peeling the silver and black paper spirally from the crayon. The credit-card machine is on the table next to this letter, and he clicks the lever up and down—each place a lever, a scale from 0 to 9—changing the numbers and their combination on the stamp as he composes. "The price still falls." On the windows in front of him are the dark sides of display signs, powered by tiny motors and flashlight batteries. The tiny electric whine rotates larger and larger gears until on the other side a Day-Glo disk moves beneath a cutout cover of sunrays and urges, as it radiates, to summerize your car. Next to it, wipers sweep back and forth over a smiling cardboard family. Racing around the dark, closed driveway, the neighborhood kids in their heavy winter coats circle on stingray bikes, running over the hoses, thinking they are ringing the bells. But either they are not heavy enough to set them off or Grandfather has turned the bells off with the lights. The only sound, besides the boring of the displays, is the running of the toilet in the ladies' room around the back. In the tank, Grandfather has hidden a delivery payment for the truckman who will come early the next day, and the balance of the plumbing tips the secret. Ed pays cash.

Ed Harz, who owns the station where Grandfather works, came to America between the wars. He found the railroads now being worked by the Irish, stayed on the Pennsy long enough to make it to Fort Wayne, where he had relatives. He worked in one of the breweries. During the Second World War, he worshipped at one of the secret masses said in German and later those Sundays led a contingent of German citizens out to the prisoner-of-war camp to give the inmates lessons in English. After the war, Ed bought the filling station and hired Grandfather. Many German residents started their own businesses and provided jobs for the prisoners who stayed after the war or came back after returning first to

Europe to gather families. Most of the service stations are run by German families. Ed also helped to start the Fort Wayne Sports Club after the influx of new German families. It was organized to support a semipro football team in a country that did not call it football. The club had since become a place to drink Bergoff beer smuggled in from Chicago and talk, in German, about the price of gasoline. Ed is at the Sports Club as my grandfather writes this letter.

Grandfather writes, "I want you to learn German in school." We are not German. At the station, he has always felt uncomfortable with the other men who could speak two languages. "Talk to a man in his own language." My family knows no other way of speaking.

Reading Grandfather's letter, I can hear Ed again.

Ed's accent now is very faint. An accent I imagine has to do with selling gasoline. The smell of gasoline. Gothic script on his breast pocket. I imagine hearing myself asking Ed for a fill-up in a low, low German voice. Something a teacher would repeat as an interesting cultural aside. Phrase-book knowledge:

Bitte volltanken!

"It is all I ask," Grandfathers writes. This is certainly true, I think as I pluck the bill from the day that was his birthday. The staple remains fixed to the letter. I set about learning another language.

I hold the envelope up to the light. The contents are masked; the return is penned out. Grandfather. Long before the price war, his station participated in a sweepstakes, a giveaway of cars and cash. With every purchase, no, maybe none was necessary, the customer received a packet of gummed stamps in sealed envelopes. The picture on the stamp, one of a number of professional football players, had to be matched with an identical picture on a playing card. Various combinations and numbers of players counted for different prizes—three won ten dollars, five won twenty-five, six won fifty, and nine won a new Mustang. The one stamp you needed never appeared. Regular customers all had the same incomplete card in the glove compartment. Grandfather would loiter around the car, polishing the outside mirrors as the customer opened the new envelope. He told them not to be disappointed when they received another Fuzzy Thurston, "why only last week a man in Huntington won ten dollars," then asked for the stamp to take home to his grandson who collected them, "if you've already got that one." Grandfather brought home cartons of the sealed envelopes and handfuls of ripped-open envelopes from losing patrons. He would go through them for me. "This is a lucky one. I can tell." I would hold each one up to the light trying to save time and avoid opening every one, but all of them were shielded and had to be ripped open anyway. I would only find another Mick Tingleoff or Gale Sayers, never the elusive Lou Groza. Now, I believe I would have been ineligible anyway. Being family. Perhaps Grandfather did not know the rules. It was after that contest that the law was changed in the state, and the company had to publish the probability of winning, with a statement about all prizes being awarded. Giveaways became less common. Many stations began selling children's toys, Corning Ware, Hummel figures. They gave away ice scrapers and ball-point pens. I think now that the winning stamp might never have been minted. Grandfather saved many of the stamps, thinking they would become valuable some day, and sticks them on the backs of the envelopes of his letters, like Christmas seals.

Grandfather writes, "Use this money to make friends." The money talks. "Buy a girl a Coke. In a glass. From a fountain. Not a can." As Grandfather writes, the wind dies in the color pennants, strung out over the dark driveway. The filling stations on the other corners are closing. Their lights go out. Their signs stop revolving. Someone leans over to a pump and takes a last reading, noting it on the clipboard dug into his hip. On a siding behind the newspaper building, boxcars of newsprint in huge rolls are being unloaded. The new construction on the hospital continues through the night. The open elevator the bricklayers use is yellow, festive, a cage of lights. They have rigged a Christmas tree on the top, and it is still there after Christmas, a skeleton with lights, going up and down.

"Who are you writing, Jim?" Betty asks Grandfather. He is sitting at Ed's desk by the phone because Ed will call in a bit. The bottle of Pepsi Grandfather has been drinking from is next to him. There are salted peanuts at the bottom that look like mixing beads in a bottle of dark polish. "You got enough light, Jim?" Betty asks. Betty has no phone in her apartment and uses the station's pay phone. "My grandson," he says. "He is learning German." And he will tell her everything. The candy bars he once took home for me. Powerhouse and PayDay. How I remind him of Efrem Zimbalist, Jr. "I send him a little something every week," he says.

The pay phone rings. She turns to answer it, then disappears behind a curtain of fan belts. Grandfather writes to tell me that another language is not easy to learn, that one way of speaking is enough for most people. I should not give up. "Think of me."

The phone rings on Ed's desk. Grandfather answers it. "How did we do, Jimmy?" says Ed. He is at the Sports Club. There would be drinking songs. Grandfather tells him of the good day. "We can afford it, what, Jimmy? Prices this low," says Ed softly. Grandfather hears him say something gruff off the phone and laughs as he returns. "The tires, Jimmy, they're in the bay?"

Grandfather walks Betty back to the Poagston Arms, and he waits in the lobby while she runs in to find a stamp for him. "I will pay you back, Bet," he says. He leaves, walking by the station. The windows of the service bay doors still have the outline of fake snow in the corners from the holiday decorations. Stopping at the mailbox, he slides his tongue across the stamp. His lips dry instantly in the cold wind. He slips the stamped letter onto the tongue of the mailbox slot. Checks that it is gone. Checks again. He reads the pickup schedule and checks his watch, cocking it to the streetlight. He notices how close the clouds are to the bank tower and how they are lined with the pure yellow sodium light of the new downtown. Two days later, the present arrives with his letter, and I go through everything again, every step he takes, two days ago, to get home.

I am learning a new language. I write to my grandfather. He writes back. "What do you want, a Willkie button?" Or I can hear him reverse the accents on the word *Broadway* as he teases about how far I think I am going, where I think I am getting off. He flexes the muscles of his forearm and says to the younger grandchildren, "You want to take a ride?" as they take turns swinging back and forth on the tense arm. He is making up stories about me. I grew up listening to my future. "The FBI. Solve mysteries. Think about the FBI." In a few days, I will receive a Willkie button. It arrives. A stylized picture of an airplane flying very high and the legend:

Straighten Up and Fly Right.

My mother writes to say she will no longer understand what I am saying. She believes that I will begin running words together in English since this is all she knows about German. At her father's insistence, she sends a German chocolate cake. I share it, as I am told to do, with the woman in the mailroom and with the postal carrier. They ask about my button, and I tell them about Wendell Willkie and the ironic expression of petty awards. My grandfather kept hundreds of facsimile campaign buttons after a promotion ended at the filling station. The company gave these buttons away with flash cards on their history. Petty awards. Grandfather kept as many Willkie buttons as he came across. A bulletin board at his home is covered with Dewey's buttons and Al Smith's and Landon's buttons with his picture surrounded by an aura of the sunflower. Around the edges of the board in the cork lining, Grandfather's union buttons proceed through the years, silver stems, changing colors annually—from orange, yellow to blue or green. If you look closely, you can see the tiny union label of the printing trade that made the button for Grandfather's union. It is there, next to the hand squeezing the bouquet of lightning.

I have learned the language well enough to translate the political slogans on the Willkie buttons. I send Grandfather a composition, in German, mainly in the present tense, referring again and again to incidents in his life. In English, I suggest that he show the above to Ed and let him judge my skills. Next Monday, Ed comes to my grandfather's house to pick up his carton of eggs. My grandfather buys a number of eggs wholesale for his friends and sells them at cost. They sit in the kitchen. Ed assembles his dozen, checking his eggs by holding them up to the light and places them in an old gray pressed-paper carton, turning the eggs the same way. Grandfather shows him this letter. Ed scans the letter quickly, stopping on a word now and then. Looking up at Grandfather, he says shyly, "Jimmy, is this true?" And Grandfather will ask what it is he has read. And Ed will only say, "All true, Jimmy, all true?" A letter will be written that night.

I receive a letter that must be from Grandfather. I recognize his hand on the envelope. I cannot see through to the letter, but I can make out the darker rectangle inside. An old football stamp seals the smile of the fold on the back. Because I have learned German, perhaps there will be two bills. More friends. Instead, I find when I open the envelope, not the usual folded scrap of paper with money but another envelope. And that is all.

The envelope is a smaller stationary size, sealed also and addressed to Grandfather, addressed with the appellation "Herr," in another hand, in real pen and ink. The envelope is an off-color, but it might once have been white. The stamp is foreign and canceled by the United States Army sometime in 1946. The return is a street in Vienna. I do not want to open it, something that has been written and sealed that long ago. I picture Grandfather slipping the envelope inside the other one and then addressing it to me. Where had he hidden it in his house? With the money? With the coffee cans of silver in the cold, summer furnace? Why had I not seen this before, an old letter, among the other things he collected—big-band albums, tire gauges, reproductions of American documents? I leave the letter unopened. The next day and the next and every day after that for several weeks, more of the same envelopes arrive in the same manner. Each with another envelope inside. They look slightly counterfeit, with the extra line for the country like a symbol more detailed than the thing it stands for. I keep the letters in a pile, careful to retain the order in which they came to me.

My mother writes, "Well, what is the story? Why aren't you writing to your grandfather?" I do not know why I am not writing to Grandfather. I suggest it is the high cost of stamps. I do not have time with my studies and all. I have nothing to say. I know I am supposed to translate those letters, and for some reason, maybe even privacy, I do not want to be involved in their meaning, in understanding them for someone else.

One weekend Grandfather calls. He is calling from the station. In the background I can hear the persistent ding of driveway bells and the exhalation of the hydraulic lift. Periodically comes the rapid fire of pneumatic drills, backing off lug nuts after tightening them, and barely comprehensible German above the racket, which becomes a shout when the noises cease.

"What, Grandfather?"

I can see cigarettes burning evenly in ashtrays by the cash register, where they have been left when the attendants went out to the pumps. Grandfather calls me a pet name, coaxing me to translate the letters. He explains how they came to him. "I heard General Mark Clark on the radio after the war and I did what he said to do." Ed's voice breaks in over the noise, the soft *w* becoming a pointed *v*. "Jimmy, Jimmy, we need you."

"Do what you can for me," Grandfather asks. That night I begin to translate the letters.

They are from a man named W. Gabauer of Vienna. The first letter, "I thank you, and my family thanks you for this paper and pen with nibs (I am not sure of this) so that I can write to you for all your gifts. This paper, this is the sheet." Grandfather seems to have found out about the Gabauers through a reconstruction scheme of the Third Army. The family is similar to his own—a young boy who has known nothing but the war and an older girl, Frieda, who "is learning English now, Mr. Payne, so that she can work in the American Army Bank."

"We have been cleared of everything now," he writes. "It is terrible to have a past." This in capitals. There is a long section recalling the inflation between the wars. "It must not happen again, Mr. Payne. Your army lets us work and controls the price of things. But we survive because of you."

Grandfather has sent them nonperishable food, paper, thread and needles, candles, perhaps some clothing, buttons, tin foil. "Your family is giving all of this up for us." Then long sections on the nature of victor and vanquished and victim. Frieda continues to learn English. He writes at length of peanut butter. They have never seen it before and are unsure what to do with it. There is a letter describing the ruins of a city, a bombed-out building, lines of people moving rubble from one pile to the next, waiting for food, for medicine. "You must not feel sorry for us, Mr. Payne. With your help, we will be just like new." This last phrase supplied, in English, by Frieda.

The packages keep arriving—picture magazines, chocolate, Spam, Quaker Oats, pencils, metal toys. Everything is duly noted, and gratitude is shown for each. The pronouns change to familiar. "The whole neighborhood came together today," he writes, "and everyone brought their American peanut butter. We eat it every way. It is so good." Ribbons, combs, rubber bands, zippers, erasers, popcorn. "What is popcorn?"

I realize that Frieda knows more and more English. She will receive the position at the bank, because she is good with numbers. She writes short notes in English which her father includes with his letters. She writes that she understands Americans better now that she understands what they say to one another. It is a funny language, full of things that mean many things.

Mr. Grabauer describes the spring in the mountains, a day in the life of the family, homesick soldiers. He is grateful for the tobacco and the pipe Grandfather has sent.

"I cannot make you understand," he writes. "You must stop sending so much. The whole family works. I do not mean to offend."

More letters arrive and Grandfather leaves them unopened, as I did, stacks them neatly, imagines what they might say, and goes to assemble another box. He crumples newspaper for packing, the classifieds so that there will be no mention of the war. Perhaps, Mr. Grabauer will read the want ads and come to America with his family. He could work for Ed. Grandfather would give him his job. Grandfather lines an old cardboard Eckrich meat box with gray paper. He thinks about what a family would need and would not ask for. He thinks of paper clips and toothpicks, towels and soap, string and marbles for the boy. Do they play marbles?

He will ask Ed indirectly. Hash, another can opener, dried milk, flour. Today, he will drive to the post office, the first time in years. He picks at the ration stamp in the corner of the windshield. There is plenty for everyone. Things haven't been this good in years.

"Why didn't you let Ed translate the letters?" I ask him.

"It was family business," he says as I spread the letters out on the kitchen table and arrange them by date.

"See, Grandfather, the little line through the *seven* so they won't confuse it with a *one*. They do that with a *Z* too. Look." I trace through the letters, stopping, now and then, to mention peanut butter or Frieda's progress toward her goal. I thank him for everything.

"No. No more," I am translating. I ask him why he didn't even open the letters.

"It was history," he says. "I saved it for you."

I translate the last few letters right there in front of him. It is the first time either of us has read them. "Write to us," it says, and I see the family in Europe one last time, still waiting for a word they could now translate. The whole correspondence running out becomes dear as I let Grandfather read along in Frieda's uncertain idiom to the point where I with my languages, where the family with its letters, where no one needs anything any more.

Lost

Mice had gotten into the basement where he slept. Someone had left the garage door open. He heard them in the dark, running over the indoor carpeting. Hugging the walls, he imagined. Once he was awake he couldn't go back to sleep. It wasn't the mice. He knew the mice wouldn't bother him. There was the sound of claws in the rug, the chatter on the linoleum by the door. He heard them working through the old toys, records, moving things on the floor, touching them. Shoes. His clothes.

He stood up and thought for a second, placing the Ping-Pong table, the air-hockey set up, the pinball. Things on legs.

Near the door he felt for the freezer, white and cold. He stood and waited for the compressor to start up. When it did he opened the chest and the light came on. It was filled with white, stone-shaped packages of the family's meat. Each was stamped with MAPLETON SLAUGHTER, NOT FOR PROCESSING. Their own steers.

He was naked and cold. He left the lid up and got his clothes from across the room. He dressed with the light from the freezer, the air above it white and swirling down over the sides. He closed all the doors and went upstairs, where he sat at the kitchen table until it was light enough to see the cornfield down in the bottom. This was the second day they would look for the boy in that cornfield.

He had called his girlfriend back East to tell her what he was doing on the farm near Turin, Iowa, again. She had been mad because he reversed the charges and forgot about the hour. The farmer had a daughter. Besides, no cornfield was that big, she said, and he tried to tell her about it. Then he said there was popcorn in the next field, and the man who owned it told him he could keep what he gleaned in the fall if he came back to help at harvest. He told her about the noise they made and the noise the helicopters made. The faint smell of chemicals.

"You should see it," he told her. He was in the back bedroom, sitting on the platform bed. Airline posters were on the walls. "They'll bring in some psychic soon. The dogs tomorrow." The psychics come after the dogs. He tried to figure how he could figure the odds on such a thing.

That morning there were lights in the field. He could see them out beyond the channeled Little Sioux River. A tractor with an implement was on the road, and the sunlight caught on the peaked irrigator. The boy's family lived in a rented house left standing at a section corner for some sentimental reasons. Someone's first home. There were many children. Everyone who was searching told him that this one always called you by both your names.

When the family he was staying with talked on the telephone, they used short sentences, a few words, as if someone were listening, as if at any moment the line would have to be cleared for some emergency. He had listened as the farmer walked back and forth with the portable phone, its antenna scraping the walls each time he turned. The farmer had said, "Yes, yes, yes," calmly.

The farmer explained it to him once. He said it was a habit of party-line days. People listened in because they had nothing better to do. Everyone knew the line was in use because the number of rings determined who the call was for and everyone's phone rang.

"It's how I learned to count," the farmer had told him. "The longer you talked, the lower the voltage would go and the more the phones got picked up." The voice you were talking to got further and further away.

"Do you want to come with?" the farmer was saying to him now. Already he could see out on the bottom and the cornfield where the boy was.

The field was known as Cottonwood for the trees that had been there, and the field ran right into the fields on all sides of it. There was no fencing anymore. The animals were pastured in the hills bordering the bottom or confined in new buildings near the old barns. The big machinery could wheel around without hitting anything.

Cars and trucks were nosing over into the ditches on either side of the road to Onawa. A crowd was gathering near a car with flashing lights. He saw all this from a great distance, so he really didn't see it at all, just imagined he saw it from the day before. The men were sitting on tailgates; the women were pouring coffee.

The farmer asked him again, and he said that he would go along. He found himself, his body and legs, stretched out in a lounge chair, covered with sections of newspapers, parts he'd read to keep awake and then spread out over himself to stay warm in the dark house.

He heard the microwave talking to the farmer, who was heating up water for coffee, the chimes and tunes of the calculator he was using to figure stops or calls or puts or something. The farmer was moving grain from last year. He sold a little bit over a long time, hedging the market. The boy was lost in this year's crop. The field was still green. The leaves on the plants still curled from the night but opening. The ears were filling out and heavy. The field they called Cottonwood was the one he helped plow in the fall. The farmer was punching a number on the wall phone in the kitchen.

He had come to Des Moines to work as an actuary for one of the insurance companies. The building where he worked was the only landmark in the city. It had a three-story, red neon umbrella on the roof. The sign looked best in the rain, at night in the rain. His girlfriend worked for one of the Big Eight firms, the one that did the Oscars. She was studying for her first actuary exam and had supervised audits in Erie and at Quaker Oats in Cedar Rapids. When she worked in Cedar Rapids, he drove up to see her, taking the only diagonal road in the state.

"It's so green," she said.

"What do you mean?" he asked her. "No greener than anything else."

"The green is different. It's not a tree green."

She had sent him a copy of the annual report filled with pictures of cylindrical grain elevators, train hoppers, tubs of oats. He worked with the farmer's daughter at the insurance company and drove her out to Turin when he had nothing better to do. In a way he believed his car needed the exercise.

Around Turin and around the farm were the loess hills, bluffs made up of windblown soil. They were rounded and green, suddenly there between the flat river bottoms. The Maple. The Soldier. The Little Sioux.

"There are hills like this in only one other place on earth, in China, and when I was little I thought that's where the dirt came from, from China. Blown all the way from China."

And the wind was the first thing he noticed once he was out of the car. It came across the bottom from Nebraska.

"That's Nebraska. That line of hills." Another time he watched a storm come from the west, watched the lightning strikes for hours walking toward him.

He walked through a bean field with her, hoeing weeds. They used a length of PVC tubing, rigged at one end with a rope wick kept saturated with the chemical inside the pipe. She still called it hoeing although all they did was touch the weeds with the wicks, careful not to touch the young bean plants. The field was full of volunteer corn, bushy because it grew from cobs lost from last year's harvest. They walked for hours. They kept the hills behind them, into the wind. They touched everything that wasn't a soybean plant, leaving behind a dewy patch on the leaves. She said it wasn't very satisfying. "When you leave the field, everything is still green and not clean, like you haven't done anything," she said. But later when he went back, he looked out into the same field only to see the brown, dying stalks of corn here and there in the neat rows of beans.

He walked through the cornfield, looking for signs of the boy. The rows were clean, cultivated early and shaded now by the crop canopy of the tall plants. He heard the men in the rows on either side of him, walking with him. They talked to one another at the same volume as the rustle produced by their brushing against the leaves. It was hard making out what was being said unless he concentrated, but then he was afraid he would miss something on the ground or on the stalks before him. The tufts of silk on the ears caught him in the same place on his leg as he went along. The tassels above him were extending like aerials, the horizontal arms intersecting each other and spreading a yellow net over the whole green field. He expected to find the boy curled up and quiet on the ground like some animal. And he did startle things. Rabbits and birds flushed and shot away at his feet.

Then they came out of the rows into a bald spot in the field where a pond had been during the planting. It might have been an acre or two and the ground still dark and soft at its lowest point and the grass coming back on the rest. The stunted corn on the edge was yellow from too much water.

He stood there with the men who had been walking on either side of him. They stopped and smoked and talked about crops and animals and the weather, ignoring him. Others moved through the corn around them. He watched the corn move as the people moved through it. In the clearing, they began to tell the stories of the other local tragedies in order to avoid mentioning the boy or the search they were part of now.

They started with fires. The last bar in Turin had been burned down by its owner, and the town was a post office away from being a town. There had been a fire at a confinement operation, and they told of the pile of burned hogs. The fires set in the bluffs. The boys drowned in a grain bin full of soybeans. They held their hands up, counting the fingers they were missing. A farmer's hand had come off clean in a binder. He didn't go into shock but walked home to wait for the helicopter. He left his son to find the hand and put it in their lunch cooler with the block of chemical ice.

"Oh, he was alive all right," someone said about another farmer. "It was a massive shock. His second." They found him the next morning. The lights were on on the combine and him all pressed up against the glass of the cab, looking at the auger still turning on the table below him. He told her on the phone that night, "He was conscious but couldn't move. He sat there. The machine still shaking."

And now the others looked at him then looked around, ready to head back into the tall corn. He didn't have anything to say though he knew about accidents. There is a list that puts a price on a foot or a whole leg, an arm, a spine. He stood there smiling. He knew his smile would seem to be caused by the bright sun. He told them who he had been staying with. They probably knew already, and they knew what he did in Des Moines, too, probably. They thanked him for coming and helping. But they wouldn't ask anything directly. They would find out in other ways if they wanted to.

He called her that night from a booth left standing near the ruins of the bar in Turin. The elevator was blowing grain from one bin to another. Bugs were sticking to the light above him in the booth. He had walked from the house so as not to bother anyone. He left the farmer reading papers, the daughter sorting her laundry. The end rows of the field edged up to the road.

The first time he called she wasn't there. He talked to the operator before he let her go, asking her where she was and what time it was.

Turin was named after the city in Italy, the daughter had told him. Someone got off a train once and said the hills were the same as those Italian hills. Starting from the post office and his phone booth, the town worked up the seams of three hills. The lights were scattered around and above to the red strobe lights of a translator tower on the crest of the highest hill.

He was always a little sick with the stars, and he looked until he found a plane blinking from east to west and another going in the opposite way. And he wished the phone would ring.

She was in the bar near her house having dinner after work, or she stopped at the convenience store and got caught up watching the neighborhood boys play the one video game the store kept in a closet near the refrigerator motors.

There had been talk while they stood in the clearing that the boy wasn't in the field at all, that maybe the dump should be checked again, the old refrigerators and car trunks.

They had not found the boy again today. The family was beginning to receive all kinds of mail, photos, and prayers. A bank account would be opened in the morning.

The soil in the field was the type that caked when it was wet, and their feet were heavy with mud, making it harder to go back into the corn to look some more.

Gumbo. The farmer had told him the name of the soil type was gumbo.

But they went back into the corn and walked the rest of the way through to the end rows. On the edge of the field were the empty fifty-gallon drums that had held the herbicides, only beginning to rust, and on the few remaining fence posts someone had speared the empty seed sacks with their black variety numbers and the cobs with wings.

The next field was fallow, set aside for some federal program, and they were grading and laying tile. He could see a long way. The ditching equipment, a Ferris wheel of buckets, was parked on a slight rise. The field was taken with grasses. Planted here and there in the green were these knee-high wires topped with Day-Glo plastic flags—blue for the buried phone cable, yellow for a gas main, orange for sewage or water or more tile. Since he was near ground level, he couldn't connect the snapping flags into lines. They looked scattered and bunched like flowers. He stood there while others cleaned the mud from their shoes with sticks.

That night by the phone booth, he heard all different types of engines in the bluffs. A tractor in road gear, an insect fogger. Listening, he heard the wind again in the big cornfields nearby. It was like the rustling of paper. Cars of kids passed him heading to the Onawa loop. He would call her tomorrow night from a booth in Onawa near the largest main street in the world. It was really four regular streets running parallel. He will have just finished eating the largest piece of meat he has ever eaten. The farmer will tell him that all the best steaks go to New York.

"Where have you been?" he said to her when he got through. She told him where she had been.

He told her about the day, the field again, the man trapped and dying in the combine. He told her about Turin, the phone-booth lights, the lights of the town, the stars.

She said she missed him, that she was thinking about him. He asked her to tell him what she was wearing, what the cat was doing now, the noise he heard. It was a bus going by on the street. And what did she have on and which way was her hair, which barrette. She said she was embarrassed and that this was costing money. And he described where he was out in the open, in the street, the cornfields on both sides. He asked her what she was doing, where she was in the room, sitting down or what, and what she was thinking of. And she said she was no good at this. Then they both said what. So he asked her again to tell him how she was sitting, where in the room so he could see her there, so he could imagine her. And then he asked her to touch herself, and she said she was, and he listened for her breathing and then asked her to talk about her body. She said she couldn't. So he just listened as best he could, concentrating on what he heard in the phone, the shell sound at his ear. He thought that he could see her, her eyes closed, the handpiece of the phone held by her shoulder against the side of her head.

Where he slept had no windows, and the door was closed against the mice. The basement was completely dark. It could be night or day, he couldn't tell. The basement had been a playroom for the kids when they were still home. Around him in the dark were stacks of board games and records and bigger games usually only found in arcades. The children had been miles from other kids their age, had played with everything here in the farmhouse basement.

He could feel the bulk of the stuff around the bed, but he couldn't see the outlines of things. So when he was unable to sleep, he felt his eyes opening in the dark, wider than they had ever been, but he still couldn't see a thing.

He thought about the boy still lost after two days of looking and what the psychics would say after seeing with their eyes closed—where he was buried, where he had been washed to. But maybe he was still in the cornfield being missed by the searches as the line swept through this section or that. He was out under the sky, under those stars, under the stand of corn as thick as a lawn.

In the dark basement, he thought of plowing the field last fall. He went back and forth again. The field seemed so much smaller from inside the heated cab. Riding up high, he could see the elevators in every direction. It took him hours to make three or four passes with the five-bottom plow.

The farmer had shown him the controls, how to call up the numbers for RPMs and exhaust temperature and speed. He touched buttons. The numbers pulsed and rearranged. He lifted and lowered the plow. The tractor folded in the middle when he turned the wheel. There was the pitching in the hydraulics. "Listen, if you miss it, just keep going into the next field." The throttle had a picture of a rabbit and a turtle. Simple. The tractor was red. He kept the wheels on the landside and in the last furrow, dropped the plow, went for miles through the bean stubble. The plow turned over ribbons of gumbo. On the radio the Sioux City public station asked for money. When he looked back he saw a cloud of seagulls above the wake of the plow, swooping down to peck at what he was turning over. More were arriving all the time, white, out of the gray sky. It was something he never expected. He looked toward the house, where he knew they kept binoculars near the window, and he could see that the sun was shining there and on the hills behind the house. And maybe he was being watched.

He wished now that the daughter would open the basement door and find her way to him through the toys. A joke, a joke he thought, but he listened for the strum on the metal stair. He imagined waking up, the daughter becoming solid in the dark, her weight on him before he knows it.

Instead he goes out so he can see again, climbs the high bluff behind the house. At the top the family has a television dish aimed up at the clear night sky.

The loess will not erode if it is cut through at a ninety-degree angle to the grade. Anything less than that and it washes away with the first rain. He can see the sharp lines and the faces of the road cuts and the road itself cutting around the base of the hill.

The television dish is like his company's logo. It is pulling things down from the air. An umbrella upended left to dry on a porch. Nearby is a pile of bones and a rack of sun-bleached antlers probably hauled there by the family dog. There are other things around too—weathered balls and a tumbled fort, a path for steers and dirt bikes. Across the bottom, he sees Nebraska. That's Nebraska.

He goes from one field to the other. His eyes go back and forth over the fields below him. That is what is always done in this country, the going back and forth. It is like reading, not like figuring. The sky is very big, and there are the few lights that farmers leave on all night long. They wouldn't find the boy. He doesn't know how he knows. But he knows.

Parting

I stutter. Badly. I always have. Through therapy, I learned that it all has to do with the way I've acquired language.

It is hard to explain but it has to do with seeing. My eyes really do roll up inside my head and I'm looking for the right word or syllable or letter. I acquired language in a mechanical age before the pulsing electronic models of the brain. I'm made up of switches, gears, brushes, contacts, solenoid springs, screws. I search by opening drawers, riffling files, sorting through the trash, the business office of metals, green and gray. My machines are the old machines.

I think it has to do with handedness, this stutter.

My father wanted a left-hander perhaps more than he wanted a son. He was always throwing things at me—balls of socks turned inside out, golf balls, Whiffle balls, Ping-Pong balls, balls of string. They came at my face, my head, and my father would project his face, his head along the path of flight. He noted which hand I moved first, which finger of which hand.

Now that I think of it, catching and throwing are the same to me. I have a facility for both in both hands. I make no distinction.

But this is a theory of mine, a hunch. The therapists didn't say one way or the other. They were treating the outward manifestation of how I acquired the language.

My father thought the movement of the left-handed more pure. Especially expressed in the asymmetry of baseball, left-handed was beautiful. I don't blame him. I don't blame him.

Writing this I am like those singers who stutter when they don't sing, whose stutter vanishes when the music begins. One word after another, like clockwork. I can stop my hand, either hand, before the long chorus line of *h*'s steps along this blue rule. What can I say?

There is that motto that circulates through the offices of the world, taped to typewriters and phones, photocopy of photocopy, with the other artifacts of the cute. The you-want-it-when keepers, comics that turn yellow, old postcards from bosses long gone. It says, Be Sure Mind Is Engaged before Putting Tongue into Gear. Exactly. A type of poetry. Rebuild the drive train around the tongue, I say—the shaft of the spine, the wires. Into the hand, the hands.

Martin, my friend, and I were in Indiana, Pennsylvania, once looking around. We had stopped there on our way to somewhere else because we were from Indiana, the state, and we were aimless enough to stop, or maybe that was the whole aim of the trip. Did we imagine a Liberia, a colony of Hoosiers, a diaspora, families keeping alive the old ways, the slow ritual of team basketball? Nevertheless, we stopped and walked around the college they have there, saying we were from the other Indiana. There were few students, gone on the same holiday we were. But when we'd see a cop or a secretary in an office, we'd say we were from the other Indiana and they would always say the same thing: We get your mail.

"That's why we're here," Martin said, "for the mail."

We ended up talking to an African student, surprised that his classrooms were empty. We found him reading the bulletin boards for explanations. We told him, "We're from the other Indiana." It was clever, we though. And he looked at us earnestly.

"Yes," he said, "my country is always sending its students to the wrong Indiana. It happens often. It's the case." He spoke English haltingly but well, searching for the words. I always marvel at anyone who knows more than one language. I could see he was the type that waited until everything was right, the grammar, agreement, before he spoke.

"We are sent away to one strange place. All we have is a name. And there are many known by that name. There is a California. A California, Pennsylvania."

I remember imagining a ship pulling away from the docks, flags popping. Everyone waves and waves. The sun sets in the wrong place. There's the dusty train station, the borrowed clothes and bag. Somewhere over there is Indiana. The end of the line.

"Why is that?" he asked. "Why is it that several places have the same name? That is not the case where I come from." His face was wide and his eyes. He wanted to know.

And Martin said without thinking, "America is so big we've run out of names."

We've run out of names. Martin.

Once, I took trips all the time with Martin, who never finished my sentences, who never knew where we were going. He waited until I was through talking and had thrown myself back in the seat. My eyes were closed and I was going through what I'd said, rubbing that place behind my ear. "What you mean to say," he would say, and tell me. And then, "Where are we?" and I'd look out, the navigator, and things would be flying by, disconnected signs, markers, arrows, signs that referred to other signs.

Martin calls the Indiana toll road the Bermuda Triangle of highway travel. It is disorienting. The cornfield, a visible magnetic field, changes intensity and color with the layout of the crop rows. The lines of cars and trucks spaced and stretched for miles. They don't move, because we're all moving at the same speed. The pull of the ditch, the siren. The main street of mid-America, the rest stops named after poets and coaches. It's a long sleep. Radios jam from all the iron dust. Time doesn't change. There are sudden sandstorms. Fog like mold on bread. Suddenly we are in Ohio, Chicago. The truck we'd been following—it bristled with antennas, its lights flicked each time it passed us—has disappeared.

This last trip I took with Martin, is it the last trip I'll take with him? I've always wondered. Will this one be? This one? The time we came back from New York—for a long time that was the last trip.

I've said good-bye to all of it, to going.

The truth is I can hardly accelerate up to the speeds necessary. I've found that I am repeating what I have just said. I haven't done that since I was a kid and the therapists suggested it as away to make me conscious of what I was saying. Word for word, under my breath, an echo. After a while I didn't think about it. I want a glass of water. I want a glass of water. The second sentence was easier, slowed down, sorted out. I saw the hooks and eyes. It wasn't an echo. It was more like going over a signature slowly, staying in the lines. I can't possibly keep up anymore. I find I am often left speechless. The subjects are tattered paper under the wheel. The strange mailbox is made out of the old plow, the pump, is behind me before I can even begin to begin to speak. It is not an echo.

The sentences are not coming back. They bounce off the world. The radar of my own language closes in on me. There is a deer. A pig. A cloud. A tree. A car. These things are coming on too fast. These things are already gone too soon. No planned trajectory. No way to plot their courses.

I'm afraid, Martin. I'm afraid.

Long trips by car were the only times we had to talk. Phone calls, impossible. The stammer on long distance, the tick of a meter. That's it, isn't it? To be in a car is to be in a moving parlor, to leave an exhaust of words.

But this last trip could be the last trip. Because it is getting harder for me to speak, and the distance between us now, the space we shuttle back and forth in, is not great enough. What? I might utter a paragraph in an hour. And patient Martin could drive a Mack truck through the silences.

Martin likes to say that the job he does now for the Labor Department is the exact same thing Kafka did for Czechoslovakia. I don't know if that's true, but he says it often.

Martin works in the District in the government's own workers' compensation office, an investigator. He is a GS-12 now, I think. His office is in one of those buildings downtown that can go no higher than thirteen floors because nothing in the city can be higher than the Liberty or Freedom on the Capitol dome. That's why it's such a sad town, Martin says. It all ends at the thirteenth floor. Unlucky—no way around it.

In that building he reads files of claims government workers make, claims of injuries suffered on the job, in the line of duty, above and beyond the call. There are the things you'd expect, the usual accidents of the motor pool, the falls from buildings, office chairs that crumple, the chemical spills, the fires in warehouses. In this way the government stimulates our world, it acts of God. But Martin must read about other accidents unique to a bureaucracy so large, the daily toll of service. The pale-green computer screen, the pastel shades of copies, the shades of language, the color of walls in offices that hum, the white lights and shirts, the colors of skin. What he hates is that he gets paid not to believe people who have headaches, undiagnosed lower-back pains. He must start from the position that the mumbling, the hand-washing have nothing to do with the job, that it's all unconnected or even faked.

Poor Martin—to work up ways not to believe, the advocate who punches holes in the cases for saints.

Maybe it's easy. I don't know.

It hasn't soured him on the species. His suspicion is professional. He leaves it on the thirteenth floor. But he carries around these stories. When he thinks of seeing, he is reminded of the blind man. When he hears, he knows he is hearing. And his limbs bud and grow all the other limbs that have been lost.

As we drive, he drives through my silences, between my words. The light is low from the instruments, just touches his cheek. The window behind him is black. Half his face is how I think about him now, his profile, round chin, the nose and mouth. That mathematical symbol, more than and equal to. And in the window, the other side of the face, milky. Skin. I remember remembering smearing white Elmer's Glue on my hand, letting it dry and peeling off long whole strips of fingers, the creases and prints, the topography and the whorls of knuckles and nails. The other side of Martin's face in the cold window kept its eye on the road.

The road was in Ohio, wide Ohio. Or Pennsylvania wider still. And Martin was telling amputation stories.

Amputation stories are like ghost stories. There is nothing to them beyond the telling of them. The ghosts make you draw closer around the campfire. Amputation stories, too, make you want to wrap your arms around yourself.

How much of me goes before I'm gone?

Really the stories are about machines. Our marriage to them. Limbs are given *to* the machines, that comes up, to the machine, a type of marriage. Machines amplify our own body's levers—the legs, the arms, the fingers. These become ghosts, lost. Machines amplify the body, make it louder.

I remember remembering the time I sat on the copier in the office and the stripped-down picture of my butt emerging, what? like something being born or passed. The new workplace is all about light and language. I remember the cold glass and the green light rolling below me, my feet not touching the ground. I gave the copy to the woman I was with. Then she rested her white breasts on the glass. She liked me, she said, because I didn't say much, and turned away to look back over her shoulder at me and laugh as the light played over her and the fan came on and rumbled the machine and the little closet where we were. It's all high contrast, her nipples black and scratchy with toner, the depth all washed out, overexposed. The mole still floating there, too, with the dust and motes of the glass. It's on good bond. There was static in the room. Our life slipped into two dimension, plane geometry, depth removed. But real amputations are still a matter of the solid and what Martin was saying sat there, something with a life of its own.

There was this man who lost all of his fingers to a machine. I think a machine that trimmed paper. It had a harness for safety that was supposed to clear the hands each time the blades descended. The device had been adjusted by the man working the machine the shift before. When the new man started this work he didn't check the play, and on the machine's first cycle, trusting it to pull his hands clear, the blades came down and all his fingers were off at once.

"Now the interesting part," Martin was saying. When the machine opened up again he could see his fingers where they had fallen perfectly, as if they had been placed there, fanned out the precise distance apart from one another. "He then reached inside, he told me this," Martin said, "he reached inside to pick up his fingers. He forgot that he didn't have anything left to pick up his fingers with. And the machine was still going. But this time when the blades closed down his hands were pulled clear by the safety device."

It was Ohio. And it must have taken me a county at least to exclaim. "Really," and then under my breath again, really, a township at least. Really.

"Really," Martin said.

I remember thinking about the engine of the car, a Dodge, the old slant six. I thought how all those different operations were happening at once. The pistons all at different points in the cycle, the cam shafts timing and the rockers lifting, the valves, the flywheel flying, the distributor distributing. And if you froze it at one instant, the whole show was being run on only one cylinder and inertia, the tendency to remain at rest or to stay in motion.

It was night in Ohio. And the radio was talking, too. The talk shows of the clear-channel stations. I had a bet with a friend that there were more songs written about telephones than cars. I though if you thought about it there would be hundreds of songs written about wrong numbers and long-distance operators and information and late-night calls and arranging rendezvous and calls to repairmen to fix the phone, no answers, busy, dead lines, crossed wires. The song is just voice. And on the phone a disembodied voice at your ear, the privacy of the private line, the party on the party line. Besides, Bell was a therapist. To him the phone was a device that facilitated the acquisition of language. The instrument is a sentimental favorite, far more terrifying to the deaf and dumb than a speeding automobile.

That songs should be written about cars seemed the conclusion everyone would jump to. It was a sucker bet.

Especially those songs about crashes, wrecks, accidents, death. Or traveling like I did with Martin, cruising on the road, a fabled love of motion and moving. You put poles and wires and miles between where you are and where you're going.

Now here at night in Ohio in a car with Martin there was a kind of nexus—the radio, the callers, the music, the road, the wires, the waves, all of these connections. The voices talking on the show of talk were making a music, a song about singing. What was said meant nothing. Talk for the hell of it. Talk just to hear oneself talk.

"The new section of the drill pipe came down from the derrick too fast," Martin was saying. "This new kid had his foot over the hole, and when the pipe came down and sumped into the hole the kid started yelling, 'Get it off my foot! Get it off my foot!' and the diesel idled down. The local said, 'Step back, son. You ain't got no foot.' "

This is indeed like stories around the campfire. I remember the story of the lovers in a car telling stories, ghost stories, being afraid, wanting to hold each other, creating stories that gave them excuses to do so. And they are telling a story about a man with hooks, a murderer, a nut. The woods, the night. There is scratching at the door of the car. The lovers tease each other. Their imagination. Then they believe and tear out of there in the car. The travel miles with the hook hooked on the door handle. It dangles there. They discover it when they are safely home.

I was always quiet around campfires. To stutter is to sound afraid. No rounds for me, no verses. The night on those nights was vast. The sparks flew up. If I spoke I sounded as if I were afraid. I was afraid to speak.

Outside now I know are strip mines. There are crossed picks on the maps. I wish I could see the shovels, the pulleys and cables, the draglines, the little houses where the operator sits, runs the machine as big as an office building. The little crossed picks don't begin to represent what is going on outside our windows as we race along.

The lovers, the car, the man, are folklore. I have heard about them and so had Martin. Perhaps he is thinking about that very story now as I do.

If I could I would have told Martin my own story. I heard it first from one of my speech teachers. I would ask Martin if what happened was technically possible. I suspect it isn't, that what I have is another tale. But it is satisfying in some ways, especially when the wife comes to say good-bye. What would she say? Her husband alive somehow but two grain hoppers coupled right through him in such a way, so tightly, my teacher said, that his insides are all packed in, his organs shoved up into his chest. There is so much violence suspended between those cars, and his legs are up off the ground. And so much loneliness, too, because he is still alive. I suppose there is shock, unconsciousness, if you can believe it at all. But the redemption, the reason I think of this, is that the man's wife works in an office near the tracks and the trainmen go and fetch her.

When I think about the story I think about the trainmen rushing in, the type clatter stopping, the women pivoting in their chairs. I think about the wife grabbing her purse from the back of the big file drawer on the lower left-hand side of her desk. When I heard the story first, they held her by the elbows. She stood on her tiptoes, whispered in her husband's ear. What? Good-bye. There was steam and the bulk of the steel, its chill atmosphere, and way off the thrumming engine, the engineer trying not to make a move. This was supposed to have happened in Decatur, Indiana, in the Central Soya yards. My teacher worked there in the summers, picked up the story on a coffee break, told it to me years later after a lesson. If it were true, what would she have said? Could he speak at all? It would be too difficult, probably out of breath, in shock. He would know what was happening. There would be that look in his eyes if they were open, the privacy, the inarticulateness of death. And then later, much later, after the wife had been led away, they'd have to separate the cars, separate what's left of him from the cars. I can see the conductor, those mule-skinner gantlets, waving the all-clear signal.

The all-clear signal.

I was finally a very good baseball player. I batted left-handed. My father hid himself during the games in the lilac bushes bordering the park. There he smoked and tried not to watch me play. The bees circled above him in the flowers, the leaves. I was in the hole. I was on deck. He was nervous, I imagine, superstitious, embarrassed perhaps. Here I begin thinking of those microscopic pictures of chromosomes tearing themselves apart in cell nuclei, now it looks like iron filings lining up on a yellow piece of paper. Magnets are beneath the paper and the slivers of metal are repelling, pulling away from each other. I was some half of him.

And there was grace. To swing left-handed, to hit the ball, to run were all one motion, the weight flowing from the left side of the body to the right as the foot steps into the pitch, then on a stride closer to first base, running, running.

And as I type this I realize, too, a slight advantage to that left hand. My *a*'s and *e*'s are strong clear strikes, no ghost images, no *z* floats below the line, the weak pinkie finger simultaneously hitting the big shift key. And the return, the big chrome spoon on this Royal manual, the twisted lever was made for the heel of my left hand. The return is effortless.

The return.

The return.

I remember the little boys out in the field in their baggy uniforms, the scratchy cotton overwashed, before the synthetic fabrics. The green grass and the redwood red outfield fence, snow fence that was rolled up at the end of the season, leaving an arch of tall uncut grass, a record of the summer. Those boys chattered insect-like while the pitcher thought on the mound. How to write it? Hey-bay. Hey-bay. Hey-bay. Swing batter swing batter swing batter swing. Firehardfirehard. All one word. Seesawing and singing, building to the pitch and starting after it from nothing. And I was in the batter's box, the catcher changing, the fielders babbling, none of it making sense. A stutter everywhere around me. I liked the sound of it. Its patterns. Its cadence. Its life.

At Breezeway we slowed and settled out from the turnpike, trying to read the yellow ticket with the boxes of numbers, the entrances and exits, and the tiny map of the road. We stalled at the booth trying to make the change.

There was still the trip through Western Maryland then and one of the redundant roads that stretches from Baltimore to Washington. The trip was nothing but an excuse.

We wound up saying good-bye in that unlucky city, in Metro Center, where there is no place to sit and all the subway lines—red, blue, yellow, green—come together. Martin was on his way to work nearby. Above. I would go on to National Airport—I had my bag—and take one of those planes that shoots straight up in the air over the Potomac, that gets out of there fast, the whole trip home in silence, suspended, known by heart.

Along the edge of the platform green lights begin to pulse when the train approaches. Air begins to flow through the station. On some other level I can hear the doorbell warning of a departing train.

I remember the therapist counting the words in the sentences I spoke, long columns of numbers on the charts. I remember them waiting for me to finish, to be sure that the pause was a period. That there was a thought completed. They were trying to determine my mean length of utterance. Just how long could I go before ruin, decay, explosion, waste, disappearance, silence. They weren't really listening to me, to what was being said, but to its ending, the harmonics of closure, that falling off in voice. And I would want to string it out, add and digress both. It was no good.

This is the way I said good-bye to Martin. I could not have said good-bye in any other way, in any way that would make sense to you.

Martin rose out of the station on moving stairs to his desk, where a man is broken on the dry blue bottom of a motel swimming pool, where the whole office is inhaling the lethal fumes of correction, white-out.

I have another friend who has made an anatomical gift on the back of his driver's license. He is giving only his lips. The card is laminated. My friend loves to think of his death. The police trying to make heads or tails out of it. Doctors being told of the donation. My friend thinks of the harvest of his body, his smile.

As I type I am concentrating, forming the words with my lips: Flesh. And blood. And metal. And light.

The Third Day of Trials

Intake

In the back of the motor home, the men played euchre loudly, trumping quickly and tossing in the hand after the first two plays. Phil and Bill Erhman looked like bowers themselves, one full-face, one profile. They were not partners at the table and argued over a loner and the number of points allowed. They were in the asphalt business, entertaining clients today, contractors mostly or state highway inspectors. Whenever the motor home hit a new patch of pavement or a new stretch of concrete on the interstate, they would all start up, listening.

"Shhh. Shhh. Shhh." Phil would say, concentrating on the pitch of the tires. "Marion. Marion, Indiana." And someone would look out the window, and there we would be, passing Marion, Indiana.

My father, sitting across the tiny galley table from me, was explaining something about football with coins, all heads up and vibrating from the road.

"The belly series," he said, "depended upon everyone doing the same thing every time, every play. Faking is the same as carrying the ball. Always covering the belly." My father had played football with the Erhmans on the 1952 mythical state champion team of Indiana. Father had been the quarterback of the full-house backfield. The Erhmans were the halfbacks. The fullback, A. C. Russian, was in prison.

"One game I started limping after each play as I carried out my fake," Father said. "Watching the end every play, sooner or later, I lulled him to sleep. He forgot about me. He though I was really hurt. And on the next play I kept the ball, put it on my hip, and rolled right around him." He scooted the dime toward me with his index finger.

We traveled down the interstate from Fort Wayne to Indianapolis.

We hit a bad bit of road and a hollow ringing bridge. "Muncie," Phil shouted from the back, and there was Armick's Truck Stop. Its lights were gravy-colored through the tinted window. Many trucks squeezed together in the lot, lights out, exhausts idling. It was still early.

This was the second weekend of time trials, the third day of the Indianapolis 500. Father took this trip every year with his friends. They started with a party the night before and left early in the morning. They continued to drink, tell stories, and do business. The Erhmans like to sell asphalt at night, when the patching and puckering of the road was invisible. We had to stand up in the motor home every time we passed over a section of the road they had paved so that we could feel it through our feet. "Take your shoes off. Walk around." After last year's major accidents at the track, they hoped to place a bid with the management to resurface the whole course. Father had nothing to do with the business but went along for the ride. To see the trials.

"On the third day of trials someone is on the bubble," he said. "That's why I like the third day because of the bubble. That means, usually, the whole field is filled up and the bumping starts. The slowest qualifying time from the first weekend is on the bubble. If someone goes faster his bubble bursts. He gets bumped out of place just like that. You want a beer?"

It was barely light by the time we reached Indianapolis. We took the sweeping banked curve with the John Deere dealership nestled behind it. The green and yellow tractors became visible. The ground around showed black, recently disked—a demonstration. The one banked curve on the straight highway anticipated the city.

"A two-stroke engine has a baffle. Have you ever heard an un-muffled engine?" my father asked. "Really?"

I had lived in Indianapolis for a while. In those moments when the whole city became quiet in the late afternoon, when the various oscillations of noise matched their pulses of hills and valleys, in the small depressions of silence, I could hear the yawn of an engine coming from the track and the tatter of a loudspeaker voice drifting after it. That would be the tire tests. Spring.

"I taught you your left and right in a car. The left hand was where the steering wheel was. The oncoming traffic messed you up again. All the daddys were on the wrong side. Fooled you."

The motor home eased on to an exit ramp, kept left and looped over the top of the highway. It then descended upon and merged with 465, belted around the whole city. Going east. The wrong way. The long way. The track was on the west side of town. This was done every year, too, a trip taken every year all the way around the city. A parade lap. The motor home wallowed back and forth between the four lanes, jockeying for no reason, responding slowly as things came up. The Erhmans lapsed into a spiel on slurry and expansion coefficients. We swayed by the first Steak-'n'-Shake drive-in, black and white, a shadow in the bell of a trumpet exchange. The striped awnings of the restaurant were already down in the new light, and a boy in white was on a ladder changing light bulbs in the sign that read dimly, In Sight It Must Be Right.

"When you were little I took you to every one of Don Hall's drive-ins," my father whispered. "Each time he had a son, Don Hall put up another drive-in. He gave them all names. His sons and his restaurants. Both the same names. Trying to get both of them right. The Hollywood next to the Roller Dome. The Stockyard. The Old Gas House. The Factory. The Prime Rip. Imagine, Prime Rib Hall. The Lantern. You had one of those car seats with the little plastic wheel. It had a little mousey horn. The parking lots were flocked with pigeons pecking crumbs."

We panned around the sun and slingshot to the south, snapped north again. The sun was on the other side of the motor home. When I lived here, I walked in Crown Hill Cemetery, the third-largest cemetery in the country. John Dillinger is buried there. Most of the land is still unused, bounded by the old canal on one side and brick walls that disappear on the other extremes. James Whitcomb Riley in his tomb on a hill, the highest point in Marion County. From there I could see most of the cemetery, the plots and tokens. At times I could catch sight of the few deer that had been walled-in long ago and continued to reproduce, living in the wooded areas. A few other people would trudge up the hill, some stopping occasionally to read the legends on the stones, pulling at the sleeve of a companion and pointing. The ends of the cemetery blended into the neighboring houses. Deep in the city someone tended the flame on the War Memorial. In a plaza, the flagpoles that raised and lowered state flags automatically using an electric eye did so every time the light changed. When a cloud closed off the sun. Clouds streamed from the east over vaults and tombs and pillars, giving the impression that the day was being manufactured just over the horizon and distributed above the city and, then, dismantled behind my back. Behind my back, I could hear the engines.

"Do you want something to eat?" my father asked. Memory interrupting memory. "Once you get inside, it will cost you an arm and a leg."

Compression

Seen through the binoculars, the sunlight streamed up from the grill and bumpers, strapping itself across the hood like wet paper. The guardrail blurred. Unmagnified, the car drifted into the banked curve, leaking light, a bearing in a roulette wheel. Trimming itself as the curve unwound, the car wedged into the shallow pool, splayed out wings of water, emerged, hit the brakes, slid until the drums dried out, then locked and skidded parenthetically 180 degrees, shifted into reverse, y-ed around, took off again through the pylons and stuttered over the railroad ties, geared down, ground and took the hill. Father and I watched International Harvester test a new model Scout. We alternated, passing the binoculars back and forth while eating French fries from a cardboard box. From where we sat among the wild carrots, we could see most of the track, the factory, and the lots packed with Transtars and army-green two-and-a-halves.

"That's right out of your future," my father said, handing me the glasses, "by at least two model years." I watched the old guard stumble up the hill toward us, one hand on his gun and the other pulling against the long grass for balance. He had come back to chase us away again.

My father was limping. Half-circled around him the freshman team he coached looked on. Central Catholic had been his high school, too. The practice field was behind St. Vincent's Children's Home. I watched him limp. I sat up on the shoulder of a giant statue of Mary that capped an outside altar. Beyond the field and the cinder track, the old New York Central tracks wound into Levin and Sons' Junk Yard. In the yard, bodies and frames of wrecked cars fit inside one another. Flattened. The usual fires burned. The trucks moved in and out of the yard, over the scales by the gate. Coming in full. Going out empty.

"Hey, kid," someone yelled from below, "come on down here." He was with a group of the orphans from the home. They were about my age. I climbed down. They wanted me to do them a favor. I was to go beg for a football from the team's manager. The orphans already had two or three helmets, kicking tees, and whistles. "Tell them you're an orphan," one of them insisted. "If you do that they'll give you anything you want." Chin straps dangled from their belts like scalps. "Yeah. Yeah." The rest now agreed and smiled, showing me the white gummy mouth guards, preformed, over their front teeth. "Yeah. Yeah," swallowing their words.

After the heats and the feature, workmen start taking apart the indoor oval, shoveling the dirt off the raked planks in the curves, and pitching the hay bales on the wagons. The scoreboard, hanging over the collapsing track, winks out and gathers into a solid black cloud suspended in the haze of dust and exhaust. I hold my scarf up to my mouth, filtering my breath through the work scented with unburned gasoline. In my head, I conjugate the winners with the races as I trot beside my father through the corridor to the ramp, descend, detouring through the exhibition hall downstairs, makeshift pits, where the midgets are being loaded on the trailers. Some are being pushed up ramps; others are running up on their own power. The trailers are hooked up to pickups with their engines running, blending together in an anxious idle. Someone touches a butterfly and then lets go as we turn. He still wears a sooty balaclava and metallic fire suit. One-third the size of the old front-engine Offys, the midgets pack up like grips, a roll bar no bigger than a handle, the decals on the cowling like those old travel stamps on steamer trunks— Champion, Monroe, STP, Goodyear, Hurst, Fram, Borg-Warner, Bell. Chains ratchet through axles. Tailgates slam, and lights come on. A truck guns and stalls and starts again. They will drive all night tonight and race tomorrow in Kokomo. We head for the doors.

Outside in the dark parking lot, the air is cold and empty. Father revs up the car and goes on and on about the way they turned *into* the skid, coaxes the car into gear and slips into the nearest street. As we slow for the first light, a pickup with a trailer coasts by. It enters the intersection as the light turns red, hits the bump at the crest of the cross street, and gives a little flip, like a fluke, as it eases down the grade on the far side and is gone in the night. Once more, because we are not moving, things begin to thicken, and the car closes in. Everything that usually escapes invisibly draws together in steam and smoke, finally heaves into a body, takes another breath, and disappears.

Power

In the trunk of my father's car there was a Polaroid camera with packets of black-and-white film, striped with bands of gray to distinguish them from color packages. There was chalk in boxes marked like crayon boxes but pale and faded. The chalk dust powdered everything, messed in with the grease of the folded tar and feathered jacks. There were tape measures as big as plates, with foldaway handles, purple snap lines in tearshaped canister, rolls of masking tape, black tarry electrician's tape on spools, and white medical tape in unopened tubes. On the first-aid kit was a green cross, and Father used an identical but empty kit for his toolbox, which he also kept in the trunk with jumper cables and two spare tires. A bright-red cartridge fire extinguisher for A, B, and C fires, and flares in red paper, rolled orange warning flags and reflectors. And a twenty-five pound bag of lime. "For the weight," he said, "in winter."

Once, when I was little, we went to a Hall's drive-in, and I used the ledge above the back seat as a table. I spilled my drink, and it drained into the trunk through the rear radio speaker. The speaker shorted; the voice gargled out beneath the paper napkins and foil I was using to blot up the mess. Father was already outside, the trunk lid up and the car rocking up and down gently, as he slid the things around with a hiss that was transmitted by the metal of the car. I watched him through the crack left between the body and the open lid. He wiped up the drink as it dripped down and mixed with the chalk dust, smearing the floor. He checked his equipment and then rearranged it. Satisfied, he slammed the trunk lid back down, and it caught on the first time for once and did not spring back up again as it usually did. He even hesitated, expecting it to pop up again. He tapped the trunk once and looked up at me in the rear window, surprised by his own strength. The car still rocked gently up and down. The pigeons circled and settled back on the ground.

Father worked as the director of safety for the phone company and used the camera and the tape measures to investigate the traffic accidents that involved the company's trucks. He spent part of every week taking pictures of wrecks, visiting accident scenes and reconstructing what had happened. At night on the dinner table, he would unroll his schematic drawings of street grids. Colored rectangles stood for cars and trucks. Sometimes he would use tokens from board games. He penciled in vectors and numbers, all done on pale-blue veined graph paper. "I know that corner," I would say. He frowned as I put a glass of milk down on a parking lot. I told him, as I chewed my sandwich, of this great crash on Spring Street or how the coral color of Jim Musbaum's Chevy at Baerfield Raceway matched the color of that car there. I pointed and smudged he picture. Father frowned again, answered that this man overdrove his headlights. Staring off, he recalled conversion tables, following distance, and reaction time. This man couldn't see and forgot about a blind spot. "He didn't honk his horn at the alley opening." Those types of things. "Don't spill," he warned.

The rest of his job concerned prevention and education. He distributed drivers' education films that always culminated in a fatality, gave tests, put warnings on windows of trucks. He modified mirrors to magnify, came up with catchy slogans such as "Look alive in '75." He also kept a black briefcase in the trunk of his car, up by the seat. Every now and then he would simulate accidents to test first-aid skills and response time of police and fire units. He used the briefcase then.

I went along one time and watched him. He had arranged for a smashed-up car to be left in a certain ditch by our house. After putting on special blood-smeared and torn clothes that he kept in his kit, he added splashes of fake blood for fresh wounds and lacerations. He put on a medical-warning bracelet that said he was allergic to sulfa drugs. To see if they would check. He then threaded a rubber tube up his sleeve and taped it to his arm. At the other end of the tube was a rubber bulb like a perfume atomizer. He held the bulb close to his chest and with his free hand pumped more blood from a plastic bag he wore suspended from his neck. The blood went through the tube and out the other end, where it spurted like a severed artery at his wrist. In his kit, he had plastic casts he could strap on a leg or arm which approximated simple, compound, or complex fractures. He had ace bandages that had been treated to look like burns, first to third degree.

He wedged himself through the broken windshield of the car, careful not to cut himself on the exposed sheet metal, and tucked his legs under the collapsed dash. Appearing to be pinned, he affected the shallow breathing of shock. His hand out the window, he tried a test beat or two from his wound and it squirted, a trick plastic flower on a lapel.

"How do I look?" he asked.

"Pretty bad," I answered truthfully.

"Good, good. Go call those numbers."

I left him there and went to a phone booth to call the police and the company's own emergency squad. By the time I returned, I could hear the sirens coming up the by-pass. I stood a little way off and looked at my father slouched and unconscious. A red trickle bled down the car door. The shadow his hair cast darkened his forehead. A rear tire had sprung a leak, and the car was settling slowly. His finger twitched.

Passing cars slowed down. Some stopped, pulled off to the side. Passengers got out and ran up to the car. There were sirens now. Someone was directing traffic. The police and the ambulance pulled up. I went closer and saw some police clearing the area, explaining to those who tried to help. They thanked them, but there was nothing anyone could do. The emergency crews cut away the door with a gasoline-powered tool that shook the car and sounded like a chain saw. My father's head rolled back and forth on the seat. Someone bent over and yelled in his ear. Someone else was holding the bleeding wrist. On the other side of the car, they broke out the window, trying to free him that way. There were more sirens now, called by passing motorists, and a television crew that must have been in the area, listening to the police band. Father was on the ground, and they could not stop the bleeding. They were bringing blankets. A man's hand was streaked red between the fingers. There was a scratch on my father's earlobe just flushed with blood. A piece of glass must have caught him when they broke the window. I could see him stretched out on the ground through the legs of people standing around. A wrecker pulled up. Its brakes coming on and a radio playing. Another man stood up from where he had been crouching over my father. There was no more blood. Someone pronounced him dead and laughed shortly, pulling back the blankets and wiping his hands on my father's shirt.

Exhaust

When we passed the sign near Penalton which warns against picking up hitch-hikers because the penitentiary is so close, the motor home slowed and pulled over. The Erhmans led everyone out the two doors, and we lined up along the drainage ditch and faced in the directions of the prison. The prison water tower was silhouetted now and then by the sweeping searchlights. Low to the ground and this far away, not much else could be seen. The men started to shout.

"Come on out, Russian," and "Now's your chance." Between each chorus, they would pause to listen, hen huddle, deciding on what to say next. Lining up again, my father would pace them, "one, two, three," directing with his hands.

"We're waiting."

A Funk Seed Hybrid sign was on the fence by the road. The cornfield was empty. There was not even an echo.

"He's not coming," someone said, and we got back in.

Starting up the road again my father said that it was a shame I had to see a year of trials when turbine cars were entered. "I miss the sound," he said. He waved his head as if following an imaginary vehicle from left to right and pursed his lips together to imply a sound, because that was what the new engines did. Imply a sound.

We stopped one more time that night. A few miles from home, we pulled off into a closed weigh station. I got out and climbed the ladder to the roof of the motor home. The siding was cold as I sat down under the TV antenna cocked like a café umbrella. Across the highway was an identical station. It was closed, too. Beyond that was a barn. Showing in the circle of the mercury light was the name of the place, Belle Acres, painted below a smiling image of the Good Sam Club that spotted the dark barn, a hex sign. Good Sam smiled broadly, eyes bugging, his halo tilted back out of the way.

My father and his friends were running races up and down the driveway. They ran heats, two or three men at a time. Someone sat at the finish line with a folding TV table and campstool keeping score. As they ran, their shadows spiraled around their feet, scooting between the pools of light.

Father ran easily, won his heat, slowed down way beyond the finish line, then turned and limped back up the apron. I applauded alone until I was interrupted by a car honking its horn as it went by on the interstate. I turned to wave. A new race started. Father, passing on his way back to the starting line, looked up at me and jerked his head from left to right performing the first half of a double take, pretending to hum along as the silent racer passed before his eyes. He hobbled back up the drive toward the hut, where his friends were jumping up and down on the scale. He bent over now and then to catch his breath.

They ran a few more heats until the man at the TV table fell asleep and put his head on his hands. The Erhmans led a walking tour north toward home, examining shoulder material. As they began to sing, they disappeared into the night.

Father and I went back inside the motor home and started up the engine, waiting for them to return. More and more trucks appeared on the highway. The sky paralleled the black field, leaving a space in between. He listened to a horn blasting down the road and to the engine beneath our feet. "Something's missing," he said, swiveling in the captain's chair. He talked until the engine died, out of gas, fitting word into word until I finished sentences he had started. I could no longer tell where we were by the sound the night was making. But by then it didn't matter; we had been carried on, by the dead center, to where it already was the next day.

Watch Out

My Story

I will write my story using English only, as my students should do. I will write about our new home and how we live. I will write about the class I teach and my very good students who will read this and who are pleased to be here in Indiana. There is the church to write about too and our Bishop Leo. But most of all I will write in English about learning it and not using my own tongue of French because we are here now and must learn this one way to talk.

Things You Must Know

I am a woman. I am five feet high. My Christian name is Catherine. In my country, I lived with the Sisters of the Sacred Hear and the Sisters of the Most Precious Blood and I remember the white, black, and gray colors of their clothes and how hot it must have been. With them, I learned French and English and the ways to teach others these languages. I worked hard and had a good time. My hair is black. My eyes too. I can drive a car. I can run a typewriter. I was afraid, of course, when I came to America. But with the help of the Diocese of Fort Wayne-South Bend and the Fort Wayne Community Schools everything is fine now. I have no family in this country, but I have a father, a mother, two brothers, a sister, two uncles and their wives who are my aunts, and several cousins. All of my grandparents are no longer living.

My Health Problem

In America there is food. In America there are all kinds of food. When I arrived in America there were signs everywhere that said Eat. But when I came here to this country with all this food, I cannot eat. The food looks like wood and tastes like mud to me. Even the food of my country that we make here no longer tastes good to me now. I lose so much weight that my boss, Mrs. Anthis, is startled each time she sees me. She pretends everything is fine, but I can see.

Where I Work

I work for the public schools under a title from the President of the United States. "We are lucky to find you," Mrs. Anthis says. This is after she pretends not to worry about me. "We were lucky to find her," she says to her bosses when I am introduced to them. These men are kind and they want to shake my hand all the time. They don't know much about my country except for the war and they don't talk about that. They say, "Why, you are so little!" I laugh. I teach English to the children of my country so that they can go to regular school one day. Everyone knows America is the land of opportunity. Here is an example.

Where We Live

Our Bishop Leo lets us live in the Central Catholic High School. Let me tell you that it is not a high school now with students and teachers. It is called CC. There are other high schools where Catholic boys and girls go to learn. Those schools are far away, on the edge of the city. Many families live here. We are waiting to find houses of our own and for the children without families to be adopted. We have made curtains for the big windows at CC. The lights are tubes filled with gas. They hum. There are many places for the children to hide. They hide in the old desks. They run down the halls and hide in the lockers in the wall. Often they will jump out at me as I walk by. There is a gym and a greenhouse on the roof where people have planted seeds they brought with them. Each family has a classroom of its very own. I live in the room with many sewing machines, refrigerators, sinks, and ovens. It was decided that it would be best if I lived here since I am alone. Now, no woman with a family will be jealous of another. Each family has its own oven and a place to put food. Water is in this room, so the washing is done here too. It dries on the roof. There are smells of cooking in my room and much laughter among the women. It is okay because I work in the school in the days and on the days I don't work I talk to the children or take them to places so they will hear English. There is a room of typewriters, too. I am there now. Every room has a clock on the wall. The thin hand is always moving. My room is quiet at night but for the refrigerators. I think to myself that they talk to one another. I hear the bells of the churches every fifteen minutes, and I hear the pigeons near the windows making their soft noises.

The Churches of Fort Wayne

There are many beautiful and interesting churches in the city. Many of the churches are near downtown, and we walk to them to hear daily mass. Sometimes we travel to the churches farther away, taking the black cars of the priests. Then we meet the people there in the new churches. We sit in the front pews with ushers standing by. The people talk to us slowly and give us boxes of cans. These are the new churches where there are many people and where they wear bright clothes and the ceilings are low and sparkle. I am thinking of St. Jude's and St. Vincent's, where the statues are smooth wood and never painted. Near to CC are the old churches. There is the cathedral of our Bishop Leo. It is called Immaculate Conception. There the stations of the cross are twice as big as life and there are banks of votive candles kept burning by the older people. There are side altars. The building is white and Mary has a crown of pure gold on her head. We have heard stories about a workman who caught on fire and fell burning from the steeple we can see from our windows at CC but lived. Nearby is a big rock here the Indians converted. There is St. Mary's made out of red sandstone. It is a church built in the old way. There are bats that live here high up near the painted ceiling. There is St. Peter and St. Paul, which is made with red brick. There is St. Patrick with one steeple. There is Precious Blood, which has two steeples and beautiful bells. There is Queen of the Angels, which is an old gym since they are so poor. There is colored paper in the windows. And there is a shrine to the Virgin near the wrecking yard and power plant where the orphanage is and near the place where football is played. Near to CC is a chapel. It is open all the time. But someone must be there praying day and night. You can see the body of Christ. There it is in the center of a golden cross inside a round window. I go to this chapel often to hear mass at noon with the workers from the banks who are not having dinner. The chapel might not remain open at night. People are afraid to be alone in the early morning. I have spent many happy hours visiting these places and talking to the friendly people.

Worry

I believe I am not doing a very good job. This happens when the children call out the windows of CC at Americans on the street. The children use their own language and slam the windows. They do not want to leave the building but play games in the hallway near the glass cases that have old awards for sports. They play near the fountains and waste water. I speak to them in English and they don't understand. I know they know some English but they are afraid too. They do not want Americans to lose patience with them. They try to tell me how things are, but I shake my head. "Say it in English please!" If I were bigger, I could do a better job.

In the Classroom

When they are not working, the parents of my students visit the classroom. They sit in the little chairs with the children on their laps. Or they sit next to the children on the floor and try to read the simple English. Then I hear them asking the children what this word is or what that one is. And I hear the children say the word in the old language. *Ball* or *dog.* I don't feel so bad then. The parents tell me it is too late for them to learn. Then they fall into silence. Then they tell the children to try harder. I say, "Let's sing a song!" With the children singing it is very nice and everyone is happier.

At CC I Am Very Busy

We all wait for the mail to come in the big bags brought by a man in a truck. People want me to read to them the letters that have come in English. Often these letters suggest buying things such as records, magazines, spoons, seeds, and food. There are other letters from leaders. Once a week, our Bishop Leo writes. And I read the *Sunday Visitor* for everyone when we all eat together. There are papers to fill out for others. And I talk to the operator when the family heads are called in other cities. I write notes for the men to take to the bank with their checks. On Sunday when Father Hamilton says mass in the little chapel, I translate the words for him. It makes me very happy to help.

Sunday Brunch

Mrs. Anthis took me to a Sunday brunch. She wanted to put meat on my bones. The Sunday brunch was at a restaurant owned by Mr. Hall. Many of the men from CC wash dishes there. There was much to eat. Bacon, ham, beef, chicken, fish, lamb, sausage, and eggs which were fried, scrambled, boiled, and eggs made a special way and given names. There was fruit. Apples, oranges, grapes, cherries, bananas, pineapples, berries, grapefruit, and many juices. There were potatoes with onions that were sliced or in long strips. There were breads that were sweet and had icing, and cakes, and bread in paper, and loaves of bread with three types of butter, one that had strawberries inside it. There was honey, and syrup for pancakes, and yellow corn bread. You could drink all the coffee you wanted. You could go back to the food tables as many times as you liked. People walked around the big room with two plates. Mrs. Anthis said, "This is our favorite place." Her husband was there and her children and other teachers. Some of the men from CC waved to me when no one else was looking. They were carrying dishes from the tables. "No wonder," Mrs. Anthis said. "Are you sure you don't want anything more?" she said. I was listening to all the English in the room, and that was enough for me.

I Become Sicker

I have gone again to the doctor. He wears a white coat, and there are folds at the bottom of his pants. There are bars on the windows, and the table where I sit is covered by a thin piece of white paper. The sister pulls out a new piece of paper from the end of the table. She pulls it tight and shiny. I am always afraid to sit on this new piece of paper and put wrinkles into it. I remember the women at CC with the hot irons and the steam and the stiff legs of their husbands' checkered pants. The women go back and forth with irons. "Go on. Sit down. It's only paper," the sister says. "You must eat," the doctor says. "Why don't you eat?" But I don't have the words to tell him why. They both look at me and I am so afraid. My hand goes back and forth on the paper. Then I cut my finger on the edge of the paper. There is some blood on the paper and we are all surprised.

Downtown

The children are like sparrows. We go downtown and they run and follow one another. They all land at one spot. They all look into the mirror that Murphy's has on their building, and then they fly, one after another, to the boxes that have newspapers. We are about the only people downtown. The people work in offices high up in the tall buildings. The children like to stop in front of the wig shop. In the window of the wig shop are black heads with all different kinds of hair that shines in the light. Most store windows are painted white and have old signs that say Closed. The clocks have stopped on the store signs. In the street I see where a railroad track has been covered over by new paving. This city is so different from the old cities. The children run from one place to another. There are only big green buses in the streets. Without the buses the streets would be empty. "Where are the people?" the children ask. "Say it in English," I say. "Hiding! They're hiding!" the children say. The children are jumping at a string of lights in a small tree without leaves. "They are up there, the people, in all of those windows. They are speaking English to one another." That is what I say to them.

In Another Classroom

I have been to the Catholic high schools to talk to students there. I tell them stories like these about what we do and how we live and about my students. Mrs. Anthis stands in the back of the room and smiles. After awhile, a bell rings and the students collect their books from the little shelves under their chairs. They go. And new students come in and sit down. I say the same things about Fort Wayne and the beautiful churches and the children and CC and the green buses. The students listen closely. They smile and look at each other. They listen hard to me. They look hard at me. I feel as if I am talking softer and softer, and I am afraid that I have not said something I said before to another class. "What, dear?" Mrs. Anthis says. "What is it?" And I can't explain with these students watching me.

The Children's Zoo

The zoo of Fort Wayne has only young animals. There are the cubs of lions and monkeys and bears and kangaroos. There are baby elephants and turtles and pigs. Everywhere there are the chicks of birds scratching the ground. The small rabbits live in a big shoe. In one building, many tiny snakes, like noodles, were under an orange light wrapped around and around each other on a bed of sawdust. My students and I rode a small train around a lake. We went into a yard where kids and lambs ran after us and sucked our fingers until we gave them bottles of milk. I pointed and called every animal by name. I told the children that the zoo was a place for children. The grown-up animals must go to other zoos. "These animals you can play with now." And my students rubbed the fur and held the animals tight, and then they tried to carry the animals away while the animals made such loud crying noises. We fed the seals also. We bought food from a machine like the candy machines at CC. I pulled on a handle and the food arrived. The noise we made with the machine was heard by the seals, and they came up out of the cold green water onto the rocks and sang as their fur dried in the sun. The children threw food to them through the air, and the heads of the seals and their long necks moved back and forth following the food as it fell.

One Night

One night the children were crying. Outside it was snowing, and the trucks that never stop were going by the building. The windows shook in the wind. The air in my room was hot and dry. It was very dark. I heard the children cry. The children were in their rooms and their crying came in under the door of my room. Then I heard mothers and fathers awake. The voices were low and they sang songs. It was like being rocked again by my mother's voice so far away. It was so hot and dry in my room. I wanted to move my bed to the floor. There near the ground would be cool air. I took off my nightshirt, which was red and pretty. I got it from the people of the church we visited. When I pulled the nightshirt over my head, I saw a flash of light. The light ran around my body and arms and legs and fingers and into my hair. Every time I moved there were more sparks and a sound like sitting on the paper in the doctor's office. The light was blue and green and it did not hurt. When I shook my head against my nightshirt there would be more sparks. I watched this for a long time. And that is why the children cried. One child woke that night and saw the light playing on the bodies of his mother and father and sisters and his brothers as they turned in bed against the sheets and blankets. He was frightened and called out. When everyone woke up and moved in the bed there was more flashing in the dark and they thought they were on fire and cried for help. The next family woke up and the same thing happened. Then everyone was awake and screaming for help. But it was nothing. It was the new clothes, something in the new clothes, that made this happen. The women came into my room to wash the clothes in the dark.

Watch Out

The next day in class, I told the children how to ask for help in English. Help me. How to say I am hurt. I am hurt. I taught them to say be careful. Be careful. I taught them to say I am afraid. I am afraid. I taught them to say I'm scared. I'm scared. The learned the words *run, move, duck.* I told them don't look and I didn't see it and be calm and get out of the way. I taught them none of your business and leave me alone and I am okay and I can't walk. I taught the children to say I am sick. I am sick. And let me sit down and rest. Let me sit down and rest. And I can't go on. I can't go on. I taught them bad, evil, wrong, pain, and death. Yes, I told them the word for death. Death. And I said "Watch out." "Say it. Watch out." "You say it now," I said. I said, "Watch out." And the children said, "Watch out." I said, "That's good." And the children said, "Watch out! Watch out!" as loud as they could.

In the Middle of Another Night

I go to the small chapel to sit and think. The people who must sit there sit together away from me in one pew. They turn to look at me when they think I am not looking but praying. I think of my family. Where they are and what they must be doing because it is day on the other side of the word. And I think at times in the old language when I think of my mother and father and I pretend they can hear me like it was prayer. When the new people come to take the place of the people who have been sitting and watching, they all turn to look at me and to whisper to each other. Then I think I am really safe here in Fort Wayne.

Later

No one is out in the downtown. There are no sounds. Nothing is open. I am not afraid to walk around. Why should I be afraid? There is no one here. I asked Mrs. Anthis this. "Why do people stay away?" And she said, "They are afraid." I said, "Afraid of what?" "Of what is downtown." I said, "Are they afraid of us?" "No, no, my dear," she said, "they are just afraid." But there is no one here but us. There is no one here at all but us. I know because I walk around at night. "You, you tiny thing?" she said. "Yes," I said. I never see anyone else. But the lights that direct the traffic still work. There are big piles of snow in the corner of the parking lots where the buildings used to be, and in the middle of the parking lots are little houses that are empty. Inside the houses, I see through the window a light is on and the cash register is open and empty. When the wind blows snow off the piles, it flows over the black ground of the empty lots like a clear shallow river, white and running fast.

A Disease

The doctor told me of a disease he thinks makes me not eat. I cried in his office sitting on the paper on his table. I cried because I am not hungry and because I am fading away to nothing. That is what the sister said when I stood on the scale. "You are fading away to nothing." I cried because I am doing something wrong. I cried because I have no one to talk to. The doctor said it was something in the air, this disease. He said that very many American girls who cannot eat are sick with it. Girls in America, he said, want to look good in bathing suits. "Do you want to look good in a bathing suit?" I cried because I had never thought of bathing suits before. The doctor can think of nothing else it can be. "That must be it," he said and then he said good-bye and left me in the little room to get dressed.

Tet

It is our first new year in America. At CC we have a party in the gym. We play records and the sound comes out of the speakers in the ceiling. The children are running around the tables. Ribbons and colored paper sail along behind them when they run. Everyone is happy. We are using white paper plates for our food, the rice cakes and pork and lemon grass and milk. And Mrs. Anthis is here and Mr. Hall and all the bosses and the man who brings us the mail. And our Bishop Leo is here too blessing everything. When I go up to him for a blessing I take his hand to kiss his ring and I cannot lift his hand in my two hands. He tells me to stand next to him on the stage and he asks me to tell him a phrase to say in celebration. He leans over and I tell him and he says it a few times to himself. Everyone is quiet when he speaks in English and now Bishop Leo says I am a good teacher. And I look at the faces. They are eating and drinking. They do not understand what has been said and are waiting for me to translate, to that I say I am a good teacher. But I say in the old language that all of you are my family, that we are here together, one body, and that we must eat all the food and not waste a bit of it.

In Another Building

We went to the top of one of the tall buildings. My students ran through the empty restaurant that is there. They ran from one big window to another and looked down carefully at the city. The restaurant was closed, so we could come in and see and not trouble anybody. Windows were everywhere and they were so big it seemed you could walk right out into the sky. Outside we saw the steeples of the churches and the green rivers way off in the distance. Below we saw the tops of the green buses and the parking lots filled with cars. We saw CC below us and the washing on the roof. Below us too were many gray pigeons flying together from one building to another. And the children asked quietly in the old language where the people were now, and I tried to show them the houses all around. But the trees made everything disappear. And the children said, "They're hiding. They're hiding." Some men from CC who work in this place were putting knives and forks and spoons on the table. The metal made a pretty sound. The children stood very close to the windows all in a line looking out. The lights of the houses and cars came on like stars in the sky. And with us in the sky, the stars began to show up. I could smell the food in the kitchen and I told everyone it was time to go. There were more and more lights all around the city, long straight lines of lights where the roads were. Why should I be this lucky one in America?

An Accident

The train would be gone by the time he got to the scene. The train had been late this morning. That might mean something. After this it would be very late into Chicago.

He drove at the speed limit. There was no radio. It was a company car.

The railway paralleled U.S. 30 between Fort Wayne and Warsaw. Conrail wanted to abandon the route. The waves in the telegraph line flattened out where an insulator had popped free of the pole, a green clot floating there in the taut wire.

It was the day after Labor Day. It was clear and bright. There had been no fog that morning in the low-lying areas. The leaves were still on the trees. The corn was tall and green in the fields. All of this could be important.

His wife wrote up the reports at the kitchen table. He did not take notes at the accidents he investigated for the company but presented the facts to her, the way he remembered them, while he ate. Rarely did he draw conclusions. She asked leading questions, partly because the forms demanded certain connections be made, partly because she was curious and thought best with a pencil in her hand. Once she got started it was hard for her to stop.

Both of them had forgotten when it was he had stopped writing. They never talked about it. He never had written much. But now he felt awkward scribbling down a phone number. He had been embarrassed when the company had given him a Cross pen and pencil set upon his promotion from craft to the safety department.

The firemen were still putting water on the truck. He judged it to be about two thousand feet from the grade crossing. The train was gone.

The driver of the truck, pronounced dead on the scene, had been taken to Fort Wayne though his home was nearby. The crossing was in a little town called Atwood and only had lights, no gate. The passenger train doesn't stop there. Its next stop is Whiting, the last stop before Chicago.

He heard the figures of 242, 312, and 276 people on board. He had talked to the other investigators there. They had given him the numbers but now what they thought about them. There were state troopers, a deputy sheriff from the county, some men from OSHA, a man from Conrail, a man from Amtrak, the railroad's insurance man and Amtrak's insurance man, the company's insurance man. The man who was killed, his insurance man. And he was here now. There were several witnesses, too, standing around talking to each other.

He stood for a second at the crossing. He saw a whistle warning, a capital *W* in the Pennsylvania keystone. The crossing was wood, splintered and bleached. A blacktop led up to it. The rails were bright, not rusted. Two tracks and a siding, unused, making for a deserted elevator. The ballast was weathered and oil-stained. There was the diesel smell and the smell of urine dumped on the tracks from the toilets of the old passenger cars Amtrak still used. A date nail dated the last maintenance to seven years ago. The creosote was gray and hard and some ties were gouged.

A column of smoke coiled up from the tires of the truck two thousand feet away. Some flares sputtered up the track. A torpedo had been left behind by the train crew and, beyond where the white rails came together, a lone signal block hovered above the track and the heat, showed red.

Along both rails was pure white sand. It started a little before the crossing and burrowed by the rails to where the train came to rest and where the truck slid down the elevation and burned. It was fine, powder, and felt, when he walked on it, like sand-blasting sand at the foot of a building. It was the same grade of sand. The same used in a kid's playground.

His wife would conclude that the train came to a gradual halt. The engineer knew he had killed the man in the truck when he hit it, had sanded freely and braked slowly at the same time, looking down on the yellow truck sliding ahead of him. The fireman was already out the cab door and out on the rail steps. The truck started to burn in the rear. Ladders spilled from the racks on its roof. There would be a big pile of sand where the engine came to rest. The passengers would have to be told what had happened. The deceleration would have felt ordinary. The train was late. What now? The conductor put the radio mike to his mouth. "Amtrak 41."

Her husband told her the speed limit was fifty-nine mile per hour and that he was probably going about that. Say sixty. The engine was painted silver with red, blue, and white striping. Two headlights and two blue strobe lights are to be on the lead unit. The fire in the truck scorched the engine's sides. Someone had to pay for that.

It was the day after Labor Day. The train was westbound from New York and Washington to Chicago. It was late. Usually it passed through Atwood around a quarter after six each morning. Today it was eight thirty-five when the truck was hit. This he got from a retired railway man who lived by the tracks.

"Did you hear the horn?" he asked him.

"Yes, I heard it."

"Once? Twice? What?"

"I heard it twice. It wasn't the engineer's fault."

"No one else says they heard it."

"I heard it. They're wrong."

"Not once?"

"Twice."

The track here runs due west. The truck crossed north to south. The sun would have been to the left of the driver. The train rising in the east.

He watched the men go about their jobs. Two of them, using a cloth tape measure, measured the distance, stretching out the tape to its full length, and then one ran by the other, stretching out the tape again in relays. Another man rolled a wheel meter. It looked like a toy. One man wrote out his notes using the roof of his car, revolving light revolving, the light washed out in the sun. The cars and trucks were yellow, orange, red, bright blue, a two-toned brown. Company colors. The radios were patched through the siren speakers and the voices flat, spitting, bitten off. From time to time he heard a bird make a sound like the sound the metal ball makes in a spray-paint can.

There had been another company truck trailing behind the one that was hit. The driver of the second truck sat in the cab, parked. The warning lights were flashing.

He said to the driver, "Backing accidents are what give us the most problems. You know if you could come up with a way to prevent them, you could make a fortune. Bell put out orange cones for a while. Do you remember? But college kids stole them. The problem is, most things work for a while and the people get used to them." He said, "Most of the time it's backing up that gives you a fit."

The driver guessed so. They listened to the tic of the lights. There was a spray of rust in the yellow panel of the truck. The rear tires were snow tires.

"What did you see?"

"I saw the taillights, and I saw him look both ways. I saw him through the rear-door window."

"Left, right, left? What? Right, left, right?"

"The other way I think. But he was across the tracks already still looking. I didn't see the train until it run into him and then just the aluminum and the windows. It was like a cartoon except the end of the train slowed down and I could see the faces. That's when I got out. I didn't hear the horn or anything. My engine runs fast until it's warmed up, and we had just come out from that restaurant over there and breakfast. We were in no hurry to work. I have orders for a splice down 30. And he didn't try to beat it across. I don't think he saw it. I didn't see it. He must have crossed here five or six times a day. If you ask me, those signal poles are too far from the crossing."

He asked the lineman if he would put that down in writing, handed him the folded forms.

The lineman said, "I'm not so good with these things."

He told him to do his best. People would understand. "That's all I do anymore." He told him to send the forms in the company mail.

Standing a little ways off were a few other men wanting to talk with the lineman. They wore ties. Two wore beepers on their belts. The other had his in his shirt pocket. The beepers were leased from the phone company. During the day a beeper would go off, and a man would walk to the pay phone by the restaurant or get in a car and drive away.

He left the lineman, crossed the track and got in his car again. He drove over the crossing without letting up on the gas. The car bucked and rocked. He did this without his seat belt on, only remembering it when he parked the car and got out on the other side of the track.

He leaned against the side of the car and reached back through the open window for the box of cigars he kept wedged between the sun visor and the roof. At home he smoked them out in the garage or in the backyard, where he looked out over the office park next door. For hours he watched the Canada geese tear at the lawns.

Later, he watched her erase a line of writing. It was different than writing one. Then her whole body leaned into the work, her head always moving steadily over the page though her eyes remained fixed on the pencil point. When she erased, she erased one letter at a time, blowing away the crumbs the color of her lips. She erased completely, never leaving ghosts of letters between or under words. She held the pencil the same way as she did when she wrote. She sat at the dining-room table. The leaf leaned against the wall. The pencil sharpener stuck to the table by means of a vacuum. Each time she used it she slid her palm over the table and then blew on the rubber diaphragm under the base of the sharpener. She set it down, worked it like a brick, and flipped the lever. It held fast. He watched her work. While she wrote, the sharpener slowly let go of the tabletop, covered with crumbs.

It was the day after Labor Day. He had spent most of the weekend watching the telethon. When he worked in craft he once had done the inside work for the telephone banks. There was a phone in every room of his house, and they all rang differently. He had cut the grass.

A Conrail truck was sliding along the track up to the crossing. It was painted blue and a yellow light flashed on the crew cab. The steel wheels jacked the truck up off the track just enough so that the rear tires could propel it along.

It stopped before the crossing, skating a bit after braking. There was no sand. The horn honked, a regular horn, and the truck crept up on to the grade, where it might have raised the steel wheels but instead kept on going smoothly up the track to where the other truck still smoldered.

He watched the other investigators scatter off the track, wave at the truck as it went by. They wore ties and hard hats. A beeper went off. He heard the door of the newspaper vending machine slam shut. A car engine started by the restaurant.

The inspection truck stopped near the wreck. Its taillights came on. Three men got out and looked down the elevation at the truck. Then, they got back in their truck and continued toward Chicago.

He talked to several witnesses who told him pretty much the same story. No one had ever seen a train hit a truck before except on TV, and those crashes were in slow motion. They all talked about how fast it had happened and how long it took the train to stop. Only the retired railroad man had heard the horn, had heard it twice. The witnesses pointed to where they had been. They told him what they had done after it was over. He gave them all his business card and they slid his in with the rest.

"I'm sorry," someone said to him.

Lunch was at the restaurant. He had chili. An OSHA man was in the booth with him having a cheeseburger and coffee. They both wore their ID badges on metal chains around their necks. The badges were flat against their ties, where they leaned into the table. It was crowded and noisy. The hard hats were on the racks by the door and on the top of the cigarette machine, along with the baby boosters.

"How can someone not see a train?" the OSHA man said. "I mean not see it when it can be seen? I mean that train was one that could be seen. The right of way had been cut back. It's a question that always plagues me. Is it a matter of concentration or what? But it's a shame, a waste. We both got better things to do. I understand there are kids. The sheriff said she took it kind of hard, but what do you expect? A train is so big and this kind of thing amazes me."

He called his wife after lunch to tell her what had happened. All the phones rang.

"I'm going to need this one in kind of a hurry since there is someone dead here."

"No, I understand. I don't mind. I like doing these things for you."

"It's a mess here," he said. "He's about a couple thousand feet down the track. I have to wait for our crew. I don't think it will be anything hard to do."

"It's all right. Did you know him?" she asked.

"I knew the name. Look, I'll tell you about it when I get home."

Whenever she finished writing and she read it to him, it never was quite right. He never would say anything to her because she would suggest he write his own damn reports. Besides, he told her everything he could remember. He went around in his mind looking through all the accidents he had been to. It was his fault, he concluded, for seeing one thing and saying another. Yes, that's it. That's good enough. Giving up.

Unless he was eating he hated sitting at a table. He told his secretary that his wife rewrote his reports so that the typing would be easy.

"How can you look at such things?" his wife asked, looking up from the yellow pad, the yellow pencil rolling over the words, her fingers spread and stretching before her on the table.

The back of the truck was scorched black. The paint was blistered. Snow tires were on the truck but badly burned.

A couple of men looked through the knee-high grass and bushes of the steep bank. One of them reached down, then held up a wrench. The salvage crew had parked down the bank on the access road. They slid the big metal toolboxes down the bank and loaded them up. They formed a line and passed along boxes of extension phones one at a time. They wrapped wire, like yarn, on their arms and carried it on their bodies like ammunition.

The investigators took pictures with old instant cameras. The prints had to be timed and the picture pulled apart after it had developed.

He looked in the cab, and the others crowded around him. There was blood on the window and down the side of the door. Blood on the wheel and dashboard. Blood on the order board. The one side was caved in. The side door sprung. The fire hadn't come this far forward. There was a wire screen, which protects the driver, between the seats and the equipment. Power tools were being taken out the back.

The mirror might have blocked his sight, the whole train hidden behind it when he looked that way.

He could hear the scratches of writing all around him. It was the only sound, for no one talked. The pencils whispered to the paper.

He saw the plastic woven cushion on the floor. He saw the pictures of children, the coins on the seat. He saw the toothpick. He saw the glove compartment popped open and the maintenance papers, the maps, and the rag for the oil dipstick. There was an upright Coke can and a spilled coffee cup in the tray above the engine. The tool belt was on the dash. He saw where he had put the decal on the windshield that said Look before Backing and he saw where it had been picked at.

The writing went on around him. The different scratch of an erasure.

The men from the company carried things down the hill.

He opened the door. A few men pushed around him into the truck. They poked around beneath the seats. The horn, the turn indicator switched on, the lights. Nothing worked.

He saw the train coming, though it was a ways off. One of its head-lights wobbled in its socket. There was heat coming off the rails and off the hoods of the engines and the black cars it was pulling. Soon, it sounded its horn, two notes, and the engines went up in pitch. Everyone looked up from the wreck as the train came nearer, picked up speed. The engineer turned on the bell and blew the horn again. It crawled by. The fireman waved. The brakeman was out the door, walking forward to the pilot as the engine moved forward. He looked down at the track, gave a wave. Black smoke stood up from the exhaust of the six engines, and the slack in the coupling was pulled in, echoed away through the cars. He saw the thin spray of sand at the wheels. The blue engines went by. The dynamic brakes hissed, kept the air even throughout the train. The black cars were identical except for the numbers, and the numbers were white and not that much out of sequence. There was a stutter over the joint in the rail. He counted 126 empty, empty coal hoppers. The others did, too.

A Short, Short Story Complete on These Two Pages

You should know right off how everything came out. Marsha is pregnant with her second, and she still looks great. She walks even straighter, and you can see the muscles through her clothes when she moves. She moves like she's saying the baby doesn't change things.

I saw her again right before Christmas at the mall where the company we used to work for, Reader's World, has a store. Every chance I get I go in and ask the new clerks, and they're always new, if I still work for Reader's World. When they answer, I ask, "Well, whatever happened to him?"

Marsha had her straight, I mean straight, black hair in a Cleopatra cut. It was like a helmet framing the white skin of her face. She has green eyes. She's one of the few people I look at when I'm talking to them. She wore her clothes clinging tight across her belly. No tent dress. Not an ounce of fat on her except maybe her breasts, which were getting ready, you know.

She let me put my hand on her stomach right there in the mall, and I mean to tell you, the results were tympanic. You forget how hard flesh can get.

I said we worked together for a summer at Reader's World but not in the store at the mall, which they opened later, but in an old English Village shopping center way the heck out. That store is closed now because the volume never was big enough. You should know that these places are supermarkets. There's no violin music, no cats rubbing up against your let as you browse. The books were paperbacks. We arranged them up and down according to the author's last name in display racks that showed you every front cover, boom. The shiny things were right there in front of you. Many books were part of a series, big numbers running from the ceiling to the floor, in order, appealing to the desire to collect them all. There were calendars galore and cute bookmarks next to the cash register. I mean, things had to move, or we pulled them. In the pockets behind the books were reorder, inventory cards. We combed through those daily. When we found a title about to get dusty, boom, on the floor it went. Boxes of the things arrived every day, fresh produce.

The place was owned by the local news agency that, heretofore, had only been wholesale, stocking, well, supermarket checkouts and the rack or two at drugstores. So they had the books. They integrated vertically.

But the main push came with magazines, and here I've got to admit it was impressive. They had, have everything, every mass-market, consumer, commercial, special-interest, slick and pulp magazine and more the bookstore ordered right from the publishers. As the only male I was hired to take care of the rack.

Marsha and I hit it off right away. The other women were much older. They popped in from tanning in their back yards to work a few hours. This is minimum-wage country, second-income city. They liked to read and talk about books with the friends who'd stop by asking if we had anything more by this one author they couldn't get enough of. Marsha and I would avoid the conversation and go out on the floor. We'd cull through the paperbacks, pulling the odd title, cleaning up the magazine rack after a kid had riffled it.

We worked alone together in the morning when the place was really deserted. I was on my knees counting magazines in and out. Marsha sat at the counter up front. She would read to me. Last month's magazines I was sending back were all around. I mean no one was in the store, and I would hear her read one of those short, short stories from the women's magazines. I'd lose track, counting, tune out a bit and come back on some lovers doing something then cut my palms on the paper as I slid *Scale Modeler* into its place.

"Well, what do you think will happen?" She'd stop like that, and we'd guess the ending of the story. I mean, you could guess the ending. She really loves her husband. Her kids are a joy even though they are brats. Her mother isn't going to be around much longer so she learns to be patient. They were the type of story where the baby everyone is worried about turns out to be Hitler or something. Things were always turning out. People came to realize.

I still think Marsha had a sentimental streak and liked these stories. She'd slowly page through last month's *Bride* looking at the old new dresses. I'd see her even though I was way down in the wrestling section. I'd see her bent over the two-page spread. The floor islands had little signs for the category of books. Romance SciFi. Detective Cookbook.

Western Religion. Of course, she looked like she was crying—all round-shouldered, heaving sighs. I don't know why.

"I don't know," I'd say. "She finds out the creep is really the one for her, that money isn't everything. I don't know." Turns out that the creep isn't a creep after all because he points out the good qualities in the man she was going to marry in the first place. He gets to be in their wedding.

We'd laugh as the things worked themselves out.

Have I given you a sense of how big this magazine rack was? It took most of the day twice a week to do a fourth of it. The copies came in bundles of ten or so apiece. More for the crosswords, less for *Atlantic*. Ten or fifteen bundles to the cardboard shipping case. Twelve or more cases. I filled most of them up again with returns. I'm not even counting the men's magazines, which were separate deliveries. I liked watching something catch on like jogging, say, sweeping through the stand, each group of magazines infecting the next—running with your dog, building your own locker room. Then there'd come new jogging magazines. Or houseplants. So even though there was the variety, it was really all the same stuff. What I'm trying to get at here is the predictability and the boredom of working in a place like Reader's World. There's reading and there's reading, you know. And this wasn't that kind of bookstore.

So we were sort of thrown together by circumstances. She was the only living thing around. I mean, the parking lot was empty most of the time.

When Marsha found something she really liked she'd read it to herself. That's how you could tell. We didn't make fun. She'd say, "Here, read this," and I'd have the queer feeling of having somebody watching when you're doing something else and I'd read the piece. This isn't to say our tastes were the same. It might have been a brief description of a place or a bit of conversation. What was I going to say, I didn't like it, when I'd have to say it looking right at her? She was sitting on the high stool with her feet up on the special-order shelf. She was a little bit older than me. "You really like it?" she said.

That was the summer of the pubic-hair wars. That's what they called it in business. *Penthouse* had taken out ads in the trade magazine. Saying that it was going rabbit hunting. *Playboy* had drawn a line a long time ago at breasts and behinds. Now suddenly in the packaging cases were all these new magazines. The pictures were changing, the women were being turned around slowly. On the cover of one the angle had changed. You could make out an aureole behind a hand that usually hid the breast. Marsha pointed it out to me. And then she went through the lot—*Gallery, Oui, Cavalier*—and put together a kind of hierarchy that had to do with hands and mouths and hair and the number of pictures on the page, the number of pages given over to pictures.

Marsha and I looked at the women, compared this month's design to last month's I'd just taken of the rack. The change was so slight. "Look," she said. She was serious. "Three fingers now, not two. She has pearls this time instead of flowers." It was that abstract to her. She was that removed.

The women in the pictures were all pretty enough in that way, the smooth airbrushed skin. Or the steam. "Vaseline on the lens," Marsha said. Cars and beds. I don't mean to be so objective; it was pretty amazing. It had the excitement and the caution, you know. Seeing it, so much subtlety, I pretended not to care, and I was kind of embarrassed, too, with Marsha so interested, studying the bodies. After all, she was a woman. "Put the thing away," I told her. She was unfolding one of the foldouts by the window.

"Look at that, a hand on a hip without a glove. It's so funny," she said without laughing.

What could I do but agree, go along with her calculations, her opinions? She had me on the spot. I didn't want to seem too interested. I was half-looking. I watched her study the shadows above a thigh. She turned a page and caught her breath. There were women now with and without tan lines, two women who might the next time touch each other or, beyond that, kiss. Now a clothed man, maybe, in the background instead of the car or white glider or mink. You could see which way that was going.

"Yeah, it's funny to think someone doing this, I mean, making the plans for it, winning ground, figuring it all out."

"Making this okay," she said, "or that. Getting us used to it."

So those were the wars, and I never did come up with the proper way to act. Certain lines weren't crossed, you can imagine. And those ladies who worked with us and their friends who came to visit didn't push back, didn't even notice the slight new angle to things, how it changed. How it was a whole new world.

I remember Marsha just looking at the little boys who were climbing all over the tiers of racks, the fat flat copies of the home and garden magazines, just to see the covers. She looked, and they took off through the door, and she came back to the counter where I was counting returns. "Boys," she said, laughing.

But I remember best her reading. Her voice was bright. A stack of slick magazines fanned out across the floor. I'd given up, taken a break. She used different voices for the different characters, tried an accent or started over with another more southern, less Texan. I rolled over on my back between some canons of books, looked up at some promotional mobile, and listened to the story about some boy and girl. I winced audibly at the dog part or the ice-cream part just to let her know I was listening.

"Do you want me to go on?" she called.

"Sure," I called back. I knew the ending. I just liked her voice and knowing that everything, and that included the rack I was working on, was neat and in place.

It was a bad location.

Like I said, the store was designed for big-volume business, and nothing was leaving the store. We just moved things in and took them off. Later they closed the store down, found other places that worked, but by then we were both gone. The pay wasn't much, but you could get free books. See, the commodity part, the legal tender of a book or magazine, is the front cover. That's the proof of purchase. That's what goes back to the publisher when you claim a refund. We got all the free stuff we wanted. Just ripped the front cover off, boom, and sent it back in with the returns. It counted. Usually they did the stripping down at the warehouse. The pulp was also destroyed there, because that's part of the deal.

I remember all of the women's magazines, a whole section by themselves. *Redbook, McCall's, Good Housekeeping, Journal.* They all had faces on the cover. There was printing on the chins or cheeks or foreheads. Huge faces. And I'm ripping these front covers off, tearing them one at a time so I can give Marsha the magazines, and the back covers with quilt ads and pictures of food and refrigerators are falling off the magazines since there is nothing to hold them on to anything anymore, and they're floating down into a pile at my feet. Then I put all these faces in a case, and they're all kind of the same—fresh, smiles. They look out, well, joyously, radiant. Happy.

I really don't know what to make of all of this. It was seeing Marsha again after all these years and thinking about all the things I've read since that summer. Good things. I was standing there in the middle of the mall with my hand on her middle, people all around. Marsha was going on, but I wasn't listening. I was looking at her face and trying to think of some lies to tell her about my own life. This is what came back to me.

Carbonation

"The first one out is a dum-dum round," Jerry said, holding up the bullet so that we all could see. "That assumes your first target is a man. You want to knock him down." The cylinder clicked as he turned it to the next chamber. "This one is armor-piercing. It'll go through anything." He tweezed the shell between his thumb and finger. "See the point," he pointed, "it's a different metal altogether. Teflon. We use this to stop escaping vehicles. After that is a shotgun shell, or it works the same. Then a round with an impact tip. Some use incendiary. Another flat-nosed round and then a regular round for targeting anyone that gets away. A long shot." Jerry reassembled the magnum, making sure the right chamber led into the pin. "It's what we call a scenario," he said.

Mr. Churn was in the house again because of the cars, and we could already hear him piling the cans on the front desk. Jerry came out front with us. Usually Jerry would not have been around this late or in his uniform, but because of the cars, he was staying all night. Last year someone poured a Coke on a Cord, ruining the finish, and the management had a hard time convincing the car owners to return this year.

Mr. Churn already had six or seven six-packs of Pepsi on the desk. They were made up of commemorative cans for the Auburn, Cord, Duesenberg festival.

"Hi," he said. "I made a little house." We knew he would be drunk. He asked about his wife. If she had been asking about him. We could see the way he had parked his jeep on the front lawn. "This should insure your loyalty," he said, indicating the cans. He was dressed in white to set off the tan he had obtained during a summer of sponsoring tennis tournaments. Mr. Churn was the president of RKO Bottlers. He was most of what was left of the company that had once filmed *King Kong* and *Citizen Kane.*

"We brought sound to film," he said to the clerk who was related to Tris Speaker. "In a big way." Last year with the antique cars parked for the night, Mr. Churn stumbled in joyously concluding that the Depression had returned and with it Prohibition and then handed out sixteen-ounce bottles of Pepsi like cigars.

Jerry and I were already drinking a can of this year's Pepsi as Mr. Churn finished his company's history by imitating the globe and tower trademark of RKO, twirling with his hands steepled above his head. "Tolu, tolu," he said radiating. "Surely you remember."

And then his mood changed. He told us he had yet to meet Tony Hulman, who was also staying here because of the cars. Mr. Hulman owned the Indianapolis 500, but his money came from his Coca-Cola concerns. Mr. Churn also reasoned that Mr. Hulman controlled the patent on the "hobble-skirt" bottle that had been designed in Terre Haute. "He's a great man," Mr. Churn added. Then he asked us what he should tell his wife.

We suggested that he use a meeting with Mr. Hulman as an alibi. And Mr. Churn said that he wouldn't be surprised if the old fart only drank Coca-Cola. "Besides I don't need an alkali; I need a story."

This reminded him of something else. "You know," he said, "life is only slices of life." And then he told us about the car auction and the balloon ascension his company sponsored and the picnic after the automobile parade. We were very nice and thanked him, reminding him that we slept during the day. We said that everyone seemed to have a good time here on Labor Day. "I was just recalling some antidotes for your benefit," Mr. Churn said. He then went back out to his jeep. He hit his head on the striped top, swatted at the fringe. He drove across the lawn, swerving close to Hitler's staff car. That's when Jerry thought he better go outside and take a look around.

A little bit later, a city policeman came in looking for a guest who might be driving a red, white, and blue jeep. We gave him one of the six-packs. Of course, we knew who it was. So I took the master ring and told the cop I would meet him by Mr. Churn's room. The other clerk would direct him there and see if we could find Jerry on the property. It seemed routine. Something to do with a traffic accident, I understood.

On my way back to the room, I heard the first shots. The pop. Pop. Different in degrees.

Where does a boy learn poetry but in his grandpa's house? "Coffee, Mawkey! Cream, Dream! Sugar, Buger!" The magic formula for a drink handed down from generation to generation. This family business. He drank coffee right after the meal. In a big milk-colored mug, he shredded a piece of stale bread and soaked it in the white coffee for dessert.

He told me the baby's first smile is caused by gas. There are other forms of expression left to the infant—spitting up, wetting, the dirt itself. But he remembers that smile.

In the summer my brother and I would put Grandpa's Pepsi in the front lawn and wait for it to explode. Two or three at a time. Which one would go first? We watched the crowns, the bottle, the Romanesque twist of sunlight. The shoulders shrugging. The percolation of incidents. And then the whole business. The whole brown column toppling over. How could they contain so much?

We knew nothing of pressure, temperature, the standard things at sea level. Grandpa would shake out the gas sometimes. He pressed his thumb over the bottle's mouth. He put his whole arm into it. The foam would rush to fill the space, flow up the neck and layer itself into beige chiffon. He let us drink through the gas. We realized in the first panic of inhaling that air could be tasted, that it was made up of portions of different things all unseen. Those simple things. Chemistry started there with Priestly, Boyle, and Lavoisier generating carbon dioxide from their imagination, hoping to imitate the holy sparkling water from the spas. The first applied science. Getting to the dead syrup underneath, we learned suspension and suspense in one swig.

He drank Pepsi for his health. How the man could belch. Healthy, he thought. At night on the back porch he sat and uttered a scale of decreasing volume or one sustained note, finished, and took another shot.

Once he listed all the strange flavors he had tasted. Tasted in soda pop.

Almond, Asphodel, Banana, Blood Orange, Calisaya, Catawba, Celery, Checkerberry, Coffee, Cream, Kola Champagne, Lactart, Maple, Orgeat, Pistachio, Rose, Sarsaparilla, Syrup of Violets, Walnut Cream, Wintergreen. No more description than that. "Soda" itself extinct as an ingredient except as part of the name.

The night sky was always expanding over the dying elm trees. He would whistle across the mouth of the empty bottle. The standard things. The one-note symphony. He would scrape the cork liner from the inside of the bottle cap.

Come on, come on. You're the Pepsi generation.

Come on, come on. Join the celebration.

Let him dissolve into this or that commercial. It seems all right for a minute. The things we contain. Snatches of songs, traces of extracts, elixirs, essences. Fusillade. Fizz. The redoubt. The delaying action. The skirmishes of half-life. The bubbles bursting in air.

"This is our life," one of the workers said, "all of us now have to work part-time jobs and then picket just to live." Three of them were sitting up on a raised platform talking to a large crowd of students. "You know that their largest customer is this university." The drivers' strike had been going on for two years now, and this was another attempt by the union to generate a boycott of Coca-Cola on campus. "Coke is a good product. I wouldn't drive for anybody else, but look what this has done to my family."

Some of the audience, even those who might have been sympathetic to the union position, sipped from the red paper cups or used empty Coke cans as ashtrays. They listened to the familiar history of walkouts, scabs, lockouts, union-busting, arbitration, harassment, suits. The conspiracy involving the Teamsters International and Coca-Cola was mentioned. Incidents of syrup trucks crossing picket lines were substantiated. It was then revealed that the university allowed the company's trucks the use of the football stadium in the off-season as means of protection from vandalism. A university official answered that the company paid rent.

One or two of the drivers wore their pin-stripe uniforms. "How can you drink that stuff?" one of them asked. "It's poison."

"It's good," someone answered from the room, meaning, I think, to be satiric. But it might have been delivered in all honesty. And the drivers left. All that remained was one to read a statement issued by the bottler, who would not come to the meeting. "In fear," he wrote, "of my life."

The strike lasted two more years. A man was shot at the football stadium.

The empty can rolled back and forth on the floor of the cab. Sometimes it would stick under the front seat when we stopped and roll back out when we stared up again. This was our first trip to the city, and we were sharing the cab with a man who had been on our airplane. He worked for the Pepsi-Cola Company, Purchase, New York, and had met Joan Crawford.

We expressed to him our fears about the safety of the city, and he assured us that in all of his travels he never felt more at home than when he was here in the city. He said that he traveled for his company and that it was his profession to ask for a Coke in establishments having an exclusive agreement with Pepsi-Cola. We could not contain our surprise that there actually were such people. We remarked that we had better watch what we say, and in his turn he related many interesting anecdotes in a matter-of-fact tone, including an incident in Paris, which he recounted in French. He was present at the dedication of the first bottling plant in the Soviet Union, where, he also told us, there is a longer line for a Coke than there is to view Lenin. "But most of my work centers around local fountains such as those." He pointed to the passing storefronts. "You would be surprised how many times I am not corrected. My company is willing to spend millions of dollars to prevent our name from slipping into lowercase." He laughed.

He suggested that we visit the Coca-Cola Museum in Atlanta, which contains the most extensive collection of proprietary bottles in the world. He traced the history of the carbonated-drink industry in America.

"I like to cite Justice Holmes." And he did. We wrote it down. It was in the case of the Coca-Cola Company versus Koke Company of America in the U.S. Supreme Court, 1921. "I find in it legitimacy," Justice Holmes, holding for Coke, wrote: "The name now characterizes a beverage to be had at almost any soda fountain. It means a single thing coming from a single source and well-known to the community. It hardly would be too much to say that the drink characterizes the name as much as the name the drink." "Italics mine," he said, but we noticed none. "You can see the ramifications?" We nodded. What could we say?

In the city proper the only things our friend would say came after we passed the Candler Building with all its billboards. "Pop contributed greatly to education. Both Tufts and Emory were founded on such fortunes. Both with medical schools demonstrating the close connection of the industry with public health. The industry's contribution to advertising is unquestioned."

When we reached our hotel he leaned over and asked, "At least you found these things interesting?"

"At the very least," we answered. I tell you it was something to run into a man who you never thought existed and have a chance to talk to him. He *was* very interesting to say the least and a wonderful introduction to what we thought was an unfriendly city.

What I think is funny is that later, when we were robbed, all that crossed my mind was that the revolver was a cola color.

One note. It begins with that and usually, out of habit, leads to another culminating in a crowd of people. Places. Things. A party. Party music.

Voices over. Or. A man alone, unconscious of any consensus doing the things he wants to do. That kind of man. By his very indifference he is chosen to lead us to drink. Culminating in consensus. The campaign. Hi-C.

He is aware, as an artist, that there are certain internal forms that one invokes to give the world some sense. This one note, the jingle writer thinks, it's the thing that satisfies best. The real thing. The Coca-Cola Company of Atlanta, his client, has just recently purchased, lock, stock, and barrel, Hi-C.

There is nowhere else to begin but on that note. It is natural. This private opening into composition.

And what follows naturally is the sixty seconds. The sixty-second notes or nearest fraction thereof. The sixty other things that convince us consuming is communal. Even when alone. The bottle. The can. The glass. Compare. Contents. Condensation always. In the air gas infused (that is the technical term) in liquid. States confused. The Calvin scale. It is a song everyone can sing. The beat of the swallow. The taste that beats the others cold. Associations. The fizz itself. The guttural pour. The splash. The crack of ice. The bubbles rising again. The name itself. Let it speak. Pop.

Empty whole notes rising to the occasion. Every good boy deserves fudge. Favors. Does fine. This satisfies. Does everyone follow. Scene. A Midwestern festival. Balloons rising. Interest in old machinery. Thresher? Combine. A way to introduce former slogans. The pause that refreshes. Longings. 1929. Candler dies. The serving trays. People laughing at how they used to look. Scene. Returning empty bottles. Boys. A wagon. A dog keeps time. Balloons rising. Satisfaction. Money back. Earned refreshment tastes better. Scene. Workers themselves happily working. Perspiration. Condensation. Much better. Skeleton of high rise. Balloons rising. Hard hats. Bottle caps. Eye-catching sandwiches. Scene. A ride in the park. Handsome hansoms. Central Park singing. The buildings rising. Balloons rising. Someone tips his hat. Bottle cap. Dissolve. Scene. A boy and his grandfather. Someone old at least. A generation. Two generations. Chord change. Can there be a sprinkler? A falling star? Balloons rising. Someone winks. The child cries. Grandpa burps. No. Scene. A man in a room at the piano. Wood floor. Sheet music. The bottle. The people. Where are the people? Balloons rising? He has finished the song they are singing. He is writing the song they have been singing. He is writing the song they have already sung. He is improvising. He is fooling around. Chopsticks. Someone sends out for Chinese. Pizza. Hamburgers. Eye-catching sandwiches. Someone burps. No.

He is stuck.

He remembers something that he read once. Written before his time.
Pepsi-Cola hits the spot.
Twelve full ounces, that's a lot.
That's better. Pause. Rest. Swig of Coke. Wash of Coke. Splash of
Coke. Inspiration. Dead. The empty bottle. The thing itself. Drawing to
it. Meaning. The universe. Space. That's catchy, but it's not filling. All the
good things. What do you want? To be done. It is, after all, a soft drink.
Perhaps a melody that lingers. An aftertaste? Is that desired? The money.
The sound of it.
Coke adds life.
Everybody wants a little life.
Coke adds life.
Everybody wants.
Let the bottle say the rest. The goods speak for themselves. Voices
over. Balloons rising. Comic afterthoughts.
A man at a window looking out across the roofs. The measure of an
automatic clip emptying. The answering rounds closer. Single shots.
Aimed.

What did we need money for? We would spend at least part of every
summer day at the drugstore. The chocolate candy would have been
replaced by the less perishable hard rock candy, Life Savers, Dum-Dum
suckers, Pez in cartoon shooters, or those paraffin disguises—huge red
lips with teeth. There were sculptured wax bottles filled with colored
sugar water. To get at it you just had to bite right through the neck.
Sometimes we would just get a flavored Coke or a phosphate in Dixie
cups with the hearts or the larger cup that said HUM DINGER. Or snow
cones, anything that would change the color of our mouths.
We got our money by returning empties. We would even take the one
that Grandma had used to dampen clothes with when she ironed. We
took out the special spigot she used and spirited away the pop bottle.
"Rats in the pantry," she would call after us. We would leave her bubble
gum from the baseball cards as an offering, knowing all the time that we
would not only have the money from the deposit but the soda from the
new bottle she would have to buy.
We would find empty bottles everywhere. Take the one Grandpa used
when he weeded the lawn, still some killer in the bottom. We loaded up
our wagons with mixed cartons of Coca-Cola and Pepsi, 7–Up, Hires,
Nehi, Nesbitt's, Dr. Pepper, RC and Orange Crush. We went to the
supermarket because they would take every brand.

One day we found a dead man in the bottle bin at the supermarket. One of the old men who worked there in semiretirement. He was just draped over the side of the cart. His hands hung down and opened by the empty bottles. His face was blue. It looked like he was just arranging something at the bottom of the bin. We were close enough to tell. My brother peered over the edge of the bin. I unloaded the wagons. All the other people in the store went on working, ringing out sales, giving stamps, sacking. He wouldn't come to life. So we just left. Left the bottles. We saw him through the windows, his back humped over. On the way home we kept looking over our shoulders. Surrounded by all those signs of death, all I remember my brother saying was, "Where is the blood?"

March of Dimes

As we walk to the next house, I tell my son to hold up. The back of his coat is folded up from sitting. It looks like a little tail. Beneath his coat I can see where his white shirt has come un-tucked. It glows raggedly against the seat of his pants. "Stand up straight." He does. He's all bundled up. His arms, in the quilted sleeves, seem to float at his sides. His hood is up and clinched around his face glowing like his shirt. His face is pale and smooth in the light so you want to touch it. In the corners of his mouth, I know there are those little smile lines made by the Dixie cup of grape Kool-Aid at the last house. "Wipe your mouth." I put the envelope and clipboard down on the ground by his feet as I kneel in front of him. Reaching around behind, I work my thumbs into the back of his elastic breeches, tucking as I go, then a quick zip around each half of the trunk of his body. "There." I yank down at the hem of his coat with both hands. The hood tightens around his head. He hops a little after each yank as if he were a compressed spring released. His arms seem only connected to his body by the sleeves of his coat. I tuck some hair back up inside his hood and touch his face.

I pick up my things and stand up. We start walking again to the next house. There are not many lights on in the houses on the block. All downstairs. The blue light of TVs or fish tanks. Cars pass rarely on the cross street up ahead. I can hear the corduroy switch of his trousers as he walks next to me. My husband thinks I bring our son along as some type of illustration. An example of good health. A general reminder.

The moon is full and in the trees. I exaggerate the swinging of my arms so that I can feel the coins slide back and forth in the envelope. Some stick in the tight corners. I can feel the face of one through the paper. My writing on the envelope is distorted by the coins beneath the surface. I can rub the pencil back and forth using the long part of the lead and make the face appear.

The next house has an enclosed porch. I can hear the slap of his oxfords on the cement walk. The jingle of coins. I never know what to do when I come to a house with an enclosed porch. I've pounded so hard the screen rattled. And I have crept into the porch with its shadows of summer furniture or old sofas, the bikes and rag rugs and tapped on the inside door. When I first hear the conversation stop or when they are just silent differently, I know they have heard something. And then I tap again until I feel their footsteps coming to the door through my own feet. I try to be but never am ready for when the door swings open and I am discovered in the half-light. I find myself in some half-room of their house. "The Mother's March," I say.

This house has a doorbell outside, and my son wants to ring it. The doorbell is lit, a little dime-sized moon. I lift him up, and when he pokes the button, the light goes off. In the house, we hear the bells, three of them, the silence and then someone coming. The doorbell light pulses on again after he lets up. "Pick up the paper so you can hand it to the lady." The porch light comes on. The inside door opens, then the storm, and then a Mrs. James Payne pads across the porch. We can see her through the porch storm. She still can't see us because the glass of the storm reflects the light inside back toward her. The overlapping louvers on the storm slowly open as she cranks them. We are watching her be cautious.

"Who's there?"

"The Mother's March," I say.

"Come in. Come in."

In a way, my husband is right. My son sits in another chair, holding a glass of something else which he supports with both hands. He never takes the glass from his lips. Tips it a bit more now and then. He swings his legs, looks around the room over the rim of the glass. The woman whose house we are in is reading through the brochures, tsking over the children with braces. Those children have brilliant smiles. She steals a glance at my son, who has focused his attention on an array of porcelain thimbles next to him on the table. I know it is a matter of touching and not touching. The newspaper, still folded, is beneath his swinging feet. She is going to get her purse, more soda.

I am unspooling that endless twine from the two red paper buttons on the back of the envelope. I have been opening and closing the envelope flap all night, and each time I do it, I wrap the string around in a different pattern. This is my first winter collecting for the March of Dimes. I am halfway through the names and addresses. My map is spotty with "at homes" and "aways." Many people still talk about Roosevelt. It is an older neighborhood. Few children. These women make me lonely with their grown-up children framed on the coffee table. My husband is only half-right. "Don't touch." I tell my son.

I wish I was able to repeat the thing my son says in the way he says them. But I can never find the words. Precious, you know, cute. But any time mothers repeat the words of their children, it never sounds quite right. It is always the parent talking. Still, children mimic their mothers and dads, I know. That is what makes them cute. Or maybe it is both ways. In any case, my husband is right about some of the uses for children. My son keeps me company between the houses even though we are silent. "Let Mommy talk," I say to him as he pushes past the neighbor holding the screen door open. He finds his own chair. Let Mommy talk, indeed. See how the words change when we use them.

It is eight o'clock and, even though we are not tired, we turn for home. The pamphlet that comes with the soliciting kit suggests this. We are walking again. He hasn't asked me to carry him. In his neighborhood the streetlights are the old candy-cane type, globes suspended over the street, the top hemisphere blackened still from the war. The vaccine's already found. My baby is already born and walking. Perfect. All his toes and fingers. He started talking early. Perfect. I am collecting for this, for him. For the time when I didn't know yet. It should be more than that. I tell him about polio and the summers his grandmother wouldn't let me swim. How, when I was his age, I was never allowed to be cold. I think quickly to ask if he is cold now. He isn't. As he switches and slaps in the dark next to me, he chants *polio* again and again. It will be his word for awhile. He'll repeat it when he is thinking to himself, as he did with the word *sum.*

When we get home, my husband is mixing blood in the kitchen. He is a safety director for the local phone company. He investigates accidents when company cars or trucks are involved and writes up the police reports in the passive voice. On the dashboards of the mangled vehicles, he has already stuck decals about backing and looking both ways. He lectures to lineman and switchmen on artificial respiration, electrocution, and shock. The blood is for some first-aid simulation he does. In the trunk of his car, there is a kit filled with realistic rubber casts of burns and fractures. He fills a special bladder with the blood. He wears it strapped beneath a beat-up shirt. Hoses are taped to his body and along his arm. He squeezes a rubber ball from an atomizer to pump the blood to a severed artery at his wrist or knee. I have seen him die a couple of times when rookie framemen applied the wrong kind of direct pressure or put the tourniquet below the wound. In times of emergencies people just yell, "Don't move him. Don't move him." He bleeds to death.

He is sprinkling an old shirt with blood, using the 7–Up bottle and the plastic spray spigot I use to dampen clothes I'm ironing.

"How did it go?" he asks, gore to the elbows.

Odd. He is the type who gets queasy at things like that, leaves the room when I do my nails because of the ether smell, turns off hospital shows. He lets me dig for splinters, pop blisters. At the doctor's, he faints when his reflexes are tested. He stumbles out of the office, sicker than ever before. As I fill the prescription he sits on the little couch with his head between his knees. He cannot stomach listening to people tell of their operations or having their hands closed in doors or even losing toenails. At night in bed, he will toss for hours, cannot sleep, if he hears his own heart beating in his ears.

"I was the one they watched in driver's education class when they showed the films," he told me. I think it is the words that bother him most of all. *Laceration* for *cut*. The slow accumulation of the sounds.

His hands are red and he squeezes me on both my arms with the inside of his.

"What did the little one bring in?" he asks.

"He's counting it now," I tell him. "We're halfway through. We'll go out again tomorrow."

He turns back to an old bowling shirt, *Tony* on the pocket. "Like an organ grinder's monkey."

I'm used to it. You get used to it.

I tip my finger in his blood, touch him lightly on the forehead, square on his football scar.

"Hey," he says.

He can't do anything about it now. His arms raised at the elbows. He looks like a surgeon with gloves on.

Our son has been counting and stacking the coins. He gets to keep all the pennies. He stores his pennies in an Old Grandad bottle his father says he came out of.

"How did we do?" I ask him.

I think he thinks it is somewhat like Hallowe'en but grown-up, without the candy, and he seems to arrange the coins like candy about him except there is less of it. He freezes most of the candy bars he gets for trick-or-treating and eats the chocolate coins wrapped in gold tin foil right away. He tells me $27.70. He has thirty-six pennies for his bottle.

"Aren't you tired?" I ask him. I'm tired. Without my glasses, the stacks of coins seem to be sprouting from the carpet, silver stocks. It has been a sheepish March. Nice during the day, chilly at night. It is supposed to snow a bit tomorrow. He has gone to get the plastic sherbet tub we keep the money in. I can hear him making faces at his father's mess and then giggles and splashes. Of course, he will come out and try and touch me with sticky hands. I am already halfway up the stairs when he reaches the bottom, hands out and clawing. Maybe when he grows up he won't be like his father that way. Used to it. He took his boosters okay as long as I was there, and he squirted the neighborhood kids with the syringe the doctor gave him. His father could not look at the Tb test on his son's arm and made him wear long sleeves in early fall. Maybe blood will never be real to him.

"Come here, you monster," I drag him by the elbows into the bathroom and wash it off into the sink. I strip him to his underwear. He is brushing his teeth, back and forth, not up and down. He stands there, using every muscle he has in his body to keep his head perfectly still. His hand saws away. I notice the button of his vaccine. It seems to be the head of the pin holding his arm on. Still, in relief, pinker than his skin, still round. The center of a black-eyed Susan. I remember when the scab fell off. We were so careful not to touch it before it did.

He pees for a long time because of all the soda and Kool-Aid. As he does he whispers something to himself.

Tucked in bed, he tells me the name of each face on the coins, wonders why Lincoln is facing the wrong way and Roosevelt's neck is too short. He says he likes going into other peoples houses and can't wait until we go out again tomorrow.

"I couldn't do it without you. You're a good helper," and catch myself from going on in this way, talking like other mothers talk. *Mommy's little helper.* Why do I want to talk this way? "I'll see you tomorrow. We'll go out again."

Downstairs, my husband is done with blood and has washed his hands. He has forgotten where I've touched him. I can still see the edges of the print beneath the fringe of hair. He is at work now, diagramming accidents on graph paper with colored pencils. Sometimes he scoots tokens from board games across the grid to give him a better feel for what happened. He goes over and over the accident, concludes, finally, it was following distance or overdriving headlights.

"You have to get the big picture," he tells me. "Drive defensively. Leave yourself an out." When he drives in his own car, he mutters at other drivers, becomes furious at old women in crosswalks. I watch him from my side of the seat as he thinks about his job. I say nothing, find my right foot pressing the floor, try not to move so he won't say, "What you jumping for? We're okay. We're okay."

My son's miscounted. $28.35. I throw in my husband's lose change. I fill in the reports. The poster child is thanking me. It looks as if she has climbed the long ladder of printed lines that scale the left margin of the page—staff, directors, honorary chairmen—to her perch in the upper corner. Roosevelt looks at her across the top of the page, through *Liberty*, chin up, haircut, without his glasses too. The date on the coin is the year of my son's birth. I dump the coins in the sherbet tub. They arrange themselves the way coins do, scalloped or scaled, deepening in sound as they deepen in the tub. The poster child has braces and metal crutches, the tops of which are strapped to her forearm. She leans out from the paper. What would she say? I draw a cartoon coming from her mouth. *Polio. Polio.* Not, *Won't you help me? Sometimes, I am weary of courage.* But a child would not talk that way.

My husband heads by me, up to bed. He runs his fingers across my shoulder as he goes.

"I'll be right there." I plan my route for the next night, sharing the streets with paperboys collecting, Girl Scouts and cookies, cars driving down the side streets with their brights on. People can't guess who is at their doors.

I look in at my son's room. I wait in the doorway until my eyes adjust. The moon is high now and in the window. The linoleum has an egg-speckled pattern on dark brown. We ironed it to the floor ourselves. I can only hear one-half of his breathing—breathing in—so it sounds as if he is making a higher-pitched sound each time he does. I see his head on its side, a shoulder and arm emerging. He looks like my coin rubbings, soft and out of focus. The light picks up something on his finger. A Band-Aid? I go over and kneel down beside him. It is a porcelain thimble. Bathroom-sink white. There is a bundle of violets painted on the collar. The little pockmarks of the tip have their own shadows, each a phase of the moon in the moonlight.

I ease it off his finger and put it on mine. I don't like the way it feels. Touching but not touching. The way being touched someplace is never the same as touching the place yourself. But touching the head of the thimble itself, its curve, its roughness is pleasing. It almost feels grainy as if instead of scoops there are spheres dotting the tip. What would it feel like if I didn't know what it was? Its opposite? The ridges of a finger?

I slip it back on one of his fingers. A different finger. Will that make him think in the morning? Wonder how it got there. His fingers walk. His thimble goes from house to house.

I am about to wake my husband and tell him, but I don't. I don't know what I would tell him. We all have our own lives in this house, and these two do not meet here. He is dreaming of game-board tokens making wrong turns, graphs of fatalities. Accidents. He wasn't drunk that night. I wasn't drunk that night. The only difference was our son, no accident. He took.

My husband's back is toward me. He has slept through the noise of his heart. I can barely see his vaccine, dimpled in his arm. A print. A daylight moon. I touch it as I fit in behind him.

About the time I became pregnant, we took the oral vaccine in the national program at the junior high. It was a Sunday, and the halls were filled with well-dressed neighbors lined against the lockers leading toward the girls' gym. We would take a couple of steps then stop. He would fiddle with the nearest locker. I read the brochures, sometimes reading parts aloud to him. The hall was close and warm. The ceiling was low. "No shots," I told him, "just sugar."

Down the ramp and into the gym. We stopped to sign our names. The hallway opened up to two stories. The sun slanted through windows with metal screens to protect them from the balls. It gave the sunshine in the gym a mottled look. The floor was linoleum. The boys' gym was wood. A doctor and several nurses handed out the sugar cubes. The way they were bricked together made them look like a junior high school project of the walls of Troy.

"Do you have some water?" my husband asked.

"You don't swallow it. Suck on it. It's just sugar."

"I'd like some water," he said.

"In the hall. Outside."

The sugar tasted sweet, of course. My teeth rang when I bit into the cube. My mouth was sticky. My husband could barely get his down. We were out by the line again, by a drinking fountain much too low for him.

"Oh, c'mon. It's not that bad," I said.

"Yeah?" he said. "I just don't like sweet things. Okay? Okay?"

People in line looked at us. Crouching, he drank with his eyes open, his face as white as the fountain. We stay on the steps outside for a long while.

Sweet thing, I am used to it. I have lived with it long enough.

There is only a powder of snow. We are marching through the neighborhood. It seems that everyone is expecting something. The porch lights are all on. This is what charity should be. Door-to-door. Face-to-face. I do not like the loose change in checkout lanes with the plastic hourglasses or the cardboard sheets with penny-loafer slots and fading football players. I'm a mother, too, not a movie star. This is my son.

The moon is full again but starting to melt. Its light looks good on the snow, white with streaks of yellow from the porches. He reads the house numbers and tries to guess the next one. Our envelope is heavy. The coins knife back and forth.

At a corner, before we cross, I ask him about the thimble. I smile to myself as his eyes widen. I know they widen even though I cannot see them. What can he say? Has he even been able to explain it to himself? He says nothing, repeats something to himself. I suggest we return it to the lady, and he agrees. Tomorrow. Yes, tomorrow. He needs it one more night. He can show it to me, now, himself.

On the bank of our yard, the one my husband hates to mow in the summer, we make very poor snow angels. The money jingles as I make the wings. There isn't enough snow here. We lie back down. The bank is steep. We are not far from standing, more like leaning backward. We blow our breath away into the night. I tell him the moon is dime-sized, no bigger. And he doesn't believe me. It is hanging there at least half-dollar size. It is the moon, after all. I sit up and unravel the flap of my envelope, reach in and feel for a dime. I find one. I tell him to hold it at arm's length and close one eye. "Put it over the moon." And he does.

Tomorrow we will go out again, collecting.

X-ray

Here, when he opened the door, the children began performing tricks, little things with their hands and finger he never understood or couldn't see in the folds of the sheets. They struck poses, mumbled songs, turned flashlights off and on, shining the light up through the plastic masks. They blurted out riddles, *Why did the moron throw a clock out the window?* When he answered, they yelled. *No*, he wasn't supposed to answer. It was their trick. The bags of candy were piled like rocks in the corner of his porch. One tall girl did flips out in the yard, out into the darkness. "Look," he said, "you don't need to do this. You don't need. That's not what a trick is."

He looked down at them. They were panting, trying to see.

"Look," he said, "it means the other trick. Something bad if I don't give you a treat, you see? Something like that. Like soap. It's a threat. I'm supposed to be scared of you. The way you look. You're scary."

He was aware of adults waiting off on the sidewalk, the air leaving his house. The tall girl in the back went up on her toes.

"Here," he said. "Here and here you go." And they thanked him.

His father could blow bubbles with his spit. He remembered watching his father. The mouth was closed but the lips working, the throat moving, inhaling air through his nose. And when he rounded his lips, he had very thin lips and the lips were wet, the tip of his tongue came out, just the tip, for a second and then the clear bubble, not like soap, heavy and clear, the size of a BB. Two or three at a time. It was the most delicate thing he remembered his father doing, the way he lifted his chin.

He could never do that. He tried. He could scoop a bubble up from behind his lower teeth and rest it on his tongue. He could do that right now. But when he moved his mouth, puckered his lips, the bubble broke.

He heard it break through the bones in his head. It sounded like his jaw cracking hollow, wooden.

When he was a boy, he always said he was double-jointed when he needed to say something like that. His friends were sitting around him belching and farting.

"Watch this," he said and dug the heel of his hand into the ground next to where he was sitting. He screwed his arm back and forth from the wrist. It wasn't much of a trick. Everyone who saw it tried it, but no one could twist the forearm, the elbow like he did without picking up a hand. He didn't know why.

He didn't know about this either. These tricks. It was more a performance, role memory. Or something made up on the spot. Everything was quickly rehearsed, even the tumbling, nothing emanating from the boredom of the long afternoons here.

There was a cicada hatch this summer. Not a big one, but the sawing was noticeable at dusk when he walked the empty streets. And downtown he saw several stunned adult insects, their wings stretched out, on the ledges of the big store windows they had hit. He had collected a large mayonnaise jar—he had emptied the mayonnaise into the bathtub—full of the golden shells he picked off the tree trunks and brick houses, the concrete light poles, the snow fences.

He liked the angle of the front legs. Now there was an insect. The broad forehead between the polished eyes, the stubby body and filmy wings. The scale, too, was right. There was a real bit of terror, a heft, when one flew by slowly, cigar butts. Dangerous. Not like the insect-sized insects—flies, bees, gnats.

No one else seemed to be gathering the shells. And now that he thought about it, the children had surprised him again. He almost worked up enough courage to invite in the next group knocking at his door and show them the jar of shells, the perfect slit down the backs. And, maybe, give some away in the light of his house, in the bags of candy. What would the parents say then? *Do you remember? Do you remember who gave you this?*

Answering the door again, he realized that he'd been here long enough now to have seen some of these children in their mother's wombs. This little one wearing a mask, the shell of a princess, her mother might have said, *It's only sound, you say.* They stared as the Polaroid developed. The thing took its shape in light, tracing a contour map, a wash on dark wax scraped with a pin. So this is how it turned out he thought to say. The princess was choking on a nursery rhyme that had to do with gardens, and the mother had asked him if everything is there where it's supposed to be.

Yes, that's the head there. There are they eyes. *It's amazing,* she said, *amazing. Can I keep this?*

By now he'd seen hundreds of the unborn children and now here they were at his door doing tricks, snapping their fingers, no longer frightening at all.

He washed his hands after handling the shells and watched television while he waited for the door to knock again. He ranged over the remote panel, his finger like a chess knight. Later, he would go to the clinic to check the candy.

As a boy, he had set a bag of dog crap on fire. He rang the doorbell and ran off the porch and around the house to the back. He could hear someone in front stomping out the flames, cursing, yelling. He was at the back door ringing the doorbell there until he heard the front door slam. Then he took off through the backyard bushes, down the cinder alley. He pictured a man tramping through the house, racing to the back door, mad, unthinking, shoes all caked, ruined. And his own heart was pounding as he ran by the open garages and ashcans. Dogs barked everywhere. He thought of it again and realized that what he saw as he ran was the inside of his own family home, the living room and the furniture, since he didn't know, couldn't imagine what the inside of his victim's home was like. He saw this stranger stumbling and raging through his kitchen as he ran toward his house. It was thrilling, an intruder there and a smelly fire on a porch someplace behind him.

When had the cicada stopped singing? The bugs in the halo of the street lamp, when had they gone? Now only the hum of the excited, inert gases. And the year of the hatching—eleven, thirteen, seventeen—why were they prime numbers? An X-ray of an insect would look like the insect. If we carried our bones outside, he'd be out of a job.

He could walk to the clinic from his house, and he did. When cars sped by, he heard syllables over the snatch of radio music. It always sounded as if they were yelling at him. It always surprised him. He though of things to yell back only after the car was long gone. He wished them accidents, wished to see them later, crumbled on his table, through the lead-lined window.

Now, as he walked through town, there were still children in the shadows, their shapes distorted by their costumes. Something round huddled near a bicycle, working the combination lock. Some cubes jumped the borders between yards hurrying to the next house before the curfew and the porch lights going out. Sneakers slapped once, twice on the cement walks then were swallowed by the lawns. The dark heads, the candy bags, swung by the hair. He heard around him the little songs, the tails of sentences rising to questions, small bursts of applauses, choruses of *thank yous.*

Children charged around him, the masks pushed up like ancient Greek helmets. Sucker sticks poked out of mouths. The children ran to the next house. The three hours almost gone. From far behind him, the voice. *What do you say?* And they shrieked, *Excuse me.*

Be careful, the voice came up through its murmuring. He didn't look around. *Be careful. Don't run with those things in your mouth.* A hiss, a scuff on the walk.

He had heard of an exhibit at a museum in the capital. It was a collection of objects people had swallowed, inhaled, and then had been removed and donated to the state. Class trips always stopped there, outside a field of yellow buses. The doctors he worked with told him about it. Pennies, paper clips, nails, tacks, keys, rings, all kinds of pins—bobby, hat, safety—marbles, thimbles, bullets. He had found some of those same things in people, the dark-edged shapes in the white clouds of flesh and the ropey smoke of bone. Nuts and bolts. He could count the threads. Read the time on the watch, see the guts behind the face, the teeth working. He saw the white faces of the schoolchildren on tour as they peered into the glass cases. These things were inside of people. Metal parts. They caught their breath. They swallowed without chewing. He had seen patients trying to see through their own skins. Saw them try not to. There is an outside and an inside.

He felt as if he had just shown up here in this town, appeared out of the air. The welcome wagon had given him coupons redeemable for things that could be dangerous—rulers with metal edges, cake cutters, tiny measuring spoons. The houses of the town started where the fields of corn left off. The highway became a street. The town grew by parking lots and blocks of houses. The windows of the houses were blue with televisions; the porch lights were out. As he went by each house, he saw, inside parts of bodies. In the windows were eclipsed heads, feet on tables. There was a wedge of shoulder, a leg flashing. He saw shadows on shades and curtain rustled. And once again, he imagined only the house he grew up in and these strangers moving around inside.

He made his way through the big crowd at the clinic up to the door. He recognized a few of the doctors with their children, the faces of people who worked downtown in stores and waited tables. All of the women looked familiar. Their children faced him, too, wormed up against their mothers' thighs. The children wore satiny clothes, smooth as if from rubbing. They clutched at the arms draped over their shoulders, pressed back. *Don't be shy. He's not going to hurt you.*

"Now folks," he said, "it'll take a bit to set up the machine." And he fumbled with his keys. A baby was crying. He could hear the paper contents of the paper bags as they were shook. The dry paper. A hand being smacked. The fluoroscope was inside the door. He took off his jacket and turned on the power.

"Folks," he said, "I've got to let the machine warm up a bit." There were cartoon characters and character types. Animals and plants. All the professions, religions, crafts. Ghosts, crooks, skeletons. Skeletons.

"How do you want to do this now? I guess you could just line up here." People moved a bit, formed lines. "I should tell you that the radiation won't harm the candy or fruit. The . . . ," he couldn't think of the word, "rays go right through the . . . and then it depends on the density of the things it goes through and the different thicknesses. The rays then hit the screen and excite things in the screen. Like your television and it lights up. That's what we'll see. Some things will be darker than others." They were all listening, turned his way. There was a vague sort of order.

"As I said, this procedure won't harm the contents of the wrapper. We'll just see if anyone has, you know. It's faster."

The machine was old and boxy. The door of the clinic wouldn't stay open. It was only recently that he understood that the stars moved at night. To watch time fly.

"And I liked all of the tricks this year. Didn't you?"

There was scattered applause and some children cheered. A girl shook her hands together over her head like a champion.

"Where I come from we didn't do tricks like those. Nice ones. We did other tricks. They weren't very good. The words we said, we meant something different. It was just the other way around." He thought then he should be quiet. "Just a few more minutes." He looked out at the crowd. Parents talked to one another again. Children were falling asleep at their feet. He looked down.

He ordered the X-ray gogs from the back of the comic book. The rubber frames had lenses of paper printed with black and white whirlpools. A hole had been cut in the eye of the storm. There, there were transparent red pieces of plastic and sandwiched inside was something that looked like a fish skeleton but turned out to be, when he tore the whole thing apart, a feather.

If you held your hand up to the light and looked through the filters, you did see something—an aura around your hand, a crazy double image. It might be bones. The instructions said to convince your friends by letting them look at their own hands. And then you were supposed to look at a pretty girl slowly, up and down, while making appreciative sounds. You'll cause a riot, it said on the package. Everyone will want to look. He just saw the red girl, the deeper shadow. He had been afraid he would be able to see her bones, afraid that his vision would go through her clothes right through her skin. Not very pretty at all.

And the pregnant women sat on this table. Their bellies splitting open their clothes, the skin almost polished clear. "It's only sound," he said. "You won't even hear it. It's harmless, harmless."

The candy disappeared behind the screen. Sometimes the metal foil would show up, the sticks without the taffy. There, the stem and wilted leaf of an apple. Its seeds scattered on the table. There, the hook of a cashew.

He though of each piece of candy as a house he wanted to see into. He wanted to find some after-image left over, a floor plan or blueprint from being in its bowl by the door as if each square of the chocolate bar was a photographic plate. He wanted to know how furniture was arranged, where the light switches were, how people talked to each other when they were alone.

The children took off their costumes while they watched him. "Where did it go?"

"It's still there," he told them. He watched the screen. Mothers look relieved and thanked him. And they left dragging their children, who were thanking him and doing tricks and eating the clean candy, behind them.

Later he did find a blade from a cheap pencil sharpener embedded in an orange marshmallow peanut.

"Here's something," he said.

The child cried after not remembering which house it came from. The mother called back at him over her shoulder while pulling the child away. "It's your fault. You brought this on. No one would have dared do this. But they knew the stuff would be checked. They knew it would be X-rayed. They knew you would find it."

The Safety Patrol

If you look on page 253 of the New College Edition of *The American Heritage Dictionary,* there, in the right margin toward the bottom of the page, you will find an aerial photograph of a cloverleaf interchange at Fort Wayne, Indiana.

Of the six cloverleaf interchanges in Fort Wayne, I am reasonably sure I know which one this is. It is not my favorite. That one is down the road. There, there was a small country cemetery right were the new interstate was going to go. I was on the citizens' committee that saved the place. You can still see it buried beneath the loops and ramps as they detour, twisted out of the way like a spring sprung. On some Sundays, I drive out there, drive around the place, entering and exiting. The interchange spreads for miles. I catch glimpses of the headstones—they're old, from before the Civil War—the patch of prairie grass and wild flowers, the picket fence. It is in the middle of the storm of concrete and cars. Saved. But there is no way to drive to it. All access limited, the site undisturbed. Like clouds, the shadows of trucks sale over the pots, change the color of the stones.

The cloverleaf pictured in the dictionary is a perfect specimen. There has been no finagling with the curving lobes of the ramp as they coil from one dual lane to the other. If you look closely you can see snow in the ditch defining the mathematical berms, shading the grade, giving it depth and perspective. A beautiful picture, one the children are proud of.

When we do dictionary drills I include the word *cloverleaf* as a kind of Crackerjack prize for the students. They cut into the big book as I've taught them, into the first third. Some feel comfortable using the finger tabs scooped out along the edge. They turn chunks of pages, getting close, getting to *C.* They peel each page back, then read the index words for *close call* and *clown,* saying the alphabet for each letter. And then, one by one, they arrive at the right page. Fingers go up and down columns. One or two gasp, then giggle. They point and whisper. They say things like "Wow." They can't wait to tell me what they've found.

The cloverleaf is there with pictures of a clothes tree, a clown licking an ice-cream cone, a clover—the plant and its buds—the cloister of San Marco in Florence, Italy, an earthworm with a clitellum, and the clipper ship *Lightning.* The pictures seem to make the words they represent more important.

The lights on the television and radio towers are always on, even during the day, when you can barely see the flush of the red lights. The newer towers have bright strobing lights, too. You see sharp simultaneous explosions all along the edges. There are revolving lights at the very tip. Guy wires angle down so taut as to vibrate the heavy air around the towers. There are a dozen at least now, and more going up. The neighborhood is zoned for towers.

I like to play games while I look at the towers. Which one is taller? Which is furthest away? Coming up State Street on my way to teach, I watch the towers as I drive. They are solid lines, the lights slowly coming into synchronization. I am waiting for a red light, watching over the cars ahead of me down the road. Each tower is beating its own red pulse. Two or three pulse together a time or two. Then they drift apart, align with other tower lights. I know if I watch long enough, if I am lucky enough and happen to glance at the right time, I'll see all the lights on all the towers switch on and off at the very same moment.

The closer I get to the towers, the lacier they become. The lattice is like a kid's picture of lightning shooting down the sides. I've been to the root of some of the towers, and they are balanced at a single point on a concrete slab. There the metal flares out in an inverted pyramid, then up slightly, tapered really, but coming together anyway past the red twirling light at the top of the lone antenna pointing to a distant vanishing point.

The closer I get to the towers the more air they become. They disappear. The red and white curtain of color where they are painted in intervals hangs in the air. The lights are nearly invisible in the sun. At that certain distance, when they disappear, it is like the red line of mercury in a thermometer held slightly off-center.

I used to worry about the houses that have been built beneath the towers. They are starter homes, small, shaped like Monopoly houses, the colors of game tokens, glossy blues and reds and greens and yellows, with a trim a shade darker but the same color. The trees are puny and new, fast-growing ginkos and Lombardy poplars quaking in the breeze and spraying up like the towers way above them. The houses are scattered and crowded into cul-de-sacs and terraces like an island village. The addition is called Tower Heights. The guy wires from the towers anchor in back-yards in deadeyes and turn buckles the sizes of automobiles. They are fenced off and landscaped with climbing flowers. The lines of one tower can slip beneath the lines of another, over still another, so the houses and yards are sewn up in a kind of net of cables arriving from the sky.

My students say the towers groan sometimes in storms. The wires twang. They tell me they like to lie looking up at the clouds sailing above the towers. The towers move against the clouds. They sway and topple. On a clear day, the shadows cast by the towers sweep over the houses in single file. My students take to geometry, all the lines and angles, acute, right, obtuse, the triangles, the compass point of the towers, the parallel lines. When I pull the blinds up on the window of my classroom, there, off in the distance, are the towers and wires. The roofs of their houses are just visible, a freehand line drawn beneath the proof.

The children this year have been very well-behaved. It is something we've all noticed and commented on in the lounge. The women think it's me. I am the only man. I teach sixth grade and take most of the gym classes. I have the basketball team. The Safety Patrol is my responsibility.

It is crazy but I am in love with all of these women in the school. Miss A, Miss B, Miss C, Miss D, Miss E, Miss F, Miss G, Miss H, Miss I, Miss J, Miss K, and Miss L who teaches kindergarten. The principal, Miss M. The nurse, Miss N, who visits twice a week, I first met during hearing tests this fall. The children were listening to earphones, curling and uncurling their index fingers in response to the pure tone. The music teacher, Miss O. The art instructor, Miss P.

How did I get here? It is difficult to say. But with each it seemed natural enough. Each relationship has a life of its own.

There is a lot of locker-room talk in the lounge and during staff meetings. When we meet in a group, I'm ignored, taken for granted, as they search around inside their brown bags for the apple, rinse the flat-ware in the sink. They talk about their boyfriends. In all cases that would be me they are talking about. None knows of my other affairs. When they yak about love they do so casually so as not to let on to the others, to tease me with this our inside joke. Their candor protects them, renders me harmless; their wantonness deflects suspicion from the room.

It is exciting. I share a preparation time with Miss D. We smooch for the half-hour in the lounge. The coffee perks. Our red pens capped. On the playground Miss C chases me playfully, jogging, then sprinting. The children are playing tether ball, box ball. They're screaming. She always almost catches me. When children from our classes are in the lavatory, I hold hands for a second with Miss G as we lean against the yellow tile brick in the hall. She turns her body around, presses her face against the cool wall. I haven't been compromised, because none of them wants to be discovered. If I am alone with one, the others leave us alone because the only time any one of them wants to be with me is when she can be alone with me. I love the moment when we all step out in the hall, look at each other and step back in the classroom, drawing the door behind us to begin teaching that day.

I am the only man, but I don't think that has much to do with the discipline of the children. Perhaps there is something in the air. It's history, I think. I like teaching history, geography, health, the big wide books that contain all of the pictures. You know the old saying about history: study history or you're doomed to repeat it. That's all wrong, I think. You study it *and* you are doomed to repeat it. Maybe even more so because you study what's happened. Get to know it and it's like it's already happened. It is the same story over and over. It is time once again for kids to raise their hands, part their hair, says "please" and "thank you," follow directions. That's all.

The Safety Patrol is in the rain. The streets are slick with oily rainbows, pooled. The gutters are full, flowing. The rain is soaking, steady. They are wearing bright yellow slickers. The water sheets down them. The bills of their yellow caps are pulled down flat between their eyes, hard against their noses like the gold helmets of heavy cavalry. The snaps are snapped beneath their chins. Their chins are tucked into their dryer chests. The flaps cover their ears, cheeks, necks. The claw fasteners shimmer down the fronts of their coats. They've polished them. They wear black rubber boots over their shoes. They stand in puddles, take the spray from passing cars without moving, their arms fixed at the proper angles, holding back the antsy students pressing to cross the streets into school.

The belts are orange, cinched tight over the shoulder, tight across the chest, over the heart, all buckled at the waist. The pools in the street turn red with the traffic light's light. The orange belts ignite as the headlights of the cars strike across them. For the instant it is just the belt floating without a body like the belt is bone in an X-ray.

The bells ring. We close the doors. Outside the patrol stays on the corners in case someone is tardy. Their heads pivot slowly checking all directions. Their faces sparkle. There are worms everywhere on the sidewalks. The towers' lights are juicy. Then from somewhere I can't see I hear the clear call of the captain. "Off do-tee." He calls again in the other direction, fainter. "Off do-tee." Each syllable held a long time. Then the lieutenants at the far ends of the school repeat the same phrasing. The patrols leave the corners one by one, covering each other's moves as they all safely cross the wet streets and come into school.

Each year I do a sociogram of my class. It helps me get a picture of how it all fits together, who the leaders are, who follow, who are lonely or lost, who are forgotten. I ask questions. Who in the class is your best friend, your worst enemy? Who is the most like a sister, a brother? Who would you never tell a secret to? Who would you ask for help? Who is strongest? Who would you help? If a boy and a girl were drowning who would you save if you could only save one? Who would you give part of your lunch to? Who would you pick to be on your team in gym class? Who would you want to pick you? Who makes you laugh? Who makes you mad? If someone told you a secret and told you not to tell it to anyone in the class, who would you tell it to? Who do you miss during summer vacations? Who would you want to call you on the telephone? Who do you walk home with? Who would you walk home with if you could? If you could rename the school, who would you name it after? If you are a girl, which boy would you like to be just for a little while? If you are a boy, which girl would you like to be just for a little while? If something has to be done in class, who would you ask? Who would you want to do your homework? Who would you want to teach you a new game? Who ignores you? If you ran away, who would you send a letter to? If you were in the hospital, who would you want to see most? If you were afraid and by yourself in the dark, who would you call out for? The children like this test because they know the answers. They sneak looks at each other as they work. Their pencils wag.

I collect the data, assign values, note names. I graph responses, plot intersections. I never question their honesty. I can map out grudges and feuds, old loves, lingering feelings, all the tribal bonds and property disputes, the pecking order, the classes in the class.

And then I have conferences with the parents. We sit on the downsized chairs. I cast out the future for their son or daughter in the language of talk shows. I dissect the peer pressure, explain the forces at work. The parents want to know about change. Is this set in stone? Can my son be a leader, a professional? Will my daughter grow up to like men? I tell them that it's hard to say, that the children are all caught up in a vast machine of beliefs and of myths. It is of this group's own making. These responses are almost instinctual now, I tell the parents. Each class has its own history, its own biology, its own math and logic. I'm just presenting what's what.

I know now who leads the class and who operates in the shadows. I know where the power is and the anguish, who shakes down who, what favors are owed, who might turn a gun on his friends, on himself.

I ask these same questions of myself. I answer Miss A, Miss B, Miss C, Miss D, and so on. Who do I trust? Who would I save? Who would I want to go home with? I wish I could ask the women as well, but the results would be skewed.

There is no place to stand, no distance. Skewed.

The Safety Patrol is in the hallway of the school before and after classes and at lunchtime. Inside, they wear the white cloth belts they launder. A bronze pin, given by the Chicago Motor Club, is attached where the belt begins to arch over the shoulder, the collar bone.

There is no running in the hall. The Patrol patrols up and down, one stationed every two or so classrooms. Stay on the right side of the hall. There is a red dashed line painted on the floor. The patrol stands at ease, straddles the line. The small children move along cautiously, try not to look around. There is a bottle neck near the piano on rollers that moves from classroom to classroom with the music teacher, Miss O. The piano is pushed keys first, against the wall. The bench is flipped on top of the upright. The legs point up like a cartoon of a dead animal. Handles are screwed on the side for easier moving. Something spills out of the intercom which only the teachers can understand. Loose squares of construction paper stapled on the bulletin boards lift and fall as kids pass by.

A Safety Patrol will speak. "What's your name?" and everyone in the hall will stop. "Yes, you," the Safety Patrol will say. Each member of the Safety Patrol can always see at least two other members. Their bright white belts cut across plaids and prints. They are never out of each other's sight.

They have arrayed themselves this way on their own, without my help.

The captain and his lieutenants have posted schedules, worked out posts and their rotation. The Safety Patrol is on the corners of Tyler and State and on the corners of Tyler and Rosemount, and one is at the crossing on Stetler with the old crossing guard who has the stop sign he uses as a crook. A Patrol walks with a passel of kindergartners all the way to Spring Street, almost a mile, to push the button on the automatic signal. He eats his lunch on the corner and walks the afternoon students back to school. A lone Patrol guards the old railroad tracks that separate the school from Tower Heights. There are Patrols at each door into the building. They are strung through the halls. There, I've seen them straightening the reproductions of famous paintings the PTA has donated. They watch over the drinking fountains. They turn lights out in empty classrooms. They roust stragglers from restrooms.

I want my students to copy each other's work. It is a theory of mine. I've put the slower ones in desks right next to the ones who get it. I've told them that it is all right by me if they ask their neighbors for the answers, fine also for the neighbors to tell.

They want to know if they own their answers.

They want to know what happens if they don't want to tell.

Fair questions. I see them covering their papers with their hands and arms as they go along, turning their backs on the copier.

"What are you protecting?" I ask them. Students can't break the habits they have of cheating. They look out of the corners of their eyes. They whisper. They sneak. They drop pencils on the floor. They don't get this, my indifference. My indulgence. If they would ask me I would tell them the answers but it never occurs to them to ask me.

We are doing European Wars. The Peloponnesian. The Punic. The Sackings. The Hundred Years. The Thirty Years. We are studying an Eskimo girl and a boy from Hawaii. Our newest states. We are doing First Aid. We are doing the Solar System. We are doing New Math. We spell every Wednesday and Friday. We read "A Man without a Country."

We have taken a field trip to one of the television stations to appear on the "Engineer John Show," a show that airs in time for the kids coming home from school. Engineer John dresses like a railroad engineer—pinstripe bib overalls, red neckerchief, crowned hat, a swan-necked oil can, big gloves. Really he is the other type of engineer who works with the transmitters, the wires, the towers, the kind in broadcasting, during the rest of the day. As a personality, he is cheap. He introduces Sergeant Preston movies and Hercules cartoons and short films provided by the

AFL-CIO called *Industry on Parade,* which show milk bottles filing on assembly lines or toasters being screwed together. There are no people in the films. The students love the show, especially the factories of machines building other machines. They think Engineer John is a clown like Bozo, who is on another station, because they don't know what the costume means. To us in the studio audience he talked about electricity while the films ran on the monitors. He talked about the humming we heard.

Later, we wound through the neighborhood in a yellow bus dwarfed by the towers, dropping students at their houses. I sat in the back of the bus next to the emergency door with Miss J, holding her hand and rubbing her leg. We both looked straight ahead. Squeezed.

The Safety Patrol made sure the windows did not drop below the lines, that hands and heads and arms stayed inside. The captain whispered directions to the driver. The stop-sign arm extended every time we stopped. All the lights flashed as if we had won something.

Every year there is a city-wide fire drill. All the schools, public and parochial, evacuated simultaneously. An insurance company provides red badges for the children, the smaller children wear fire hats. They are sent home with a checklist of hazards and explore their houses. Piles of rags and papers. Pennies in the fuse box. Paint cans near the water heater. I know they watch as their parents smoke. They inventory matches. They plan escapes from every room, crawl along floors. They touch doors quickly to see if they are hot before they open them. Extension cords. They set fire to their own pajamas.

In school they discuss their findings with each other, formed up in circles of chairs. They draw posters. They do skits.

On the day of the drill a fire company visited. Their pumper was in the parking lot gleaming. A radio station, WOWO, broadcast messages from the chief and the mayor and the superintendent. These were piped through to our classroom. A voice counted down the time to the moment when a little girl in a Lutheran elementary school this year would throw the switch and all the buzzers and bells in every other school would ring. Of course, this drill is never a surprise. That's not the point. Usually the alarm just sounds, and those assigned to close the windows close the windows. They turn out the lights. They leave everything. My students form into single file, are quiet for instructions, no shoving, no panic, know by heart where to go, what area of the playground to collect in, how to turn and watch the school, listen for the all-clear or the distant wail of sirens.

I arrive at school in the dark. The Safety Patrol is already sowing salt along the sidewalks. Their belts quilt their heavy overcoats. They are scooping sand from the orange barrel that is stored at an angle in a wooden frame on the corner with the little hill. The captain watches over the dim streets as others spread the sand in sweeping arcs. Going by, the few cars crush the new snow. In the still air, I can clearly hear them chopping ice and shoveling the snow.

I gave all the women sample-sized bottles of cheap perfume I bought at Woolworth's. Their desks were covered with tiny packages wrapped in color comics and aluminum foil, gifts from their students. I smelled the musky odor everywhere in the school for months later.

Miss J sent me a note one day. A fifth-grader, one size too small, handed it up to me. It was on lined notebook paper. Three of the five holes ruptured when she pulled it from the ring notebook. In the beautiful blue penmanship many of the women have: *Do you like me? Yes or No.* She had drawn in little empty squares behind yes and no. The fifth-grader waited nervously just outside the door. My class in the middle of base two watched me as I filled in the *yes* square and folded up the paper. I sealed it with a foil star, sent the child back to the room. My own students watched me closely. I knew they were trying to guess the meaning of what I did.

I thought I saw them all blink at the same time. I couldn't be sure, because I can't see all the eyes at once, but it was a general impression, a feeling, a sense I had, a moment totally my own in my classroom when what I did was not observed.

In the lounge the smell of the perfume is strongest, overpowering the cool purple smell of mimeograph, the gray cigarette smoke, the green mint breath, the brown crushed smell of the wet Fort Howard paper towels.

Miss A has drawn our initials, big block printing, in her right palm, stitched together with a plus sign. Her hands are inscribed with whorls and stars, marks against cooties and answers to problems. If I just touch her she thrills and titers, runs and hides, rubbing her body all over with her streaked hands.

In Fort Wayne we say that there are more cars per capita than in any other city in the United States except Los Angeles. I believe it when I am caught in traffic on State Street. Up ahead are the school and the axle factory and a little beyond them the towers. We creep along one to a car through a neighborhood built after the war. All the houses have shutters with cutouts of sailboats or moons or pine trees.

I drive a Valiant. I shift gears by pushing buttons on the dash, an idea that didn't catch on.

In the middle of the intersection I am waiting to turn across the oncoming lane. The Safety Patrol watches me, knows my funny old car. It has no seat belts. The way they hold their hands, their heads, it's like a crucifixion. Their faces are fixed.

I am stopped again by the crossing guard in the street. He leans heavily on the striped dazzling pole. I have seen him swat the hoods of cars that have come too close. The Safety Patrol is behind him, funneling the children along the crosswalk of reflecting paint smeared in slashes on the street.

The guard has told me a story that may be true. He says when he was a boy he saw his kid brother die at the first traffic light in Fort Wayne. The light had no yellow, only the green and red flags snapping up and down. The boys knew what it meant, crossed with the light, but the driver came on through, peeled the one brother from the other. It was a time, the guard has said, when signs meant nothing.

He has played in the street. When he was a boy, he told me, he played in the street, Calhoun, Jefferson, highways now, throwing a baseball back and forth with his brother. They didn't have to move all day. He drove cattle down Main Street, cows home to be milked twice a day, then back out to pasture.

He remembers when all the land the school is on and all the land around was a golf course, and before that a swamp. All of this was a swamp, he says.

I like old things. I like the old times. It doesn't take long for things to get old. Everything seems to have been here all along but often it is not old.

Our principal tells us one day there will be no students, the neighborhood is aging, running out of babies, but there is no evidence of that. The school is teeming every year, spontaneous generation. We do that old experiment each year in the spring. The cheesecloth over the spoiled and rotting meat grows its fur of maggots. The children love this.

Getting out of my car in the parking lot I am almost hit by something. It zips by my ear. Something skitters across the pavement. Nearby Miss F flings acorns my way, Brazils, cashews, mixed nuts. When we're alone she pinches me long and hard, won't let up, kicks me on the shins. She bites when we kiss. She says she likes me, she doesn't mean to hurt me. She wants me so much she wants to eat me up.

This is an elementary school. The sprawling one-story was built in the 1950s with Indiana limestone, a flat roof, and panels in primary colors. Its silhouette is reminiscent of the superstructures of the last luxury liners—the SS *United States*, the *France*—streamlined with false ledges and gutters trailing off the leeward edges, giving the illusion of swift movement.

The Safety Patrol makes a big deal of raising and lowering the flag. Three or four members and always an officer parade out in the court-yard. There are salutes and an exaggerated hand-over-hand as the flag that flew over the nation's Capitol goes up and down. They fold the flag in the prescribed way, leaving, when done properly, that pastry of stars which one of them holds over his or her breast.

Finally, you can never be emotionally involved with any of this. That's a fact, not a warning.

This is an elementary school. The children move on. I have their homeroom assignments for junior high school. It's all alphabetical from now on. I come to the school believing it is some kind of sacred precinct. Teachers are fond of saying how much we learn from the children, how when we paddle it will hurt us more than it will hurt them. Tests test what? What was learned or how it was taught? Children are like any other phenomenon in nature.

The first steps in the scientific methods according to the book are to observe, collect data. An hypothesis would be an intimate act. All the experiments would be failures. I know my job. I am supposed to not know more than I do now. No research. I repeat each year the elemental knowledge I embody, the things I learned a long time ago.

I watch the seasons change on the bulletin boards. I take down the leaves for the turkeys and the pilgrims, and the leaves leave a shadow of their shapes burned into the yellow and orange and brown construction paper. The sun has faded the background. The stencils and straight pins, colored tacks and yarns, the cotton-ball snow, the folded doily flakes, no two like. The eggshell flowers are in the spring. The grass cut into a fringe on a strip of green paper is curled bluntly through the scissors. The summer is cork.

The Safety Patrol folds its belts like flags. At the end of the school day they are sitting at their desks folding their belts to store them away. The other children have already been ferried across the streets. It is like a puzzle or trying to fold a map. The trick is to master the funny angle of the crossing belt, the adjusting slides, the heavy buckle. It's like folding parachutes. They leave the packets in the center of their desktops, the bronze pin on top of each.

I go home and watch the "Engineer John Show." There are so many kinds of people that exist now only on TV—milkmen, nuns in habit, people who live in lighthouses, newsboys who yell "Extra." Engineer John arrives with the sound of a steam engine.

We know that when tornadoes happen they are supposed to sound like freight trains. It is spring and the season for tornadoes, which Fort Wayne is never supposed to have according to an old Indian belief, still repeated, that the three rivers ward them off. We will drill. The students sit Indian-fashion under their desks, backs to the windows. Or in the hall the bigger children cover their smaller brothers and sisters.

During our visit, Engineer John told us about the ground. How electricity goes back to it, finds it. I though of the towers as a type of well. These pictures gushing from the field, a rich deposit. The electrons pump up and down the shafts.

In storms, the children say they watch the lightning hit the towers. They turn their sets off and watch. The towers are sometimes up inside the clouds. The clouds light up like lampshades. I think a lot of people watch the towers, know which windows in their houses face that way. They sit up and watch when the storm keeps them awake. Or when they can't sleep in general, maybe they stare out at all the soothing, all the warning lights.

The sixth-grade girls are gathered in one room to watch the movie even I have never seen. I have the boys. They are looking up words in the dictionary. I tell them that dictionaries have very little to do with spelling but with history, with where the word comes from, how long it has been used and understood.

Miss K calls me out in the hall. The doors are closed and she leads me to the nearest girls' restroom and pulls me inside. I always feel funny in the wrong washroom, hate to open the door even to yell in "Hurry up" to my girls, who are just beginning to use makeup and are dawdling over the sinks and mirrors.

We cram into the furthest stall, and Miss K unbuttons her dress, which has her initials embroidered on her collar —AMR. We have played doctor before in the nurse's room, where there are screens, couches and gowns. There are even some cold metal instruments ready on a towel. She is in her underwear when we hear the doors wheeze, and someone comes in. A far stall door clicks closed and we hear the rustle of clothes and the tinkle. Miss K worms around me, crouches down to look beneath the partition. Elastic snaps. The flush. We hear hands being washed in the sink, dried on paper towels.

When we're alone again Miss K finishes undressing. She clutches pieces of her clothes in each hand, covers her body and then quickly opens her arm. She lets me look at her, turns around lifting her hands over her head, clothes spilling down, taking rapid tiny steps in place. She tucks her clothes into the wedge of her elbows, hugging the bundle next to her breast, her bronze nipple. She reaches down between her legs with her other hand, watching me as she does so, trying not to giggle. Then she shows me her hand. There is some blood on her fingers, she thinks it is so funny. She couldn't sit through the movie.

Perhaps all of the women in the school are bleeding at the same moment, at this moment, by chance or accident, through sympathy, gravity, vibration. It's possible. It could be triggered by suggestion, by a school year of living out blocks of time, periods of periods, drinking the same water, breathing the same air. And what if it had happened, is happening? Would it be any worse if the planets all aligned or if everyone in the world jumped up in the air at the same time? The school, a little worse for wear a few days each month, tense, cramped, even horny, a word my students always giggle at. And now that some of them are alone with dictionaries I know they are looking up all the words they've never said and know they should never say.

The bright yellow tractors are back cutting the grass around the school. The litter in the lawn is mulched and shot out the side with the clippings. The driver takes roughly a square pattern, conforming to the shape of the lawn, the patches fitting inside each other. The green stripe is a different shade depending upon the angle of the light—flat green, the window of cut grass and the bright lush grass still standing. The tractors emit those bleating sounds when they back up, trimming around trees.

I see all of this through my wall of windows. The Safety Patrol on their corners cover their ears as the tractors come near. I can see them shouting to the other children, waving at them, yanking them around. Their voices lost in the roar of the mowers. They mean to take the shrapnel of shredded branches, stones, crushed brick, the needles of grass into their own bodies. A heroic gesture they must have learned from television.

The word *carnival* means "the putting away of flesh," according to *The American Heritage Dictionary*. I feel as if no one knows this as I thread through the crowded school halls.

Parents and neighbors and high-school kids have come to the carnival. We're just trying to raise money for audio-visual equipment, tumbling apparati, maybe buy a few more trees. The students are here, many with their faces painted like clowns, one of the attractions. Some fifth-graders are following me around since they have learned I'll be their teacher next year. They're drinking drinks that a fast-food place donates. Their lips and tongues are orange or purple or red or a combination of those colors. Underfoot a carpet of popcorn pops where we walk. The floors are papered with discarded spin art and scissored silhouettes. People are wearing lighter clothes, brighter clothes. They form clots in the hall, push and shove. Children are crying or waving long strips of the blue tickets above their heads, hitting others as they go by. It is a job, this having fun.

Each room has a different game run by the teachers and room mothers. I am floating from one place to the other, bringing messages and change, tickets and cheap prizes. One room has the fish pond. I see the outline of Miss B working furiously behind the white sheet, attaching prizes to the hooks. Children are on the other side of the sheet holding long tapering bamboo poles. In another room is the candy wheel. Another has a plastic pool filled with water and identical plastic ducks. There are rooms where balls are tossed at hoops and silver bottles. There is the cakewalk. One room is even a nursery where mothers are nursing or changing their babies. In all the rooms are the cards of letters—Aa Bb Cc Dd Ee, some in cursive Aa Bb Cc Dd Ee with tiny arrows indicating the stroke of the pen. There are green blackboards, cloakrooms, the same clock, the drinking fountain, and the illuminated exit sign over the door.

In the cafetorium adults are having coffee. Children are rolling in the mats. Pigs in blankets are being served, beans, Jell-O. Up on the stage behind the heavy curtains is the Spook House. Four tickets. There is a long line.

In the dark you are made to stumble and fall. Strings and crepe streamers propelled by fans whip your face. There are tugs on your clothes, your shoes, your fingers. There are noises, growls, shrieks, laughs. Things are revealed to you, such as heads in boxes, spiders, skulls, chattering teeth.

All the time you can hear the muttering of the picnic outside damped by the curtain, the thrumming of conversation. And your eyes just get used to the dark when you come upon a table set with plates each labeled clearly: Eyeballs, Fingers, Guts, Hearts, Blood, Brains. You can see clearly now the cocktail onions, the chocolate pudding, the ketchup, the Tootsie Rolls, the rice, everything edible. The tongue, tongue. Someone is whispering over and over "touch it, touch it." And it's hard to, even though you know what these things really are. Or you want to because you know you never would touch the real things.

I go outside up on the roof, I have the key, to sneak a smoke. The Safety Patrol is out in the parking lot. The towers are sputtering off in the distance. For a couple of tickets you take a couple swings with a sledge hammer at an older car. The car looks very much like mine.

The glass is all removed, the sharp edges. It only looks dangerous. The sound reaches me a heartbeat after I see the hammer come down. People like the thin metal of the roof, the hood and trunk, the fine work around the head and taillights. The grill splinters. The door that covers the gas cap is a favorite target.

The Safety Patrol rings the crumpled car, holding back the watching crowd a prudent distance. Their belts together are a kind of hound's tooth pattern. In the moonlight the metal of the car shines through the dented enamel and catches fire. The car has been spray-painted with dares and taunts. A blow takes the hammer through the door, and there is chanting. Again. Again. Again. And the Safety Patrol joins hands.

From Fort Wayne Is
Seventh on Hitler's List

Fort Wayne Is Seventh on Hitler's List

This is a city of poets. Every Wednesday, when the sirens go off, a poet will tell you that, after thirty years, Fort Wayne is still seventh on Hitler's bombing list. And you half expect to hear the planes, a pitch lower than the sirens. their names as recognizable as those of automobiles. Heinkels lumber out of the east, coast up Taylor Street, or follow the Pennsy from one GE plant to another. Stukas dive on the wire-and-die works, starting their run at the International Harvester bell tower, left standing on purpose, and finish by strafing the Tokheim yards. Junkers wheel, and Messerschmitts circle. All the time there would be sirens.

Grandfather keeps his scrapbooks upstairs in the window seat of the empty bedroom. When he dies, they are to be mine, and I am to give them to the Air Force Museum at Wright-Patterson Air Force Base. Grandfather started keeping these scrapbooks when he felt the time was right for war. He felt the war coming. In the years before the war, the scrapbooks that he kept were pieces of the world he found-a field outside of Peking where old people go to die, a man being buried alive, all the All-American football teams of those years, the bar of soap Dillinger used at the Crown Point jail, a man cut into three parts by a train, a Somalian warrior with no clothes on. These things made sense to Grandfather.

A real poet knows how to bomb his own city.

In the window seat where Grandfather keeps his finished scrapbooks, there is also his collection of missals, all the handouts from Wendell Willkie's campaign, and everything Father Coughlin ever wrote. The scrapbooks have interesting covers. There is one with a mallard duck on the wing worked into the leather. One is made of wood and has an oak leaf carved into it. Most, though, have only company names or *Season's Greetings.*

I have never been able to read all the scrapbooks. They are in no order, and nothing in them is. Every page is dated with the newspaper itself. He went straight through the hook. One day I can read about the Battle of Britain, the next day VE day, the next the Soviet Pact. I have never gotten to the bottom of the window seat.

Once I found Hitler's list.

There are cottonwoods along the rivers. In the spring, a poet will look up at the undefended sky and announce, "At any moment we could be destroyed."

When I was little, I would practice making bomb noises, the whistling sound of a bomb falling. I would take a deep breath, form my lips, begin. I could make it sound as if the bomb were falling away from me, or on me, by modulating the volume, adjusting its fade or rise. I preferred the perspective of the plane, starting with the loud high note. A second or two of silence as the bomb is out of earshot. Then the tiny puff of air reaching me from the ground.

This is why old men smoke at night in the middle of parks. To attract bombers.

Mother remembers certain things about the war. She remembers making dolls out of hollyhocks, taping butcher paper on the windows, and not being able to look at the newspaper until Grandfather had cut out the things he wanted. Once, in the A&P, she lost her underwear while waiting in line to buy milk. There was no rubber to hold up the underwear. She tells me this story every time I think I have troubles. Mother danced in the USO shows for the troops from Baer Field and Casad. Once she shared the stage with Bob Hope.

The whole city watches as the skywriter finishes the word.

SURRENDER

Before going through the scrapbooks, I would sit on the window seat as if to hold the lid on. I would look out over the front lawn, across Poinsette to Hamilton Park. Through the pine trees and the blooming cherries, I could see the playground and the circling tether ball, the pavilion, the war memorial, the courts. I wasn't old enough to change the world.

At a high school bake sale, the frosted gingerbread men remind a teacher of her students drilling on the football field during the war. They wore letter jackets with shiny white sleeves, or bright sweaters with stripes and decorations. They carried brooms at trail arms in the sunset.
How does evil get into the world?
Witches. Or children crying, "Catch me, if you can."

I watch Mother feed a baby."Nnnnaaawwwhh," she goes, "here it comes in for a landing." She conducts the spoon on a yawing course, approaching. "Open the hangar door," she orders.
Mother looks at me as the baby sucks the spoon. "Remember?" she says.
"I remember," I say.
She sends out the second wave of creamed cereal.

In the fall, the new Chevrolets arrive, and Hafner sets up his old searchlight. It is surplus from the war, painted silver now. The diesel motor rotates the light. The light itself comes from a flame magnified and reflected into a beam. People come across the street to look. They look at the new cars lined up.
From Hafner's lot, you can look across the St. Joe River, south, to where three other beams sweep back and forth in the night. Those are coming from Allen County Motors, Jim Kelley Buick, and DeHaven Chevrolet. From the west is the lone light of Means Cadillac tracing a tight circle and toppling over into a broad arc, catching for an instant the tip of the bank building downtown and righting itself like a top. To the north is another battery of lights playing off one another, intersecting, some moving faster than others. Toward you and away. Bench's AMC, Northway Plymouth, Ayres' Pontiac. The illusion of depth in the night. The general vicinity of each source.
What are they looking for?
Something new is in the world.

There was a Looney Tunes cartoon Engineer John showed almost every day on his TV show, It was made during the war. Miller, upset with the way the war is going, flies a mission himself, only to have the plane dismantled over Russia by "Gremlins from the Kremlin."
I would look through the scrapbooks to see how it really happened.

There has been a plane circling all day. There appears to be a streak of smoke coming from its tail. But I'm sure it's some kind of banner too high to read.

In the scrapbook with the wood cover, there is a picture of Gypsy Rose Lee selling war bonds.

This is the only picture in all of Grandfather s scrapbooks where he's made a note. It says: *I bet the Lord is pleased.*

During the war, the top hemispheres of the streetlight globes were painted with a black opaque glaze. They stayed that way after the war. No one seems to mind. Parts of dead insects show in the lower half of the globe. There's more and more of them in there summer after summer.

Grandfather read meters for his living. During the war, he was made block warden because everyone remembered the way he'd kept calm during *The War of the Worlds.* They also figured that he knew a little bit about electricity.

The city practiced blackouts all the time because they'd heard that Fort Wayne was seventh on the list. One night everyone stumbled into Hamilton Park for a demonstration. A man from the Civil Defense wanted to emphasize the importance of absolute dark, lights really out. Grandfather said that the man lit a match when the rest of the city was all dark. He said that you could see the whole park and the faces of everyone in the park. They were all looking at the match. He said you could see the houses. He said you could read the street sign. *Poinsette.*

The man blew out the match with one breath. The people went home in the dark.

Were they wishing they could do something about the stars?

They kept German prisoners in camps near the Nickel Plate yards. People would go out to the camps and look at the prisoners. Everyone felt very safe, even the women. Many of the prisoners had worked on streets downtown, or in the neighborhoods, and were friendly with the people.

Some of these prisoners stayed in town after the war. Some sent for their families. You ask them, they'll tell you—Fort Wayne is a good place to live.

In one of Grandfather's scrapbooks, there is a series of pictures taken from the nose of a B-17. The first picture is of the bombs falling away from the plane. In the background are the city streets already burning. In the second picture, the nose of an-other bomber is working its way into the frame and under the bombs, smaller now by seconds. The third picture shows the plane in the path of the falling bombs. One has already taken away the stabilizer without exploding. The perspective is really terrifying. The fourth picture shows the plane skidding into its tailspin. All this time the bombs are falling. And the fifth picture is the plane falling with the bombs.

Grandfather has arranged these pictures to be read down the page. One after the other.

Casad is a GSO depot built during the war just outside of town. I go there sometimes to watch them dust the fields nearby, the fertile strip near the bend in the Maumee. High school kids race by on the township roads on their way to Ohio to drink. I don't know if they even use Casad for anything now.

Casad was built to be confusing from the air. All you can see, even from across the road, are mounds of different-colored stones. Some of the piles are real, others are only camouflaged roofs. If you look closely at some of them, you can see a small ventilation pipe or maybe some type of window. The important things are underground. There are stories that date from the war of one-ton chunks of rubber in storage. They feared the damage that would be caused if they dropped any during transportation. Tin, copper, nickel, tungsten, and mercury were all supposed to have been stored there. From the road, quarry piles and sandpiper tents hump out of sight through the cornfield to the river.

It must all look pretty harmless from the sky.

The high school kids will stop on the way back. Late at night, they will sit on the hoods of their cars guessing which of the shadows are real. They are waiting to sober up and weave home.

Mother remembers his Prospero at the Civic Theatre. He lived here years ago. The only time I saw Robert Lansing act was on the TV show where he played the wing commander and flew B-17s. All I remember now are the shots in the cramped cockpit with the flights of bombers in the background. Most of the action took place on that tiny set, two seats and the man in the turret, aft, always moving as the actors talked or rocked from the flak or were riddled by "bandits" or feathered the number three engine.

Robert Lansing visited our high school and talked about acting.

He said there was a method that allowed him to use his past experiences in new situations. He said he was afraid to fly. He told us this standing in the middle of the gym floor, targeted in the cross hairs of the time-line.

In the stores downtown, there are bowls of lemon drops and cherry drops next to the cash registers. The merchants have broken into some of the supplies of the bomb shelters in the basements of their stores. They found that the water had soured years ago in the tins. The candy is sweet even though it is over twenty years old. They say the candy and water have been replaced in the bomb shelters. "No sense letting anything go to waste," they say. Every time you buy something, the person running the register will say, "have some candy." And then they will mention where the candy comes from.

The small drums the candy came in are being used as wastebaskets. They are painted drab. Sometimes, the stenciled CANDY has been crossed out. The Civil Defense emblem can still be seen—the pyramid in the circle, pointing up to the sky.

Grandfather saw Bob Hope in the coffee shop of the Hotel Anthony. He showed him the clipping he had been carrying around for years, the one about mother dancing in Bob Hope's show. Grandfather said that he wished Bob Hope could be home for Christmas but was grateful that someone did what Bob Hope did.

In the fall, the wind turns the trees to silent puffs of smoke.

Grandfather wants to know why I want to be a poet. He shows me a clipping of Eldon Lapp, who goes to our church. There is a picture of Eldon in his flight jacket and soft hat. During the war, Eldon was shot down over Germany. Before his capture, he lived for months in the Black Forest. He survived that long with the aid of another flyer who had been trained as a Boy Scout and had been in Germany during a world jamboree. This flyer knew all the tricks—how to fish with a line and makeshift hook, how to conceal a trail, how to secure a camp, how to read signs. Eldon swore then that if he got out of this alive he would dedicate his life to scouting.

"That's vocation," Grandfather says to me.

The Kiwanis Club sponsors airplane rides all summer. Taking off from Baer Field, the tour flies over most of the city. I saw the Wayne Knitting Mill's tall smokestack, *Wayne* built right into the bricks. I flew by the elevators, followed Main Street downtown and circled the courthouse.

Then over the Old Fort, looking defenseless, and the filtration plant with the ponds. I followed the Maumee from the three rivers downstream, sweeping by the old Studebaker plant, Zollner Piston, all the wire-and-die works, Magnavox. Then banking up the bypass, north, over the shopping centers and malls and their parking lots, over Eckrich and the campus, to my house.

I could see my house. I knew it even from the air. There were people in the front yard I did not know, looking up, shielding their eyes, waving.

Grandfather, all you can see are the contrails. The plodding lines of the bombers and the lyric corkscrews of their escort. It is how this city chooses to die. Daylight raids, everyone is watching. This is the American Way. To see it coming. The bombs are inverted exclamations at the beginning of their sentence.

I can hear the planes looking for the city each night. I keep my eves closed as they fly over the house. Their engines pulse like the sirens. It is a patient sound. And I wait too.

I wait for them to drop the flares, or for a few of them to come in lower. We did not ask for this. They fly by overhead. You can hear them, but you cannot see them. They are showing no lights. Low clouds. No stars.

They go on, on some heading to the west. But they will be back later. Then, further east, there will come the panting sound, almost comic, as they drop the bombs randomly, hoping to hit something, and then, empty, go back to where they came from.

Tarsk and Hartup have been taking aerial photographs for years. All the merchants and the schools, each new mayor, every public place has one of their pictures. Sometimes the picture is of one building and at other times of whole blocks. There are calendars, too, that everyone gets from Lincoln Life. In Mike's Car Wash people will try to find their house in the picture that hangs in the lobby while their car is being dried. Every day Tarsk and Hartup fly over the city taking pictures—but no matter what picture you look at, someone will always point out what is missing, or what has since disappeared.

Three Postcards from Indiana

Santa Claus

"A watch means that conditions are right for a tornado." As we drove, I explained the difference between a watch and a warning. This was her first summer in Indiana, and every time she turned on the radio she found herself in another depression, pressure dropping. An imaginary line extending just north of and passing through the counties of La la la and Mmmmm. The Balkan states of the weather map. It would be in effect for a couple of hours.

"Is that us?" she said.

"It's just a watch," I said, and I told her what to look for, though I had never seen one myself. I remembered sightings, hearing of funnels over towns. One Easter. One Palm Sunday. "If you see one, we get in a ditch. Some place low." I remembered feeling this way every spring and summer—too hot, too still. You can hear better. There was this picture in the grocery store encyclopedia of a drinking straw driven into the trunk of an elm. She had seen violent storms in Baltimore but only the leavings of hurricanes, not this kind of wind—all eye and finger, one that can see and feel.

Of course, it started raining, and the voice on the radio tracked the storms, interrupted by the sizzle of static—soft or loud, close or far away. I'm here now, the static said. Teasing. Moving.

"It's not us," I said.

In the half-light we passed the Statue of Santa Claus, melted limestone, in a field surrounded by broken skeletons of farm implements slick with rain and submerged in mud. Horses, startled by the lightning, shied and ran sideways away from the sound. The book said the statue said: For the Children of the World

Triple A just mentioned the St. Nicholas Inn, the only motel in Santa Claus. It was made up of little bungalows, Munchkin-size, scattered behind a gas station.

"A mite windy," said the woman, letting us into number 3. The baby riding on her hip yelped each time it thundered. "No one stays here. They drive up from Louisville or down from Naplis to see Santa Claus. My baby sees him every day."

We went into our room and found everything half-sized—the TV, the end table, the bed. "Think, she said, "to grow up seeing Santa Claus even day but Christmas." Yes, in the part of the world where flying is easy— lawn deer, flamingos, silked jockies.

As we slept did we shrink? Were we that small? Did our feet touch the ground? Did we count each other's sheep as they clouded that tiny room? We heard the baby cry all night through the storm.

The next morning I knew the sky was clear before she pulled the drapes and turned on the morning news. Eyes still closed, I heard that a tornado had touched down in the Baltimore zoo the day before. A woman reported that she survived by being blown into the hippo house. A miracle. The world is full of miracles. Closing my eyes again, I see the woman blown into the hippo house. One puff, a blow to the belly, arms and legs trailing, millions of shrimp swimming backwards into the hippo house. Size has no scale. I am asleep again.

Later we wrote our postcards in the car, parked next to the post office. The doors were open. To keep the post office, the natives changed the name of their town from Sante Fe to Santa Claus. Now, besides the amusement park, the post office is the town's only industry. All the letters come here. All the ones addressed to the North Pole. All the lists. All the directions home. We came here to mail some from the eye of the storm. All the stamps were airmail. It is too hot for Christmas, too still. You could hear the sleigh bells.

"Look. Look." I said, pointing across, the evaporating parking lot to the back gate of Santa Claus Land, Santa Claus. In shirt sleeves and bermudas, he swung a Mack lunchbox as he went to work. He was sweating and he wasn't whistling. She didn't look up.

"Where?" she said.

But he was already gone through the gate and hidden behind the scraps of newspaper caught in the cyclone fence. I pointed with my finger.

"There."

French Lick

We came into the valley from Santa Claus and skirted the grand hotel fronting the road, a walled city. We crossed the old Monon tracks, the spur where the private cars from Chicago were switched right up to the door of the resort. "Monon," you say. I told you again about Hoosier, who's there. The French in Indiana. We stayed down the road in a motel-half in French Lick, half in West Baden, Alsace-Lorraine. "A lick," I said, "was for the wild game. The seasoning in the ground." I will show you the salt blocks in the supermarket.

"Kiss me, there," you said.

We walked back over to the grand hotel. In the coffee shop you had a tongue sandwich, and the waitress behind the counter said I was the first to order a bagel and cream cheese "since I've worked here. What do I do?" Next to us on the little stools, a couple argued about the food. She complained about her peas in French. He scolded her in English. We came for the waters you said. But really you only wanted your postcards canceled with French Lick. We played Space Invaders in the arcade, and they kept coming. Then, we lingered on the veranda, following the deck chairs to the spring. The spring was in a gazebo, bubbling through a pool of green water. "Kiss me, here," you said, but the sulfur smell was too strong. "If nature can't Pluto will." You read the sign. "This is what they came for?" you said. "This is what they came for, the presidents and gangsters?"

The next morning you wrote your postcards, naked, at the desk. Maids were making up the next room. I watched David Letterman on TV as he made jokes about Muncie. Turning, you said, "Lets," licking 10 cents Justice, "go there next." On my way to the shower, I stopped behind you. You were writing that animals need their licks. The sounds you make, the ones that are not quite language, name nothing.

"Knock, knock," I say in your ear. "Who's there?" you say from another world.

Muncie

In Muncie, we are staying at the Hotel Roberts, downtown. And, though the elevator is automatic, they have a man wearing a Nickel Plate conductor's hat who pushes the buttons. We have learned that the third Middletown study is in progress. We are mistaken for sociologists by the old men we sit with in the lobby when we watch TV. Before we can quiet them with the truth, they are speaking of their church affiliations and bathroom practices.

The first night here, we ordered a pizza by phone from a campus take-out to be delivered to our room. Since then we have gone through the yellow pages for anything that will be delivered. When it arrives, Theresa answers the door wrapped in the hotel bath towel. After awhile we begin to receive all sorts of things we never ordered—pints of macaroni salad, goldfish cartons of fried rice, heads of lettuce. They are delivered by college boys wearing Ball U T-shirts, who then sculpture obscene animals with the warm tin foil. Everything seems to have the same tomato paste base.

If we leave the Roberts at all, it is to watch the summer basketball leagues play on a court next to one leg of the high school drag. The cars go by honking. The players glisten in the single scoop lamp. The backboard is perforated metal used in temporary runways. The hoop is a red halo with not even a metal chain net dangling from the rim. Or we go to the Ball factory and watch them make mason jars, press the rubber lips to the tin lids. They have shelves of jars the Ball brothers canned seventy-five years ago. The seal holds stewed tomatoes with yellow seeds, embryonic eggplants, black butter chips and sweet gerkins no one will taste, okra, of all things. We have been there several times, and unlike other factory tours, there is nothing to sample unless we care to can and wait a season. We do keep our loose pennies in a Ball jar, and Theresa makes the boys reach in it for their tip, a monkey trap. They can't withdraw their clenched fist through the narrow mouth of the jar without letting go of the money. She leaves them laughing, closing the door against them with the flat of her foot.

But all of this is typical here, or, because we do it in Muncie, it is typical. We have seen the sociologists on the sidewalks, shielding their eyes with their clipboards, trying to cross the street. They take pictures of barber shops and trophy stores. Or they sit and count cars in and out of the parking lot or look for butts beneath their feet. In every room there are questions to be answered with special pencils. "What brings you here?" In each case, love. We write that our dream is to open all the jars one at a time and to eat vegetables older than our grandfathers. We want everything delivered to us. Theresa wears nothing but two pasties of pepperoni. I am reading books on pickling. The scientists will figure out what is going on here.

From Seeing Eye

The Mayor of the Sister City Talks to the Chamber of Commerce in Klamath Falls, Oregon

"It was after the raid on Tokyo. We children were told to collect scraps of cloth. Anything we could find. We picked over the countryside; we stripped the scarecrows. I remember this remnant from my sister's obi. Red silk suns bounced like balls. And these patches were quilted together by the women in the prefecture. The seams were waxed as if to make the stitches rainproof. Instead they held air, gasses, and the rags billowed out into balloons, the heavy heads of chrysanthemums. The balloons bobbed as the soldiers attached the bombs. And then they rose up to the high wind, so many, like planets, heading into the rising sun and America...."

I had stopped translating before he reached this point. I let his words fly away. It was a luncheon meeting. I looked down at the tables. The white napkins looked like mountain peaks of a range hung with clouds. We were high above them on the stage. I am *yonsei,* the fourth American generation. Four is an unlucky number in Japan. The old man, the mayor, was trying to say that the world was knit together with threads we could not see, that the wind was a bridge between people. It was a hot day. I told these beat businessmen about children long ago releasing the bright balloons, how they disappeared ages and ages ago. And all of them looked up as if to catch the first sight of the balloons returning to earth, a bright scrap of joy.

Dish Night

Every Wednesday was Dish Night at the Wells Theatre. And it worked because she was there, week in and week out. She sat through the movie to get her white bone china. A saucer. A cup. The ushers stood on chairs by the doors and reached into the big wooden crates. There was straw all over the floor of the lobby and balls of newspaper from strange cities. I knew she was the girl for me. I'd walk her home. She'd hug the dish to her chest. The street lights would be on and the moon behind the trees. She'd talk about collecting enough pieces for our family of eight. "Oh, it's everyday and I know it," she'd say, holding it at arm's length. "They're so modern and simple and something we'll have a long time after we forget about the movies."

I forget just what happened then. She heard about Pearl Harbor at a Sunday matinee. They stopped the movie, and a man came out on stage. The blue stage lights flooded the gold curtain. It was dark in there, but outside it was bright and cold. They didn't finish the show. Business would pick up then, and the Wells Theatre wouldn't need a Dish Night to bring the people in. The one we had gone to the week before was the last one ever and we hadn't known it. The gravy boat looked like a slipper. I went to the war, to Europe where she'd write to me on lined school paper and never failed to mention we were a few pieces shy of the full set.

This would be the movie of my life, this walking home under the moon from a movie with a girl holding a dinner plate under her arm like a book. I believed this is what I was fighting for. Everywhere in Europe I saw broken pieces of crockery. In the farmhouses, the cafés. Along the roads were drifts of smashed china. On a beach, in the sand where I was crawling, I found a bit of it the sea washed in, all smooth with blue veins of a pattern.

I came home and washed the dishes every night, and she stacked them away, bowls nesting on bowls as if we were moving the next day.

The green field is covered with these tables. The sky is huge and spread with clouds. The pickup trucks and wagons are backed in close to each table so that people can sit on the lowered tailgates. On the tables are thousands of dishes. She walks ahead of me. Picks up a cup then sets it down again. A plate. She runs her finger around a rim. The green field rises slightly as we walk, all the places set at the tables. She hopes she will find someone else who saw the movies she saw on Dish Night. The theater was filled with people. I was there. We do this every Sunday after church.

Lice

I was waiting for the girls to come out of their mother's trailer so I decided to check the tires with a penny I found on the passenger seat. On the left front, the tread wasn't deep enough to reach Lincoln's nose and I could see all the rest were more or less bald. That's when the girls blew out the trailer door. Their coats were half on and half off. It looked like they had a couple of extra arms each, their hair flying.

I stood up and threw the penny away. As soon as I did it I felt sorry. I wanted the penny back right away and looked for it in the tall brown grass. I looked away from the trailer out into the yard which was turning all copper as the sun went down. I'd never find it.

It was almost winter again. Straw bales were stuffed around the trailer, hiding the wheels and the hitch. The propane tank was newly painted silver. They paint metal silver. That penny was still somewhere in the grass. The girls were pulling each other's hair, and I felt the car sink with the weight of them. I felt it sink under my butt where I leaned on the fender and looked over the cornfield newly gleaned next to where the trailer was parked.

"Daddy," the kids said, "look at us."

My car is silver. The seats are black. The girls were in the nest of their things in back. Paper, rope, arms from old dolls, clothes, books with gold spines, and bent up plastic straws. They were already reading.

Their mother followed them out this time. She showed me the paper from the school. She hadn't read the note until I'd pulled up in the drive when she was getting the girls' things together. She checked their hair right there while they wormed around in their coats by the door. She combed through the fine hairs behind their ears and in the scruff of their necks and found the ropes of eggs leading down to the scalps and there the lice.

And I stood there a second with her. I thought about the time I let one die overnight on a piece of notebook paper. It clung for hours to a loose hair I put beside it like the grass the girls throw in with lightning bugs. I wanted to see if it was true about needing warm bodies to survive. It was true. And I blew the paper clean.

"We took a nap," she said. And it took me a while to understand what she meant. We were both leaning on the car. She had her head hanging down. Her arms were straight and her hands were jammed into her sweater pockets. I felt my fingers on her scalp, and I leaned in toward the whirlpool of her hair.

Meat

Because I could play baseball, I never went to Korea.

I was standing on the dock in San Francisco with my entire company. We all wore helmets, parade rest, and were loaded down with winter and summer gear. We were ready to embark. My name was called. I remember saying excuse me to the men in rank as I tried to get by with my equipment. Then I sat on my duffle and watched them file aboard, bumping up the side of the ship, the cables flexing. There was rust in the bilge. I could hear the water below me. Sailors laughed way over my head. It only took a few hours. There were some people there to wave good-bye though not for the soldiers since our shipping out was something secret.

Nothing was ever said. I was transferred to another unit where all the troops were baseball players. I played second base on the Third Army team. I batted seventh and bunted a lot. We traveled by train from one base to another in Texas, Georgia, and on up into New Jersey for the summer. We had a few cars to ourselves including a parlor with an open platform. The rest of the train was made up of reefers full of frozen meat. The train was aluminum and streamlined. We could stand in the vestibules or in the open doorway of the baggage car where we kept the bags of bats and balls and the pinstriped uniforms hung on rods and look out over the pink flat deserts. There wouldn't be a cinder from the engine, its wheels a blur. You would see it up ahead on the slow curves, the white smoke of the whistle trailing back over the silver boxcars of meat and then the whistle. Some cars still had to be iced so we'd stop in sad, little towns, play catch and pepper while the blocks melted in the sun and the sawdust turned dark and clotty on the platform. We'd hit long fly balls to the local kids who'd hang around. We left them broken bats to nail and tape.

The meat was our duty. It was what we said we did even though everyone knew we played baseball. The Army wanted us to use frozen meat instead of fresh. We ran the tests in messes to see if the men could tell the difference. We stood by the garbage cans and took the plates to scrape and separate the scraps of meat to weigh for waste. A red plate meant the meat was fresh. The bone, the chewed gristle, the fat. I picked it out of the cold peas and potatoes. Sometimes whole pieces would come back, gray and hard. The gravy had to be wiped off before it went on the scale. Those halls were huge, with thousands of men hunched over the long tables eating. We stood by watching, waiting to do our job.

It made no difference, fresh or frozen, to the men. This pleased the Army. Things were changing. Surplus from the war was being given to the UN for the action in Korea. There were new kinds of boots and rifles. Then every camp still had walk-in lockers. The sides of meat hung on racks. The cold blew through you. Blue inspection stamps bled into the yellow fat of the carcasses. All gone now. That's what I did in the service.

But the baseball didn't change. The ball still found my glove. There were the old rituals at home. I rubbed my hands in the dirt then wiped them on my pants, took the bat and rapped it on the plate. The pitch that followed always took me by surprise—hard and high, breaking away. The pitcher spun the ball like a dial on a safe. And trains still sound the same when they run through this town. At night, one will shake our house (we live near an overpass) and I can't go back to sleep. I'll count the men who walked up that gangway to the ship. The train wheels squeal and sing. It might as well be hauling the cargo of my dreams.

What I See

I was killing time at the ranger station in West Glacier, twirling the postcard racks by the door. There was an old one of some teenagers around a campfire near Swift Current Lake. They have on dude ranch clothes, indigo jeans with the legs rolled into wide cuffs. The boys have flat tops. There is a yuke. One girl, staring into the fire, wears saddle shoes. The colors are old colors. Colors from the time women all wore red lipstick. Beyond the steel blue lake the white glaciers are smearing down the mountain sides. I saw the glaciers even though it was night in the card. They gave off their own light. No one ever took this card, not even as a joke. I was looking at this card when a woman walked in with her son. They mounted the stair above the model of the park. The models of the mountains were like piles of green and brown laundry, the glaciers sheets. The lakes were blue plastic. A red ribbon stood for the Going to the Sun Highway. It all looked manageable. The mother pointed. In the corner was the little house. You are here. She said to me then: Is there any place we can go to overlook the grizzlies?

This year the wolves have moved back into the park. And number 23 had mauled a camper, his third this year, but didn't kill her. Children walk through the station with bells on their feet. When the wind is right you can hear the songs drifting in from the higher trails. We were told there would be more people here this season because of the way the world has turned. There are too many people here for this place ever to be wild wild.

The cable's come as far as Cutbank. I rent a room in town my days off and watch the old movies they've juiced up with color. But the colors are as pale as an old rug. They look like they've already faded from old age. Now the blue sky outside looks manufactured, transported here from the other side of the mountain, its own conveyer belt. A bolt of dyed cloth. It is dripping with color. And my shorts here are khaki which is Urdu for the word dirt. Sometimes my eyes hurt from seeing the situation so clearly. Every ten minutes or so I hear the ice tumble in the machine out on the breezeway. Then the condenser kicks on. Beyond the hot table land I can see the five white fingers of the glacier.

All of what I know about the world worms its way to me from Atlanta. The news is to stay put. They have a park in Atlanta. In it is the Cyclorama, a huge picture with no edges. The battle of Atlanta is everywhere. The painting keeps wrapping around me so even out of the corner of my eyes I see nothing but the smoke and the smoky bodies falling about me. Atlanta is a mustard yellow in the distance. Sherman rides up in front of me. The battle ends and it begins again. I climb out of the painting through a hole in the floor. There is no place to overlook it. In the basement of the building is the famous steam locomotive THE GENERAL. I see Ted Turner has just painted that movie.

And it strikes me now that I looked like Buster Keaton, my campaign hat is tilted like his hat, as I stood next to King on the memorial steps. The monument behind us was white, even its shadows were white. King's suit had a sheen like feathers or skin. The white shirts glowed. Everyone wore white shirts except for my khaki since color hadn't been invented yet. The Muslims wore white. Their caps were white. And the crowd spilling down the steps looked like marble in white to stay cool. It was swampy near the river. They showed the speech around his birthday. I am always there, a ghost over his left shoulder. I was so young. I look as if nothing could surprise me. A ranger look. It always surprises me now. Now I know how it all came out, what happened to that man. I look like a statue. King flickers. I kept him in the corner of my eye. I watched the crowd. What I see is me seeing. I don't see what is coming. When they color it they will get the color of my eyes wrong.

In the window of the motel, I watch the day move. I have made a career with Interior. The range is being painted over by a deep blue sky. The glacier grips the mountain top then lets go to form a cloud. Then everything just goes.

The Teakwood Deck of the USS Indiana

I stabbed a man in Zulu. It had to do with a woman. I remember it was a pearled pen knife I'd got from a garage. I'd used it for whittling and the letters were wearing off. It broke off in his thigh and nicked the bone. It must have hurt like hell.

I did the time in Michigan City in the metal shop where I would brush on flux and other men would solder. Smoke would be going up all over the room. They made the denim clothes right there in the prison. The pants were as sharp as the sheet metal we were folding into dustpans and flour scoops. It was like I was a paper doll and they'd folded the jacket on me with the tabs creased over my shoulders. And the stuff never seemed to soften up but come back from the laundry shrunk and rumpled, just as stiff until the one time when all the starch would be gone and your clothes were rags and you got some new.

There was a man in there who was building a ship. When I first saw it, he had just laid down the keel and the hull looked like a shiny new coffin. This guy was in for life and he kept busy building a model of a battleship, the USS Indiana. He had hammered rejected license plates, flattened the numbers out. He'd fold and hammer. In the corner of the shop he'd pinned up the plans, a blue ship floated on the white paper. He had models made from balsa, the ribs showing through in parts. He had these molds of parts he would use to cast jigs and dies. His tools were blades and snips. The needles he used to sew the tiny flags, he used in the model as antennas. The ship was 1/48th size of the real thing, as big as a canoe. The men who walked the deck had heads the size of peas. He painted each face differently, the ratings on their blue sleeves. He told me stories about each man frozen there on the bridge, here tucking into a turret, here popping out of a hatch way. He showed me letters from the same men. He had written to them sending samples of the paint he had mixed asking the men who had actually scraped and painted the real ship if this was anywhere near. He knew the hour, the minute, of the day his ship was sailing, the moment he was modeling.

But this was years later. At first I saw the hull. I saw the pile of rivets he collected from the temples of old eyeglasses. He collected spools for depth charges, straws for gun barrels, window screen for the radar. He collected scraps from the floor of the shop and stockpiled them near the ship. Toothpicks, thimbles, bars of soap, gum wrappers. Lifesavers that were lifesavers, caps from tubes for valves and knobs, pins for shell casings. Everything was something else.

At first he started building only the ship but knew soon enough he'd finish. So he went back and made each part more detailed, the guns and funnels, then stopped again and made even the parts of parts. The pistons in the engines, light bulbs in the sockets.

Some men do this kind of thing. I whittled but I took a stick down to nothing. I watched the black knots of the branches under the bark grow smaller with each smooth strip until they finally disappeared. Maybe I'd sharpen the stick but that got old. Finally it is the shavings thin like the evening paper at my feet. That was what I was after. Strip things so fine that suddenly there is nothing there but the edge of the knife and the first layer of skin over my knuckle.

One of the anchors of the real battleship is on the lawn of the Memorial Coliseum in Fort Wayne. The anchor is gray and as big as a house. I took my then wife to see it. We looked around that state for the other one. But only found deck guns on lawns of the VFW, a whole battery at the football stadium near the university. In other towns, scrap had been melted and turned into statues of sailors looking up and tiny ships plowing through lead waves.

The deck of the model was the only real thing. He said the wood was salvaged from the deck. A guard brought him a plank of it. He let me plane it, strip the varnish and splinter it into boards. A smell still rose from it of pitch, maybe the sea. And I didn't want to stop. I've seen other pieces of the deck since then in junior high schools made into plaques for good citizens. It is beautiful wood. The metal plates engraved with names and dates are bolted on and near the bottom there is another smaller one that says this wood is from the deck of the battleship. It is like a piece of the true cross. And that is why I came to the capitol in Indianapolis to see the governor's desk. I heard it was made from the teakwood deck of the USS Indiana.

So imagine my surprise when in the rotunda of the building I find the finished model of the ship in a glass case with a little legend about the prisoner in Michigan City. He'd finished it before he'd died. The port-hole windows were cellophane cut from cigarette packs. The signal flags spelled out his name. It was painted that spooky gray, the color between the sea and sky, and the stern a blue airplane was actually taking off and had already climbed above the gleaming deck where a few seamen waved.

I felt sad for that con. He spent his life building this. He never got it right. It wasn't big enough or something.

I walked right into the governor's office. I'm a taxpayer. And the lady told me he wasn't there, but I told her I was more interested in the desk. So she let me in. "It's beautiful, isn't it?" she said opening the curtains for the light that skidded across the top cut to the shape of the state. One edge was pretty straight and the other, where the river ran, looked as if that end had melted like a piece of butter into toast. I ran my hand along the length of it, felt how smooth it was—the grain runs north and south—when the governor walked in with his state trooper.

"It's something," he said. He's a Republican. The trooper followed and stood behind him. "It has its own light."

The trooper wore a sea blue uniform with sky blue patches at the shoulders and the cuff. Belts hung all over him. Stripes and creases ran down his legs. Braids and chains. The pants were wool. He watched me. And I looked at him.

Jesus, you've got to love a man in uniform.

I stepped up to the desk and saw my face and the shadow of my body deep inside the swirling wood. I took my finger and pointed to the spot not far from Zulu where I knifed a man and said, "Right there." I pushed hard with my nail. "That's where I was born."

Limited

I saw the rock, saw the boy who threw it. I saw it hit the window next to the seat in front of me. Saw the window shatter instantly. Saw that now I couldn't see through the window anymore.

And we were gone out of Warsaw on the Broadway Limited. We hadn't stopped at Warsaw but gone through at sixty miles an hour. I saw the boy and the rock and his friends around him on their bicycles, and I imagined our train rocking the town, pushing the sound of the horn ahead along the tracks. Not stopping.

Now the whole car, everyone, is talking and pointing at the window. There is a high-pitched whistle. The light is different in the window since the windows are tinted. And the guy who sits there has just come back from the club car, dumb with luck, not drunk enough yet. I could have been sitting there, he says again. Everyone is talking about the kid with the rock and the window and outside now are cornfields and a few houses and the highway far away.

The conductor is looking out the rear door of this last car, and it looks like he is shaving. He is not shaving but whispering into a radio while he looks back at the tracks coming together.

I saw the rock, saw the boy, I tell him. He says that it's not the first time. Called someone who'll call the police. He's an old man. He's seen it all. He can't understand it.

I saw the rock float along with us at our speed, saw it barely catch up to us. I saw the boys on the bikes holding up their arms, jubilant, already tearing away from the place. The window went white.

He waited. Waited for the engines and the baggage cars, the coaches, the dome, the sleepers, the diner, the cafe. He waited, the rock already in his hand. More sleepers, more coaches, this last car. He waits, sees the people in the windows. Something so big and so much metal. Silver and blue. His whole town shaking. One long horn. He can't hear his friends egging him on. This rock won't stop a thing, won't slow nothing down. He throws it, and it's gone.

Three Tales of the Sister City

1.

If the Chamber had known he was arriving on the last United flight that evening someone would surely have been there to welcome him.

At first he waited near the doors that led out to the apron and the parked airplanes. It was raining. The airport is not equipped with the ramps that connect the planes to the terminal. Instead, passengers that night were given red, white, or blue umbrellas.

He looked outside. In the dark, he could see only the huge umbrellas bobbing, the colored panels and the white ones stained red by the flashing lights of the electric carts unloading the luggage. The umbrellas floated back to the airplane and up the metal stairs. The rain was a sheet on the white fuselage.

Passengers entered the terminal. A man in coveralls collected the umbrellas. Some were left open and some closed but not rolled. He hugged the umbrellas to his chest. Water dripped down the leg of his suit. After a bit, the man ran back out through the rain, rocking the bundle of umbrellas, three of them still open and shooting out about him. He pushed up the stairs to deliver the umbrellas to a steward handing them to passengers at the door of the airplane.

In the terminal some angry men shoved the umbrellas from themselves as they came in the door. The umbrellas flew across the waiting room, hitting across chairs and skidding over the floor. They kicked at the umbrellas on the floor. The carpet was dark from the water. He stood near the door, waiting for someone to come up to him, umbrellas scattered around him.

He was dressed in a white uniform—shoes, pants, tunic. The kerchief he wore when he worked at a table was in his pocket. He wore a white hat. His hair was wet. The only English he knew was *Don Hall,* the man who opened Takaoka, the restaurant named for our sister city, and who had invited him here. There were small groups of loud people all around him in the corridor. He went on up the ramp to claim his luggage.

The new conveyor wound around the room. The belt skimmed along just above the floor, curved back on itself, bulged, detoured around ceiling columns. The suitcases and flight bags went from one clutch of people to another, sniffed at their heels for an owner, wheeled around, meandered toward a businessman with a coat over his shoulder, and then disappeared behind the rubber strips in the wall.

His bags did not appear.

He stared at the black sheets moving by his feet. Only the women at the rental desk remained—red, green, orange, yellow—placing envelopes in lighted boards on the walls. There were a few men at telephones.

At last, the small case that held his knives appeared at his feet. The bright yellow tag had been placed on its handle. The knives had been taken away as he boarded a plane. He had tried to explain. They had given him a yellow tag instead.

He chased after the case, catching up to it in a few strides. Together they waited for more luggage. The conveyor stopped. Across the empty room he saw a few clumps of unclaimed luggage, none of it his.

Later that evening, he was in a restaurant kitchen. It wasn't clear that this was the restaurant where he was to work. He had been saying Don Hall to everyone, and now he was in a restaurant and here he felt more at home.

The woman who had shown him to the kitchen sat across from him at the shining steel table. The kitchen had been cleaned at closing, and the metal sang in the bright light. There were chrome panels on the walls, woven aluminum racks, nickel trim on the oven doors. The sinks, the freezer doors, the shelves stacked with bone dishes were of stainless. He was stirring the burnishing balls with his hand. He lifted a dozen to his face, let them spill through his fingers back into the bright tin can. The drains were minted coins set into the floor.

The woman had been gesturing all the time. She lifted a silver hood on one of the tables. He saw tubs of butters and white pastes, yellow and red sauces, shaved meats and dried cheeses. She placed before him a loaf of bread and a pale green head of lettuce.

He opened his case and took out his knives, crossing two before him on his oiled cutting board. He held the head of lettuce in both hands for a second then set it down firmly as if he were setting a stone.

He cut into the little finger of his left hand on one of the first slices through the lettuce but did not realize it. There were drops of blood on the almost white leaves. He saw the darker veins running through the pale leaf.

The woman ran for help. He pressed the wound against the leg of his pants. He still wasn't afraid, but he was alone again.

2.

The man who was the official photographer for the Chamber came from one of those countries that has no language of its own.

He was the last known immigrant to the city.

He was taking pictures of the summer parade and was allowed to walk in the street. The children on the curb were waving Japanese flags. He wore several cameras each with different lenses.

In the parade, the embassy from our sister city rode in a yellow bus. They wore blue kimonos and leaned out through the open windows of the bus. They took pictures of the children on the curb waving the Japanese flags. Their wide blue sleeves swung along the yellow sides of the bus. Red lights flashed.

He saw her in the window beneath the black image of a bird. A black pinstripe ran the length of the bus. He walked along taking her picture—her white face, her black hair, the blue kimono and the knot of the white obi.

When she arrived at his house that evening, he could barely hide his disappointment. She wore western dress.

In the basement where he had his studio and darkroom he showed her the framed pictures of his daughter that hung on every wall.

She turned from one picture, touched her own breast, and pointed at his daughter. He looked down through his glasses, his head tilted away, at his daughter's chest. He saw below each full breast a small dark nipple.

He turned back to the woman who now looked at the popcorn she held in her cupped hands. She brought the popcorn up to her face and with her tongue took one kernel into her mouth. Some other kernels had fallen on the wood table below her knees, and he saw that each kernel looked like an orchid. Their metallic throats were the fragments of the shell, the seed turned inside out.

3.

We had no way of knowing they were mad at each other.

When they arrived in Fort Wayne, we thought they looked enough alike to be brothers.

At our noon meetings at the Chamber, they uncrated the boxes that had been delivered that day. They held up shovels and brushed off the packing straw; they oiled the clippers while we watched. We saw the rakes and the brooms, the trowels and the hoes. When the boulders began to arrive they took turns telling stories of discovering each stone, of wanting that one to go to America, to the Sister City. The stones spoke saying so.

Everything followed. The smaller rocks and the pebbles in jars, the envelopes of pine needles, the stone lanterns, the bamboo pipe. The plants and the trees were waved through customs. Even some water came from Japan with a note from the mayor.

They were given a backhoe to use and instructions on how to run it. They were shown the stretch of yard east of the Performing Arts Building that had been set aside.

And they worked well enough together, setting stones, the dwarf pines, the creeping evergreens. It began to take shape in our minds.

Then they began fighting. They knocked over piles of rock, stepped on the dam of pebbles and sand they had made to form the pools. They stopped people as they walked from the parking lots to work.

"This or this?" they asked. "This or this?"

No one knew what to do. They worked on opposite sides of the plot, and we heard that they threatened each other with tools. We watched from office buildings. People took sack lunches outside and watched for the hour. Sides were being taken. Pools and lotteries were being formed. Bets placed. We talked of little else.

No one could talk to them. They stopped talking to each other. Our local architect, the men from the city greenhouse, the women who had taken the flower arranging course in our sister city all tried to explain to them how we felt.

Really, we could see no difference between them. It all looked Japanese. We liked the colors next to the red brick of the building.

Finally one of them abandoned the project site altogether, drove the backhoe to another part of the newly sodded lawn, and started digging. The other one paid no attention, poured goldfish into the shallow pond.

The delegation had come from Takaoka to escort the gardeners home. At the airport the Japanese were dressed to the hilt. We all bowed to say good-bye. We muttered a few words we knew. We had arranged ourselves around the brown waiting area and kept the two of them far apart. They sat silently, heads bowed. All of us pretended none of this had happened.

The runway stretched on and on.

A woman from our city broke the silence, suggested that we sing the state song, that everyone should sing.

The out-of-town businessmen stood up, charmed by the silk and smiles.

We pretended to sing. The woman had a clear, high voice. She sang the state song—a song about the rivers, the trees, the meadows, the hills, the unimproved beauty of our state.

Guam

The time in Indiana never changes. I grew up minutes from the Ohio line, and in the spring, the clocks leapt forward there. But in Indiana we'd lose an hour without trying.

A pack of us in my father's Olds crossed over to Van Wert and a bar there called Mr. Entertainer and got smashed on 3.2 beer, legal for minors. In the summers the nights were long, longer than the bars were open, and we waited for the dawn, parked on some township road, the car wading in the corn. It was the funniest thing to us, buzzed as we were, to race the sun back to Indiana. There were five guys in the back seat. We took off, the tail of my father's car dragging in the gravel. Even floored, it took a quarter section before the overdrive cut in, and then, maybe, we hit a grade at an intersection or the road tossed us up when it switched to tar or oil. The shocks heaved, and we were flying, the eight knocking and the tires revving off the ground. This was dawn. Maybe there was a farmer on a Case, scything the ditch weed with a sickle bar. All of us stuck our arms out the windows, flapping our wings. I blew the horn, and we watched ourselves pass the sound. We saw it roll off the fenders and tumble into the dust, bounce a few times behind us like something we'd killed. We were moving so fast, we weren't moving, like the times all of us had sat in our fathers' parked cars and pretended to drive, that fast. And then we jumped over another road and into Indiana, and there, it was an hour before we left the bar, and we felt like we had cheated on several things and gotten away with it all.

I could tell this hadn't impressed her. A frat house friend from college had set us up. This was the year after graduation when I was sharing a flat the company owned with some other guys. It was on the west side, and for the first couple of weeks I lived there I watched the sun set in a smudge on the other side of the river at the end of our street. Her name was Doreen, and this was the only time I ever took her out.

"So, where you from, Doreen?" I asked. We were walking around Times Square looking for something to do.

"We moved around a lot," she said.

This was kind of a lie, I found out. Later, at the comedy club where we ended up, all the comics taking turns at the open mic started their routines by telling us we were a good looking crowd and asking us where we were from.

"Guam!" Doreen shouted louder than the rest of us could shout where we were from. And all the comics picked her out of the noise of states and cities.

"You're kidding. You're from Guam!" they'd say, adjusting the microphone stand to their height. Guam is a funny enough word, and they all had jokes they'd fire off as they settled into their timing and material.

Doreen rolled her drink between her hands. Her neck snapped back when she laughed. Things dangled from her ears. She'd say, "Guam!" when the next guy came on and asked, nervous and squinting in the lights, where we where from. And Guam again for the guy after that. It was funny because none of the comics had heard the one before him, passing the time in the green room backstage. So the last several were getting laughs just for throwing off the question. The house sat still to let Doreen answer the question he had forgotten, in the silence, he had asked. "Guam! I'm from Guam!" and the comic would recover with a joke about food or sex, thanking her with his eyes and the cock of his head for such a straight line. But by this time I couldn't laugh anymore because I had laughed so much already at all the other comics who'd come before. They had been funny. I felt bad that there was no way to let the last ones know they were funny but by laughing, and I just couldn't anymore.

It was early in the morning when we left. A new comic was asking what remained of the audience where they were from. We started walking home.

"So, what was Guam like?" I asked Doreen. I imagined island beaches of ground volcanoes, cinder block houses painted after-dinner mint colors, reefs made from rusted hulks of sunken ships. Everyone is related and looks the same.

"I was only born there," Doreen said, "I'm from no place really. But I remember it like every place else I've lived. Quonset huts, lots of Quonset huts."

It was early in the morning, and I was trying to think how to get us to an after hours club downtown my roommate had told me about. There, no one would expect me to laugh, just dance and drink, and I could get close to Doreen and shout in her ear, ask her more questions she wouldn't answer. I still didn't know then how the night would turn out.

Tomorrow's market in Tokyo had already closed. Hong Kong had fixed the price of gold. Their yesterdays already heading this way. In my office, I kept a laundered shirt in my desk drawer. No need to go home. There were no cabs. There never are. We were standing on a traffic island in the middle of Broadway, back to back and circling each other, concentrating on the cars as they rushed by. Above us, the lights of the big signs sputtered all around. I began my story about where I was from and what I did when I was there. I thought about Guam again while I was talking. I thought of the surge of water the moon pushes ahead of itself every day, bearing down on that pile of sand. And I thought about the people there, just getting up or just going to bed, laughing at each other, never thinking that I was thinking about them, here and at this very moment on the other side of the world.

The War That Never Ends

That summer I followed the trucks as they cut down the trees. I sold ice cream to the kids who watched, drawn by the pitch of the chainsaws and the wood chipper. Our convoy snaked through the terraced neighborhoods. The green city 2 and ½, the cherry picker folded on top, hauled the chipper, a yellow cannon. And trailing behind, the dump truck, its bed mounded with chips, pulled the leggy circular saw skirted with canvas that ground down the stumps. The trucks' lights flashed. They bucked in low gear. Their drivers rode the brakes, looking for the trees marked with the white X's. I pedaled hard behind them, thumbing the bells when I thought about it, jacking the freezer box back and forth as I cranked up a hill. I breathed in their trail of sickly sweet fresh-cut green wood and burned sap. The trees arched over us, leafless and dying.

More kids banged out of the screen doors, clutching change in their fists. They jumped on their chopped bikes and swerved in behind me. Their axle cleaners, strips of leather riveted together with a cheap reflector, plunked the spokes of their wheels when we coasted, sounding like a flat oriental instrument.

I sold chocolate bombs with soft centers and popsicle rockets I broke in two on the edge of the cart, plugs of ribboned ice cream in paper cups they ate with flat wooden spoons that came wrapped in wax paper I ripped from a belt, tubes of orange pushups with pointed sticks, fudge bars that crusted over white in the humidity, sandwiches with the wafers peeling in strips, and dreamsicles evaporating into thin air. The kids sat on the curbs, a splatter of drips around their feet in the gutters. A man in a bucket up in the trees tied a cable around the biggest limb while men on the ground snipped off branches with the long handled pruners. The foreman, wearing a tie, pointed to the place he wanted the trunk to fall. I let a piece of dry ice smoke on the lid of the box.

I needed the money to stay in college and out of the draft. The popsicles sold for 7 cents. I cleared a penny after the rent on the trike. I had thought about enrolling in a safe academy, the Coast Guard or the Merchant Marine, wait out the war learning to shoot stars and spend my summers on long training cruises aboard old mine sweepers made of wood and non-magnetic metals. I had too many fillings to get in, cavities being a general indication of health, the applications said. Then, they could afford to be choosy.

"You sure you want that?" I said. The little boys still had their milk teeth. They stood around the cart and sucked the red syrup from the cherry pop, turning it into a chunk of pink ice on a stick. An older girl ran back home with the grimy change and a drumstick for her mother who stood in the shade of her front door.

The trees came apart so easily. Two or three chainsaws whined at once. Then one idled, putting, as its operator considered his next cut. The sawdust sifted down. Leg-length logs were lowered by rope like scenery on a stage. In the street a man swept the dust and twigs into neat piles with a new push broom, tapping the stiff bristles twice after each swipe.

The chipper ran on its own engine, chewing up the logs and brittle branches. The man on the ground hurled the wood into the blades like he was throwing spears. They caught and the engine coughed and almost stalled until the grinding drum inside bit in and screamed, ripping through the limbs that shot out in shreds up the stack. It had a rhythm like the locusts in the trees at night, and the sound brought the mothers out to watch. I sat waiting, flicking the tinkley bells on the handlebar between the wails that sounded above the sputtering engine. A mother drifted up to my cart and bought something and watched until the trunk crashed down and was sectioned into wheels and rolled away. All the time she held the mushy wrapper away from her body. Then she threw the stained stick on the piles of sawdust and brown leaves.

The houses had been shaded, softened by the canopy above. Now after the trees were cut the houses looked stark and new again, just built, the lawn bald where the children had played. The sky lifted, and I could make out the shapes of dormers and eaves and see the sickly TV antennas twisted on the roofs, saplings that didn't survive the winter.

I had lived through an age of service. Bread trucks delivered then. Men sharpened knives at your door. There were brushes for everything. Milk in bottles appeared on the stoop. The milk cartons now are printed with faces of newsboys who've disappeared. They identify the dead with dental records. All that summer the trees kept dying and the city crews, their saws calling back and forth to each other, cut every elm.

I didn't cheat the war but went. In the cities they blew up trucks with hand grenades dropped into fuel tanks. A rubber band held the plunger in until the gas dissolved the rubber. There were always two explosions in Saigon. The first to bring the crowd. The streets were filled with bicycles. As they flowed by me, they made a soft sawing sound as soft as chirping crickets.

When I came home, I rode a bike along streets I didn't recognize. The trees the city planted, the gingkos and the crimson maples, had filled in. Along the fences the Chinese elms sprayed up, weeds, from all the trimming. The houses were smaller. The hills were steeper. The telephone poles still towered above the new trees, their cables sagging. At one pole a wire angled out from the top and ran to the ground. A long time ago the wire had grown into a tree branch. When they cut that tree down, they cut on either side of the wire leaving the gray slice behind, still suspended, floating above me. Straddling my bike, I stood there awhile keeping that disk of wood between me and the sun, trying to imagine the time it took for the tree to absorb the wire. The wire hasn't let go, even now when the disease is dead.

Chatty Cathy Falls into the Wrong Hands

Let me tell you that the boys who stole me from Baby Face, lusting after the secret of this voice, their own hearts racing when they screwed their eyes down to the scale of my dress tipping the scales that shut mine, as good as they were with their hands, came away disappointed when all they found after they found no easy way in (and they had ways) was a whorl of perforations in my chest more like a pattern left by a mustard plaster or a Band-Aid than the actual ventilation of my views; and I told them all I was admitting was sound, all I was allowing was conversation as they tossed me away without so much as another word like a live grenade seconds before I blew, pin pulled out, as if I had the short fuse, armed and fertile as I was without a loop to hang on; if they only would have stopped to hear what I had to say instead of hearing their own inarticulate insides, I would have told them how things work in this world, all right; can a man imitate speech? I ask you; I was born talking, talking borne, wired and whining, content enough to be a thing itself, a person and a place, made to lie on my back and run on, coming to understand why those boys were so uncomfortable with the hollow part of language, and imagining a woman who talks too much; and I find that even if, after plugging me a time or two, the boys had decided to unscrew my noggin to look inside, to uncoil what was left of this doll's notion and then send my fuller-brush head back to Baby Face on a Mattel tea plate with my eyes rolled up inside my brain, a replica of screams, a fabrication (after all) of speech playing dumb, I would, always, even as we speak, let that other part of me go on talking (listen to me) until the line runs in

Evaporation

Your mother can't even remember why I never drink. She sits upstairs by the bedroom window until the timed diamond lights switch off, repeats every question I ask her.

"What are you doing?"

"What are you doing?" she says.

Kids on bikes racing on the infield drag clouds of dirt from base to base. The softball players drink beer in the stands, telling each other stories about the game they have just played. Their voices carry. It's against park rules. It's a public park.

"They shouldn't be drinking."

"They shouldn't be drinking," your mother says, her face reflected like smoke in the window. I had turned on the light on the chest of drawers to write some letters while I was thinking of it. One to Bill Kaple down at the City Light and another to the reporter I like at WKJG. The next morning, I went and picked up the beer cans from beneath the bleachers, filled the yellow fifty gallon drum the park board leaves for trash. I flicked out the dregs from each can onto the dust. The beer dribbled into shimmering balls of gray powered mud almost like mercury before the ground got dry again.

I've told you how in 1930 I was working for the Pennsy when the foreman said, "We're going to have to lay you off, Jimmy." I was a management trainee, but that day I was a gandy dancer learning the ropes. "Just for a little while," he said. I wasn't called back until 1938, but by that time I was working for the City Light, turning off the electricity when people ran up there light bills while they were paying down their gas bills and setting meters again when they paid off the light bill. But I was lucky in 1930 when they laid me off from the Pennsy. I got another job right away as an orderly at the Irene Byron outside of town. I had to live on the grounds, in the ward and come home only on the weekend. I left you and your mother early every Sunday and walked up the Kendalville Road, out into the country to the county farm and the children's home to the sanatorium where I wheeled the TB patients through the big French doors out onto the screened in porches even in winter.

I listened to them breathe on those cold nights, the moon throwing shadows of the screens like a net over their wrapped up bodies. Their breath smoked. The screens rattled in their frames when the wind blew. The big engines of the night trains on the Big Four track slipped climbing the steep grade behind the powerhouse, lost their head of steam and panted up the hill.

This was before the repeal of Prohibition. Hospitals were granted an allowance for evaporation of the alcohol they could use. We all knew this. Most of the orderlies stole a teaspoon or two from each big jug, the theft disguised as a part of the fraction that was lost naturally. I kept a Nehi bottle hidden in the steam tunnels too. The tunnels connected all the wards and the cottages to the powerhouse. We used them in winter to go from place to place. The pipes hissed at the joints and sweated hugging the wet walls underground. A few bulbs strung overhead lit the junctions where the tunnels forked off with little puddles of light. I saw the sparkle of other bottles stuffed behind a knot of valves or beneath the wooden duck board on the floor. I wrapped my bottle in asbestos batting so it looked like a section of discarded scrap pipe.

Your mother doesn't remember this. We lived then with your grandmother who was failing, and once you all had to hide behind the curtains when the landlord came for the rent. I collapsed those weekends after the long walk home from the country. Your mother forgets, forgets how we worried, how we saved everything, and how I told her the alcohol accumulated drop by drop, more than a swallow, past a couple of fingers. Those nights I slept with her I listened to her breathe. I woke up after midnight, screwed up from the shift I worked. Her breathing catches when she sleeps, not so much a snore as a click back in her throat that sounds like a clock ticking or a leaky faucet. And I figured in every exchange of air we were losing something. We were falling behind. Soon the act of breathing itself wouldn't be worth a good goddamn. I was so tired. Some nights finally I hoped she wouldn't be able to persuade herself to try again, just settle into a last long sigh. I held my breath those nights so I could hear her, hear if this was it or this one or the next. But then the room would lighten enough for me to see the blankets rise and fall, and I had to leave before you even woke up to make it back to the sanatorium in time.

I told you how we went to a party after the repeal, how things were looking up. The alcohol we skimmed was still illegal but in a different way now. The party was out in Huntington. We were going to drink it all, toast the end of our bootlegging. Ed Patton, who's past away now, and I took the first belt. We were lucky. We had eaten a lot of potato salad, ham sandwiches, and deviled eggs while we mixed together the hooch in a wash tub, cutting it with lime rickey. Somebody had replaced the grain alcohol we stole with the rubbing kind, and both of us were out cold before we knew it. I've told you this. I came to under the kitchen sink. Back then there were three pipes—one for the hot, one for the cold, and one for something I can't remember. I woke looking up at those bars and knew I was in jail.

"Ed," I had said to him after taking the first swallow, "this is sure hard to get down." It's the last thing I remember before the pipes. They pumped my stomach and Ed's too who froze both his feet later at the Battle of the Bulge and in the hospital then all the doctors asked him if he was related to the general, and he just said, "Hell, no!"

That was my last party and an end to all my drinking. People had come drunk to it, drunk on moonshine rye and smuggled Canadian whiskey. Perry Monet said he could walk a straight line and walked straight over the kitchen table and up and over the back of the davenport and on out the door and into the backyard. Your mother and Marcella Voltz put ForestNorton in the ringer washer and turned it on. He went around and round. I never knew who switched the alcohol. He might have been at the party, already pissed from the real stuff, too scared or stupid to say a word. I've been a sober man ever since.

At the sanatorium, one thing I had to do was massage the patients. I remember the chill it left on my hands when I swabbed the rubbing alcohol over someone's back, the way the skin drew up tight. From then on the vapor always made me a little sick, so I held my breath until I could feel the skin turn rough and warm. A doctor explained it to me once, how a liquid warms to the degree it takes to turn it to air and how it stays at the temperature, even if you add more heat, until the liquid's all gone.

Not much later, I was walking the alleys for the City Light. Tramps had scrawled these picture messages in chalk on the utility poles. *A dishonest man lives here.* A circle with an X inside marked a house good for a handout. A jagged line of triangles meant to tell a pitiful story. A bunch of lines was food for chores. You learned to draw the smiling cat you found scribbled on the paving bricks behind our house on Oakland Street. A kind-hearted woman, a kind-hearted woman lives here. You listened to the men on the back steps while they ate their fried egg sandwiches your mother made for them. And those weekend nights when I was home, you told me their stories, and they were always the same, how they'd heard of work in town, how they had a kid like you at home.

People waited. Once I had to shut off the power to a house on Brandroff Street. The meter was in the basement. I had to go through a bulk head in the back. In the backyard around a card table were six or seven men all out of work playing euchre or watching the game. They stopped and turned toward me, looked at me standing in a clump of hollyhocks and ashes while the tenant fiddled with the lock on the door. I expected something would happen, for them to run me off. Instead they spend the moment just staring at me, as if I wasn't worth the effort. The patients too, on the breezeways and porches, shrinking inside their rugs, watched the moon rise and then set. And your mother, back then, sitting with her mother, trying to pry her mouth open with a spoonful of broth.

Your mother sleeps all the time now, even in the chair beside the window. In the park, a yellow tractor comes each day to drag the field smooth again with an old piece of chain link fence. The cloud of dust it raises drifts this way. I try to remember when it started happening, how we got to here. That ratchet in her throat cranks her head down, her chin to her chest.

"Blanche," I say, "Blanche, wake up."

She starts. "Wake up," she says. "Wake up."

And I try to think of something more to say.

Miners

Going east, I cross the Ohio by a bridge that empties on the west side, smack into a mountain face tunneled through to Wheeling. Set back from the highway on the old roadbeds are the miners' houses. Mountains are at their backdoors. The highway cuts through the mountains, and on the sheer faces of the cliffs on both sides, I see where they've bored and set the charges like a pencil split in two and the lead removed.

I think about the products of coal. The stockings you wear. The records you play. The aspirin you take. The pencil you write with. These are mine. What would we do without carbon?

The face of the land is changing. I am going east so I can write to you.

The hillsides are quarries mining men. The men are going home where they will discover that all the waters in Shakespeare will not clean them. This life has gotten under their skins. They make love in smudges.

I am going further east where men are inside of things, where they own things inside and out.

I am writing this with a pencil painted yellow and printed with a silhouette of a woman with no arms.

I wish I were a miner so that when you turned your back to me and the face of the land changed, before I would go back underground, I would reach out and write with my black finger some graphite text on the places you could not reach.

"You," it would say, "are mine."

The War of Northern Aggression

Sometimes we are mistaken for Nazis. We are not Nazis. It is our blond hair. It is our white skins. The names are not Latin. Johnston, Buell, Early, and Jackson. We speak English to each other when we wish not to be understood. We marry our cousins and stay within the walls of our villas. We have been here generations now, but cannot forget the country we have left behind. Our ancestors burned their ships in the harbors. Pilgrims, my friend. But do not call us Yankees. Never call us Yankees.

We have traveled to Bogota from our homes in the mountains to see the North American vice presidents when they make their state visits. We are curious about such men. We watch as the *campesinos* pelt the limousines with eggs and paving stones from the plazas. I myself liked Señor Nixon, his face the color of newsprint. How he smiled and waved even as the masses swamped his sweating blue Cadillac.

For awhile we grew rubber. Then for a long time bananas, but the bananas are all dying now. You do not know this yet in the north. A fungus infests the plantations, staining the leaves of the trees. The plants are all of the same variety, interbred, like us, our white flesh like the flesh of the banana, vulnerable to such things. We collect the toy Spanish horses now, grow a little coffee and broker chocolate, even some cotton. We grow the cashew, too, along with other crops.

My family owned land outside of Atlanta. Sherman slept there, my granddaddy told the children, one night during the siege. Refusing the master bedroom, he pitched a tent in the gardens. Tara, yes, like the movie. The flowers bloomed and the sky turned red with flame. I have never been there. My picture of the mansion comes from the books of the time, little Greek temples surrounded by weeping trees. I think of the acropolis in Athens, where I have been on business, the white porches and the fluted columns. When I was there, they were restoring the Parthenon, encased in scaffolding, not to the way it looked before the Turks blew it up but to its previous state of decay. It had grown shabby. It had melted like a cake in the heat of the exhaust, the *nefos*, the Greeks call it, the cloud of smoke. I think of the house in Atlanta that way. Still smoldering, always smoldering. The white walls scorched and pocked from countless bullets. Zouaves, who look like Turks, are carrying away the portraits of my forebears and their dogs. The slaves, dazed, attach themselves as contraband to the Union invader.

Now, we sing the old hymns in English still. Here, where we feel in our bones, the seasons in reverse, we grow nostalgic. We have avoided our whole history by leaving the south of the north. We import cases of Coca-Cola from Atlanta for our cotillions in the fall where I wear the moth-eaten gray and yellow tunic of my great granddaddy. The ladies, caged in ancient contraptions of whalebone and browning silk, sip from the heavy glass bottles of Coke. The salted peanuts blanch, dissolve in the dregs of the flat black syrup.

We watch the burning of Atlanta every year on television. We know the lines of the movie by heart. The dish is in the nearest grove of our dying banana trees. The rotting leaves collect in its shallow palm breaking up reception. On our screens, the scratchy snow is an image of the mosaic disease infecting our dying banana trees. Today on CNN, through bursts of static, we watched the pictures of North American helicopters settling in our own jungles like falling leaves. The *guardia* set fire to the bales of coca. Then we looked out of our windows and saw the coiling trunks of the new forest of smoke, growing on the slopes of the blue hills beyond. And then you came to take us back with you.

Listen, no place is home but this home for us. You North Americans should know how we feel. To be extraditable. A nation such as yours made up of people who have come from elsewhere, you should know. But you forget, you forget, my friend, the bitter taste of leaving for good. For who has left the garden of North America once they have arrived. Here, we still celebrate the Fourth of July by not noticing its passing, still mourning the fall of Vicksburg long ago. We Southerners are one example. We left and never thought to go back. And there is the colony of free black men and women all named Doe, who we think of as kin, killing each other as we speak in their postage stamp country on the green equatorial shores of western Africa.

Elkhart, There, at the End of the World

The roads are lined with produce stands. There is no cider or ear corn as there would be in early fall but the feral fruit of mid-summer, strawberries and melons. Little is left in the shacks—empty wicker quarts and pecks, fragile chain scales, U-Pick-Em signs. I head toward Elkhart, Indiana, where reed and brass instruments are made. The wind whistles through the car, and I follow a station wagon of migrant workers, tailgate down, leaking the brown exhaust of legs and arms, up from Lincoln Highway toward Michigan to cherries and tomatoes. I pass the sod farms where the sprinklers stutter and the overhead systems, struts and hoses, walk with water across the turf to the ruled black strips left after the grass is rolled away.

In Elkhart I stop for a train. Somewhere Conn makes clarinets and trumpets and the good high school bands have their pick of instruments. The marching bands spend their summers in travel and parades in all the nearby towns.

The train skates for Chicago as parts of houses back up the street behind me. Tractors pulling trailers of modular homes, "Oversized Load" attached to their bumpers. The stalled lead cars and the trailing cars flash their yellow warning lights. We wait and the wind comes up to stir the red pennants and the clear plastic sheets that cover the open half of the house.

Somewhere in the middle of this I think that there is a place that produces a lasting thing. What stays when even the earth gets up and moves away? It is the season when the hot sky touches the ground and draws the water away. The earth cools too quickly and things keep moving toward high wind, tornadoes.

The train squeals by, and across the right-of-way the flat sound of siding dins again from the trailer factories. A bottom to the wind.

A horn. A horn. I move.

Blue Hair

Mister Pepe lowers the clear plastic canopy over my head, flicks a few switches, the engines throb to life. My blue hair, woven into whistling rollers, a snug helmet, bristles with bobby pins. The women on either side of me thumb through their magazines, but I am flying, flying over the checkerboard of friendly fields. The leafy woods below look like mats of hair on a linoleum floor. The engines roar. My wing men tuck in beside me, our staggered flight piecing together the formation of the whole bomb group. Now the contrails peel off our leading edges. We bank together, coming to the heading that will take us back to the Ruhr. The sky, severely clear. Mister Pepe pokes a puffy cloud with his rat tail comb. The starched white cliffs of Dover drape away below us. The flashing sliver of shears darts in and out. Nimble pursuit planes. Escorts with belly tanks nipping at our stragglers.

Years ago, I knew the war was over when the bombers left the plants with their aluminum skins unpainted. No need to camouflage the Boeings with that European forest green. It was only a matter of time. Hair, too, a matter of time. My hair would grow back. I watched as wave after wave of silver Forts lumbered over, climbed above the sound, the pounding of their engines rattling the bones in my head, my bare neck chilled by the breeze blowing in off the water.

"The hair, it is dead," Mister Pepe whispered in my ear. This was later when I first came here. He rinsed my hair of color, the tarnished yellow coiling down the drain. He had me peer into a microscope in the backroom of his salon. Curling in behind me, he tweezed the knobs on the machine. I saw the shaft of the hair he had plucked from my scalp rip apart then reassemble, watched as my sight dove right through the splitting hair, my vision melting then turning hard.

"There," I said when it came into view, kinked and barked like a tree limb, blue as ice.

"Let me see," Mister Pepe said, wedging in to look. "It is damaged, no? The over-treated hair. The frazzled ends. You need my help, yes?"

And years before that the general had said, "You cannot tell anyone why you cut your hair." I was a young girl in Seattle. My parents stood in the doorway of our kitchen hugging each other as they watched the WAC snip a few locks. She held them up to the light then draped the strands across the outstretched arms of a warrant officer. He slid the hair through his fingers, stretched it out straight, and lowered it into a box like the one florists use for long stemmed roses.

I was a blond, and my hair had never been crimped or permed or ironed. I never knotted it up into braids, only trimmed the fraying. It was naturally straight. I brushed it every night a hundred times and shampooed it with eggs and honey. When I slept, my hair nestled in behind me like another person slipping up against my back as I breathed, a heavy purring weight.

"It's a secret," the WAC had said, evening the ends. "Let me look at you." She held my chin in her palm, her fingers squeezing my cheeks. "You look all grown up now. Not a word until the war is over. Tell people it was too much bother, a waste of water washing it." She plucked one single strand that clung to my sleeve as if she were pulling a stitch through me. She pulled until the other end swung free, and then she placed it with the rest in the box.

And only last week with my hair all done up, I was flying. From the air, the Rockies looked flattened down. The way the shadows fell fooled me into thinking the peaks were really craters. Then the clouds piled up below, and the jet climbed to evade the weather. The Air Force had bought the seat next to me for the bomb sight. It was in its crate sitting there.

The cadets in Colorado had given it to me. An honor guard had marched across a checkerboard courtyard. And now it is home on the coffee table with the magazines, a conversation piece. It looks as if it should be potted with some viny plant, its tendrils hooking on to the knobs and buttons. Flying home after the ceremony, I wrestled it out of the box and plunked it down on my lap. It had the heft of a head, a lover gazing up at me and me stroking his hair. I leaned forward, lowering myself to the cold metal. It smelled of oil and polish. I squinted through the lens as the plane bumped beneath me, riding the turbulence over the mountains. There was just enough light, a white dime-sized hole of light. I saw the cross-hairs, crisp and sharp, my dead hair, half a century old, sandwiched between the glass, deep within the machine. Outside the clouds broke apart, and in the Great Basin, the lights of each tiny city lit up as the sunset fell on each of them.

And now, I have been staring at this *Redbook* spread on my lap, and my eyes won't see the words. The dryers want to lull me to sleep. From up here, the letters on the page look like the ruined walls of buildings, remains of burned foundations, blocks of pitted houses, alley ways that lead to nowhere. I follow the footprints of bombs. I was reading about hair, about its history, about its chemistry, about how we know more about it now than ever before. Below me, the words explode as I read them. One after the other. There is the roar in my ears. I sit here waiting. Soon it will be my turn again.

It's Time

I remember the time each year when my husband cut back the raspberry bushes. I always thought he took too much, afterwards a row of whittled spikes where once a tangled mass of brambles boiled along the fence. He ripped out the dead canes altogether, brittle straws, pruned the branches down to nothing. He dug up the newly rooted tips where last year's growth had bowed over to the ground and took hold, the first long stride into the garden. Every spring, I believed they would never grow back, but in a few weeks, with the days lengthening, the stubby canes streaked with red, budded, shot up overnight.

Does it count as a first word? The other raspberry, the sound my daughter made, her tongue melting into slobber between her lips, stirring before dawn in the tiny bedroom down the hall. It was dark, and the wet blasts helped me navigate, the floors covered with her blocks and toys. Her room was pitch, the only light the daubs of radium I swiped from the factory outlining the rails and bars of her crib. At night it looked like a bridge lit up, suspended over the varnished surface of a wide, still river. The paint had dripped on the floor, formed a tiny drifting phosphorescent slick. My daughter tottered about. I could see only her shadow, her shape blotting out the dew of pulsing light behind her. She sprayed her one note greeting. When I picked her up, her tongue rasped next to my ear. I felt her whole body going into the sound, her breath dying down, her spit a mist on my cheek.

"Don't go," my husband had said. "Stay in bed. She's not crying. Ten minutes more. Let her go."

I could see he was looking at the time. I watched the luminous dial of his watch float up off the night stand. The little wedge the hands made rotated as he fumbled to right the face. From eleven o'clock the time spun to a little past six thirty. "She's up early," I heard him say. The little constellation spiraled back to the table.

Often there were flecks of paint in my hair. He said he could always find me in the dark. He'd kiss me through a cloud of stars. I'd shake my head and the sparks spilled down onto the pillow, sprinkling his face. My finger tips too lit up, stained where I held the brush and the tiny pot. I became distracted with my own caresses, streaks of light tracing his back, neck, hips. Flakes of light caught in the hairs on his chest and eyebrows, blinked on and off as he opened and closed his eyes. Where I kissed him I left welts of throbbing light. His lips grew brighter. It seemed like the fire should die out but it didn't, would only disappear with the dawn in the windows. We could see everything then and still hear our daughter down the hall cooing to herself, inventing a language to call me to her.

This was in Orange right after the war. They used women at the factory there to paint the clocks. Our hands were steady. We were patient, perfect for the delicate trimming, outlining the numerals with the radium, down to the marks on the sweep face, sketching hairlines on the minute hand. I had sable brushes I rolled on my tongue to hone a point sharp enough to jewel each second. The paint was sweet and thick like a frosting laced with a fruity essence. We'd thin it with our spit. Rich and heavy like the loam in the garden. It was piece work. At the long tables we'd race through the piles of parts, my hands brushing the other hands, reaching in for the next face or stem. The room was noisy. Alvina sang to herself. Blanche reeled off recipes. Marcella clucked. We talked with our eyes crossed over our work, "She had to get married. They went to Havre de Grace by train and were back by noon the next day." We paused between each sentence or verse as we dabbed the brushes to our lips. It was as if our voices came from somewhere else. I'd look away, out the huge windows to the brilliant sky. I can still hear the buzz above the table as something separate from the people there, another kind of radiation in the room that never seemed to burn out. The stories and the songs blend into one ache.

What more is there to tell? Our bones began to break under the slightest pressure—getting out of bed, climbing stairs. Our hair rinsed out of our scalps. Our fingertips turned black and the black spread along the fingers by the first knuckle while the skin held a wet sheen. Our hands were negatives of hands. The brittle black fingernails were etched with bone white.

But this was after so many of those afternoons at the Undark plant with its steady northern light. I remember cursing an eyelash that fluttered onto a face and smeared my work, how I damned my body for the few pennies I had lost, the several wasted minutes of work. "I'll race you, Myrna!" There were many factories in Orange, and their quitting whistles at the end of the day were all pitched differently. The white tables emptied, the heaps of silver parts, like ashes, at each place. Another shift, the night one, would collect the glowing work and ship it somewhere else to be assembled. We ran to the gates, to the streetcars waiting, to the movies that never stopped running. It was all about time, this life, and we couldn't see it.

At the trial, not one of us would speak, and the newspapers said how happy we were considering the sentences already imposed. We sat there with our smiles painted over our lips to hide our teeth. During recess in the ladies, we powdered over the bruises again. We couldn't blot the lipstick since our skin was so tender. Four clowns in the mirror, mouths like targets, stared back at us. We couldn't cry. It would ruin our work. In court, we listened to the evidence and covered our faces when we laughed at what was being said. I watched the clerk who recorded everything, his pencil stirring down the page. Sometimes he would be called upon to read testimony back, and I was taken by the accuracy of his words. I remembered the speeches that way. It seemed right, right down to some of the sounds he noted, pausing to insert *laughter* or *unintelligible.* I liked these moments best when the words were the only solid things left in court. The lawyers, the witnesses, the gallery, the jury were all poised, listening to the clerk. They might have been an audience from another time. The only thing left of us was that string of knots on paper, the one sound in the room.

My daughter loved the fresh raspberries in milk. The white milk coated the scoring between the tiny globes on each berry in the bowl. It looked like the milk drying on her tongue. The berries as they steeped turned the milk pink. She grabbed at the fruit, crushing it into her fist and then sliding the pulp into her mouth.

I haven't been able to speak since soon after the trial, and eating now, even the raspberries so ripe they liquefied when I picked them, is painful. The berries have seeds that shouldn't hurt the way they do. I can't explain this to my husband who sits reading the newspaper on the other side of the table, his fingers smudged with ink. I make the same sounds now the baby made, little whines and grunts. He's already used to it. I feel I am being whittled away like the nub of the pencil I write this with then sharpen with the paring knife. Why do people lick the lead point? Perhaps it is just a gesture of thought, a habit, hoping that the sound of a voice will rub off.

I'm not afraid. I know this now. It happened this morning when I was picking the berries. The bees were in the late blossoms on the canes above me. The canes trembled, about ready to bow over. Sweat scalded the skin of my arms and neck. The berries hung in clusters everywhere among the thorns and sharp leaves. I have no feeling left in the tips of my fingers, and as I watched my black hand close on each berry, the fruit seemed to leap from the stem into the numb folds on my palm. So little had held the berry in place, a shriveled ball and socket. The berry, a dusty matte red that soaked up the light, bled a little, a pool in my palm. I thought about sucking the raspberry into my mouth, straining it through what was left of my teeth. Instead, I reached out for another berry and then another, dumped them into the pint baskets squashed and ruptured, and rushed them into the house. I found a pencil and a piece of paper to write this down. Each word fell on the page, a burning tongue.

Fidel

My husband, I'll call him David, left me for my best friend. I'll call her Linda. Since then, I have found it difficult to sleep.

I have taken to listening to the radio through the night. The radio is next to the bed, an old floor model filled with tubes that heat up and glow through the joints in the wood frame. My father gave it to me when I left home to live with my husband I'm calling David. I used it then only as an end table next to the bed. I painted it a gloss red and covered it with house and garden magazines, the bottom one's back cover still sticks to the tacky enamel surface. I live in a city I'll call Fort Wayne.

I listen to a local station, I'll call WOWO. It is the oldest station in town. It's been on the air since the beginning of radio. My father listened to the same station ever since he bought the radio consol on time. I have seen the payment schedule. He kept it in the drawer beneath the sad face of the staring dials and the frowning window scaled with AM numbers. He penciled in 37¢ each week after he walked downtown to a store I'll call The Grand Leader to turn over the installment.

One night, when I couldn't sleep, I rolled over in bed and noticed for the first time since I had painted the radio red the two clunky knobs the size and shape of cherry cordials, one to tune and the other the power switch that also controls the volume. Without touching the tuning knob, I turned the radio on, but nothing happened. Nothing happened even after I waited the amount of time I thought it would need to warm up. I turned on the brass table lamp perched atop the pile of wrinkled magazines. I had never plugged in the old radio. I rolled out of bed and onto the floor. Behind the radio was an outlet where the table lamp and the modern clock radio were connected. I had the other radio's plug in hand as I pulled out what I thought would be the plug for the clock radio. It was the plug for the lamp instead. In the dark, I scraped the walls of the bedroom with the prongs of the radio's plug looking for the outlet never thinking to reinsert the plug of the lamp. I had painted the walls a linen white about the same time I had painted the radio red. When I found the outlet the radio lit up inside, green light leaking out every seam and joint. I was sitting on the floor when WOWO faded in, the station my father listened to years ago when he listened to this radio before I was even born.

The next few weeks I listened through the nights and into the morning. I left the radio on during the day for the cats who I'll call Amber, Silky, and Scooter as I stumbled off to work each day. They liked the purring box. In the evenings when I staggered back in I'd find them attached like furry limpets to shiny skin of the radio. The paint, constantly baked by the glowing tubes, gave off the stink of drying paint again and steeped the bedroom in that hopeful new smell it had when I first moved here with the man I am calling David.

The later it got at night the further back in time WOWO seemed to go with the music it played. After midnight scratchy recordings of Big Bands were introduced by Listo Fisher who pretended the broadcast still came from the ballrooms of the Hotel Indiana. Alfonse Bott, Tyrone Denig and the Draft Sisters, the brothers Melvin and Merv LeClair and their orchestras, Smoke Sessions and his Round Sound, the crooner Dick Jergens who sang with Bernard "Fudge" Royal and his band or with Whitney Pratt's Whirlwinds, and Bliss James singing the old standards. It was as if I had tuned into my father's era, the music slow, unamplified, and breathy. Toward morning the sound was like a syrup with wind instruments scored in octave steps, the brass all muted, the snares sanded, and the bass dripping.

Bob Sievers, who had been the morning farm show host at WOWO for as long as I could remember, came on at five. I had first seen him, though I had heard him for a long time before that, when I was in high school. On television, he was selling prepaid funerals to old people. He didn't look like his voice. And now I heard that voice again thanking Listo Fisher for standing watch at night and then cueing the Red Birds, a local quartet, to sing "Little Red Barn" as he dialed the first of ten Highway Patrol barracks to ask what the night had been like in the state I am calling Indiana.

The sputtering ring of the telephones on the radio sounded swaddled in cotton. It was five in the morning. My head melted into the flannel of the pillow slip. The only sound was the mumble of the connection as a desk sergeant answered in a place called Evansville. He whispered a sleepy monaural hello encased in the heavy Bakelite of an ancient telephone. Bob Sievers, his bass voice lowered a register, identified himself and ask about the weather down there in the southern part of the state. The flat accents of the trooper reported snow had fallen overnight but that the major roads were salted and plowed.

I waited for the next question, lifting my head from the pillow. Bob Sievers voice dove even lower, "And Sergeant, were there any fatals overnight." For a second I listened to the snow of static, the voltage of the phone picked up by the sensitive studio microphones. "No, Bob," the trooper answered, "a quiet night." Instantly I would hear the ratchet of the next number being dialed, the drowsy cop, the weather outside Vincennes, then South Bend, Terre Haute, Jasper, then on the toll road in Gary, Indianapolis, Mount Vernon, Monon, and finally Peru. At each post, the search for causalities, the crumbs of accidents. Every now and then someone would have died in a crash. The trooper sketched in the details. The road, its conditions, the stationary objects, the vehicles involved, and the units dispatched withholding the identities of the deceased until the notification of the next of kin.

There were nights I waited for such notification. I saw my husband behind the wheel of my best friend's car, his face stained by the dash light of the radio. He is listening to WOWO, the big bands of the early morning, when the car begins to pirouette on the parquet of black ice. I know that the radio is still playing, a miracle, after the car buries itself in a ditch of clattering cattails sprouting from the crusted snow. The last thing he hears, the car battery dying, is the quick muffled dialing of Bob Sieves, his morning round of calls, and the hoarse routine replies. I think to myself I am still some kind of kin. Those nights, I practiced my responses to the news brought to me by men in blue wool serge huddled on my stoop.

WOWO is a clear channel station, 50,000 watts. At sunset smaller stations on nearby interfering frequencies stop broadcasting and the signal can be picked up as far south as Florida and out west to the Rockies. Just north, the iron in the soil damps the power, soaking up the magnetic waves before they spread into Canada. Listening, I felt connected to the truck drivers in Texas and the night auditors on the outer banks who called into Listo Fisher and told him they were listening. Often they would ask "Where is Fort Wayne?" as if they had tuned into a strange new part of the planet. Listo Fisher would take requests, explain patiently the physics and the atmospheric quirks that allowed the callers to hear themselves on the radio they were listening to broadcast by a station days of travel away from where they were. "It's a miracle," some yahoo in a swamp would yodel.

One night in the middle of a beguine, a voice came on the radio speaking what I found out later was Spanish. For a moment in my sand bag state, I thought it must be part of the song, a conductor or an announcer turning to a ballroom full of people in a hotel, both the people and the hotel now long turned to dust and the evening just charged molecules on magnetic tape, saying to them good night and good-bye. Thank you for the lovely evening. We've been brought to you by United Fruit and now are returning you to your local studios. But the voice kept talking, rising and falling, the *r*'s rolling and the *k*'s clotting together. Every once and again I would recognize a word, its syllables all bitten through and the whole thing rounded out by a vowel that seemed endless, howling or whispered.

The telephone rang. It was three in the morning.

"What the hell is that?" my father asked. The words were in both my ears now. I could hear the speech in peaks playing on his radio across town, like a range of mountains floating above clouds.

"Dad, what are you doing up?"

"Listening to the radio when this blather came over it."

I asked him why he wasn't asleep instead. The radios continued to emit the speech, a rhythm had begun to emerge beneath the words, not unlike the beguine it had preempted. Just then there was a huge crash of static. I heard my father say, "What the," but it wasn't static it was applause, and as it trailed off, I heard the voice say the same phrase over again a few times, starting up again, as the cheering subsided.

"Oh," my father said, "you're awake then."

"Of course, I'm awake," I lied to him. "You woke me up." I asked him again why he was awake.

"I haven't slept in years."

"Well, go to sleep, Dad."

"You go to sleep then."

"I am asleep. I've been asleep," I said.

"What's that crap on the radio?"

"Change the station, Dad. Maybe it's the station."

"But I always listen to WOWO.

I hung up and listened to WOWO. The speech continued for two more hours punctuated by bursts of applause the sound then breaking into a chirping chant, steady at first then going out of phase, melting back into itself and the rising hiss of more applause. The voice would be there again. It seemed to plead or joke. It warned, begged. It egged on. It blamed and denied, sniffed its nose. It sneered. It promised. I could hear it tell a story. It explained what it had meant. It revised. It wooed. Toward the morning it grew hoarse. It grew hoarse and dried up. It wound up repeating a word, which seemed too long to me, again and again until that word was picked up by the listeners on the radio who amplified it into a cloud of noise that this time was static. Then Bob Sievers was on the radio and his theme song was playing:

Let me lay my head on a bed of new mown hay, hey hey!

There are so many secrets in this world. About the time my husband, who I'll call David, and my best friend, who I'll call Linda, started sleeping together, two silver blimps were launched in a swamp south of a city I'll call Miami. They were tethered there to slabs of freshly cured concrete a thousand feet below. I think of those balloons floating there, drifting toward each other, perhaps bumping together finally, and rebounding in excruciating slow-motion. The wires connecting them to the ground shored them up, I imagine, so their nuzzling was reigned in, the arc of rotation proscribed. They moved hugely, deliberately like whales in a tropic bay. Their shadows shifted on the spongy ground below. I am almost asleep, dreaming, when the nodding blimps turn into the slick bodies of my husband and my best friend sliding beneath a skin of sheets, moving as deliberately and as coyly until they are tangled up in each others embrace and then that Zeppelin in New Jersey bursts into flames and melts into itself, the fire spilling from the night sky. There is a voice on the radio crying how horrible, how horrible to see the skeleton of the airship support, for an instant, a white skin of flames.

The curious in south Florida were told that the bobbing balloons were part of a weather experiment, a lie. Their real purpose was to hold aloft a radio antenna aimed at Cuba. It was propaganda radio. The voice I had heard was Castro's Cuban radio's response, jamming the signal spilling south from the balloons, overflowing on the clear channel all the way north.

For a long time our government denied what was going on and the speeches continued through the night. I bought a Spanish to English dictionary and translated one word I'd catch out of the one thousand perhaps that flashed by, leafing through the book until I found something I thought sounded like what I had heard. He's talking about a ship, I'd think. And he is sitting or he sat once. Overlooking the sea specked with ships. Now there are roosters. Ships, the holds filled with roosters, who crow out the watch. Mothers waiting for the ships, I thought, at the docks, shielding their eyes in the sun, empty baskets balanced on their heads.

WOWO's ratings went up as people stayed awake late into the night to listen to the interruptions, the speeches with the static of applause. And, as if they realized they now had an audience, the programmers in Havana began to salt the broadcast with cuts of Latin music, bosa novas and sambas, anthems and pretty folk songs plucked out on guitars with squeaky strings. Downtown, during the day, I began to see people napping at their desks, sleepwalking to the copying rooms and the coffee machines. More men smoked cigars. High school Spanish classes were assigned to listen to the station at night, meeting at their teachers' houses for slumber parties. So tired, we were infected by our dreams. The days grew warmer. I had been unable to sleep for so long the measured pace of the people around me matched my own endless daily swim through the thick sunlit air. We moved like my cats, lounged and yawned, stared at each other with half-closed eyes.

I listened for Fidel at night. Over time, I counted on him. I translated his rambling monologues in my own dreamy way as he talked about his island with its green unpronounceable trees, the blooming pampas where butterflies from the north nested in the fall, lazy games of catch performed by children in starchy white uniforms chattering in a dialect that predates Columbus. You see, I was ready for someone to talk to me, to explain everything to me. How I looked like a movie star in those sunglasses I wore continually. How fires smell in the cane fields as the sugar carmelizes. I thought I understood romance for once and martyrdom, maybe even revolution. This ropey language, the syrup of its sound, an elixir, was on the air now all the time, crept into my bed each night.

What would my father say? It filled me up, crowding out the mortgaged furniture, the old sad music, the phone calls to the police, and all the names, especially the names I've now forgotten were ever attached to those other frequencies through which I drifted.

Seeing Eye

The kids on the stoops with the dogs are still confused. They tackle the overgrown puppies, tangling themselves in the harnesses and leads as the whining dogs lunge and stumble. Panting. Lots of panting.

"It's the Mailman Lady," the kids shout. I kind of throw the mail their way with just enough velocity for the postcards to strip away from the bundle, startling the dogs, who soundlessly bark at the spinning envelopes. The kids hang on, use their sweaty faces to spear an animal back, grope for a purchase of fur and skin.

"Letter carrier," I say over my shoulder. Each stride a sidewalk square. The next stoop of the rowhouse has another dog, another kid already mixing it up. The dog's ears are pointing my way. It's stepping all over the kid. And now the whole block of children and animals senses me. "The Mailman Lady," they howl. The dogs bob and focus, then snap and tumble with the kids, slough them off, cock themselves again. The dogs know. The kids are still confused, don't know what to make of me. Never seen one of me before. The dogs are attentive to ancient messages. The uniform. The territory. I smell just as sweet.

I'm a letter carrier in a town whose main industry is raising dogs. Guide dogs for the blind. Shepherds and retrievers mostly. Big brains and bones. Steady mutts with substantial paws, plodding beasts. Slobberingly loyal. Obedient, of course. Easy to clean. It's still a mystery to me just how the training works. The school is on another route, but I've seen the Quonset huts, the kennels, the field of stripped obstacles at the school. Every year the newspaper does a feature story with a page of pictures of the graduating dogs staring into the calm faces of their new masters. I only know the puppies come here to this bedroom community and are parceled out to families who keep them just like pets. After awhile you'll see the dog in the station wagon. A mom is driving, dropping her husband off at the platform, the kids at school. The dog commutes to work also, comes home for the night, a pillow to a pile of kids in front of the TV.

I run into the older dogs, already on the special lead, as volunteers walk them around the town. There isn't a street where you won't see a couple pairs plowing the sidewalks. The sighted volunteers, waving to each other, nudge their dogs around a corner. They slug their way through a cul-de-sac. At the corners, there are patient instructions. They wait for the light to change and for the scramble bell to sound. The dogs walk through the aisles of the stores downtown. They wait in packs for the special bus that distributes them in the neighborhoods. In fact, the town is overly complicated for its size, presenting to the dogs every possible distraction. Too many cats. Dummy fire hydrants. Revolving doors in the butcher shop. The park has been landscaped in levels. Stairs lead by fountains and reflecting pools. I see the dogs taking cab rides. There is an escalator leading down to a subway station with turnstiles but no trains. They take the elevator back to the surface where there are flower carts, news kiosks, street singers, three card monte games, people selling watches spread out on towels and other volunteers who pretend to be drunk and passed out on benches. Everywhere there are trees. Lots of trees. And people who have signed up to be people today walk their dogs and eat ice cream, read newspapers they then throw in the white wire trash bins scattered everywhere on the avenues. The dogs slog through it all as a car, slow enough to chase, cruises by blowing its horn. I'm part of this too, I know, though the mail I deliver is real. My satchel is strapped to the back of this tricycle cart, and I slalom through the plodding dogs and trainers on the street. The dogs sniff the wheels of the cart. The walkers, for a second tense, lose the strange connection with the animal. My cart speeds up, pulls me along. Up ahead, a wailing fire truck skids around the corner on its way to an imaginary fire.

Along with the letters, we all carry a repellent. It comes in a canister with a pump action like a purse-size cologne. It is standard issue with the uniform and fits neatly in a leather holster. At Brateman's, the store that carries all the uniforms, I attracted a crowd of men—cops and firefighters, other postal workers, meter readers—as I tried on the new uniforms. The skirt, the shorts, the dusty blue acrylic cardigan still patchless but with stamped buttons. The baseball cap, the pith helmet. I'd step out from the dark dressing room, wire hangers jingling, and the men stopped talking with the clerk who was sucking on pins. They leaned on the glass cases of badges, whistles, and utility belts and watched me look at myself in the mirrors. There were piles of canvas coveralls on the floors, boxes of steel toed shoes. I tried on a yellow slicker. "How does that feel?" the clerk asked, his mouth full of pins. It felt slick already with sweat. A sheriff's deputy twirled through a stand of string ties. They talked under their breath, examined a handcuff key. A dog and trainer glided through the racks of khaki shirts. I came out in pants that I had rolled up. I have always liked the stripe, that darker shade of blue, and the permanent crease that lets me fold everything back into the shape it started with. The clerk soaped the altered cuffs. In the dressing room, I stood there in the dark, my new clothes folding themselves into neat piles. I listened to the damped voices of the men outside, the dog whining, then yawning, and scratching, panting outside the door. The clerk made out the bill, punched the register. I had clothes for every weather and season, a week of shirts and calf-length socks. Shoes. At last he handed on the key chain and the repellent in its shiny case. "To keep the boys away," he said. I smiled thanked him, poised over the charge slip ready for the total. I knew it would take at least two trips out and back to the car to load the uniforms.

The mural above the Postmaster's door in the lobby is being restored to the way it looked when it was painted during the Depression. Scaffolding hides most of it now. The painters move deliberately in the rigging, scooting on their backs or stomachs. It seems to me they are too close to the work. The mural is about the guide dogs. The dogs are marching, leading a parade of blind workers. In the background are ghostly St. Bernards, border collies, and bloodhounds, all the working dogs working. The sky rolls with clouds, the rolling hills gesture like a cursive hand. The road they walk is like a signature, too. The painter signed his name in Braille, the code of bumps shaded to make it look raised on the flat wall.

In the lobby, the county association for the blind runs the news concession selling candy bars and newspapers, stationery supplies, and maps of the city's streets. They let Mabel, who mans the stand, smoke behind the counter. Her dog, a black Lab, curls around the stool, the stiff lead angling upward like a harpoon. Mabel's eyes are a kind of nougat. She never wears glasses. Smoking artlessly, she picks the tobacco off her tongue. It stays on her moist fingers.

My final job of the day is to clear sidewalk boxes outside the station in time to make the last dispatch. She hears me blowing through the lobby with the carton filled mainly with the metered mail in bundles.

"I always know it's you," she says, "You walk on your toes. I can't smell you." She feels her watch on her wrist, "Same time every day, too." I run through the lobby to the back with the mail. On my way out again, I stand by her stand untucking my shirt, letting myself cool down.

After weeks of this routine I say to her without thinking,

"You're the only blind person I know." It isn't that she looks at me, of course. The dog on the floor does look up. She pauses and cocks her head.

"You can see, can't you?" She waits for me to answer yes, begins the elaborate ritual of lighting another cigarette. "I don't know too many blind people either. It's not like we run in packs."

The Postal Service has a secret. There is only one key that opens everything. It only makes sense. We can't be walking around with a ring of keys for all we have to open. The banks of boxes in apartment lobbies open at once with the key. The corner collection boxes. The green relay boxes. The padlocks we use. The box at the end of the glass chute between the elevators in the old hotels. Same key. In that way a substitute on the route already has all the keys needed. One key.

I guess it is not much of a secret. If you worked for the post office you know, or if you even thought about it some, you could guess. There it is at the end of that long chain. One key.

They make a big deal about the key at the office. *Do Not Duplicate* is stamped on it twice. I find I am always fingering the key, my hand in the pocket with it as I walk. In cross-section it has an S shape. It has several deepening grooves and bristles with teeth. I want it to not only open up the boxes of the post office but to turn in every lock, a true skeleton key, opening all the houses on my route. Inside I could arrange the mail further, piles for each family member, on the marble mantel or the little table by the door. As it is, I find myself looking into houses through the mail slot, holding up the brass flap to see the slice of floor and the envelopes and flyers splayed out randomly there. I feel the cool air rush out in the summer. Adjusting my line of sight, I can see walls of framed pictures of grown children who send the postcards I've read from all the islands, the color envelopes thick with pictures of grandkids. Clocks hang on the walls. Coats on racks. And sometimes one of the dogs—I've heard it bark in the back of the house—will come clicking on the linoleum. Huffing around the corner of the entry hall, he is ready to blow the door down from the inside. A snarl and chomp. The flap on the mail slot is already back in place. That's when that black nose points through the door, the nostrils blinking, opening and closing, trying to take in all the smells of me. The fear, the loneliness, my own secret combination of nerves.

Years after the trained dogs leave this city, their owners bring them back. They leave with a new dog.

I'm out at the airport picking up the orange bags of overnight mail when a dog and its owner will come limping across the tarmac. One of the props of the plane they flew in on still revs while the little trucks, run on propane, weave around with baggage and fuel. The dog and the man were the last down the metal stairway, led by an attendant to the terminal. The dog's muzzle is white. Its tongue is out, slipping off to the side of its mouth. There is no color left in the dog's eyes. The dog's almost blind. Its head is down. The shoulders roll. Someone from the school meets them. They wait in the van as the luggage is stowed. I can see the dog's head for a second next to its owner. It shakes itself and collapses beneath the window.

And I sometimes read the notes on the postcards they write home, postcards of the school, a color photograph of a German Shepherd at attention rigged out and ready to go. The notes are about Spike or Lady, how the dog took the flight, how the dog is off its food, how the dog seems to remember this place. The writing is little and cramped or big as if magnified. The ink smears on the coated glossy stock of the card. They always love the town, the children on the street. The new dog will take some getting used to. "Buster is making new friends with all the retired pooches." On and on. It's too much to bear. I read these cards and think of losing them someplace or sending them out on the wrong dispatch. By the time they make it home, the writer will have returned to his or her life. "Oh that. I'd forgotten I'd sent it. It's just what I told you."

I read these cards in the new white trucks with the right-handed drive and no windows in the back. You have to use the mirrors to see and everything is distorted.

My family never writes but calls. My mail is window mail, stamped with the odd denominations of the definitive issues, the transportation series. Each stamp is a special class. Every one's soliciting. The stamps depict all these obsolete forms of movement. Canal boats, milk wagons, stagecoaches, pushcarts, carretas, railroad mail cars, a wheelchair with hand-cranked transmission. Bulk rates, presorted, ZIP-plus-4 discounting, carrier route sorting. When it isn't bills, it is charity, non-profit dunning. Tandem bicycles, steamships, dog sleds. I read my name through the plastic window on the envelope. I try not to imagine what lists I am on, what those lists say about me. My family calls when they have to with important family news. "The mail takes too long to get there," they say. I am too far away to do anything with the news I get. I sign a sympathy note or write a check during the commercials on TV.

I get other calls in the evening or in the morning as I am dressing for work. I answer, and there is silence on the line for a second or two, then the disconnection. This happens often. I shout hello, hello into the static. I can't seem to not answer the telephone. You never know. It could be news. For awhile I just picked up the phone without saying a word, listened hard to the silence and then the line going dead. I have to sort my route first thing in the morning. I go to bed early. In the dark the phone rings. I let it ring for a long time. When I answer it, there is that moment of silence and that soft click. Just checking. Just checking. There is nothing to be done. I leave the phone off the hook and wait through the warning alarms of the phone company, the recorded message telling me to replace the phone in its cradle. And then even that gives up.

I have a screened-in porch, and in the summer I sit on the swing as the neighborhood gets dark. With the light out, the kids who come through collecting for newspapers, cookies, band uniforms, birth defects can't see me through the gray mesh. I stop rocking. They rattle the screen door and peer in. Their dogs are circling in the quiet street. Positioning themselves at the foot of the dying oak trees, they crane to look up at the roosting starlings. I let the kids wonder for a bit if I am home, then I go to answer the door. It gets darker. The street lights come on. The wheezing birds wind down, and the locusts begin to saw. Across the street the lawn sprinklers start up, and the water pools in the street, a syrup on the blacktop. The bug traps sizzle, the blue light breaking into a cloud of sparks. Mosquitoes aren't attracted to the light. I know at least one is on the porch hanging in the still air, sniffing out the heat I'm giving off. Shadows of cats shoot under a parked car. A blind man comes up the street with a new dog. He is talking to the dog. Commands, encouragements, suggestions all just below my hearing. I can just make out the gist of things, the cooing and the nickering. A few paces back a trainer from the school walks in the wet grass, skips over the concrete walks. He turns all the way around as he tags along making sure no one is following.

Once a month the magazines arrive and the clerks will break into a few copies, never from the same address, leaving them scattered on the tables in the break room. After a few days they put the handled magazines in shrink-wrapped bags labeled with a form. Checked explanations for the condition of the enclosed: *Destroyed on conveyor. Fire damaged. Automatic equipment error.* And sometimes someone will go the extra distance, tear a few pages, pour on some liquid smoke. Customers suspect. They always suspect. I am stopped on the street, asked about the handling codes stamped on the back of the envelope. A *C6* floats in the sky of a sunset on a card from Florida. And *NB* in red tumbles into it. What's this? The bar code embossed beneath the address like stitches closing an incision. "You read the mail don't you?" I'm told. "I don't have time." I try to explain. "Things get lost. Overlooked," I tell them.

The men at the station like to think they are the first in town to see the pictures in the magazines. One will turn the pages when the other two have said they are through. Their free hands are wrapped around the steaming coffee cups, as their heads float from one cluster of pictures to the other. I'm stuck with the cover girl. I look for the hidden rabbit's head. This time a tattoo. It could be the run in her stocking. The inky smell of the after-shave ads leaks into the room. Business return cards collect on the floor by their feet. They'll forget after a while that I am watching them. Forget to whoop and point. They'll forget to turn the magazine my way, holding it like grade school teachers do when they read to the class. They'll forget, and their eyes will skip and flutter over the pages, the beams crossing and focusing. At last their eyes will be the only movement.

The dogs who don't guide, the pets, the ones too friendly, who can't refrain from jumping up and licking your face, the surely ones broken when they were puppies. We all have our routes. The dogs shuffling through each stop read the streets and hedges and utility poles. These dogs know when something is new. The trash can, the parked car, breaks up the picture in their heads. River pilots and the river. Their noses scour out a new channel, revise the map they carry in their bones. They pull their owners along the cluttered streets. These dogs see through their memory.

I hate to surprise an unleashed dog while he's intent on his rounds. I turn down an alley. A mutt is snapping at a pair of cabbage butterflies. His muzzle draws little circles in the air, tracking the flitting white wings. His eyes are crossed. I can hear his teeth snip. The butterflies are like a little whirlwind, scraps of alley paper. Now they tumble around the dog's body, and the dog begins to turn back on his tail, his wagging, until he dives into his own fur on his flanks, collapses and rolls, barks and paws at the insects hovering above his belly. Then, upside down, he sees me watching him. Instantly he is on his feet, pivoting on his nose. His eyes never leave mine. He is growling but backing up. His embarrassment is human, shuffling his feet, clearing his throat. He shrugs his shoulders, scratches his ear, then changes the subject, woofing right at me. I have the repellent out of its case. My arm is straight out, and I am aiming for the eyes. The dog circles, barking, trying to convince the backyards that he knew all along I was there. He takes a few steps closer, the skin on his face tight and his body rigid. It frightens me that I can read him so easily, how the gestures of people inform his every move. But still, I don't know dogs. There is no way for me to enter into his thinking, foolish of me for even thinking, at this moment, that there is a way to explain everything, a way to connect. I think of the spritz of chemical, its sting. I think of the one cord of muscle in my forearm used only when I squeeze the trigger or beat an egg. And just then the dog's eyebrows arch and his jaw relaxes and he starts to pant, a kind of laugh.

Now that the mural in the lobby of the office has been restored, it is much harder to see the dogs, the blind workers. It's as if they bleached the images away. The phantom working dogs have disappeared into the background of sky and clouds now all blended into a hazy yellow soup. Perhaps the paints were cheap during the Depression, unstable out of the tube. Or maybe the restorers didn't know when to quit stripping off age and went under into the rough sketch, the outlines, the patches of mixed paint. The workers seem less uniform but more tubercular. They find their own way. The dogs they hold on to now look hairless. I think it's a shame but that's just because I knew the mural before. If I'm here long enough, I'll have to get used to it the way it is. I'll forget the old painting, the gray dust the marching kicked up in the picture and the dust itself layered on the painting like shellac.

I almost tell Mabel about the new painting, but I think better of it. Her booth was built in the fifties. It looks like a wrecked spaceship in the marble lobby. Blond wood, goosenecked metal lamps, streamlined steel cash register. The aluminum dashboard candy rack is enamel-plated with extinct brands. I hear the physical plant people talk on break about her concession. What to do with Mabel is the problem. She sits behind the counter touching piles of different things, tightening stacks of bubble gum, riffling town maps. After awhile she'll reach down and touch her dog on the floor.

During the Depression drifters would scrawl messages on light poles indicating what houses were good for a handout. There would be arrows on the sidewalks, a soaped X on the brick by the mailbox. So I've heard. Now I just see the kids' games boxed out in colored chalk or maybe a name scraped on the sidewalk with a quartz rock from a gravel drive. I never walk on them and they last.

It's a sad town. The kids are always giving up their dogs. Their mothers give them popsicles, and they sit quietly together on the porch gliders, pick at the unraveling strands of the wicker furniture.

"Hey, Mailman Lady," one of them says. "My dog left." What can you say?

I say, "I don't know too much about dogs."

The kid says almost at the same time, "He went to help a blind person."

"Well, you've got to be happy about that, right?"

"I guess."

It goes on this way, a cycle of mourning visiting most houses on my route. In the summer the child, collapsed on the lawn, stares up at the sky. In the winter, he is chewing snow. The kids get a new dog soon, but it is a chronic ache like a stone in my shoes.

On the corner I take out the one key to open a relay box. Inside, the bundles of mail have been delivered to me for the last leg of my route. I try not to think about the messages I am delivering. I file the mail into my cart, stand in a forest of telephone poles, streetlights, fire alarms, police call boxes. The square is crawling with dogs.

The dogs find ways through the crowded streets. They don't stop when children pet them. They ignore each other. They don't see me. They don't bark. They keep going.

Outside Peru

I was cutting the alfalfa with the H when two A-10s skimmed over my head low enough for me to feel the heat from the exhaust.

The H is a tractor. It's red and the first one McCormick streamlined so that the radiator hood looks like a melting ice cube, a charging locomotive, a bullet. The A-10 is an attack aircraft with stubby square wings, a forked tail, and two huge fan jets stuck on the rear of the fuselage. That day, they were painted five shades of green, a northern European camouflage of pine and lichens. Over the years I've watched the patterns and the colors on the planes mutate—the iridescent splashes of tropic jungles to near eastern sand studded with yellow rock, a white tundra splotched with brown. The designs advertise the way trouble grazes around the globe. My cows are always spooked by the fly-bys. I saw them scatter off the rise in the clover field next to the one I was cutting, angling for the electric fence it took me that morning to string.

The jets are pretty quiet to begin with and the Farmall chugs a bit when I use the power take off. The breeze I was heading into stripped the sound away. The jets cracked over my head at the same time the air they pushed in front of them slammed against my back. And then the fans whined overhead. The engines reared back like they were hawking spit. I had been a target. The planes are weapons platforms built to kill tanks. They are slow, haul a huge payload of ordnance, can hang over a battlefield like a kite. The pilots wobbled their wings. I could see the control surfaces, the rudders flex, the flaps and leading edges extended on the blunt wings. They were on the threshold of stalling. Then they broke apart from each other, one going left, the other right, and banked around the cornfield in front of me, meeting up again at the grove of trees near the section road. Without climbing, they tucked in together, the wing of one notched into the waist of the other, nosed over the horizon heading back to Grissom. I let the clutch out again on the tractor and the sickle mower, a long wing sweeping off to my right, bit into the alfalfa collapsing it into windrows. I nudged the throttle. The engine gulped and caught up with itself. The first cutting, rich, green and leafy. I settled back to work. Soon, I felt like I was flying myself, sailing at tree top level.

The first calf since I came back to the farm I named Amelia. With another chance to farm, I was going to do everything right this time. Mom dug out the herd book they kept when I was a boy, the records skidding to a stop around the time all of us kids were in high school. I remember some of those cows. They clouded the barn. Those winters in high school I came home late and stayed up for the milking in the steaming barn. I sat there in the dark, smoking, the radio tuned to WOWO. The cows, heaps in each stanchion, waited for my father to come into the milk house and turn on the vacuum. The herd book has silhouettes of cows, outlines of heads, all scored over with a grid to map the markings. We've always raised Holsteins. The black and white looks best on new grass. I looked at the sketches my mom had made back then. There was Amy with the blob on her shoulder. The crooked man spilling down Apple's flank. As I looked at the old book, I sat down next to the hutch I had just made for the new calves. I flipped through the spiral book to an unmarked silhouette. The new calf's tongue wrapped around the woven fence. She was mostly white except for a spray of black dime-sized spots along the ridge of her right hip and dwindling back down her thigh. Ringing her neck, another chain of black islands aimed toward her eye. There was this ocean of pure milk, white between the black markings. And I stared at her for a long time after charting those few patches. I thought Amelia would be a good name. An A since she was Apple's calf. And an A for Amelia Earhart, the flyer, lost between archipelagos, at sea.

We had just moved to this farm, I was eight, when the plane buried itself in the big field next to the road. The field was planted to corn that year, and the corn had just tasseled. A silver F-86 flamed out on take-off, the pilot ejected, and the plane arched over and swooped down on to our farm. It disintegrated as it plowed up the field scorching the ground, flattening the corn, and spraying fragments of the airframe along its path. It came to rest in the ditch looking like an exploded cigar, the engine ashy beneath the peeled aluminum skin. The swath it had cut through the corn was a precise vector pointing back to the base. Disking the field this spring I turned over more pieces from the crash, a bit of fused Plexiglass, part of a shock absorber, the casing of a running light. I threw them in the tool box of the 20 we use to plow and brought the finds back to the shed, to my dad who keeps all his scrap. The pile in the back corner looks like a reconstruction of a dinosaur, the whole imagined from a few bits. The wing tip, dented and discolored, resting on the floor far away from the main wreckage of bones, implies the missing wing. Dad has suspended a panel of the vertical stabilizer from the beam of the shed. It twists there, unconnected, could prove the rotation of the earth. The first time we went into Peru after the crash I found a plastic model of the jet at the hobby store. I put it together quickly then with a soldering iron melted off the wings and canopy trying to sculpt the ruin in the field. For a long while the whole incident felt heroic. The pilot had chosen our farm to ditch into. I reasoned that from the air our dusty road must have looked like an emergency runway. Later I realized that the pilot hadn't thought twice about it. As he pulled the shield over his face triggering the ejection seat, he believed that no one was down there, his ship would fall into the green uninhabited place on his charts.

Early in the morning, waiting to milk, I've always looked up at the night sky. There are no city lights washing out the view. I watch the falling stars and the meteor showers. I can see a few satellites streak by and below them the puttering airliners. I think to myself, a kind of homing beacon. Here I am, here I am, come and get me.

My father has offered money for a tractor tire someone was using for a sandbox. He scavenges. It's the only way we could farm these eighty acres. We are surrounded by corn this year. To the west and north, the land is owned by an Italian industrialist. To the east and south an insurance company, a thousand acres each. Beyond that, I'm not sure anymore, an incorporated family, rented parcels, more insurance companies. From the air our little grove of trees and the spread of buildings and the strips of grass and small grain stitched together with threads of muddy lanes must look like the center of a dart board encircled by the alternating eight row stripes of corn. The bull's eye would be Wilbur, our bull, lolling in the pen next to the red barn. We can keep this place because my dad never throws anything away and never buys anything new. "You never know," he says, "You never know." Under the old cottonwood trees he has parked the remains of 20s and Hs we've cannibalized and there are all the implements we'll ever need—the manure spreaders, the balers with crates of twine, the Deere two row planters and the corn picker that fits like fake glasses and a nose on the brow of the tractor. Wagons with bang boards, discs and harrows, a rusting mower conditioner, even a sulky plow though Dad says he never liked horses. People pay him to haul the stuff away. Now that I am home he has more time to scout around. I do both the milkings. His knees are shot. He walks like he's been dropped from altitude and his legs looked shoved up into his body. They fall straight from his shoulders. We make do with this junk we've got. They can't touch us as long as we don't long for things we don't need. As long as we don't desire to live in the out-side world.

I told my mother about the jets zeroing in on me because I knew it would remind her of the summer the red-winged black birds buzzed her as she mowed the alleys in her orchard. She wears a baseball hat now while tracing compulsory figures around the apple trees on the Toro. She hates to see my dad go into town because each way has its own junk yard or flea market. Once he came back in a new old pickup hauling a new trailer carrying the old Continental he was driving when he left.

I went to Purdue and majored in ice cream. The food labs I worked in were vast expanses of tooth-colored tile with eruptions of sparkling stainless and nickel chrome appliances spaced about the room. I wore white smocks and paper hats and wrote papers on stabilizing fruit rib-bons and fudge swirls. In the gleaming kitchens, I was a long way from the wreckage of our farm. The milk too had been transformed into something else. I thought of ice cream as milk raised up to a pure art form. There was quarried butter fat to dabble on a palette of ingre-dients—exotic nuts and berries, fragrances shipped to us in plastic tubs, extracts of roots and seed pods, raisins soaked in rum so they wouldn't freeze. I worked in the Union's snack bar too waiting for pharmacy students to sample all the flavors. They stood there, deep in thought, licking the wooden spoons. I scooped up double scoops for couples who couldn't decide and crossed their cones like they were interviewing each other about the taste. Professors' kids ordered bubble gum, embarrassing their parents who predicted the disasters just as the first dips cascaded to the floor.

Every spring, back on the farm, the barn swallows build their nests in same places in the rafters. About the time we turned the cows out after a winter inside the barn, the swallows swooped through the top of the dutch door, jinking around the post and level out just under the mow floor stirring the cirrus clouds of cobwebs. Then they peel off, flapping their wings once, back out the door. I am scraping the shit into the gutters and plowing it toward the far door to shovel into the spreader. The yard is already mud, the cows mired, moo, their skins twitching and ears flapping. The swallows shoot in and out daubing the beams with mud and straw. There will be one nest right over Jean's stanchion whose black back weathers the summer of droppings from above as if her coat is wearing away.

My parents thought I'd never come home.

If you farm a dairy, you can never get away. That is, if you are milking cows, you have to be on the farm all the time. Milking is twice a day. When I first came back to the farm after quitting school, I tried milking three times a day to increase the yield. Slowly, I broke the herd's habits. The production fell way off. That's to be expected. There was nothing scientific in my methods. I weighed the cans before I poured the milk into the holding tank and marked a piece of scrap paper with the pounds of each. If I had the time between the milkings, I'd draw a line to connect the dots on my rude chart. It looked like a cardiograph. Molly came on in the afternoon when Clover was falling off. Amy made a sawtooth pattern, like she was singing scales. The vacuum pumps breathed all the time. I was inside the heartbeat of the barn. And I'd hear the cows' big heartbeats through their sides as I rested my head against them hooking up the claws. Over time, the weight came back up. I could feel it in the cans as I lugged them up the alley. They got used to the new routine, the extra scoop of sweet oats. But I gave it up. I was milking all the time. When I had a chance to sleep, I dreamed of the purple iodine dip I used to disinfect the teats. My whole body was stained. I fell asleep twitching, dreaming about the wet warm muck of the brown paper towels I used to massage the bags to get them to let down.

Now that I am back on the farm working, I don't like to ask my Dad to do the chores. His knees are bad from the stooping he did all his life. But sometimes I have to get away. I like to take the Continental into Peru. It is the same blue-black topless model that Kennedy was riding in when he was shot. It has the backward opening suicide doors. I nose into the line of hot rods cruising in downtown Peru and imagine those rear doors popped out, scooping up a bystander off the street into the back seat surprised but ready to go. Instead, the high school kids always say my car turns the loop into a funeral procession. Watching from the parking lot of the Kum & Go, they see the Zapruder film. A creepy car. I am too old for this anyway. I end up buying some cigarettes for my dad and then point the endless hood of the car back to the farm and get home in time to muck out the stalls.

Those nights after I've come back home from those silly trips to town, I hear my parents worrying about me. Their whispers come up to my bedroom through a floor grate there to conduct the heat. I never heard words but sighs that have nothing to do with passion. My mother never changed my room when I went away to school. All the silver model airplanes are still tethered to the light fixture on the ceiling with yellow rotting string. I never had enough patience to paint them. The glue on my fingers had fogged the clear plastic canopies. The decals are dry and peeling. The planes twist above me, in that rising updraft of worry, like compass needles looking for a true north. On the walls are posters of prize-winning 4-H cows. Behind the planes, they look like a backdrop of clouds, billowing thunderheads, dappled skies. In those pictures, the cows are posed with their front legs resting on little hills that are covered over with turf. They are supposed to look more beautiful elevated slightly like that. But I always think the step-up hill takes away from the picture no matter how artfully it is hidden. I hung up my sketches of the new calves. I ripped them from the herd book. In the shadows, they could be mechanical drawings of camouflaged transport planes. My mother taped up the drawing Annie did when she visited the farm, the butt ends of the herd in a row of stalls at milking time, their pin bones forming a range of snow capped mountains.

That night after the planes buzzed me in the alfalfa field, I asked my parents if I could go into town. I called them from Peru, from the phone booth in the parking lot of the Kum & Go. Pilots from the base still in their green nylon flight suits, perhaps the ones who flew over me that day, got into the midnight blue van. A national guard unit on maneuvers. The four of them had popsicles. I told my Mom I thought I'd head on down to Purdue, maybe stay a night.

"Whatever," she said. She wrote down the feeding instructions I gave her for Dad to use. I told her who the vet had treated for mastitis. The milk would go to the calves and cats.

I said, "I hope this isn't too much trouble." Moths were batting at the light in the booth so I opened the door to turn it off. I heard the sound of jets taking off over at the base, a sound like ripping cloth.

"You know your father likes to keep his hand in. I'll keep him company." I could see her that night. She would tune the radio to one of those magic stations where the songs have no words and then spread the lime thicker than I do in the alley way. When I got back it would look like it had snowed inside the barn.

"Say hello to Annie for us," she said.

I brought Annie home to the farm once for a weekend when we were both in school. She was from the Region, in northern Indiana, and had never been on a farm. I went up to Hobart once with her, back then, and she took me to the dunes. We stared at Lake Michigan. I remember it looked like it could be farmed, flat and dusty. We huddled on some riprap and saw the lights of Chicago flare up where the sun set. It is the only body of water I've been to where I couldn't see the shore on other side, and it scared me. Annie said she felt the same way walking the lanes around the farm. The land just seemed to go on forever.

"When I was a kid my mother told me to not go near the corn," I told her. In the late summer you can get lost in it and panic. It swallows you up.

The weekend she visited the farm, I helped Dad clear out some scrap wood piled next to the barn. We all stood around while he decided what to move where. My mother teased Annie about the rats that would be hiding underneath the lumber.

"Stick your pant legs inside your boots, Annie," she said. "They'll go right up your leg. It looks like a burrow to them."

Dad jiggled a 2 by 4. I stood back a ways with a pitch fork. Annie curled over and stuffed her jeans inside her boots neatly. She did this straight-legged like she was stretching before a morning jog, her hair falling over her head. The rat broke out from beneath some barn wood and window frames, parting the dried grass, faking first toward my father who tried to club it with a stick, then me, then my mother who was stomping, but then it angled straight toward Annie as if it had heard my mother's prediction. Annie stood perfectly still, her legs pressed together. I saw her shiver. The rat spun around toward me standing between it and the wood pile. I pulled the fork back above my shoulders aiming at it as it sliced through the grass. I hesitated because I didn't really want to kill it in front of Annie. The rat should be killed. His burrow was beneath the grain bin. I just couldn't be gleeful about it. My mother was squealing. I sensed Dad lumbering toward me, thrilled by the chase. Annie stood like a post as if she rammed her boots into the ground when she had taken care of her cuffs. Her face was pale and blank. At my feet, I could see how fat the rat was, how sleek and brown like a bubble of earth was squeezing along under the dead grass. Then, surrounded, the rat stopped dead still. And then, it flew. It took off straight up, reaching the peak of its climb at my eye-level where we looked at each other. It hung there it seemed for a long time. The rat's little legs were stretched out as if they were wings. It flashed its teeth then ducked its head and dove through my hands. I was twirling the pitchfork like a propeller, trying to find a way to bring the tines or the handle around to defend myself. I yelled. The rat disappeared again in the junk by the barn. We all stood there panting, clouds of dust wound round our faces. Our eyes were fixed on the spot in the air where the rat had hovered between us. I couldn't get Annie to come into focus again. She was a blur a few paces beyond the clear empty space.

That night, Annie and I sat on the couch pretending to watch television. I turned the sound down low so I could hear my dad snoring, the sound drifting through the registers from the room next door. The lights were off. Annie's white shirt turned blue in the flicker of the television. I tugged at her shirt, untucking it from her pants the way she pulled her pant legs from her boots after the rat had disappeared and we all walked back to the house for dinner. As we kissed, I slid my hand up inside her shirt and covered her left breast. Then, my hands weren't as hard as they were when I lived and worked at home. The only callus left was on my thumb, worn there by the trigger of the ice cream scoop. I rolled the nipple between my fingers and thumb. Even then I couldn't help but think what she was thinking. Just that day she had watched me strip the milk from the cow's tits. I'd wrapped my hand around her hands as she squeezed and pulled on the udders. Self-conscious, I traced a circle around her nipple a few times not to seem abrupt then ran my hand over her ribs and let it fall on the flair of her hip. She shivered and turned her head away.

"What?" I said.

"Your nails," she said, "that rat."

This all happened a while ago. It has been two years now since I've seen her.

The road to Purdue follows the remains of the old Wabash Canal. In some places the ditch is dry and leafy. In other places, black water has pooled, steeping logs slick with green slime. The tow path bristles with saplings and a ground fog of wild berry canes. Through the sycamores, sometimes, you can see the river itself green from the tea of rotting leaves. Once, it had been important to hook the Great Lakes up with the Ohio and the Mississippi. The state went broke doing it. To the north is good farm land, a flat table leveled by the glaciers, but along the river the road rolls over the rubble of what they have left behind.

In the low slung Continental, I was flying. The car leapt off the crests of the rolling hills then settled again, the mushy shocks lunging with the revving engine. It was still early though most people were already in bed. The security lamps in the farm yards and small towns draped streaks of light along the long hood like straps of wet paper. In fields beside the road, I saw the hulks of lulling cattle, the debris of herds scattered around like boulders in the glacial till these pastures are built on. The car couldn't go fast enough to escape the gravity of the farm. I thought of my own herd drifting through the clover after Dad had turned them out. All their markings bleed together in the dark so that they become these lanky shadows, blotting out the stars rising behind them. I had raked the alfalfa in the neighboring field into wiggling windrows. The stink of the drying leaves hugs the ground and levels it again with a thick mist, the lightning bugs rising to its surface. For a second, my hands are on the yoke in the cockpit of the matte jet buzzing that field. The cows shimmer in the infrared goggles like hot coals in a pool of oil. The mown field pulses, smoldering with the heat of its own curing. The insects bubble through the haze to sparkle in the air. And I am looking down at myself sitting on the molten tractor, smoking, inhaling the fire of my finger tips, my sweat turning to light. I snapped out of the barrel roll, honked the horn twice, and coasted down the hill into Lafayette.

I got lost in the court of tin shacks where Annie lives, turned around on the rutted, dusty roads in the dark. Somewhere, she rented a half of one of the Quonset huts the university put up during the war and never tore down. Any effort to remove them brings howls of protest from sentimental alumni who remember conceiving their first children in one barrack or the other, and the university administration loses interest in renovation. It is cheap housing, a place to store the international students who grow strange grains and vegetables in the empty plots that open up randomly in the court. The spaces mark where a shack has blown up, a yearly occurrence, torched by a malfunctioning gas heater, furnace, or range. The shacks all look alike though some are decorated with flower boxes rigged by this term's inmate. Bikes nose together in the long grass up against the corrugated siding of the houses. The galvanized metal of the buildings has oxidized over time, so now it has a finish akin to leather, grained and dull. I crept through the rows of shacks looking for the right number.

I had called her too. Her directions were highly detailed but useless to me since I didn't know this place intimately enough to see the details. They were camouflaged by the repetition of forms. I was lost in a neighborhood of Monopoly houses. I only found her because she was sitting on the stoop outside her house watching for the car. When she saw me skittering along the cross street she stood up and waved her arms over her head and whistled.

"The house is like an oven," she told me. "I was an idiot to cook." She had put on macaroni and cheese when she heard I was coming, and we ate sitting on the front stoop, our bowls balanced on our squeezed together knees. I could feel the heat on my back as it poured out the screen door. There were clouds of bugs shading the street lights. Every once and awhile another car, looking lost, would shuffle down the street dragging the dust behind it.

We talked. I did say hello from my parents. Annie had been working this summer as an illustrator for the veterinary college, rendering organs, muscles, and bones of various domesticated animals. We set our bowls aside, and she brought out several drawings, turning on the porch light as she stepped through the door. She handed me a bone the size of a rolled up newspaper, Sunday.

"A cow's femur," she said. I was never much for the insides of things. I was raised on a farm and should be comfortable with the guts of animals. My father delights in eating the brains and hearts and tongues. I have watched my mother ring the water from kidneys and roll the shiny liver in her hands. I think to myself that I should love, to the point of consuming, the whole animals I tend. Still, something sticks in my throat. When I moved back to the farm, I castrated the first bull calf born. I wanted to raise a steer and slaughter it myself. I named him Orville. He was docile and fat. He did dress out nicely when the time came, but I let the locker do it. I can't get used to it. Sometimes during calving, a cow's uterus will prolapse. I'll find it spreading in the gutter behind her. I can tell myself I know what it is, I know what to do, but when I see guts it's as if my guts are doing the thinking. I stop seeing the animal as a kind of a machine to scrap or fix. Even dairymen need a distance. Maybe especially dairymen.

"Do they still have the cow at the vet school with the window in her side," I asked her. I would go over there between classes and make myself watch the regurgitating stomachs squeeze and stretch. The cow was alive, chewing her cud. A flap had been cut in her side for studying. I always admired her patience, the way she stood in the special stall letting the technician dab antiseptic around the opening.

"I don't know if it is the same one you saw," Annie said, "but they still have one. The elementary school science classes still are herded in to take a look. They want to not look but can't help themselves."

I could feel my stomach working under my skin, wrapping itself around the stringy elbow noodles, plumbing within plumbing. The bone was in the grass at our feet weighing down the newsprint sheet with its unfinished sketch. She used a kind of stippling style, all points of ink that clustered into shadow for depth, so that the bone on paper looked worn as smooth as paper, porous as bone, chipped like the china bowls. The dots looked like a chain of volcanic islands on a map of a huge sea just tracing the fault hidden under the water.

I told her about my own drawing, the sketches in the herd book. "I wish I had your eye," I told her. Even with the coordinate grid, it was still so awkward transferring the markings to paper. "It's just a mess. There are gray smears where I've erased. It looks like they have some kind of mange."

"You like cows a lot though, don't you?" she said then.

"Yeah, I guess I do. I guess I'd have to to do what I am doing."

"But don't you miss," she said, "don't you miss the noise of other people. I remember the farm being so quiet and how you never talked. I never knew what you were thinking."

I sat there on the stoop in the yellow light of the bug bulb thinking about the farm and how I missed the cows, the green fields, and the piles of junk when I was here at school. I thought of the chatter of my own thoughts, how when I work I am always telling myself what I am doing. I am opening the gate now. I am walking into the barnyard. I am driving the cows into the lower field. My boots sinking into the kneaded mud of the yard.

"I love cows too," she said. "The big eyes. The way they just stand there. You look away and then look back and they look like they haven't moved but they have. The arrangement is all different."

"Yeah," I said. "That's true."

"It's like drawing waves in a lake. The calm motion." She shivered. "Spooky after a while."

That night I slept in the front room on a couch that came with the place. The apartment had aired out with the windows and the doors propped open. Annie had tucked in white sheets around the cushions. The vault of the Quonset hut created a kind of organic cavity, and the ribbed walls were papered with her washes of organs and glands. The sink on the dividing wall between the two apartments gurgled when the neighbors came home. I stayed awake, listening to the rattle of their language that seemed pitched just right to start the sheet metal of the building buzzing. They played strange music that ratcheted up and down the walls like a thumbnail on a washboard. Later still, when they had disappeared deeper into their side of the building, I tried to imagine them. I gave them a family life, a routine, classes to take, diplomas they would haul back to the other side of the world where they would wade in paddies, follow cattle along a packed earth road. And I thought of Annie too, on the other side of the inside wall. I hovered over her bed and watched her slowly rearrange herself, articulating arms, the white rollers breaking along the shore as she stretched a leg beneath the sheet, the tide of her breathing. How she used up every inch of space in her bed, asleep but constantly moving.

Before I left the next day, I wandered over to the Union and had some ice cream, chocolate, in a dish. Students were cutting through the building for a bit of air conditioning before dashing on to the next classroom. Some would stop and buy a cone, stand and lick the ice cream smooth on all sides, manageable, before they rushed off. The Union is camouflaged with Tudor beams of darkly stained wood and stuccoed walls. I hadn't remembered it being this much like a barn. Lumps of students sleeping in leather club chairs or single ones swaying in study carrels, reading, tucked in nooks behind squat square columns. I knew where the milk had come from to make the ice cream, but no longer remembered the origin of chocolate. South America? Perhaps Peru. Which was the more exotic ingredient, the stranger place?

I drifted over to the library across the street from the Union. It was hot out, and I promised myself I would hang around the campus til the sun went down then drive back home in the dark. When I was a student, I liked to look at the special collections the library had on flyers and airplanes. Neil Armstrong went to Purdue. A lot of astronauts did. I don't know why. And the plane Amelia Earhart disappeared in was owned partly by the school. At the time she was a professor of aviation or something. There are pictures of her in her flying jacket and slacks having tea with women students. They crowd around her. I love the pictures of her posed with the silver Electra, pouring over maps of the world in this very room of the library. The room seemed even more crowded now with trophy cases, photos, charts, and models. There were navigation instruments and facsimiles of her notes and letters. I looked at a milky white scarf arranged as if casually flung along the black velvet shelf encased in glass. A librarian was typing labels in an office off the main room. Behind her there was a picture of the librarian receiving the school flag from two astronauts. It looked like the ceremony was taking place during the half time of a basketball game.

"The flag had just come back from the moon," she told me. "I have it here someplace."

I told her I was interested in Amelia Earhart's time at Purdue. I like to think of her circling above the countryside, perhaps looking down on our farm. It isn't that far away. I sat down at a polished table where she brought me an album stuffed with local news clippings, brittle and yellowed, pasted to the black pages.

"They found her, you know" the librarian said. "They think they found her."

"What?" I said.

"Or what remains of her," she said, "on an island in the middle of nowhere. They found a navigator's aluminum case washed up on an atoll. They're going back this summer to find the plane and what's left of the bones. They came here to look at the photos, to see if they could see that same case in one of the pictures."

That night, I drove home with the top down on the Continental. I climbed and stalled and dove through the hills along the Wabash. The metal skin of the car was the color of the night and the road. I let myself lose track of what was what. All that was left was this little ellipse of upholstered light I sat in, gliding through space, adhering to the twisting white rails emitted by the low beams. Annie had sent her love to my parents, and I thought of it, her love, as a slick, gleaming, and, as yet, undocumented organ I was keeping right here in my silver navigator's case. It had been easy, the librarian had said, to find the little island in the middle of the Pacific once the searchers guessed the slight miscalculation that led Amelia Earhart off her course. They followed the string of physics into the sea. As I drove, my cows drifted from the light of the barn, sifting through the gates and alleys to the highest part of the farm, the rise in the clover field, there to catch the slight stirring breeze. In their own way, they tell themselves what comes next. Wait, they say, and the next moment they say wait again. Me, I wanted right then to get lost on my way home in the middle of Indiana, but I knew, deep in my heart, that that was next to impossible.

Turning the *Constellation*

I try to see the stars through the rigging and the old reefed sails. The lights from Pratt Street bounce off the edge of the still water in the Inner Harbor. Beyond the pavilions of Harbor Place, downtown Baltimore steps back in terraced, flood lit cliffs with outcroppings of red neon logos. The light seems to steam off the buildings.

The soft pools of light from the paper Japanese lanterns strung above the deck spot the polished fir. Couples shuffle around the masts and hatches, keeping time with the brushed snare of the combo set up in the stern. Once, boys they called the Powder Monkeys smothered this deck with sand right before a battle so the bare feet of the crew could gain a purchase on the planking. It mentions this in the souvenir program of the evening. The old wood frigate must be turned each year so that she'll last longer as a static display. They've made the maintenance into an event. Half of Baltimore is on the docks to see us shove off. We party on the deck while the crew casts away the lines. The tugs nose up against the sides of the ship. The launches taxi back and forth over the black water.

In the still water of the Inner Harbor, I think I see a sky full of stars. Then I remember that the bay is saltier this year, and the sea nettles and the Portuguese men-of-war have been drawn into the estuary. Tonight, they give off their own phosphorescent light in a frequency below the sodium vapors coating the downtown. Shading my eyes, I can almost see into that sky of water as those stars wheel with us and turn on the high tide.

They shipped Nelson's body home from Trafalgar in a cask of brandy. You say, "Byron's too!" I wonder how it worked. Were the barrels big enough for the bodies to float? Or were they doubled over, embryos again, ingeniously folded as grape leaves in a jar? Our brandy sloshes around the sides of the snifters. We glide by the dark hulks of the submarine and the lightship at their slips. More museum ships. The water churns white from the bite of the tugs' screws. The pilot boats sweep the deck with flood light. The liquor catches and then shatters it. Bright jewels bob above your cupped hand.

It is close below on the gun deck. A few naked bulbs patch together some light. In the shadows the sleeping hammocks strung between the beams look like ancient cobwebs. The rose odor of gasoline drifts up from a few decks below where the generators rasp away, and beneath that the bilge pumps pant. We dance a step or two. We're not supposed to be here, but the empty deck looks like an old ballroom. Only the masts break up the space. Above our heads the upright bass sends a beat into the timber, and the whole ship seems to resonate. We are dancing in the guts of a guitar, the sound, all around us. "What a fine coffin," you say.

A soggy breeze laps at us as we look out of an open gun port. We're closing on the Domino Sugar sign which, from this angle, looks like a city burning on a hill. Sliding my hand along the lip of the loop, I lodge a splinter in my finger. "Some sailor you are," you say and hold my hand to your face. Your eyes cross, and you catch the tip of your tongue in your teeth. "It will wait until we get home," you say. "I'll have to use a needle." The light from the burning sugar sign polishes the dollop of blood you've squeezed from the wound.

I am in retirement from retirement. I hope to forget what I did at Social Security all those years. I wrote letters. I listened to stories, a fiduciary chandler outfitting final voyages. I tended all those sputtering candles, a bank of votive lights. I reassigned the numbers when the checks came back unsigned. The computers there were as big as ships. And you teach composition to midshipmen down the bay. The literature of salt and Odysseus returning home each spring term. I imagine you looking out your office window, watching the sculls cut through the Severn and, out further, the little sunfish stagger around a buoy in yet another race. This is our shipboard romance, not very important people among the other invited guests: the crooked politicians, the tarnished navy brass, the Rouse company execs and the doctors from Hopkins Hospital, the flush philanthropists, the car salesmen and restaurateurs, *Evening Magazine,* the odd Oriole signing starched white shirt fronts.

Imagine the wounds from the wood when it splintered in those broad-sides. The double shot leaving the muzzle was slow enough to see, the trajectory as flat as a throw to the plate. The wood, elastic, shrugged off the balls but not before they chewed off a slice of pine or pulverized the oak, turning it into a kind of atmosphere the gun crews breathed in with the black ignited powder. You say this as you dig into my wounded finger with your nails. All this wood. England cut down every oak to smash them up at sea. You read about the endless voyages of wooden ships bound in books so thick they could stop a bullet. And there was the pulp my department floated on: the tractor fed girdle of paper run through the printers, the newsprint barked with chips, and the legal pads laced with a dust of fibers as fine as the motes that float in the fluid inside your eyes.

I bought you a star. I used my Visa when the call came during dinner from a boiler room scam in Ohio. Thirty-five bucks. They sent a certifi-cate and sky charts with the star, a speck of puny magnitude, highlighted with a yellow marker. I thought once out in the harbor away from the lights of the city we'd be able to see it ground beneath the heel of a twin. The charts are in my pocket. The zodiac all stitched together. I never was any good at seeing the tacked up hides of the old stories in the night sky, took other people's word that they existed at all. Even the single drip of the North Star can't lead me back to the Dipper. Or is it the jewel in the handle's crook? I've always liked the shooting stars, the showers of sparks struck off the dome of heaven I can only catch in the corner of my eye. By the time I turn to look, the streak's extinguished, so I'm not even sure it was there, a kind of memo that's sent to the shredder. Look, there's one now.

There. A red navigation light strobes on top of the old shot tower. The rest of the red brick is black in the night. It blots out the skyline behind it, a gap in a grin. We'll have time now for all this history. I can see us climbing the spiral staircase like smoke in a chimney, up to the platform where they dropped the boiling lead, letting it fall into the vat of water six stories below, the hot rain freezing into hail. The cove and creek bottoms of the Eastern shore are silted with shot that falls back to earth. The ducks scoop up the pellets for their gizzards. The lead that missed them on the wing kills them finally. And we'll go next door to the Flag House where the star-spangled banner was pieced together. The ensign, big enough to wrap the little row house, clouded the rooms with bunting. The woman picked through the cloth as it crept over her lap. One white star dwarfed the whole front parlor. We'll have to see it, the way the flag was folded into the house, another miracle of packing, like the whole sky tucked into my pocket or those bodies steeping in their kegs.

"What are you doing down here?" the marine says. He jogs toward us, skipping over cables. He wears a bowler hat and a short green jacket. We're not supposed to be below but up above with the party. We hear them hailing the little sailboats and inboards swarming alongside. The branch has widened here, and the channel is newly dredged. The boats wallow in the wake of the tugs. We follow the volunteer aft along the gun deck. He's from Highlandtown, a jar head in Korea. He draws a pension from Bethlehem. Now he mends his uniforms for the summer of re-enactments. "The Civil War's the war," he says. "The encampment down at Manassas is near as big as the battle was." He slips in and out of character. There is so much to save now, he thinks. He's part of the industry of preservation. We watch you climb the open ladder up into the night. I remember you climbing back into the upper berth of the Pullman we took to Chicago. That silly ladder hooked into the loft. With the overhead lights off, we had slid the shade up and left on the one pale blue light near my bed. There was no way for you to be graceful, each rung forced you to splay your knees apart. The train rocked. You threw your body into the bed above me. Below, my vantage all screwy, you foreshortened, and your toes turned white on the last step. You floated into a heaven of webbed luggage while the porter felt for our shoes in the locker by the door. I don't tell the marine this, but follow you up to the main deck, my face in your skirts.

The traffic helicopters from the television stations seem to be caught in the yards of the foremost tops. The pennants there begin to stir as if the light from the helicopters' swiveling spots drove the air. The choppers pivot on the beams shining down. Their long tapering tails stir around. Miss Ethel Ennis is singing a jazzed up version of the National Anthem with the fort just off the starboard, and the guests can't make up their minds if this rendition counts enough to settle down and salute. There is champagne with cold soft crab sandwiches. The governor takes a turn at the helm, spinning the unconnected wheel after a brief toast. The cameras in the helicopters never stop moving. The lights on the deck spin beneath them. Watching the news tomorrow, we'll be hung over enough to forget how to see, how to make the cameras pan. Instead the ship will roll and yaw, the masts raking at us dodging the streams of light.

Most of the dignitaries have been piped off the ship, sailing away in a fleet of speed boats towards Fells Point. We've talked the crew into letting us stow away to wait with them for the morning tide and the ride back to port. The band is packing up on the quarter deck. The bass player, in shadow, wrestles the body of his instrument into the case. We watch the caterers break down the tables, snitch swipes of crab salad on crackers before it turns in the heat. The Constellation will ride the night out here in the bay with its skeleton crew. She'll head in tomorrow with the tide, to her berth, her bowsprit now poking in toward the upper windows of the shopping mall she poses next to. She'll weather more evenly, the marine had said, the weather hitting her like a slower broadside. We watch the divers in the dark water. Their heads tip forward. They disappear together. They are inspecting the hull. Blind, they feel along the keel and try to imagine what has cemented itself to the old copper sheets below the water line. We wait for the divers to surface, their black rubber suits shedding the light of the full moon, an oily sheen. We try to guess where they'll appear in the black water, but they never do.

I say, "A friend of mine died, and he had always wanted to be buried from his boat, wrapped in a sail and tipped overboard into the bay. His will charged a group of us with handling the details. So we looked into it. We thought it would be simple, a few pieces of paper. But the state of Maryland requires a crypt with the coffin, a big concrete vault that would have sunk his little boat if we even could have gotten it on board. We thought of hiring a dredge with enough room for the casket and its casket, and we realized the estate would be eaten up with the costs. The body still had to be embalmed, permits obtained for dumping chemicals into the water. So, on a night like this, we wrapped the body up in canvas and lead sinkers and sailed out to the ship channel where the tankers rode at anchor as they waited for a chance to dock and dropped him in the deepest water we could find inside the Bay Bridge. We buried the empty casket in a crypt in a cemetery on Belair Road."

You say, "You are such a liar. Who was this friend who died? Who were the friends who helped you? Did you buy off the undertaker to look the other way when you loaded the body into the trunk of your car? Wouldn't the body be tonged up by some startled waterman sooner or later? I know you too well. I've heard you tell the story at too many barbecues with a glass of champagne you use as a model of the little ketch heeling in the bay and in the lobbies of funeral homes where your real dead friends are being shown. After you've taken a glance at the body, you say 'A ghastly business, this viewing.' And in some versions, it isn't even you at the tiller on that moonlit night. Another friend of yours has done the deed. He has told you the story at a wake of a mutual buddy as you stand by the body. A cold nose, like a luffing sail, just shows above the open hatch of the casket with its spray of taffeta. But I love the story because it is the story you tell over and over. It's a spell, another form with carbons, to ward off the bureaucracy of time. It is a bribe to get around the rules. You've lived through another night. You've buried your stand-in at sea. You whisper the story in the parlors of funeral homes while, kneeling near the body in the next room, the old women race through the rosary, the sorrowful and the joyful mysteries. Listen, the last stitch the sail maker made when he made the shroud at sea went through the stiff's nose. A detail from a book I read. Its pages sewn together too, that ancient repetitive gesture of time and storytelling."

The moon is so fat it can't lift itself much higher than the Key Bridge, a fresh suture in the sky. Its mealy face is ready to blister like paint on a balloon. The old skin will slough off. This has been going on a long time, this moon turning old. There is enough light to wash out the stars after all. Mars, always heading toward us, follows the moon toward Virginia. The very old light from the biggest stars happens to reach our eyes at this moment. We are stretched out on the deck looking up through the nets in the rigging. The live oak in her frame is decaying in measurable amounts, an ambient rot. The souvenir program says the wood is original, America's secret weapon. It gets harder in brine. They couldn't work it 200 years ago. When they pulled it from the swamps and bogs of the

Carolinas, their saws and chisels blunted. My tux is rented, has its own history of sweat. Along my back, I feel the splinters of radiation prickle my body with its own stores of carbon, its rings of skin. I say that sliver of wood in my hand will fester, the infection will streak toward my heart. "Baby," you say, "it will work its way out."

The telescope they sent up into space was supposed to prove there are other planets around the suns we see as stars. It is floating above us now, a blind hulk, its perfect mirror ground to the wrong formula. All that preserved junk of fabricated senses spirals around us as we spin. I would have aimed the thing back down at us, a civil spy satellite, with a bank of scientists interpreting the semaphore of, say, two human bodies in a bed, reading them like letters on a page.

Getting ready for the day, the crew is hoisting signal flags, pennants, ensigns, and Perry's battle flag quoting the dying Lawrence on the Chesapeake. There are no poems for this ship. Who remembers the quasi-war with France, Truxton, the hostages held by the beys of the Middle East? Here we are, drowsy, on watch on the poop of an old ship. The moon has gone, and the breeze has freshened, blowing the swamp away toward the Eastern shore. There the stars are finally opening their eyes, and nobody can see us.

The fire boats have come out to greet our return voyage, and the light is breaking up in the arching water of their canons. The mist on the water smolders. The sun behind us chisels from the haze the row houses climbing Broadway. Everything is new or ancient. We can just see the piers crowded with people. The cranes and the gantries of the city's construction could be the rigging of tall ships. I am getting too old for this. My archaic joints are ungreased wood, creaking like the frigate, her spars rattling in the headway she is making. But I unfold myself and stand into the wind. On the wind is the smell of Baltimore, the spices from the factories on Light Street that survive near the shopping malls, offices, and hotels. The spices mask the frightening stench of sluggish water, suggest the orient, a new port opening to trade. The dried fruits and crushed leaves of another season preserve us all, home after a long passage, anoint our memories at the same time they come flooding back before us.

From Pensées:

The Thoughts of Dan Quayle

On the Highway of Vice Presidents

Even from this distance, it looks like a brain. As big as an Air Stream trailer and shiny like polished, dented aluminum, its skin is shrunk and crinkled, pitted and fissured.

My notes tell me it is a bioherm and that I am to blow it up which I do. It is one of my first acts as Vice President. I am wearing a yellow hardhat when I ram down the demolition plunger as they do in action movies. The plunger makes a ripping sound like fishing line being stripped from a reel by a well-hooked bass. The engineer had told me this is the sound of an electric current being generated, *rrrrr* like a siren. We wait.

It surprised me that it took awhile for the electricity I had generated to reach the charge. They had showed me the dynamite, red paper sticks bundled together with black electrician's tape. It looked like dynamite, but the fuse didn't burn like it does in cartoons. We followed the wires back to the black box where someone stripped them and attached them to the plunger by turning thumb screws. Then another person raised a flag, a whistle blew, and a siren went off that sounded throaty and hoarse like the sound of the plunger I pushed when they said I should. We waited.

And I thought for a second about the old dinosaurs, the huge ones with long necks and long tails, and how they had walnut-sized brains and needed all these other littler brains to relay a message from the tip of the tail to the bigger brain in the head. *Hey something is biting you back here. Hey something is biting you back here. Hey something is biting you back here.* Until it got the message: *Hey something is biting me back there.*

Boom! The charge goes off. The brain-thing, which was, just the moment before, sparkling with a slick fluid of light as if it had been freshly scooped from a skull, now bursts into a brain-shaped cloud that hangs there for the longest time. Its different hemispheres bulge, contracting and squinting like it is thinking real hard. I imagine it is thinking: *What the hell happened?*

The engineer had told me that a bioherm is an ancient fossil reef built over centuries by shells of dead mollusks sinking to the floor of an ancient inland sea, cementing themselves together layer after layer. To think that Indiana was once the bottom of such a sea. I looked hard at the bioherm before we blew it up. We stood around, a group of us, having our pictures taken in front of it. I wore a yellow hardhat. I saw things that looked like snails and worms, whelk shells and mussels and clams all stuck to one another like different kinds of noodles fused together after being left in a strainer in a sink overnight. But bigger. Much bigger.

I thought about my own brain made up of all those tiny cells, each one storing the flesh of something special, a memory, say, like this one when I blew up this huge rock that wasn't a rock at all but a kind of bone sponge to make way for a highway that will by-pass my hometown. I have not talked to any experts about this. It is probably the case that a brain does not work this way at all, that the cells in my head are not like ranks of offices along long corridors that account for just one scrape of information. I shuffled through these thoughts as I thumbed through my index cards. I read a little speech then.

I remember the trucks that rumbled through Huntington, my hometown, on old 24 painted circus colors and coughing up exhaust from the stack behind the cab as they downshifted on the grade leading to the Wabash. I sat there on the hot white sidewalk and shot my hand up over my head then yanked it down and with it came the blast of the air horn from the passing truck loud enough to rattle the picture window in its frame. They liked me, I thought then, and waved. Things would happen if I made the right gestures. I could snatch the sound right out of the air, wall it away in some deep crevice in a fold of a wrinkle in my head.

Now the cloud before us in the field has lost all its glue and has turned into a gauzy curtain of sparkling powder. Through it, I see the clunky yellow earth-movers scraping along the staked out route of what will be called the Highway of Vice Presidents. The machines have a gait like crabs, their huge balloon tires stepping over the rolling floor of what my notes tell me was once an ancient inland sea.

And, later, in the Marine helicopter, my aids shouting out the briefing for the next stop of the day, we'll hover a few feet above the ground. I'll wave to the crowd gathered below. They are staggered by the blast from the prop. The dust begins to boil at their feet. The helicopter pivots on its main rotor, the long green tail lashing out and around in an arch that turns us north. I'll nod my head slightly. We'll dip forward and pick up speed, climbing. And from a distance, I'll look down as the bulldozers creep toward the scorched crater I leave behind. Huntington will be somewhere over there. With any luck I won't need to come back this way until Coats runs again for the Senate.

On the State of the Union

The Speaker bangs the gavel for order. The gavel is a gift to the United States from the people of India, the largest democracy to the world's oldest. Order.

I'm standing in front of my swivel chair next to the Speaker. I'm the President of the Senate. At the beginning of his speech the President of the United States will call me Mr. President.

The party members are still on their feet. Some are whistling, fingers stretching lips, like fans at a basketball game. The red light bounces from camera to camera around the house. The Majority is settling in, looking before they sit, picking up the text that has been distributed to their seats. Some are riffling through its pages. Others are shouting into their neighbors ears while they continue to applaud routinely. Order.

The gavel is made of pale marble and ivory fitted with brass trim. The Speaker rests his weight on his knuckles, the gavel's handle squeezed in one fist. He looks like my father, his chin lowered, looking out at the house through his bushy brow. It makes me want to do something bad, and the boys in our party on the floor start up again after the Speaker has introduced the President just as much to see that stern mask set deeper on the Speaker's Neanderthal face as to cheer the President on.

I watch the red light on the cameras as it goes off and on around the room. I try to guess where it will alight next. The one in the lobby doorway. The one fixed on the mezzanine wall. The one behind the Speaker that shows the fanned seating of the floor. The angle that captures the various Secretaries and Generals and Ambassadors. I never know when the camera will focus on me. I am looking thoughtful, I think, as I applaud. The light flickers on the camera aimed at the wives in the gallery above. I follow the vector from the that camera, its lens slowly extending for a tight close-up on the First Lady, who stands by the railing in the blue dress with big buttons, pearls bubbling at her throat, her eyes glassy, as always, applauding effortlessly. I see her over the President's right shoulder as she smoothes her skirt around her hips as she sits down. And we all sit down.

Her husband begins to speak, and I remind myself to count the number of times he will be interrupted by applause. I know the words that are cues. The Whips have briefed us in caucus. There are plants salted in the gallery to trigger responses. The pauses are scripted. I always tell myself that I will keep track of the applause to match the number with the talking heads at the networks. But I lose track. My thoughts flit away from me like that light that now burns on the camera in the center aisle below us suddenly extinguishing itself and suddenly flaring up again after completing a circuit of the room during an interlude of cheering.

They've been working on the President. I can see the line of pancake on his neck where the napkin masked his white collar. Color has been brushed on the cheek he turns toward me when his head scans the room. His hair is freshly dyed, the television lights polishing the contours, each strand lacquered into place.

I know what people are thinking. They see me brooding behind the President. I have touched up my own temples with a hint of gray. It is important that we all forget about the President's mortality. I alone am allowed to age. I imagine the Members on the floor squirming in their seats, adjusting their angles of vision, using the bulk of the President to blot me and then the thought of me out of their minds. The President's most recent collapse, captured on television, has brought me back into their thoughts that now are drifting away from the prepared text, the paragraph on infrastructure they have been following halfheartedly, and into that percentage of every minute each has allotted to daydream, fantasy, or prayer. I walk in the corridors of some skulls out there. The possibility of me. The blue-eyed, bushy-tailed fact of me.

To get back at them, I employ the old Toastmaster trick of imagining the audience naked, and they sit there like dollops of frosting, their famous gray heads collapsing into puddles of fat that fill the seat. The esteemed colleague from Rhode Island is a smear of freckles. There, Howie has a rash that itches. I see secret tattoos. Trickles of sweat deliberately trace the topography of Teddy's sagging breast. The thighs worn smooth, shiny, and white by a life dedicated to always wearing trousers straddles the shriveled assortment of penises, the Members' members, that now are listening to their owners' own state of the union, a message of hope and resurrection punctuated by a worn catalogue of past and very private images. Order. Order.

Up on the toes of their naked feet, cheering, their flesh jiggles and sways, breaks out in splotches of color. Bill's thighs have been stripped of veins for his bypass. The gentleman from New Jersey has new plugs. They are otherwise unremarkable, marked only for death they have convinced themselves for now does not exist for them. The cancer ticks in a chest, a strangled heart, a brain that forgets to remember. There is another nakedness beneath the twill layer of beige skin. And it is, perhaps, only accessible to me from my strange vantage on this dais looking out at them all. I see into them. My job description gives me this vision since all I do is wait on death. I am the official mourner. The shadow of death cast a few polite paces behind the aging President.

Above us all, the First Lady, also naked, her face framed by an aurora of hair, rises from her seat and continues to rise to hover near the ceiling. A gesture of etched lines divides her body into hemispheres of breasts and belly and clefts of her butt, a kind of ancient statue, veined marble and ivory. She cleaves apart suddenly. The parts whirling into a system of orbiting planets. The President looks up at the glowing constellation of his wife.

The President's speech continues. All of it has already been distributed. It is being delivered as if by a machine. I witness the essential part of him leave himself for a moment, shedding the shell of his suit, to float up above the august chamber of the House of Representatives, joining the animated and precious flesh of his wife.

I think such thoughts because the President thinks such thoughts. Much of what we do is fantasy. It is my job to dream his dreams. In case he is unable to complete his constitutional duties, I am ready to step into his place.

I chair, at the pleasure of the President, a commission on space. I see in his dark suit the deep black fabric of the universe. There are still flakes of white dandruff on the shoulders and the back. I stare into the depths between those flecks of white transforming into twinkling stars. It is a map of heavenly bodies. This vacuum has a texture. I lose my way in its blackness. I no longer hear the speech. On television, I will appear lost in grave thought. I have forgotten the spontaneous applause. The infinite silence between those stars terrifies me.

On the Tomb of the Unknown Soldier

Who were these soldiers? The hairless living ones who helped me place the wreath at the Tomb of the Unknown Soldier. One of them was black. One was white. But what I saw of what was left of their faces (the glossy brim of their caps squashed down on their noses and the straps hid the lips outlining the metallic exterior jaws) were identical grim expressions made up of the least expressive parts, the plane geometry of their cheeks and chins. Their hands were gloved and gripped the green florist wire stand that connected them as if it ran out of their palms and extruded through their squeezing fingers. Their skeletons must have been made of the same pinched wire running through the clay. When they moved, they moved only the moving part. Marching, the legs didn't disturb the head or torso. When they lifted the flowers, their hands alone snatched them up. Their wrists ratcheted to a predetermined calibration in the joints. A pause and then their heads snapped forward together leaving their bodies still facing the wreath they held motionless between them. Another pause then their left legs stepped toward the tomb, Egyptian, the mechanism of the hips hidden beneath the flare of their blue-belted jackets. The air reeked of carnations and roses and mothballs that had steeped their wool uniforms. I followed them conscious of the wobble in my limbs, my wrinkled suit, my puckered face, my hair blowing into my eyes.

As a congressman, I had sent visiting constituents out to Arlington to see the show, shaking their hands at the door of the hired cab. Sometimes, I went myself and took the kids if they were out of school in time to watch the changing of the guard. I counted the twenty-one gliding steps along the red carpet, the twenty-one seconds of silence between the pivots and the echoing heel clicks, the twenty-one steps back past the tomb. Suddenly the replacement and an officer would appear, enter into the rhythm. They barked at each other. The officer inspected the rifles. His hands breaking open the breech. His head snapping his chin to his chest as he looked from behind his dark aviator glasses at the gleaming round in the exposed chamber. Twenty-one steps. Twenty-one seconds. The officer and relieved soldier slid off the runway when the new guard stopped to click his heels. They disappeared behind the cedar trees that screen the barracks.

My grandmother took the copper bracelet she wore in memory of the missing Navy flier of the Vietnam War with her to her grave. I remember reading the name and dates on the green band around her wrist as the family removed the other jewelry before the casket was closed. We decided to leave it on since he'd never been found and because my grandmother always said the copper helped with her arthritis. We left the hearing aid in her ear as well, her plates. The pacemaker was buried, buried in her chest. She had an artificial hip of titanium and gold made by a company in Warsaw, Indiana, in my old district. It is guaranteed to survive forever.

I saluted as the soldiers placed the flowers before the tomb. Beneath the slabs of marble at my feet there were unknown remains of American soldiers from the other wars that followed. World War II and Korea. We have gotten better at knowing though. There is a marker for the Vietnam War but nobody from that war is unknown really, everyone has been accounted for. Everyone is alive, dead, or missing. Say a tooth turns up in a riddle sifting the dirt from a crash site in a Delta paddy. It is rushed to the lab in Hawaii, and they puzzle it out and match the tooth with a name. The classifications shift. There is nothing left to find in the jungle that will now leave us ignorant. You are either lost or found. But not unknown.

So just what is interred here? Perhaps we've created a Gothic monster in reverse, not animated after being stitched together from pilfered corpses, but a fake pile of remains constructed out of the stolen wax limbs of movie monsters posing in Hollywood museums. What is buried here is still only known to God; it just isn't human. The only part of it that is human at all is the lie that placed an empty coffin here, that sustains the fiction. We buried a symbol. We buried not knowing. But we know. We know we know.

In Disneyland they maintain a Hall of Presidents, a stage filled with jerking dummies of the dead Commander-in-Chiefs. After I'm dead, if all has gone right, something that looks like me will nod its head sagely seated next to the smiling hulks of Lincoln and Hoover. The engineers have worked so hard to encode grace and gesture into my lower right arm. They move from tendon to muscle and back again, experiment with a new substance more like cartilage, import artificial femurs and rotor cuffs from the factory in Warsaw, Indiana. Programs to scratch an ear run for thousands of pages.

On this other stage, these living boys of The President's Own Guard, having practiced alone in their barracks, wish to extinguish every twitch. They force themselves not to blink. They wire their jaws shut with will. They attach governors to their stride, unlearning their bodies. Who are they? As taps played, I concentrated, trying to catch one of them breathing. I could hear in the silence between the sad notes only the whirr of the cameras winding after the hiss of the shutters.

Before all this pomp, between the world wars, families came to the cemetery and used the marble tomb as a table for picnics. They looked out over the new sod of a field of Civil War dead. The place was only occasionally guarded then by groups of veterans who would police the area for the scored wax paper, the chicken bones, and the child's ball left behind. Who knows? Perhaps it was a better ceremony to stretch out on the marble table after a big dinner and let the sun feast on your itching skin. Perhaps better than a wreath. Watching the unflinching bodies of the soldiers at attention, I imagined losing myself. I was a statue come to life, tap dancing on the plinth of the Unknown Soldier, looking out over the Potomac to the distant white memorials melting in the haze.

The crowd of people assembled for that Memorial Day applauded as I walked away. They know who I am, they think. I let them think what they think.

On Late-Night TV

The television is second hand from the White House, an early color model dating from the Johnson administration. The mahogany cabinet, gaudy as a casket, holds three screens. I can tune each to different channels, watch the same network on all three. It has been modified for remote. It is cable ready and three VCRs have been hooked up. Johnson had it built so he could watch simultaneously the three versions of the evening news. The maps of Vietnam were in different colors. He must have had an aide at the ready, turning the volume controls by hand. "Let me hear Cronkite, the bastard," he would bark. Or maybe he just left on all the sound. He would have to distinguish who said what the way you pick out instruments in a symphony. I can see him, slouched in a swivel chair, his tie loosened, his eyes skipping from screen to screen to screen, the room filled with the babbling voices. I watched the same war on WISH-TV in Indianapolis never dreaming that it would come out like this.

Most of the furniture we have here at the old Naval Observatory was once in the White House. Each new resident sweeping clean, sends tables and chairs, portraits and drapes, mantel clocks and mirrors over in the GSA vans. The first floor looks like a furniture showroom. The televisions, however, I had sent up to our room. In the evenings, propped up in the waterbed we brought with us to Washington, I watch the televisions. The mattress is slightly baffled to dampen the waves. Still, it is soothing, the gentle rocking. I float watching the late night shows.

Marilyn falls asleep each night after the local weather. Curled away from me under the light blanket, she wears a frilly blindfold like the ones panelists wore on old game shows. The elastic band bunches her hair together into a dark helmet. She snores politely beside me. The sheets are silk. There is a slight roll in the mattress. The polyester in the blanket will discharge static from time to time, faint sparks tracing her hair and shoulders, letting me know she is here.

On the far wall, the televisions are on. The screens seem to float too, a slight flicker in the pictures. I like to arrange the programs from left to right. I have a remote in both hands, and I am good enough now to read the buttons with my thumbs like Braille. I can start with Carson on the first screen, then move to Arsenio in the middle. While I am watching him, noting the strange new design cut into his hair, I can leapfrog Johnny's image to the screen on the right, catching him as he turns toward Doc. My fingers are busy moving Arsenio from the middle screen left, nudging the volume up there so that I can hear his first joke while I watch Carson, arms behind his back, lean forward toward the audience like a figure on a ship's prow. I cue up Ted Koppel on the middle set just to find out tonight's subject. If I'm not interested, I'll switch to the comedy channel with its parade of club stand-ups or run the tape of the morning talk shows, scanning for any reference to me until it is time for Dennis Miller to come on after *Nightline* on ABC.

If I am alert enough, I can record the jokes on the other two VCRs. I now sense when a joke is coming. When Leno stands in for Johnny, he uses me last after a string of gags based on the day's headlines. He likes to end with me. Arsenio seems embarrassed, the punchline swallowed, buried in his nervous guffaw. It is almost as if he feels compelled to make a joke about me. I am able to catch a couple of these jokes a night, save them on one of the two 120-minute cassettes.

Late at night, after all the talk shows are over and the overnight news shows are on the networks, I'll run the tape, one long string of jokes about me. I want to remember who said what. There are the nightly bits that turn on my stupidity, and then the frenzy of jokes when I have done or said something silly. "Did you see where our vice president visited Los Angeles?" The comic shakes his head. "This is true," he says. "He had a few things to say about television." The audience is already howling. He goes on with the joke. Quiet, I think, I want to hear this. I want to know what's true, you bastard. Tell me what's true.

On the other screens, I like to run the weather channels with their shifts of nameless hosts pointing at loops of computer enhanced weather swirling left to right across the map of the nation. The comics stand between two computer enhanced maps of the country. The storm warnings are boxed out, the line of storms a slash of red.

Weather people look like ordinary people. Rumpled and tired. Their suits are off the rack. Their jokes are corny, harmless. I like to watch the weather dancing behind them. I know it isn't actually there but projected on the screen, blended into the signal by the control room mixers. The screen they point to is really blank and they must look at a monitor off stage to see the map. They learn to do this by watching television. I could watch them do this for hours.

While I was in law school, I did watch David Letterman do the weather on that Indianapolis station, sticking pictures of umbrellas and smiling suns in sunglasses on an airbrushed map of Indiana. He drew arrows that meant nothing, made up forecasts on the spot, and teased the anchors who smiled back at him. The other students thought he was funny. My study group took a break to watch him every night. He would spend his time asking on the air what a flurry was, who had seen high pressure, why was Indiana always colored pink.

And now I have him on all three screens. He fiddles with his suit, licks his teeth with his tongue, presses his face into the camera. His jokes aren't funny, and the audience doesn't laugh. But the funny part is, I think, that that is what is supposed to happen. The audience groans and boos. The harder he works, the more it fails, the better the audience likes it. I don't get this being dumb. I don't get it.

At two a.m. the dogs in Washington start barking. I can hear sirens going up and down Massachusetts Avenue. I have been watching the weather. There will be snow in Vail and sunshine in Palm Beach. It's a great country. You can ski or play golf on the same day. I've been watching a show-length commercial for a new kind of paint brush and, on several channels, the pictures of the pouting women who say they will talk with me live if I call them right now.

All the phone traffic is logged here at the residency. I couldn't get away with dialing a 900 number. There would be a leak. Word would get out. I can anticipate the jokes late at night, the winks. I can almost make them up myself.

Marilyn snores, and her snoring sets up a rocking in the bed. The water sloshes. She rolls over, and her face turns toward me. Her eyes are masked, but I can see the twinkling blue screens reflected deep within the black satin.

I want to walk onto the Tonight Show in the middle of someone's time in the guest chair the way Bob Hope does. Perhaps on Carson's very last show. I want to straighten this whole thing out. Let people see me as I really am.

"I can only stay a minute, Johnny," I'd say. He apologizes for that evening's joke during the monologue. "Hey, I understand. I'm used to it." I can take it. I'd show them.

I watch the televisions. I start with the one on the left. The later it gets, the more ads there are for private conversations. The women say they are standing by, waiting for the phones to ring. I could call right now. I could. I would tell them who I am. And they believe me right away. I say, "I'm the Vice President." I say, "No, really. I'm not making this up. I am the Vice President. I am. I am."

On Anesthesia

The naval officer with the football clutches it like, well, a football, tucked under one arm and the other arm wrapped over the top. We call it the football, but it's not a football. It's a silver briefcase stuffed with all the secret codes for launching the missiles and the bombers. He slumps in his chair at the far end of the Oval Office. Secret Service agents, packed into the couches, read old *People* magazines. The lenses of their dark glasses lighten automatically the longer they're inside. They've let me sit at the President's desk in the big leather swivel chair. Now my back is to them. I'm looking out at the Rose Garden where the white buckets weighted down with bricks protect the plants. On the bureau beneath the window, the President has a ton of pictures. His kids and grandkids. His brothers and sisters. Shots of Christmases. The house in Maine. His wife. The dog. I don't see me. Little elephants are scattered among the frames. Carved in stone or wood or cast in polished metal, they all head the same direction, their trunks raised and trumpeting.

Every few minutes I like to turn dramatically around to face the room. Nothing happens. The agents flip through the magazines licking their thumbs to turn the pages. Other aides huddle by the door fingering each other's label pins. The naval officer with the football has a rag out now. He breathes on the briefcase then rubs the fog off the shiny surface.

I get to be President for about twenty minutes more. The real President is under anesthesia at Bethesda. In the big cabinet room the chiefs of staff are watching the operation on a closed circuit hook-up. A stenographer is taking down everything that's being said. They asked me if I wanted to watch with them, but I get squeamish at the sight of blood. I'd wait in the Oval Office I told them. An amendment to the Constitution lets me be Acting President in such situations, but there is nothing for me to do. We've been ignoring the press. No sense mentioning it.

I've been doodling on White House stationery I found in the desk drawer. I always draw parallel zig-zagging lines, connecting them up to form steps. When I am finished I can look at the steps the regular way and then I can make myself see them upside down, flipping back and forth in my head from one way to the other. I arrange the pens on the desk blotter after I've used them as if I am going to give them out as souvenirs.

They let me make a few phone calls. I called a supporter in Phoenix but I forgot about the time difference and I woke him up. What could I say? I'm sorry. I left a message for the Governor of Indiana, a Democrat I play golf with some times. His father, when he was a senator, wrote the amendment that let me be President for a few hours. "Just tell him the President called," I said. I wanted to rub it in. I called Janine, my high school girl friend, who is an actuary in Chicago. I don't know her politics. "Guess where I am," I said. She couldn't guess. When I traveled commercial I used to call her at her home from O'Hare on a stopover. I let her know I was a Congressman, a Senator. I wanted her to know I was on my way someplace.

"Try," I said. "From where I sit I can see the Washington Memorial." That wasn't true. I was looking at the Commander with the football. She told me she was running late, that her eggs were getting cold. Janine had a view of the lake, I imagined, her building near a beach on the North Shore.

"I've got to go," I said, "this is on the taxpayer's nickel." I wanted everyone to hear me. The men in the room, I could see, were trying hard not to look like they were listening.

I was anesthetized once. This was a few years ago. All four of my wisdom teeth were impacted. Before they put me under, I had to read a form and sign it. It said I understood all the things that could go wrong. The procedure was usually performed on patients much younger. Nerves could get cut. Dry sockets. Shattered jaw bones. I don't like blood or guts, so I signed it quickly to stop thinking about the possibilities. I signed, sitting in the chair while the oral surgeon held up the syringe, squirting out drops of the drug from the gleaming needle.

"We are going to put you into twilight sleep," the doctor told me. "Not really sleep. Not deep enough to dream. You'll just be very relaxed," he said slapping at my arm to find a vein. "If we weren't going to work in your mouth, you'd tell us all your secrets. You'd just let go."

I was out like a light. It felt like sleeping in a seat on an airplane. I remember thinking I wish I knew what my secrets were, what I really thought. But the drug that made me tell the truth also put me into twilight sleep so that I never really knew what I said. I know I was talking, telling them everything. I kept rocking along through the dark night. Then, the doctor and the nurses were looking at me strangely. Had they heard me say something, the muttering I had been making becoming clear when they swabbed up the blood or turned away to pick up another instrument? Did they stop and listen?

Tell me what I said, I said to them. But it came out nonsense. I could just begin to feel my face again, feel it swelling up. My lips and tongue had vanished.

"Who stole my tongue?" I said

"Is someone coming to drive you home?" they asked as they walked me into another room.

"Ma mamph," I said. I could hear again. I was vaguely aware of other bodies on cots scattered around the room. The doctor and the nurse eased me onto my own cot. They stuck a sheet of instructions in my hands and slid a small envelope into my shirt pocket.

"Those are your teeth," they said. I had wanted to do something with the molars, polish them up and have them made into jewelry or shellac them for a paperweight. But when I opened the envelope later all that spilled out were splinters of bone, crumbs of teeth. They had to be chiseled out the doctor told me when I called. "They didn't want to budge," he said.

I looked at the pile of fragments on my desk. Here and there I could see a smooth contour of a tooth, the tip of a root, the sliced off crown like a flat bottomed cloud. I pushed the parts around on the desk. Most were ragged, caked with clotted blood and bits of browning tissue. The pulpy nerves crumpled to dust. I poked the pieces into four piles, the bits making a scratching sound as they slid across the stationery they were on. I had drawn stairs on the paper, and I climbed them up and down, up and down.

Maybe it was the painkiller I was still taking. I sat there staring at the piles of dust thinking: These are all my secrets reduced to ashes.

"It's the drugs," Marilyn said when I told her how sad my wisdom teeth had made me. I tried to explain that the operation had pried something out of me. I couldn't begin to explain it. "It's the drugs talking," she said.

The kitchen timer the Secret Service set bings on the end table, and they all stand up from the couches. They toss the *People* magazines in a heap on the coffee table. I turn back to the window and see the navy officer sprinting for the helicopter revving up on the lawn. He'll fly directly to Walter Reed. The official White House photographer snaps a few pictures of me at the desk. A Secret Service agent rushes my doodles to the shredder in the closet. You want me to dial the phone I ask, sign a few papers? What?

"Just act natural," the photographer says as aides usher Marilyn into the room. I stand up, push the chair from the desk. We kiss in front of the bureau, the elephants sniffing up at us. I hear the snap, snap, snap of the camera, sense the white flash on my eyelids.

I am sentimental, I think. I feel lots of things. I just don't let anyone know. No one will know how it felt to be the President of the United States for a few hours. Janine, on her way to work, cannot begin to imagine the depth of my feelings. Everyone else, the whole country waking up and getting ready for the new day, they can't begin to imagine what I feel I feel.

The photographer wants another picture of us kissing. Marilyn leans into me again, her eyes closed, her head cocked to the right. I could kiss her on the cheek or on her mouth. Kissing is all different now. After the extraction of my teeth I found that feeling would never return to my lips, the nerve endings crushed or severed by the operation. I don't like to think about that, nerves and tissues. I decide to kiss her mouth, and I do. It is a sensation I've grown to like. The numbness.

On Barbie

"What is your real name?" I ask the women who is Barbie. She is shivering next to me as we stand in the open doorway at the end of the assembly line. The satin sash she wears matches the ribbon we are supposed to cut. The sky is gray, and the pigeons, scared up by the band music, are spiraling back down to the holes in the eaves and windows of the unused part of the factory where they roost. She tells me her name as she takes my arm. Her hardhat floats on top of her thick hair.

"You could be Ken," she whispers to me. "Let's pretend."

The CEO and owner of this plant is speaking to a crowd of workers and reporters who spill out to the big parking lot. I've thought of that. I could be Ken. I have that block-shaped head. The hairline and the line of the jaw are Ken's. I smile at her, imagining the way we look. I am holding the giant pair of scissors with my other hand. Barbie and Ken and a pair of scissors scaled to make us look doll-sized. Our smiles are frozen on our faces. You have to practice this. Yes, I could be Ken. He's a good looking guy. I take it as a compliment.

The Corvettes spaced along the line are pink. This factory now makes all kinds of electric cars for kids. The cars have two forward speeds and one in reverse controlled by pedals and gear shifts. The detailing of the paint and upholstery matches the vehicle it is modeled on. But I am told it is the novelty of the keys that come with the car, starting it up and shutting it off, that sells the product. Children in elementary school love them. They carry their jingling key rings to class for show and tell.

"It is like a real car," the CEO told me earlier. The Corvettes are just one line called Barbie's Corvette. It's a licensing agreement with Mattel. "And it comes in any color you want," the CEO said, "as long as it is pink."

I thought it was a bad idea driving one of the Corvettes around the parking lot. The CEO and the PR people had hoped I would take one for a spin. I thought of Dukakis in the tank. I pictured myself wedged in the tiny cockpit, my knees up by my ears, my hands on the steering wheel between my feet. The Secret Service were to act as pylons. Stiff as posts, staring from behind their dark glasses at everything except me, I would scoot around their legs in the car, turning a complete circle around one agent, then slalom back through their dispersed pattern on the parking lot, a test track. I would try to cut the corners as close as possible, trench coats slapping my face.

Instead of driving one of the cars, I admired them during a photo opportunity. One turned slowly on a table-top turntable, the television lights playing over its pink gloss finish. Barbie stroked the fenders with the fingers of her long hand. This was my first look at the car. The ribbon cutting ceremony at the end of the assembly line came later. We were to take a tour of the plant and the factory show room where salesmen walked among the highly polished demonstration models handing out brochures. When we got there, we picked our way through the cars at our feet, the miniature Mercedes and tiny Jeeps. We stopped to marvel at a replica of a '57 T-Bird coupe.

"Oh," Barbie said bending over to pet it, "so cute."

This is what Vice Presidents do. Bury the dead and open factories. This factory had once made tractors for semi-trailers, Trans Stars for the local van line company, and green Army Two-and-a-Halfs. The white star stenciled on the door. The factory is in Fort Wayne, in my home district. It had been a ruin for ten years ever since the Harvester closed the plant in favor of one in Springfield, Missouri.

When I was a kid, my father brought me up here. He was covering a roll-out for the paper then. Crammed onto a reviewing stand, we watched the trucks blast around the banked track, stutter over a patch of cobble stones, then plow through a shallow pool splaying a wake of water from beneath each wheel. I got to climb up in the cab as the engine idled and rumbled beneath the seat. With my arms stretched wide I couldn't hold both sides of the steering wheel.

On the way back to Huntington, my father tried to explain the future to me. The truck I had been in was just an idea, its model year two or three years away. I didn't get it. I had smelled the diesel fumes, heard the sneeze of the air brakes. "Who knows," my father said, "a lot could happen."

I let them love me in Fort Wayne. I swung a grant their way. Jawboned the locals for tax relief. Some people are working again. Let them blame that on me.

"I am really Malibu Barbie," Barbie says to me. "The doll comes with a

Frisbee, a tote bag, and a beach umbrella." That is why she is wearing the swimsuit on this early spring day. The sky is as dirty as the grime on the big windows. Off in the distance, at the other end of the property, is the red brick bell tower. The old company logo, the small *i* bisecting the capital *H* to look like a gear shift pattern, still hangs crookedly just beneath the roof. The stink of the drawn copper from the wire works next door begins to coat my tongue.

"You from around here?" I ask her. Her neck is long and thin. Her swimsuit is made out of a miracle fabric in an animal hide print. She is wearing sheer hose that sparkle even in the bad light and hiss like scissor blades cutting construction paper when she walks.

Earlier, we toured the whole factory, even the abandoned parts. The new assembly line took up a fraction of the acres under roof. The toy car company had been started in the owner's garage. At first he just made go carts for the neighborhood kids. Then, as business grew, he moved to a Quonset hut in an industrial park. There is plenty of room to expand now.

Barbie's heels snipped over the steel plate on the floor that had covered the conduits for cables that feed the old machines long removed. On the terrazzo I could see where they had been positioned from the footprints of discolored flooring outlined with filth. Here and there were rusting heaps of metal that could not be salvaged and yellowing scraps of paper that looked like scaling fungus on rotting trees. The factory opened up to three stories, the web of girders supporting the roof lost in the gloom. Dripping water from somewhere matched Barbie's cadence. We stopped in the middle of the vast hall to rest. There was a little oasis of gun metal stools and desk chairs on coasters. The Secret Service drifted on, their backs to us, spreading apart to form a perimeter, right on the edge of being seen. No one spoke. What light there was seemed to be drawn to Barbie, who swiveled slowly in the office chair. Her legs, crossed at the ankles, stretched out to keep her pointed feet off the floor. Her head was thrown back, the hardhat adhering to her hair. She closed her eyes as if she were sun bathing. She shimmered, bobbing like a needle in a toy compass slowly nudging north. I could hear the pigeons cooing in the rafters and then suddenly flapping after launching out, gliding into sight to land on the floor across the room.

"You know," I said to Barbie, "we always live in the age of lead. We stand on the shoulders of giants." I looked at her to see what impression I had made.

"Oh, I know," she said. "Look at the toys these days. Nothing is left to the imagination"

I felt like an accessory in a new playset. Call it Barbie's Factory. Action figures and clothes sold separately. Any moment the vast roof could crack open, the walls hinging out. I am Midwestern Ken. A seed cap, dungarees, and a farmer's tan.

Barbie is a head taller than I am. I sat quietly and watched her turn in the chair, propelled by invisible forces. The Secret Service whispered to each other in the shadows.

At the end of the day, we cut the ribbon. I grasp one handle with both my hands. Barbie has the other. I remember again the gigantic wheel of the truck. I am confused, confused again by size. I never fit. I never fit no matter what I do. The scissors are useless at cutting through the ribbon, the fabric folding then slipping between the blades. We end up tearing through it after the threads of the edge have been frayed enough by our frantic efforts. We pull the handles apart, then hurl them back together. The blades slicing closed smack with a kiss.

Barbie leans over and gives me a kiss. Her lips are waxy on my cheek. We pose that way. Barbie's long neck stretched out as she nuzzles my face. A hand on each of my shoulders for support. I am smiling at the cameras. This is what I am thinking. I'm thinking: It's a small moment of triumph no matter how you look at it.

The air is permeated with the tang of metal. I hold out in front of me the shiny keys that fit the brand new pink Barbie Corvette I was given that the Secret Service will later carry out to my limousine and store in the trunk like a spare to begin our trip back to Washington. And later still, in an intimate ceremony on the Mall, I will donate the car to the Smithsonian. Mattel will send another Barbie, this one dressed in a gold gown that might have been worn at an inaugural. Together, with the pink car roped off in one corner of the museum, we will have staked out our own little piece of history.

On Hoosier Hysteria

This is true. During the annual high school basketball tournaments in Indiana, the winning small towns send a team to the cities for the regional or semi-state finals. Those towns empty completely for the games, the whole population evacuated by yellow buses and strings of private sedans and wagons. The Governor declares an emergency and sends a few state troopers or a truck load of the Guard to patrol the deserted streets.

I got sent to Marion one spring when that team was playing up in Fort Wayne. I was attached to a clerical unit stationed at Fort Benjamin Harrison outside of Indianapolis. We convoyed up from the south and parked on the outskirts of the ville as the residents streamed north. We could hear the horns. A muscle car sped by camouflaged with crepe paper and tempera. We were humping it into town, two files, one to a gutter, along the main street. The lieutenant sent a squad down a side street. Dogs barked. Up ahead was the small downtown of two-storied stores and offices. Hovering just above the brick buildings, a huge water tower seemed to float like a dark cloud, its supporting legs obscured by the buildings and trees. There was writing on its side that couldn't be read from where I was, the town name and zip code perhaps, the sense of it stretched around out of sight. We had to hold the town for the day, and, if the team won its afternoon game, stay the night in bivouac set up on the high school football field.

It took us a few hours or so to walk the streets and rattle some door handles. Tacked up on every garage was a scuffed backboard and rotting net. I looked in the windows of the empty homes, saw the big glossy house and garden magazines scalloped on the coffee tables, the dish rag draped over the faucet in the kitchen, an old pitcher filled with pussy willow branches in the middle of the dining table. Some places were unlocked, and I poked my head in, shouting to make sure no one was there. As I walked through one house, I listened to the clocks ticking. There was Eckrich meat in the refrigerator. I turned on the television and stood in front of it as it warmed up. The game was on, live, the boys going through warm-up drills at each end of the court. Somewhere in the crowd, the people who lived in that house shook pom-poms behind the cheerleaders. I stood there, too close to the set, in the living room, in full gear, my helmet on my head, cradling my rifle in my arms. The boys in their shiny outfits did lay-up after lay-up. Each of them took a little skip as he started to break for the hoop, meeting the feeding pass in mid-stride, the ball then rolling off his fingers, kissing the glass. A sergeant tapped on the picture window. "Quayle," he said, his voice filtering into the house, "get your butt out here."

I followed a squad down an oiled street. The sidewalks had crumbled into dust. The Kiwanis had tapped the maple trees growing along the side of the road, the sap plunking inside the tin buckets. We formed up at the end of the block where the town met the surrounding field of corn stubble. The field went on for miles broken only by a stand of trees, a cluster of buildings, a cloud of crows rising up from the ground. We stood there waiting for something to happen. How strange and empty the world had become. In a few more weeks spring would be here for good, but you would never guess it from the way things looked. It was as if we had survived something horrible. I felt frightened and relieved. Then, the sergeant told us to saddle up and get back to town.

Later, we watched the game on a television we brought with us from the armory. The little diesel generator sputtered outside the tent. Marion won and would play again that night. We ate K rations while we watched, fruit salad in army green tins. I saved the cherries for the last after eating the peaches, the pears, the pineapple, and the grapes in that order.

And later still, I climbed the water tower and circled the tank on the wire catwalk, looking down on the town. I saw the grid of street lights come on automatically in patches down below. A sentry in one neighborhood waded through the puddles of light. A truck or a car would rumble up the main street and brake at the check point near the square. On the wall of the water tank, high school kids had scratched their initials in the paint, coupling them together with the stitch of plus signs. Now I was too close to read the huge letters of the town name and the legend that declared Marion was the Home of the Little Giants and the numbers of the years they had won the state championship. You had to read that from the ground. In my pocket was a souvenir I'd pilfered from a house below, a gravy boat from a corner cupboard. I have it still.

And when Marion won the game that night, I could hear the troops shouting that the home team had won. I watched from the platform on the water tower as all the patrolling soldiers came running from their posts to see the team cut down the nets. From my perch, I looked north to the haze of light where Fort Wayne was supposed to be, recreating in my own mind the whole celebration I knew by heart.

I was floating above a peaceful Indiana in the dark. Out there, there were winners and losers. After tonight, we'd be down to the final four. I thought then, and I think now, that this is what we were fighting for.

On 911

He used to walk everywhere, Ed, the incumbent I beat for the congressional seat that got me to Washington. His campaign consisted of taking walks. He'd walk through a neighborhood in Fort Wayne, going up and knocking on a few doors, waving at cars as they passed by him. He gave out stickers in the shape of footprints and in the outline of shoes. He'd walk out into the country, out to Zulu and Avilla, Markle and Noblesville. The few reporters that trailed along tired after a few miles, caught a ride back downtown. He was a tall thin man. He slung his jacket over his shoulder, his shirt sleeves rolled up to his elbows. His pants were too short. Along Indiana 3, he'd wade through the patches of wild carrot and golden rod. He was bombed by the angry black birds. He had thin hair and wore glasses with clear plastic frames. Near Leo, the Amish, who don't even vote, passed him by in their buggies. He would stop at a farm house for a drink of water from a well. He'd get his picture in *The Journal*, the Democratic paper, kicking an empty can along the gutter in the streets of the new suburbs of St. Joe Township. He was always alone, hardly talked to anyone that mattered. No one walked anymore. His shoes were always dusty. It was a cinch.

After I won and Ed was showing me around the Hill, he refused to ride the Capitol subway over to his office. He put me on board, and we left him behind to walk over by himself. His aides even rode with me. They didn't bother looking back to see him shrink in the poor light of the dark tunnel beneath the streets of Washington.

He was too pitiful for words. He had more than enough rope to hang himself. The few rumors we fanned at Rotary Clubs and the Zonta were enough. His skin was milky. His voice was pitched too high. He smoked a pipe. The pictures you saw in *The Journal* always showed him from behind, the loose white shirt draped with that summer weight jacket. Such a target, his back exposed, brought the best out of the voters. I salivated along with my staff as we watched him walk through the fall.

His one piece of legislation was the bill that established an emergency telephone number, 911. Something a child could remember and dial. I can just imagine the debate. Who would oppose it? What could be wrong with it?

I imagine him right now sitting in his rec room watching television, perhaps the show that dramatizes the rescues once someone has called the emergency number. Every time I watch that program, I think of him in his recliner, feeling good about his public life, the stories he watches a kind of endless testimonial to his goodness.

When I was a kid, I believed in creating a kind of chronic discomfort, using the telephone to disrupt the work-a-day world. "Do you have Prince Edward in the can? You do? Well, you better let him out." I dialed the numbers randomly, "Is your refrigerator running? It is? Well, you better go chase it." I flipped through the phone book looking for funny names, calling the Frankensteins or the Cockburns. I liked transforming the telephone into something dangerous. People being startled by the bell, their hands frozen for a moment before reaching the rest of the way to pick-up. My little voice, a needle in their ears, creating these anxious moments. Let him out! Go chase it! I'd make up fictions to clear the party line so that I could call my girlfriend. Or I would listen to the neighbors talking to each other, letting them know I was there. I would always be there.

A guy like you, Ed, would keep on answering the phone, would think after all the heavy breathing I'd want to talk with you. You believe in signs, in what they say. The tinkling bells of the ice cream truck would have you racing down the street. You answer the phone with out a second thought. Is your refrigerator running?

Poor Ed. Everything in the world can be used, used in ways you'd never dream, used against you. Twisted. Devoured. Pulled inside out. I like to imagine you cringing in your dark rec room, the flicker of your television slapping you around, your sweaty skin sticking to the gummy vinyl of your lounger. I broke your legs. I made you crawl. You were so easy to kick. I watched you drag yourself along the oiled back roads, the uncut ditches of Allen County where well-bred children who hurl rocks at the Amish buggies just to hear the wood splinter took aim at you.

In the bedrooms of America, no one ever entertains the fantasy of a liberal with a whip. They desire something more, something more like me but dressed to the hilt in black uniforms and patent leather, professional looking, someone who might be truly dangerous. It's in the eyes. It's there in the tight smile. In the privacy of their own rec rooms some people like to dress up. People like to be hurt. People like to hurt. They play out their own amateur versions of epic conflicts. Here words don't mean the same things. Saying stop doesn't work. Stop means keep on going. Try to imagine it. What to yell when things get out of hand, when the stimulation in these dramas exceeds the threshold of endurance? I've heard they scream or mutter: 911. 911. The number you invented has been absorbed into this language of love.

I hate to think about these things at all. But we live in the sickest of times. It's a still matter of trust. Your partner will stop if you find the right thing to say. What can I say, Ed? What number can I call? It seems I can't exist without these dramas. There are the good guys and the bad guys. I like that. Someone gets hurt. Someone does the hurting. And the bells keep ringing.

On *Quayleito*

I know now how it works. I spent one afternoon in my office with an eye glasses repair kit dismantling the thing. I unscrewed the little screws that held the tiny hinges, unhooked the rubber bands, untied the threads with tweezers, freed the minute springs as fine as hair. The pieces lay scattered on my desk blotter. I put the various parts in the empty squares of days mapped out on the appointment calendar. I had been ordered to lay low awhile, rehabilitate myself.

I never drink the water anywhere. It can make you sick. But in Chile, I waded into one of their outdoor markets to look for something local to ingest. I wasn't going to be a Nixon holed up in the limousine rushing through the *platas* pelted by eggs. I believe native populations can smell the fear. Gorbachev kissed babies on a street in Washington, DC. I can shake a few hands and handle some grapes in Santiago.

Marilyn waited back at the embassy. I was sandwiched in a three car motorcade. "Stop the car," I ordered. "How do I say 'How much?'"

The car was already floundering in the market crowd. I like to move through a thick mass of people this way, the ring of security wedging me along, hands, disconnected from the faces they belong to reach through to touch me, to try to grab my hands. "Steady, lads," I barked out to the agents.

The squids were huge, draped over clotheslines like parachutes. The shrimps looked like stomachs. Chickens squawked when the vendors held them up to me by their feet. We'd move from the sun to the shade made by awnings of brightly colored blankets and gauzy dresses. I could smell coffee roasting. The potatoes were the size of golf balls and colored like breakfast cereal. Rabbits in wooden cages watched what must have been skinned rabbits skewered on spits turning over charcoal fires.

Where we walked, the ground was covered with the skins of smashed vegetables and crushed leaves and tissue wrappers. I slipped on a banana peel.

I pointed at fruit I had never seen before. The crowd that had been drifting along with us hushed to a whisper. The farmer brushed the flies away from melons that looked like pictures of organs in an anatomy book. Striped, gland-sized berries secreted gummy juices. The apples had thorns and were orange. Another fruit had been split open to show it was choking with sacks of blood red liquid. The flies swarmed around the farmer's hand as he pointed from one bushel to the next. He threw some plums into a sack and waved away the aide who tried to pay him.

"*Gracia,*" I said, reaching in for one. I pulled it out and held it up. The crowd cheered. The press took pictures of me eating the plum. I felt like a matador, the crowd cheering me on. The translator said something about water. I told him I didn't want any, that I never drink it. But he had meant that the plum should be washed. It should have been washed before I bit into it. Too late. The bite I took went to the pit. I survived though I was sick later. It didn't matter. I was going to get sick one way or the other. The plum was good. It tasted like a plum.

On the way back to the car, we bumped into a stand filled with carved wood figures of little men. I thought they must be souvenirs like the dolls of baseball or football players you get at the stadiums back home whose bobbing plaster heads are attached to the uniformed bodies by a bouncy spring.

"*Cuanto vale?*" I asked the surprised seller. The translator told me what he said.

"Is that the right price?" I asked the translator.

He shrugged. "Seems fair," he said. And I told him to tell the man I'd take one.

I held the figure in my hands admiring the workmanship. Though crude, there was a deftness to the carving, the way the clothes hung on the body. The bright paint seemed festive and foreign. People in the crowd jockeyed around to get a look. The statue was lighter than I imagined, hollow. I shook it and heard something rattle inside. I noticed an unglued seam at the waist. The crowd was shouting at me now.

"What are they saying?" I asked the translator. He told me they were shouting instructions on how it worked. As he said that, I was pulling gently on the doll's head. Just then, the joint below the shirt cracked open and a little flesh-painted pee pee sprung up. The crowd went wild.

Back then, when I bought the doll, I laughed it off. I told the press it was a gift for my wife. I jerked its head a time or two to show what happened. Everyone in the crowd was smiling and giggling. Security, too, looked back at me over their shoulders to catch a glimpse of the exposition, the flesh-colored splinter tipped with the head of a match.

When I returned to the embassy, I didn't tell Marilyn what the doll did. She found out after listening to the Voice of America on the short wave. Nothing was mentioned at the state dinner that evening. "Get rid of it," was all she said before turning off the lights and rolling over in bed.

Maybe I should have washed the plums. I was up all night in the bathroom. I brought the doll in there with me. As I sat in the bright tile light, I contemplated the thing. Its enigmatic smile, the way one eye seemed to wink, how its arms and hands and fingers looked like vines grown into the trunk of its body, what did it mean?

Everything I touch transforms into things I cannot begin to understand. I was terrified when I squeezed from my own penis its first drop of semen. I was twelve, taking a bath, soaping myself hard when I felt the shiver. I thought it was the chill in the air of the room then I saw the little white pill slip out of me. It was soap, I thought. It burned. It had gotten inside. But it wasn't soap. What had I done? Who could I tell? I had hurt myself badly, I thought, and once I thought that, it did not surprise me to then think that I had gotten what I deserved. I have always gotten what I deserved. I washed and washed myself. Years after that, here I was sick again in a strange bathroom in Chile, and a souvenir that didn't have a name regarded me as my insides rearranged themselves spontaneously.

In Chile, I found out later, the ending *ito* gets glued to every name. It means little, *ito*. It's affectionate. Little this, little that. And the kind of doll I bought that day in the market are now called *Quayleito* after me.

The guts of the thing are all spread out on my desk. I know now how it works. The springs, the trap door, the counterweights, the whole mechanism of the joke. I still don't know its purpose, why it was made. Poor little *Quayleito*. What to do now? My days are empty. Idle hands. Devil's playground.

On *The Little Prince*

The children are out in front selling lemonade to raise money for Jerry's Kids. One of them comes running in for more mix. It's a holiday so we all have to shift for ourselves. The old Naval Observatory where we live is near the neighborhood of embassies. A pack of Africans in native dress have surrounded the card table, drinking from the tiny Dixie cups while the kids are dumping the powdered mix into the picnic jug and wetting it down with the hose. I can see this from the house. Foreigners don't understand why we have a labor day at the end of summer instead of in May. They are all working today, even the Marxists who live down the road. They are heading back to their desks after lunch, killing time at the stand.

I've got the television tuned to the telethon. Crystal Gayle, who is from Wabash, Indiana, is supposed to be on soon. Jerry staggers around the stage. His eyes are crossed, and he's yammering out of the side of his mouth. The French think he is a genius. I hear that all the time. How the French think he is a genius. Personally, I liked him better when he was teamed up with Dean Martin whose suave manners stood out against his sidekick's clowning. I like the movie where Lewis plays a goofy caddy for Martin who is a smooth golf pro. The high pitched whining, bending the clubs, the divots. Martin gets the girl, wins the open. Now, Jerry looks doughy, the sheen on his hair matches the satin stripes on his formal trousers. My God, it's time already to undo the bow tie. What the French say about him has to have gone to his head. He rants at enemies then leers buck-toothed, eyes bulging. He wears aviator glasses that look like copies of the pair the President wears.

French is still the language of diplomacy, I guess. It makes sense since everything they seem to say says the opposite of what should be said.

Jerry Lewis is a genius. They use language as a kind of disguise for what they really mean. They praise adults who act like children. Is a genius, Jerry Lewis. I would have studied it in high school where they made it hard on purpose, all those little *la*'s and *le*'s, to weed out the Z lane kids who were routed into Spanish. I took Latin because it didn't move around, because it would help me with my English, and because I was going to be a lawyer.

When they were younger, I read to my kids. I took turns when I could and chose the stories with a lot of words and few pictures assuming that, after a while, I would look up and the kids would be asleep, their faces smashed into their pillows, their arms hanging over the sides of the bunk beds. That's the biggest myth that bedtime stories put kids to sleep. It revs them up, and after I had closed the book, I had to hang around in the dark and answer questions about the strangest things. They always wanted to know if I was there when the story happened and was the story different when I was their age. I'd rock while they thrashed in their blankets pretending they were characters from a book, that there was something scary in the closet. "Settle down. Settle down." I thought of torts and contracts, the stories of the man who falls down an old dry well, posted but uncovered, on a neighbor's property while he was cutting the lawn as a repayment of a previous debt. Who can sue who? On what grounds? There were ways out of those stories. It ends up being settled. One could walk away, fall asleep.

I could have killed the Little Prince. Reading his story, I felt so guilty for growing up and having no imagination anymore. But one night, I understood that that was the point. I was supposed to feel bad because I no longer had an imagination. The French. This thing they have for innocence. "Go to sleep!" I always wound up screaming. "Pipe down!" I'd storm out of the room, the children whimpering. "Grow up!" I'd yell and yell at them until, one day it seemed, they had done just that, grown up.

I stay away from them now. They have their own lives, their lemonade stands. The Africans must be thirsty. They crowd the table. Somewhere among them are my children refilling their glasses with lemonade that is not lemonade.

Let me try to explain it to myself. Those books never are about what they are supposed to be. Reading transmits a disease that you get through your eyes. A thing like *The Little Prince* gives it to you. You feel worse. You feel like you have lost something you'll never get back. But you never had it and that makes you feel bad too. Therefore: Don't read. Stop now. Don't even crack the book open. In every story there is a dangerous formula hidden in the forest of the letters. It is there already, always.

On *The Planet of the Apes*

I was always one of those who hid in the trunk. You paid by the head at the Lincolndale Drive-In off U.S. 30 on the north edge of Fort Wayne. There was an orange A&W shack across the highway from the entrance. We stopped there just as the sun was going down and drank root beers, sitting on the bumpers of somebody's father's car. The parking lot had been oiled and the heat of the day had squeezed out little blobs of tar breaded with dust. You flashed your lights on and off when you were finished, and a car hop who knew we were from the county and ignored us came over to gather up the mugs. Then three or four of us climbed into the trunk fitting ourselves together like a puzzle. Two others always rode up front, somebody alone would be suspicious. One of them would drop the lid on us, bouncing it a time or two to make sure it latched.

At first, the dark smelled like rubber, the rubber of the spare tire and someone's sneaker in my face. The car rolled slowly over the packed dirt of the lot, stepped around the ruts, then made a short burst across the highway to join the conga line of cars leading up to the theater gates. It was hot inching our way up to the box office. The trunk was lined with a stadium blanket. Who knows what we were breathing, the moth balls, the exhaust from the idling car. The brakes clinched next to my head. The radio from the cabin was muffled by the seat. I always thought I would almost faint from the lack of oxygen, and then I would. I went light-headed, floating in space, my limbs all pins and needles and the roof of the world pricked by stars.

"Dan O!" They called me Dan O then. They hauled me out of the trunk by the cuffs on my jeans. The car had its nose up, beached on the little hill that aimed it toward the screen. I slumped on the rim of the trunk sniffing the air, looking at the next swell of dirt, a line of cars surfing its crest, moored by the speaker cords to silver posts. It was wrong. I swore I would never do it again. I staggered up out of the trunk, afraid I was turning into some kind of juvenile delinquent. "Book me," I yelled to my friends as they filtered between the cars toward the cinder brick refreshment stand to buy overpriced burgers and fries with the money we saved sneaking in.

I was telling this to Chuck Heston in the green room of the convention. The green room was a trailer with no windows parked beneath the scaffolding of the podium. The crowd on the floor above sounded like the wind, and Chuck looked scoured and bronzed. He listened intently, his smile frozen on his face.

"Do you remember where you were from in *The Planet of the Apes*?" I asked him.

"From earth?" he asked without moving his lips.

"That's right," I said, "But where on earth?" I could see again the inquisitor ape in white robes interrogating the crazed astronaut. This is before we know about the beach with the broken Statue of Liberty buried in the sand. Chuck had been huge on the screen at the drive-in, his head as big and as brilliant as a moon. The screen is now a ruin itself, plywood plates have popped out of its backing exposing the girders rank with pigeons. The box office is abandoned. The neon has been picked over and scavenged. The high fences are sunk in the weeds.

I saw them all, I told him. *The Planet of the Apes. Beneath the Planet of the Apes. Escape from the Planet of the Apes. Conquest of the Planet of the Apes. Battle for the Planet of the Apes.* I saw the first one with my high school friends at the Lincolndale that summer after law school. As a joke they put me in the trunk by myself where I rattled around with the tire iron and the jack.

"I could have been disbarred before I was even barred," I told Chuck. That night at the drive-in, my friends and I sifted through the rows of cars to the playground of swings and seesaws under the screen. I climbed up into the monkey bars and talked with my friends about the future. The huge clock projected above our heads slowly ticked down the time remaining until the movie started.

That night, before I had even seen the movie, I sensed that I was different from the rest, an alien walking among them. I imagined that the amphitheater of parked cars stretching into the dark had come to see me caught inside a cage. I looked out over the expanse of cars. Clouds of dust floating along the lanes were illuminated by the headlights for a moment before they were extinguished. There was the murmur of the speakers, hundreds of repeating messages reverberating in each car. I thought, I'm your man. I'm the one you're looking for.

Chuck hadn't moved. He had stared at me while I talked, his face sagging some as I went on with my reminiscence. Above us the convention crowd howled, a gale force. We would be on soon.

"You," I said, "were from Fort Wayne in the movie." And he looked a little relieved. "The astronaut you played was from Fort Wayne, and the apes took that as another bit of evidence of your hostile intention."

"Oh," he said, "I had forgotten."

"I'm from near there," I said.

I wanted to tell him that back then it had been important that someone like himself had come from that part of the planet even if it was all made up. And now I was here with him waiting for what would happen next.

His head was huge, I remember. As big as the moon. And when the news of his character's nativity seeped into the cockpit of the car, we pounded fists on the padded dash, hooting and whistling. We flashed the car lights and honked the horn until the steering wheel rang. For several minutes, all the cars rocked and flashed, the blaring horns drowning out what was being said on screen. It seemed at any second these hunks of metal we rode in would rise up and come alive. But they didn't.

On Snipe Hunting

They told me to wait, so I wait. They gave me a burlap sack and pushed me out of the car into the ditch next to a field. I watched the taillights disappear. They told me they would drive the snipes my way. "Wait here." And I do.

Stars are in the sky. I'm in a mint field. The branches of the low bushes brush against my legs, releasing the reeking smell.

I think, suddenly, they are not coming back. Back home, they are waiting for me to figure out they are not coming back. They are thinking of this moment, the one happening now, when I think this thought, that they are not coming back, and then come home on my own.

But, I think, I'll wait. While waiting, I'll think of them waiting for me to return home with the empty burlap sack. They'll think that I haven't thought, yet, that I was left here in the mint field, that I am waiting for them to drive the snipes my way. I'll let them think that.

In the morning, I'll be here, waiting. They will come back looking for me. Dew will have collected on the mint bushes. The stars will be there but will be invisible. And I won't have thought that thought yet, the one they wanted me to think.

The imaginary quarry is still real and still being driven my way.

Uncollected Fiction

Borges in Indiana

The Pan Am Stewardess Saying Good-Bye in the Door of the Airplane at the Airport in Indianapolis
He paused on the platform at the top of the stairs and said, "Ah, Indiana. It smells like corn."

The Comp Lit Student Who Had a Car
From Indianapolis to Bloomington, about an hour trip, I counted between him and the prof seven languages. But I was distracted by the new car.

A Farmer in a Field of Clover Near Martinsville Spreading Manure
I saw a big new car going by, south, fast.

The Pharmacist on Walnut Street
He says, indicating this other guy next to him, "This is Borges, and he has a head cold."

A Grease Monkey at the Standard Station
The filler cap was hidden behind the license plate. Little flappy thing. I saw him in the rear seat nodding his head.

The Brakeman of a Northbound Illinois Central Freight Waiting to Set a Switch on the Other Side of the Viaduct as a Car Passes Beneath
Smelled like rain.

The Junior High School Art Teacher Supervising the Elaborate Painting of Fire Plugs to Represent Various Patriots in Honor of the Nation's Bicentennial

This car stopped, and he asked me—he had an accent—to describe what I was doing. Can you believe it?

The Track Team Manager Scooping Out Dollops of Analgesic Balm with a Wooden Tongue Depressor
A car went by honking its horn.

The Morning Baker at the Sugar 'N' Spice in the Memorial Union Serving Him an Iced Fruit Bar Cookie
He said, "It has no nuts, yes? I can't eat nuts. Nuts give me gas." Something like that.

A Student in Front of the Von Lee Theater on Kirkwood Watching Bees Collect Around the Trash Bin There Attracted by the Dried Syrup of Spilled Cola
I told him: Careful. Bees.

A Waitress in the "Frangipani" Room Explaining How the Perfume Was Popular at the Time Hoagie Carmichael Wrote the Words for the Alma Mater Changing the I to an A so It Would Rhyme with Indiana
No, I am wearing musk.

The Flagman on 3rd Directing Traffic Around the Asphalting Being Done There Near the Green House
They were rolling up their windows real fast. The kid who was driving didn't want to take the new car down the wet street. He had no choice, see.

The Audio-Visual Guy Running the Lights at the Lecture
He erased the blackboard then clapped the erasers together a couple of times which made a huge cloud of chalk dust which he then walked through which coated him.

A Student Who Had Broken a Leg Slipping on a Freshly Mopped Terrazzo Floor Listening to the Lecture from His Hospital Bed
He was just beginning to say how he was reminded of Buenos Aires when the orderly starts to slop the floor with Lysol. I told him to knock it off.

The Union Board Representative Leading Him to the Podium
He sniffed the microphone before he spoke like it was a rose or something.

The Mayor's Wife Giving Him a Bouquet of Roses after His Speech
And then he held them up to his mouth like he was going to speak to them or eat them. I don't think he can see so well.

The Daughter of the Professor Who Sponsored His Visit (a Toddler at the Time) Recalling the Visit Years Later in Her Best-selling Memoir
With a crayon I had drawn on the wall and I was rubbing my little nose against it and this sweet old man with moth-bally clothes who can hardly see, my dad always says when he tells me this story, leans way over right next to me to get a good look at the wall with my scribbles.

A Librarian Who Brought the University's Collection of Books to Be Signed Standing in the Back of the Hall Cradling the Editions
He knew I was a librarian. How the hell did he know I was a librarian? I must have reeked of it.

A Freshman Who Was Required to Attend Falling Asleep and Dreaming He Was Mowing the Front Lawn of His Parents' House in South Bend
I can't remember.

In the Darkened Light Booth a Theta Making Love for the First Time Coming, Her Face Pressing Against a Humming Electrical Panel Where She Saw Out of the Corner of Her Eye the Twitching Needle in a Glowing Dial Indicating the Fluctuating Sound Levels Emanating from the Stage
It was great. Just great.

A Teenager Pissing into the Empire Quarry Thinking He Had Been Caught
I was naked and I about shit my pants.

The Stock Boy at the A&P Grinding a Big Bag of Eight O'clock Coffee
The old guy, he didn't say nothing but held his breath.

An Old Woman in the Back Seat of the Third Car of a Funeral Procession Seeing a Man on the Corner of the Square Eating Popcorn from a Bag
I thought it was my dead husband.

Her Father Sitting Next to Her
I thought it was me.

A Clerk in Howard's Bookstore Watching Through the Window of the Store and Through the Windows of the Passing Funeral Procession
I was licking my thumb, counting money in the till.

A Yearling Gilt Roasting on the Spit of a Portable Barbecue Set Up for the Occasion on Dunn Meadow

At Night a Group of Fraternity Boys About to Pour a Large Box of Detergent into Showalter Fountain
This big old car circles around and the geezer in the back rolls down the window in the back to have a look-see.

A Reporter for The Herald-Telephone *Lighting a Cigarette*
He spoke to me in Spanish. Asked me for a smoke.

A Doctor at the Heath Center Washing His Hands After Taking a VD Swab Out of a Young Man's Penis Telling the Person Knocking to Come In
It's a Borges in two. He says he has a head cold and fever.

Mr. Frango Mincing Garlic for his Pizzas
"Can I have change on the phone?" Honest to God, that's what he said. Honest to God.

A Graduate Student Who Was Reading Borges on a Bench Making a Mental Note to Give Her Dog a Bath When Her French Lover Who Left Her Two Years Before to Go to Algiers Sits Down Next to Her on the Bench
I said, "Philippe, what are you doing here?" And he said, "Looking for you."

A Trumpet Major Blowing the Spit Out of His Trumpet Just as Borges Presses His Nose Against the Small Window in the Practice Room Door
I said hi, but he couldn't hear me. Soundproof.

A Sophomore Poet in a Workshop Watching the Great Man Slap Himself in the Face with the Paper Each Time He Is Handed a Worksheet
It was a ditto, man. He wanted the high.

Twenty Years After the Visit, a Sound Lab Technician Listening to a Tape of the Lecture
This platform is the stone ages. Scratchy, you bet. How should we label it?

Borges, Calling Home from a Phone Booth in a Pizza Parlor in Indiana Inhales, as He Speaks, the Scent of Talc Left by a Previous Caller
"It is snowing here," he said in Spanish.

A Man at the Counter of the Gun Store Sighting Down a Barrel of a Surplus M-1 Garand at an Old Man Across the Street Looking Up at the Courthouse
It had been recently oiled.

A Fireman Flushing the Hydrants on 10th Noticing in Passing How Small People Are in the Distance
Jesus, these plugs. They're a disaster.

The Night Auditor at the Union Hotel Running Room and Tax on 415 at 3:07 in the Morning
There was a pick-up error of nine cents on that folio which threw the house out of balance. I found it around five before he checked out. It was direct billed so it didn't matter much really.

At RCA a Quality Control Inspector Fine Tuning a Set for Shipping
His head is blue. OK. His face is red. OK. And now it is blue. OK. Now it is green. OK. Now it is red again. And that's OK.

At the Waffle House Eating Corned Beef Hash a Graduate Student Translating Says He Said
The eggs. The sunny-side up eggs. They look like eyes. Like eggs. Look, like eyes. Something. Something. Something. . . .

On an Indiana Bell Pole a Lineman Completing a Splice Listening
It was in Spanish, I think. Spanish. I don't really know since I don't really know Spanish.

An Undergraduate in the Language Lab Listening to an Elementary Tape
These guys come in and look us over. I couldn't hear what they were saying, but for a second it looked like their lips were moving to what I was hearing on the tape. You know, *le chat est sur la table*, stuff like that.

On the Edge of Town a Woman Selling Concrete Lawn Ornaments
There. There, a deer. A chicken and a chicken with chicks. A frog. A

frog. A frog. Another deer. A deer, there, there, there, and there. Ducks. Two deers. This goes on.

A Dog Tracking Something on the Lawn of a Limestone Ranch House

The Engineer of the Southbound Monon Freight Waving at the First Car Waiting at the Grade Crossing on 15th
It was ditch weed, you bet. I told the Maintenance of Way. Plain as the nose on my face.

A Bum in the Open Doorway of the 23rd Car of the Southbound Monon Freight
Spoiled grain. Old cardboard. Never get off where there ain't no shade.

The Conductor on the Rear Platform Turning and Walking into the Caboose as the Gates Begin to Lift
Something's burning.

A Man at the Next Urinal in the Rest Room of the Airport
I couldn't say anything to him under the circumstances.

The First Officer Asking If He Would Like to See the Flight Deck
It was pretty close quarters up there.

A Woman in Seat 7A Turning Her Head Away in Disgust
Oh, I knew I was pregnant.

A Radar Operator Noting an Anomaly at 0744 and Informing His Supervisor
It smelled like trouble, but it wasn't nothing.

Species

Our teeth will last the longest. We hide them now behind our kiss. Our tongues are scholars in caves, and this archeology a type of destruction. A red dawn cuts its teeth on the ridge outside the window as these lines erupt predictably, moving forward from the breccia of my genes. Bound together, we splint each other, each other's die and caste, a lucky fossil in the dig. The light changes. The sun's dentition promises something quite primitive. Strange burial practices. Diastema, we fit together—lower jaw, upper jaw. You bite my shoulder every time you die. Then, as we watch, these mute dissertations disappear like specimens en route to Western museums.

7

*Two More Things to Do
When in Indiana*

The World Headquarters of World Headquarterses

Given its central location geographically and its abundant supply of fresh water, the municipality of Indianapolis, which also serves as the state's capital, has become an attractive location where various corporate entities, trade associations, and fraternal organizations have established a significant number of world headquarterses, home offices, and central distribution warehouses. What follows is an abbreviated list representing a baker's dozen of such sites, many open for tours and often containing museums, libraries, company cafeterias, dioramas, animated displays, and/or gift shops available to the public. The vast majority of world headquarterses may be found along the city's principle paved motor artery, Meridian Street, which runs north and south through the center of Indianapolis, tracing exactly the geographical 86 degree west meridian for thirty-seven miles.

1. World Headquarters
The Glutinous Maximus Corporation
8317 North Meridian Street

Next to the United States Postal Service's National Center for Affixation of Post-Addressed Postal Labels and Notices (USPS-APAPLN), the world headquarters of The Glutinous Maximus Corporation (GMC)—the nation's third largest producer of adhesives, pastes, glues, putties, sealants, and caulking—houses the financial offices as well as the chemical research laboratories. On the site of the original abattoir, the grounds still include the historic stockyards, re-visioned, by the architect Michael Graves, as an extensive topiary garden featuring trained shrubbery mimicking domesticated animals and which includes, at the rear of the property, a small Museum of the Tongue.

2. World Headquarters
Gramm's Globes
On the island in the middle of the 8000 block of
North Meridian Street

Designed by the architect Michael Graves, the spherical president's office and astronomical observatory on the roof of the thirty-seven story tower, rests on a titanium gimbal and is motorized in such a manner as to replicate the rotation of the earth. In 1999, the entire production of globes was moved to unrevealed locations overseas, leaving thirty-five of the other thirty-six floors vacant and a picket line of cashiered members of the International Amalgamated Brotherhood of Globe Workers, Local 27, circling the ground floor continually since the lay-offs. However, the bank of twenty-four glass lifts fully exposed on the building's north facade will still serve as the site for the summer's World Elevator Surfing Championships, sponsored by the company's hydrology and atmospheric departments and broadcast on ESPN2.

3. World Headquarters
The Association of Normals
6250 North Meridian Street

Administrative offices share space with a conference center and convention hall in this renovated, by the architect Michael Graves, ranch-style house operated by a coalition of cities named "Normal." The association publishes a newsletter, *The Thermostat*, and, each year, during its annual banquet, presents its annual award, The Golden #2 Pencil, acknowledging an individual who most exemplifies the group's tenets and principles. With the money it generates during this event, the association continues to fund research into the design of squirrel-resistant bird-feeders and for the technology needed to compress further the segment of the radio band spectrum allocated to automatic garage door openers.

4. World Headquarters and Hall of Fame
League of Basketball Managers and Officials
5932 North Meridian Street

Indianapolis's renaissance has been a result of a community and governmental strategy which actively pursued amateur and professional athletic events and organizations, making the city a necessary destination for competitors and competitions. The offices of the League of Basketball Managers and Officials relocated here from Martinsville, Indiana, in

1973. Among its many projects, the League provides the seat of the Court of Final Technical Appeals where games played under protest receive their ultimate adjudication and the Grand Union Hall where the world's pool of referees and timekeepers competitively bid their weekly games based on seniority. The Hall of Fame, built from plans based on sketches rendered by the architect Michael Graves, hosts an active program in the archiving and preservation of whistles, analgesic balm, and shoes.

5. World Headquarters
The Hellenistic Consultancy
4444 North Meridian Street

Housed in the refurbished, by the architect Michael Graves, Gattling Homestead, this research and design firm works exclusively with the world's Greek letter social sororities and fraternities in the development of their graphic and cultural identity. Field representative report here on the continuity and the degradation of the millions of secrets utilized or compromised on campuses while, at the same time, generating, during special brainstorming sessions in the Brainstorming Room, a fresh supply of handshakes, passwords, and ancient rituals. The Map in the Map Room tracks every active or probationary chapter by means of blinking displays. The Hellenistic Consultancy also acts as the official depository for the proprietary branding of the various organizations. In its ongoing effort to maintain the integrity of this process, the firm employs the use of the largest Cray computer in the state.

6. The Mother Church
The Society of Mary Gravida
Square Mary, North Meridian and 38th Streets

In addition to the geodesic domed chapel, the architect Michael Graves's master's thesis project when at Ball State University, the grounds also include The Grotto, The Home for the Unwed Mother, and The Chancellery Office for this excommunicated heretical holy order. The Grotto features the fifty-foot limestone statue of Mary Expectant. The clients of The Home, during their residency, manufacture, in a variety of media and in several scales, reproductions of the statue in the hope of fulfilling the prophecy, delivered by The Virgin Mother on this site in 1872, to propagate only representations depicting Our Lady as pregnant with the Son of God. The Gift Shop is open 24 hours a day, everyday throughout the year.

7. World Headquarters
LOVE Incorporated
3628 North Meridian Street

Operating out of an "L" shaped building that is the architect Michael Grave's homage to Richard Meier, LOVE Corp administers the assets of the estate derived from the artist Robert Indiana's LOVE work, including the management of all royalties derived from the ongoing sale of the postage stamp and the .000005 cent fee levied on the everyday use of the word. The LOVE Foundation, located on the mezzanine, supports, philanthropically, the proliferation of benday and pantone to the Third World. The Gallery on the first floor displays the artist's early drafts, sketches, models, and alternate versions of the masterpiece which include a galvanized "V," an "LE" in India Rubber, a series of "O" studies in aspic, a feldspar "LL," and the adobe, "OVL," the top two cross-strokes of the "E" having deteriorated over time.

8. World Headquarters
The Great States Company
1510 North Meridian Street

The only remaining manufacturer in the world of push lawn mowers, the Great States Company utilizes the former Stutz Bearcat automobile plant, originally designed by Kurt Vonnegut, Sr., to produce a gross of machines each day The twelve acre roof of the factory has been converted into the test track, planted in stripes of varietal grass strains which are kept viable throughout the year with heat and moisture disbursed by a subterranean system of tiling and pipes. The steam the system transports is created by a co-generation process derived from the world's largest compost heap in the company's adjacent parking lot. During the Memorial Day festivities, the company sponsors reel mower races at the facility which are televised locally by means of cameras mounted aboard helicopters hovering overhead.

9. World Headquarters
The Re-reinsurance Insurance Company
1300 North Meridian Street

In this nondescript building, reminiscent of the early work of the architect Michael Graves, the actuaries of the Re-reinsurance Insurance Company calculate the risk of insuring insurance companies which insure insurance companies. The company offers to these corporate clients, through it sales staff, a variety of re-reinsurance policies that are said to set the industry standard. The daily Re-Re Index scoring the twenty leading re-insurers is published in *The Wall Street Journal* and on a blackboard propped on an easel in the small front lobby. A vestibule off the lobby contains a Depression Era soda fountain and grill run by the Marion County Association for the Blind.

10. World Headquarters
Mikes of America
22 Monument Circle

The oldest nominal club in the country, Mikes of America boasts that it is also the world's largest organization of same-named individuals with an active membership of over twelve million "Mikes," "Michaels," "Micheles," and "Michaelas" according to the most recent available figures. This total, it must be said, also includes the auxiliary of "Micks" and "Mickeys." The Italianate campanile, designed by club member Michael Graves, pays homage to the nearby state monument honoring Indiana's soldiers and sailors which dominates the circle's center. The spire's interior circular ramp is lined by a constantly circulating gallery of portraits depicting the club's more recognizable members such as "Michael" Graves, Leonard "Michaels," and David "Michael" Letterman.

11. World Headquarters
FC2
South Meridian and McCarthy Streets

In a second floor suite of offices above a laundry and Shapiro's Delicatessen in Indianapolis's famous Chinatown, FC2, the publisher of the Blue Guide to Indiana series of travel books, makes its corporate home. Staffed entirely by temporary employees who must demonstrate they are at least second generation Hoosier natives, the media company constantly updates its several outlets of tourist information, including its real time internet video feed, its errata chain letter network, and the 300 foot crawl light display which wraps around the building. On the roof, the famous PoMo dovecot and carrier pigeon roost, designed by the architect Michael Graves, stand next to the sand and platform volleyball courts where the employee teams, routine competitors on the I States Semi-pro Tour, practice during their half-hour lunch breaks.

12. World Headquarters
The Need for Some Home Assembly Furniture Institute
3245 South Meridian

Located in a Quonset hut designed by the school of Michael Graves, this think-tank reports to the eponymic producers of portable home furnishings. Its testing laboratories simulate conditions for domestic construction and do-it-yourself finishing of the merchandise and authenticates and verifies time estimates given for the various tasks. Its literary office translates English translations into the English found on enclosed package instructions and is a leading contributor to the International Signage Initiative. There is an interesting collection of veneer in the sculpture garden along with Claus Oldenberg's monumental *Allen Wrench*.

13. World Headquarters
Central Beetle Breeding
South Meridian and County Line Road

This family-owned enterprise has been raising free-range Scarabaeid on this site since 1901 when patriarch Hiram "Hi" Floria domesticated his first wild "doodle bug." The intermodal transhipping terminal, designed by the architect Michael Graves, has the capacity to handle up to six boxcars of live insects each day while off-loading liquid manure from a like number of dedicated tankers. In addition to supplying the farm market with a reliable source of dung beetles, the concern also provides certified beetle semen for private use in small scale AI programs as well as a collection of hybridize carrion, *scarabaeus sacer*, for use by natural history museums, taxidermists, and religious organizations.

The Thirty-Year Salad Bar War:
An Appendix to *The Blue Guide to Indiana*

Opening Moves
December 2, 1952

At dawn on December 2, 1952, forces of the Salad Axis in alliance with the Cafe Owners and Independent Truck Stops League stage a surprise preemptive attack on the Hobart Restaurant Equipment Company in Hobart, destroying the prototype mock-ups and machine tools used in the manufacturing of the newly invented deep fat fryer. At the same time, elements of the Tea Room Operators and mercenaries in the employ of public school cafeteria managers launch a siege on the Jenn-Air Range and Oven plant in Indianapolis. The Future Franchiser's of America and the Legion of Lard respond by imposing an embargo of cucumber and pimento, seizing these and other vegetable contraband at the border crossings with Ohio, Michigan, and Illinois.

The Battle of Wawasee
Glorious June 11, 1953

In a Pyrrhic victory, privateers loyal to deviled eggs, cottage cheese, and macaroni salad sink twelve ships in a convoy of canal barges transporting a vital supply of charcoal briquettes provided on lend/lease by a profiteering Henry Ford. The raiders lose their aircraft carrier, *Parsley,* when it becomes lost in the smoke generated by the barbecue pits on board the enemy's flotilla of destroyer escorts.

The Attempted Assassination of Colonel Harlan Sanders
Mayday, 1954

In the parking lot of The Hobby House restaurant, Colonel Sanders comes under attack by a fusillade of celery spears. The Condiment Brotherhood issues a denial of responsibility on WOWO radio and reports their membership has mixed feelings about the introduction of Kentucky Fried Chicken as it utilizes a pressure cooker in the process and, therefore, falls outside the strict interpretation of the rules of engagement declared against the forces of fried food.

McDonald's Enters the War
Election Day, 1956

With the suspicious explosion of a tractor-trailer hauling spatulas under the McDonald's flag at the Theodore Dreiser truck stop on the Indiana Toll Road, the short order franchise inflates the incident in order to intervene in the statewide conflict. Its forces flood across the 43rd parallel and the Ohio River, decimating the small Pakistani peacekeeping force sent there to observe by the United Nations.

A Plea from the Pope
October 12, 1959

The Vatican releases an ambiguous statement. In a delicately worded bull, Pope John the 23rd reiterates the Holy See's position on natural food but suggests that the Holy Spirit inspired Fry-O-Later facilitates the celebration of "lean days" and the abstention of meat during Lent and on all Fridays by making appetizing the abundance of lake perch found in the state.

The Opening of the Trans-Indiana Mayonnaise Pipeline
New Year's Day, 1960

The second Eisenhower administration opens the pipeline running between Chicago and Cincinnati through the egg and soybean rich heartland. Both sides claim this public work as a victory. The forces allied with salad hail the mayonnaise as essential to the dressings of their various dishes. The opposition claims mayonnaise as one of the secret ingredients in their secret sauces.

The Great French Fry Famine
1961–65

Blight devastates the potato crop forcing the emigration of thousands of Hoosiers to Ohio, and contributes to the ketchup panic at the Chicago Board of Trade. Conspiracy theories abound, suggesting the natural disaster was actually the work of the turnip and parsnip interests. A long-term consequence is that the agreed upon spelling of the tuber's proper name falls into obscurity.

The Fall of Azar's Big Boy
Greek Orthodox Easter, 1968

The first chain of fast food restaurants in Indiana, Azar's Big Boy, collapses after opposition forces demanding the bread of the Buddy Boy sandwiches be served crustless invade its counters. Under the cover of darkness, Alex Azar flees Fort Wayne for Detroit in a Railway Express Agency truck. Arriving in Detroit and under the protection of the Elias Brothers and the Stroh Brewery, Azar vows he will return.

The Last Stand of the Watercress Sandwich
Bastille Day, 1969

At the sidewalk cafe of W&D's Department Store, the final watercress sandwich is served by Cindy Hall to Mrs. Bud Latz who eats it and who, afterward, addresses the crowd of several thousand gathered to witness the event. In that crowd, the disgruntled unemployed sous chef, Bob Earle, carves decorative rosettes from hydroponic radishes.

The Geneva Convention
Spring Equinox, 1971

Signed in Geneva, Indiana, the convention forces the signatories to adhere to certain rules of war including the treatment and exchange of prisoners and the abstention from the use of food borne pathogens. The instrument also establishes certain zoning ordinances and prohibits the construction of a sandwich of more than three decks.

A Second Front
Ash Wednesday, 1975

Partisan skirmishes erupt between The Syracuse China Company aligned with Oneida Flatware and Libby Glass against the incursion of disposable utensils, dishes, and cups. Volunteer brigades of dishwashers and silver polishers attack the phalanx of Greek Evzones and Turkish Zouaves hired to smash china while dancing.

Field Marshal Ron Popil
Boxing Day, 1977

The assembled Army of the Raw and the supporting Relish Legion are lead by Field Marshal Ron Popil, the Kitchen Fox, who has equipped them with the Veg-a-Matic as standard issue appliance. Popil is later implicated in the botched kidnapping attempt on Duncan Hines at the Evansville K-Mart.

The Breaded Pork Tenderloin Is Dropped on Muncie
August 16, 1978

John of John's Awful Awful (Awful Big, Awful Good) introduces the dreaded Breaded Pork Tenderloin sandwich at his restaurant near Ball State University. It is crucial that the thinly sliced, dredged, and tenderized slab of fried pork extend significantly beyond its accompanying white bread bun and, in most cases, its serving plate. The design is widely copied and proliferates throughout the state. An early prototype falls into enemy hands. During an experiment at the secret laboratories of Purdue, five grad students in hotel and motel management are killed in a suspicious grease explosion.

The Sneeze Offensive
The Eve of St. Agnes, 1980

Paramilitary units infiltrate cafes, buffets, cafeteria, and restaurants that deploy the new endless salad bars. In suicide sneeze attacks, they contaminate the colorful array of side items and salads before succumbing to their own self-inflicted respiratory disorders. There are reports of other fifth column sympathizers ignoring the new-plate-for-each-trip rule, filling their plates up up to three times with second helpings.

The Eleventh Hour Crouton
Armistice Day, 1981

At the eleventh hour the crouton is introduced. It is golden brown and crispy like fried foods yet is allied with salad. Confusion reins.

Pudding Is Declared a Vegetable
VJ Day, 1982

The Supreme Court, in a sharply divided ruling, certifies pudding with class standing and finds that pudding, especially chocolate pudding, to be a vegetable, endowed with all the rights and privileges inherent to legumes and enumerated in Article 37 of the U.S. Constitution. The decision brings an uneasy truce to the war after protracted and contested negotiations by the belligerents at an A&W Root Beer stand in Huntington on the Wabash River.

*Three Contributor's Notes
and a Review of Michael
Martone*

Contributor's Note (1)

Michael Martone was born in Fort Wayne, Indiana, and grew up in a small house, white with green trim, 1812 Clover Lane, in the neighborhood known as North Highlands. His neighbors across the street were the Mensings, Ed and Mildred. Mr. Mensing was a fireman, but he no longer lived and worked in a firehouse. He was an assistant chief. That meant he had a white helmet he kept on the back shelf of his fire-engine red department car he drove home at night from work. His work was fire prevention. In his dress uniform, he left each day just as Martone was leaving to walk to school (Price Elementary, Franklin Junior High School, North Side High School). Mr. Mensing would get into his bright red and polished chrome car and drive to inspect factories, offices, theaters, and schools. Martone saw him inspecting his schools and would say hello as Mr. Mensing checked the panic bars on doors or the recharge records of extinguishers. Mr. Mensing also went to construction sites and ran tests on the new automatic sprinkler systems, the dry standpipes, and the emergency overrides on elevators and escalators. Martone saw him at the high school basketball tournament games at the Memorial Coliseum, counting the cheering fans sitting in the stands and standing in the aisles and hallways. Probably most exciting, however, was when, every fall, Martone saw his neighbor on television during Fire Prevention Week when all the schools in the city school system participated in one huge fire drill, the only fire drill that wasn't a surprise. Martone watched as Mr. Mensing (surrounded by the mayor, the school superintendent, other fire chiefs, insurance agents, radio announcers announcing, and television weathermen commenting) pushed a button after all the other officials made speeches about fire safety. When Mr. Mensing, dressed up in his formal white hat and gloves, pushed the button, the fire alarms sounded all over the city: the sirens, whistles, horns, buzzers, bells. Everyone pretended the whole city was a blaze. And, each fall, no matter what school Martone was attending, he would get up from his desk and walk quickly yet orderly to the designated exit, clear the building, and assemble with his classmates at the safe specified distance away from the school, then turn and face the building and wait for further instructions. Usually on those days there was a fire truck nearby the students inspected during their lunch breaks or recesses. It was still warm, and the sun reflected off of the bright polished hardware of the fire engines or ladder trucks and blazed on the reflecting stripes taped to the helmets and coats of the bored firemen. Mr. Mensing always had extra badges and plastic fireman's hats left over from the event. The hard red plastic badges and hats were donated by the Hartford Insurance Company and featured a picture of a deer with huge antlers. He gave them out as treats for Halloween, pinning a badge on a ghost or pirate who might also don a helmet that became part of the costume for the rest of the night. Mr. Mensing did not like to turn on his lights in his house on Halloween or on any other night of the year. He delayed turning on a light and when he did it was a single fixture, dim and dull. Martone never knew if this habit hoped to save money or demonstrated some basic mistrust of electricity or revealed some knowledge of its inherent danger. For as long as he could, Mr. Mensing read the evening newspaper, *The News-Sentinel*, while sitting in a lawn chair just inside his glass storm door, his back to the door, what little light there was falling over his shoulder to illumine the open pages he held up. He was there in the morning too, reading the morning newspaper, *The Journal-Gazette*, sitting in the webbed lawn chair inside his door. Even in winter, he sat in the doorway, collecting what little light there was through the frosted glass. When the winters were cold, Mr. Mensing would have to climb the city's water towers and make sure the elevated water in the tanks that put pressure on the system, pressure that the fire department needed at the hydrants, hadn't frozen. One particular cold spell, he spent several nights in a rubber dingy floating inside one of the huge tanks that read on the outside FORT WAYNE, agitating the water with an oar so it wouldn't skim over with ice and then freeze solid and shut of the water. In the spring, there would be floods in Fort Wayne, and Martone when in high school helped fill sandbags and shore up the leaky levies. Mr. Mensing spent the floods wading beside and guiding boatloads of rescued people to dry land. He told Martone that floods were worse than fires. Manhole covers popped out of place from the pressure of the rising water, and the muddy water prevented someone walking a boat or raft from seeing the ground below.

Suddenly, the solid street wasn't there, and you fell right through the hole, down under the street, impossible to see the way back up to the surface. Not like falling through ice, Mr. Mensing told Martone. With ice you swam up, escaping by ignoring the light, the solid ice illuminated by the sun. The way out was the only one above you not lit up. Against your instincts, he told Martone, swim to the spot that looks the blackest.

Contributor's Note (2)

Michael Martone was born in Fort Wayne, Indiana, and grew up there attending North Side High School where he earned his single ruby pin from the National Forensic League, a speech and debate honorary. His mother who also participated in speech and debate during her years at North Side debated a team from Oxford University in the chambers of the state legislature in Indianapolis when she was in college. It was Martone's own lack of enthusiasm for debate that prevented him from obtaining the double ruby. He found the cross-examination format of presentation and rebuttals difficult. He disliked the high-speed speaking style employed to introduce the reams of evidence gleaned for the 3x5 note cards in each 20 minute section. He was unable to accurately keep flow charts of the arguments on the yellow legal pads and would inevitably neglect one line of interrogation out of the many to be covered when it was his turn to question his opportunities/needs case on such topics as *Resolved that the jury system be significantly changed.* Instead Martone preferred preparing for weekend speech meets where he participated enthusiastically in impromptu, extemporaneous, after dinner, poetry interpretation, or original oratory where he went to the state finals with a speech entitled "Circles" and placed third. Martone's debate partner, Les Seiling, carried the team. He was equally adept at affirmative or negative positions and enjoyed creating arguments he knew had not been covered in the casebooks or evidence card files to which high school teams subscribed. He proposed ecclesiastical courts handle divorces, quoting canon law to the effect of no man tearing asunder. Instead of preparing, Seiling liked to play RISK with his teammates and after conquering the known world show them the potato masher grenades and Soviet burp gun his father had salvaged during the war. After high school,

Seiling became a line chef then later the sous chef at the Win Schuler's at the Marriott on I-69 and for several summers after that Martone and the other debate team members accompanied Seiling up to Marshal, Michigan, to eat in the original Win Schuler's and return to Fort Wayne with a case of strawberries for the restaurant there. Win Schuler's was know for its complimentary pot of Swedish meatballs placed at the table when the guests were seated. Seiling speculated that the very first meatball might still be in circulation as the leftovers of each table's pots were returned to a giant one in the kitchen to be redistributed. Later, Seiling joined the Navy and served on the Aleutian Island of Adak at a listening post a few miles from the Soviet Union's frontier. Not long after Seiling left the Navy, Martone received a telephone call from a man who identified himself as an agent of the FBI wishing to ask Martone a few questions about Seiling and his application for clearance to work in a Federal agency. Did Martone think Leslie Seiling was a loyal American? Did Leslie Seiling belong to any organizations advocating the violent overthrow of the United States? Is Leslie Seiling capable of contributing to the collapse of the United States? Martone answered all the questions in a way he hoped the agent from the FBI and his debate partner, Les Seiling, would have wanted him to answer. The agent from the FBI thanked him and Martone never heard from him or Les Seiling again.

Contributor's Note (3)

Michael Martone was born and grew up in Fort Wayne, Indiana. He has worked in a variety of jobs, including night auditor at a hotel and stock clerk in a bookstore. One Christmas he helped kill cattle in Michigan because he was in love. The woman Martone was in love with was named Karen K. Potts who was born and grew up in Detroit and was then a veterinary student at Michigan State. It was the Bicentennial year and some months before the gas crisis. Martone drove up to East Lansing from Fort Wayne, borrowing the huge green Pontiac Bonneville from his parents who were disappointed he would miss Christmas, the first, with them in order to kill cattle in Michigan. In Michigan, a few years before this Christmas, a fire retardant chemical had been, inadvertently, mixed into feed dairy farmers then fed to their herds. The chemical residue called PBB contaminated the milk supply. Milk had to be dumped. Whole herds were destroyed. A television movie was made starring Ron Howard whose character in the film ended up slaughtering his cows and calves. Martone remembers the scene where Howard uses a bulldozer to dig a big trench to bury the carcasses. PBB was thought to be persistent. That Christmas, it was being said that the chemical would be in the milk supply for years. Martone imagines it might still be in the milk supply. Once, while kissing Martone, Karen K. Potts stopped, looked into his eyes, and said, "I love cows." Martone believed her. She had worked her way through vet school rendering anatomical drawings for the large animal surgeries and dissections. She contributed some of these drawings to textbooks her professors were writing. She had a meticulous style of stippling with pen and India ink, patiently pixeling the porous bones and shading the creases of the vital organs. She gave Martone a life-size drawing in three colors of a bovine heart that he still has framed above his desk. As it was Christmas, the campus was deserted, almost all of the students going home to be with their families. Karen K. Potts had volunteered to stay and tend a barn where the school was conducting an experiment on the long-term effects of PBB in dairy cattle. There were some thirty head in all, weaned calves mostly, heifers and steers, but some milking cows. Martone helped to muck the stalls and stanchions. The calves were still young enough to kick and prance in the fresh straw Martone forked in for bedding, but they were clearly sick, many with a rheumy barking cough. The PBB was in the feed that was kept in big garbage cans. When Martone removed the lid, the sound it made alerted the friskier calves that trotted from the loafing parlor over to where he worked shoveling the laced grain into the manger. While the cattle ate, Martone helped Karen K. Potts pitch the fouled bedding and manure into the gutters and then slide it all to a spreader parked outside in a paddock. It was a cold night and had already started snowing. The muck at their feet steamed. Somewhere else on the campus was a control barn filled with cattle not being poisoned. Other students took care of those animals. Karen K. Potts was a good quarter foot taller than Martone and wore a real Irish cable knit sweater with the lanolin still in the wool, designer jeans, and Frye boots she fit into rubber Wellies when she worked. Before she went to the barn Martone watched her put on eye make-up, a dab of rouge, and some colorless lip gloss. She changed her earrings to another set of dangling silver hoops she bought on trips she made over to Ann Arbor. Martone stayed a week, Christmas day not that much different from the other ones before and after it. They visited other barns on the university farm, driving around campus in Karen K. Potts's red VW Beetle. He saw the bulls kept in tight pens where they were milked for their semen, sows that were farrowing, and the elaborate charts kept on the university's milking herd noting the pounds of milk each produced, their calves' birth weight and gain, and an estimate on when they were due to freshen. At the turkey coops, she told him a funny story about the birds who would gobble in waves as she talked. It isn't the case, Karen K. Potts told him, that domesticated turkeys are too stupid to mate. Artificial insemination has to be used because the toms are bred too big to mount the hens. Poultry scientists at Michigan State thought they solved the problem when they developed a kind of saddle to fit the hens and better distribute the tom's crushing weight. But then the turkey's stupidity was demonstrated. With all the hens wearing the special saddles, the toms no longer recognized them as turkeys and didn't even try to mate. It snowed most of the time Martone was in East Lansing that Christmas, and it turned very cold. He had left the lights on when he parked the Pontiac a week ago, and the battery was dead when he tried to start the car to return home. His parents, already angry with him for leaving at Christmas, would now be even more furious that it would cost money for the repair of the car. He had to call them to tell them he would be delayed another day in order to replace the battery then drive back to Indiana in time for New Year's. While he was on the phone, Karen K. Potts, whose skin, Martone remembers, was like milk, stood by the sink and drank a big glass of milk as she looked out the window at the snow. She then gathered her things to drive him to the service station where his parents' car had been towed.

Review

Michael Martone was born in Fort Wayne, Indiana. He began writing thinly disguised autobiographical stories while at North Side High School, a response to the annual romantic tragedy he suffered when he broke up with Janine B————, a cheerleader, each year during the basketball season. Martone, who was not a basketball player, anxiously anticipated the opening tip-off that then precipitated his girlfriend's return of the inexpensive yet tasteful promise ring and her subsequent dating, until the team's elimination in the sectional tournament, of Tom S————, the power forward. In the meantime, Martone took to his books and found solace in the seeming prevalence of and preference for adultery-themed narratives. As if by divine intervention, *Othello*, he noted with mixed emotions, had been substituted for *Macbeth* as the junior year's Shakespeare offering. During his now abundant spare time, he tried his hand at rendering overwrought and generally sentimental tales of revenge, attempting, in a severely tortured manner, to rewrite his history of torture, but he discovered that like actual torture torture, this attempt to coerce and rekindle love and affection from his girlfriend by means of literature proved not only painful but inefficient to say the least. As if she even read his brittle stories of apologetic ingénues reuniting in the dénouement. And as an ameliorative, his juvenilia itself proved even less of a personal balm, the machinations of revenge served lukewarm. Yet, in those dark weeks and months, as he sat alone, it seemed, in the packed gymnasium bleachers, watching his estranged girlfriend perform the traditional school cheer, the mere act of physically scribbling out in long-hand his thoughts and feeling created a certain distraction, allowed him, at last, to take his eye off the ball, so to speak, just as Tom S———— made another gangly cut for the hoop. Later, at Indiana University, Martone, still attempting to write his way out of failed and failing relationships learned about the New Criticism, which criticized the proceeding critical penchant for lifting the thin veils of biographical disguise. Martone sat silently in his workshops as his colleagues gamely attempted to overlook him sitting silently and considered Martone's work before them, judging its efficacy and élan in terms of authenticated masterworks. "To His Coy Mistress" was routinely invoked in both the poetry and prose writing classrooms. The students puzzled endlessly over not "what" the work meant but "how" it meant or, more exactly, "how" it meant to mean. In his silence, Martone noticed how deftly the participants of the workshop skipped over the veiled and not so veiled allusions to their own work embedded in Martone's own, how he deftly settled a score after score, hash after hash. They seemed not to notice how the coy mistress at hand in Martone's story had more than a passing resemblance to Susan V———, a daughter of an Indianapolis dermatologist, sitting at the opposite end of the table, who had just a week before during the writing of the story she was, along with the others in class, now considering, given Martone the old heave-ho, had informed him that her previous lover, Philippe, had returned unexpectedly from France, the homecoming to Bloomington captured in Susan V———'s own story, considered just prior to Martone's story now under consideration, with an evocative meet cute:

"Michel!" I screamed, "What are you doing here?"

Taking me into his arms, Michel whispered, "Looking for you."

And later at Johns Hopkins University where Martone took a class on The Moderns with Hugh Kenner, the prohibition against the use of the biographical became more problematic. Hugh Kenner told Martone's class that Ezra Pound told Hugh Kenner to visit the great men of his, Hugh Kenner's, time and Hugh Kenner had. Later Kenner reading aloud William Carlos Williams's poem called "The Sea Elephant."

> . . . But I
> am love. I am
> from the sea—
> Blouaugh!

The *Blouaugh* part was supposed to be the sound the sea elephant made Kenner said, and he read it, he said, just like WCW had read it, even though Kenner's lisp made most of what he read sound, at first, quite similar to the nasal interjection emitted by the sea elephant. Finishing the poem, Kenner shared a series of anecdotes from the lives of the writers under scrutiny gleaned from his visits with them. *Waiting for Godot* could be explained, he explained, if you knew Samuel Beckett, his stint with the resistance. How many times did Beckett himself wait at a clandestine rendezvous for an alias-bearing contact to appear? Well the answer was several because Samuel Beckett informed the young Hugh Kenner while they walked picturesquely along the Seine. Martone's fiction writing teacher at Johns Hopkins, John Barth, instructed all of his students to think twice about reviewing books one way or the other. Criticism, he said, was best left to our Gillman Hall colleagues in the English Department. He had made a pact with his muse in this regard, he said, believing the consequences would prove dire. Undeterred, Martone himself has tried his hand at a little reviewing, writing brief essays on T. C. B——— and Stanley E——— for a literary magazine. For the *Philadelphia Inquirer*, Martone dabbled, filing reviews of books by Richard B———, John C———, and Steven M———. But his heart wasn't in it, especially the last one where he really didn't know what to say. It was difficult, he thought, when one did not know the writers in question. He didn't want to hurt anyone's feelings, especially feelings he didn't know. Praising the books seemed even more dangerous because Martone was confronted with his own secret feelings of being a fraud after all, attaining what little authority he did have not from any amount of intrinsic merit or native talent (Martone secretly believed he had none) but that his success as a writer, what there was of it, was derived from chance, fortuitous meetings with people of real talent and a charitable nature. To write reviews then seemed to expose Martone to the real risk of personal exposure. Far more than his fiction that was merely a clever mask disguising the actual elements of his own history, Martone felt a book review felt far more dangerous. Far more than revealing the nature and quality of the book being reviewed, a review carried the risk of revealing the reviewer by exposing the revelations emanating from the reviewer. Martone soon shied away from reviewing, but he stayed in the literary marketplace. He continued to make friends in high places, patiently waited for contacts who said they would come and didn't, dropped names whenever he could, made a series of spontaneous inflected noises, camouflaged the camouflage of his life with stories about his life. Keeping to himself, Martone soon discovered he had kept himself from himself.

Michael Martone was born in Fort Wayne, Indiana, and grew up there. He attended Butler University and graduated from Indiana University. He holds an M.A. from The Writing Seminars of The Johns Hopkins University. Martone has taught writing at Iowa State University, Harvard University where he was the Briggs-Copland Lecturer on Fiction, and Syracuse University. He currently teaches in the Program for Creative Writing at the University of Alabama and is on the faculty of the M.F.A. Program for Writers at Warren Wilson College. He is the author of a dozen books of fiction and nonfiction and has edited seven other volumes. His stories and essays have appeared many magazines and journals including *3rd Bed, Ascent, Benzene, Brooklyn Rail, Epoch, Flyway, Harper's, Iowa Review, McSweeney's, Mid-American Review, Ninth Letter, North American Review,* and *Parakeet.* His work has been recognized with two fellowships from the National Endowment for the Arts, the AWP Book Award for Nonfiction, the Bruno Arcudi Literature Prize, an Ingram Merrill Foundation Award, and as winner of The World's Greatest Short Short Story Contest. Work has been reprinted in both the Pushcart Prize and Best American Essays annual anthologies. He edits Story County Books in Tuscaloosa, Alabama, where he lives with the poet Theresa Pappas and their two sons, Sam and Nick.